THE TWO MRS. CARLYLES

THE TWO MRS. CARLYLES

SUZANNE RINDELL

G. P. PUTNAM'S SONS | NEW YORK

PUTNAM
— EST. 1838 —

G. P. Putnam's Sons
Publishers Since 1838
An imprint of Penguin Random House LLC
penguinrandomhouse.com

ISBN: 9780525539209
ebook ISBN: 9780525539223

Printed in the United States of America
1   3   5   7   9   10   8   6   4   2

Book design by Elke Sigal

For Jayme

THE TWO MRS. CARLYLES

PROLOGUE

Ghosts.

If you asked me a few months ago, do I believe in ghosts, I would have given one of those pragmatic, empirical answers that most people provide when pressed. I might not have said no, perhaps, but neither would I have said yes.

All these new doctors—the ones who specialize in the psyche and who administer to the mind—insist there can be no such thing; they are figments of an overactive imagination. After all, women see them three times more often than men do. Proof that so-called "ghosts" are nothing more than flights of fancy—because women are hysterics, of course.

Spiritualists say differently. And while I'm not a worldly girl by any means, I've heard stories about the séances that have grown so popular among the fashionable set. In velvet-curtained parlors all over the city, newfangled electric lights are snapped off, candles are lit, and men and women sit around a table, begging the spirits to knock once for "yes," and twice for "no." It is interesting to note, in most of these cases, that the spirits are more communicative when a bit of coin changes hands.

At St. Hilda's Home for Girls, they taught us about the Holy Ghost, but nothing about the spectral kind. I remember, though, once asking Sister Maggie if she believed in ghosts—if she believed they could be real. I can't recall exactly *why* I was asking. Perhaps, as an orphan, I hoped to someday communicate with the parents I'd known too briefly. Or perhaps I hoped there might be something other than myself to blame for the episodes of misbehavior I got up to.

Sister Maggie didn't chastise me for asking such a blasphemous question—others might have given me lashes—nor did she insist that the existence of ghosts was impossible. Instead, she simply said: *There are those who believe spirits return to the earth because they cannot rest; they have not finished with their earthly business. Others will tell you that a ghost is a living mind acting out its troubles. Either way, Violet, can't we find it within ourselves to pity the haunted?*

Years later, I've come to admire the ambiguity of her reply. *Spirits that cannot rest. A living mind acting out its troubles.* Sister Maggie didn't see the need to pick one, because one doesn't rule the other out. I've come to understand that "ambiguity" can likewise describe a simple sentence pared down to its smaller parts, when you can't decide which is the adjective that ought to come first and which is the defining noun. For instance: *A murderous accident. An accidental murder.*

Come to think, if you asked me a few months ago if I believed in ghosts, I would have more likely said no than yes. I'm fairly certain of it.

I was not haunted then.

I

efore the great earthquake of 1906, I was not haunted, but it would
be inaccurate to say my mind was entirely at peace.

From the time I was a small child, I'd suffered from what the sisters
called "spells"—strange, trancelike episodes of which I have no memory.
I'd be found, say, with a broken toy but no understanding of how I'd
broken it. I was raised to see these spells as an undesirable flaw in my
person—my *curse*, really.

In fact, I have always had reason to believe that my spells had something to do with my winding up in an orphanage. Most of the other
girls had arrived at St. Hilda's Home for Girls by the traditional route:
that is, as infants, by way of a basket left outside the main gate. But I
was seven when I was brought to St. Hilda's. I still have memories of a
house. Richly colored rugs. A chest full of toys. A fireplace and a room
filled with books. I must have been around six when my mother and
father died. I suffered a terrible spell around the same time and, in

consequence, did not learn the particulars. The most I have been told since is that they took sick and that there was simply nothing for it.

An aunt with three children of her own took me in for a short time, but I'm told that when my spells began to take the form of hysterical, violent crying, her nerves were stretched to the limit. My aunt dealt with me as best she could, mostly by putting a drop or two of laudanum in a glass of milk and ordering me to drink it down.

She kept me in her care for just shy of a year, at which point she had a change of heart about her duty—or so I assume, because she brought me to St. Hilda's and left me, with stunning detachment, in the care of the nuns who greeted us at the gate. I was confused when we first arrived. My aunt bade me stand a few paces behind her and whispered something to them I couldn't hear, until her voice rose a little as she went on.

Surely you understand. I can't have that kind of wickedness in my house. She's beyond my help!

The nuns bobbed their heads. I was admitted without further interrogation. I never saw my aunt again. It was then that I realized most of life is divided up into a series of "befores" and "afters":

Before my mother and father died, and after.

Before my aunt brought me to the orphanage, and after.

Before I made friends with Cora and Flossie, and after.

Before the orphanage caught fire and burned to the ground, and after.

Each event marked a sea change and divided my life with a sense of permanence. There was no going back, no reconciling the dichotomy.

Even now, this feels true, for most San Franciscans will tell you there are two cities: the one that existed before the earthquake, and the one that was rebuilt after.

What the 'quake itself did not topple in 1906, the fires razed. Afterwards, the world was hungry for modernization, and eventually, the "new" San Francisco boasted wide streets thronged with automobiles and tourists. The steel-blue waters of the Bay began to buzz with pleasure cruises. Modern department stores sprang up in Union Square, their shiny display windows winking in the sun.

But the San Francisco that existed *before* the earthquake was a piece of the Old West, a place that had been slapped together hastily to cater to the needs of the '49ers.

Nowhere was this truer than in the infamous neighborhood nicknamed the "Barbary Coast," where the sidewalks stank of piss and ale. Even as civilization tried to nudge its way in, the neighborhood still hosted the occasional barbaric shoot-out. Horses nickered impatiently, tied up outside the area's many saloons. Ragtime and sawdust spilled out of every open doorway. The streets were narrow alleyways frequented by sailors and prostitutes. It was a place where a man might still be "shanghai'ed"—kidnapped after falling into a whiskey-induced stupor, only to wake up aboard a ship bound for the Orient and forced into work. Even the fog that rolled into the city during the late afternoons moved as though on the prowl.

During our days at the orphanage, Cora, Flossie, and I had only glimpsed the streets of the Barbary Coast a handful of times. I suppose in our initial impressions we were rather blind to the neighborhood's more unsavory characteristics. We did not notice the stench; we did not observe the hollow, opium-addled gazes of the men and women who walked the streets. Instead, to us, it felt as though the rebellious spirit of the Wild West was still alive, and to our young, foolish eyes, the Barbary Coast appeared an exciting, merry place.

We observed what naïve girls do: Cora took special note of the colorful, flashy dresses worn by the dancehall girls. Flossie noticed that these girls often jingled with coins. As for me, I noted their laughter, which seemed loud and constant. Surely, people who laughed like that were having a gay time.

When we run away, Cora mused. *That's where we'll go. We'll wear bright dresses and dance, and no one will order us about, ever again.*

Cora hated life at the orphanage. Like all wrongfully imprisoned heroes, she insisted her presence there was a mistake: she ought have been born to royalty, or, at the very least, a great robber baron. Of course, the way most people reacted to Cora's scarlet hair and striking beauty did not help to disabuse her of this notion. She took to flouting the sisters' rules and obsessively plotting her escape. As Flossie and I were her closest friends, she planned for all three of us to run away together.

Cora was full of ambitious dreams, but if there was anyone who might actually see one of Cora's plans to fruition, it was Flossie; she had a knack for shrewd planning. Flossie was slim, narrow-hipped, and as straight as an arrow. She had lank blonde hair the color of pale straw, a long neck, and very large, very round blue eyes that seemed to take you in one feature at a time, as a bird might. Whenever her eyes lit up in that birdlike way, you could be sure she was making careful calculations.

But, as it turned out, it didn't take much plotting for us to run away. When St. Hilda's mysteriously caught fire, we were presented with a natural opportunity. I can still recall those first days roaming the streets of the Barbary Coast; it was *then* that we first glimpsed the neighborhood's rougher side. It was like seeing behind the curtain at a magic show. The atmosphere of merriment that had so charmed us before was laced with dark frenzy, and sometime between night and morning the sounds of laughter too often turned to the screams of violent argument. I found myself newly intimidated. Flossie appeared unsurprised but leery. Only Cora remained doggedly optimistic.

"It's only because we're on the streets all night," she insisted. "I'm sure anywhere you go, four o'clock in the morning isn't bound to be very pretty."

When we arrived, we hardly knew what to do, but the cheerful *plinkety-plonk* of the player pianos kept our steps light even as our stomachs growled, and kept us hoping that the answer would come. Later, of course, the irony of this dawned on me—we'd taken heart from music produced by mechanisms with no heart at all. We couldn't have guessed then, but this was symbolic of the Barbary Coast: merry on the surface, but cold and mercenary underneath.

By then we'd managed to piece together what had happened to our former home. *A Terrible Act of Arson*, the newspapers all read. St. Hilda's had been utterly reduced to cinders. A handful of girls had died of smoke inhalation, as had one of the sisters, Sister Edwina. The remainder of the orphanage's former occupants were scattered upon the winds of charity that carried them in haphazard manner to five other similar establishments—one as far away as Oregon. If we had lingered instead of running away, we surely would have been separated. This would have proved unbearable: the three of us were family, tied together by a bond even stronger than blood.

We wandered aimlessly for a few days, until Flossie set her sharp mind to ensuring our survival. She procured a name—Mr. Horace Tackett— and the address of the boardinghouse he ran.

"I hear not only will he take us in, he'll help us find employment," Flossie said. "He owns the dancehall down the lane."

Cora mulled this over, brightening. I could see she was already imagining herself wearing a colorful dress.

"But what will I do?" I asked.

Cora and Flossie were sixteen then, but I was not quite fourteen and scrawny, with the figure of a boy. I was a mousy little sister with few defining features other than my atypical passion for books, which I very much doubted would help me pass for a dancing girl.

"Hmm." As Flossie looked me over, it was plain she was wondering the same thing. "I'll think of something," she promised.

After a particularly uncomfortable night sleeping in an alley, we agreed to give Tackett's a try. We'd long ago divided ourselves according to our specialties. It was Flossie's job to do the negotiating. It was Cora's job to be witty and fetching. And it was my job to be invisible—or as close to it as I could manage. It was entirely likely that Tackett might want to turn me away, but Flossie set her mind to convincing him I'd make a suitable—and cheap—scullery maid.

When we arrived on his doorstep, Tackett asked our ages, and did not seem to notice nor care that we carried on our persons the scent of burned char. Likewise, he was either unaware or unconcerned with the fact that a girls' home some small distance away on the other side of town had recently burned to the ground. He clearly did not consider it his duty to bring wayward orphans to the attention of authorities.

I snuck looks at Tackett while Flossie employed her most persuasive appeals. He possessed a clashing air of old age and wiry youth. His face was angular and leathery, like a pirate's, but his body was surprisingly robust. I also noticed that his hair—presumably gray—had been dyed with so much black, it took on a bluish tint.

As fortune would have it, Tackett was down a couple of girls at the dancehall, and eager to replenish this deficit sooner rather than later. Convincing Tackett that my presence was somehow necessary in the whole bargain was trickier—but Flossie, soft-spoken genius that she was, managed to win him round, and Tackett began to approve of the idea of a servant that he didn't have to pay outright.

"You could tell folks that she's your ward," Flossie persuaded him. "After all, if you *did* have a ward, it would be only natural for her to earn her keep."

Soon enough, Tackett saw the beauty of it all—and, more importantly, the economy. I would be cook and maid. Blanche, the girl who'd had the longest tenure at the boardinghouse and who fancied herself Tackett's second-in-command, handed me a bedroll and showed me to a slightly sooty alcove in the kitchen where I was to sleep. Being so near the oven fire, it was, at least, quite warm.

Cora and Flossie were to have a small bedroom each. While my work was to begin immediately, Tackett generously insisted that Cora and Flossie remain idle for the week, taking some time to get to know the other girls, and learn the can-can the girls sometimes danced when they were not being ferried about the dance floor by a customer. He ordered Blanche to help them rustle up some suitable dresses.

The week passed quickly. My first memories of the boardinghouse are spotty, impressionistic; I was utterly overwhelmed by this sudden new life. I attempted to survey my surroundings, but it was extremely dim inside the house; I found out later this was because Tackett had a miserly streak, and insisted the gas jets be kept turned down low. And while the house itself was quite large, the rooms were small and cramped, as if they'd been squeezed together by some impulsive, slapdash architect. The floors creaked; the stairs were rickety. The privy, I learned, was out back, through a tiny yard, and put up a horrible smell.

Nevertheless, I threw myself diligently into my work, eager to prove my worth—anything to remain near Cora and Flossie. Between chores, I was curious to see what my friends might get up to, and one afternoon I spied Cora practicing dancing in the tight space of her room. I was startled by a cough behind me and whirled around to see Flossie had caught me snooping through the crack in Cora's door.

"We're meant to join the girls at the dancehall for the first time tomorrow night," she reminded me. I couldn't read her expression—if she was excited or apprehensive. But Flossie could be like that; she was so practical, she often appeared emotionless.

The next day, as late afternoon teetered on the precipice of early evening, the girls began getting ready—Cora and Flossie included. There was a small room with a bathtub inside the main house, and I was charged with boiling water for the girls' bath. They were each to bathe with the same water in succession, starting with Blanche and ending with the house's newest additions. I could tell this did not appeal to Cora's queenly inclinations, but she bit her tongue, excited to get dressed with rouge and dyed petticoats—things we'd never have been allowed to wear in the orphanage.

When all the girls were dressed, they lined up in the hall at the bottom of the stairs. I gasped when I caught sight of Cora. She wore an emerald dress with black stockings and a black frilly petticoat peeking out from under the shortened front hemline. Her scarlet hair was pinned in a lavish bouffant and her cheeks had been powdered and rouged. It was all very garish, and yet, on Cora, it was also shockingly beautiful. Flossie was dressed similarly, but on her the clothing and maquillage had an unfortunate clownish effect; evidently her pale coloring was no match for one crimson swipe applied from the pot of lip paint.

Tackett descended the rickety stairs, and after he gave each girl a once-over, the entire group trooped out the front door. When the door clicked shut and I was parted from Cora and Flossie—even if only temporarily—I felt lost.

I can't recall how I filled those hours, but by the time the front door swung open again on its creaky hinges, it was nearly morning, and I had long since retired to my bedroll in the kitchen alcove. At first, I sat up, thinking to go and greet them. But then I flinched to hear male voices— more than one, and rowdy. I crept to the door that led into the sitting room and peeped cautiously within. There they were; I saw no trace of Cora and Flossie, but I spied several of the other girls. And with them were three very drunk men. As I looked on, I detected a strained note to their hilarity. One of the girls, a friendly, rotund woman named Henrietta, attempted to smooth the tension by cranking up the player piano. The cheerful tinny banging of ragtime filled the air. A joke was made and everyone laughed.

But the scene was interrupted when the front door opened again and slapped shut. I caught a flash of Cora going up the stairs, with Flossie following close at her heels. I made a quick dash to the staircase and followed suit.

I found them in Cora's room.

"What's wrong?" I begged Flossie.

Both of them looked a little worse for the wear. Their rouge had streaked down their faces in rivulets that suggested dried perspiration. Cora's eyes looked red, either with anger or tears; I couldn't tell which.

"What's wrong?" I repeated. "Who are those men downstairs?"

At this, Cora's eyes flashed in my direction, green and angry as a cat's. She ripped the black velvet ribbon from her neck and threw it in my direction.

"Get out, Violet!" she snapped at me.

I was stung. Cora had never spoken to me with such hatred. Flossie hurried to take my arm and usher me out. Once we were in the hallway, she dropped her voice.

"She's . . . well, she's disappointed. She wants to leave," Flossie confided.

"Shall I get my things?" I asked, thinking of the meager bundle of trinkets I had hidden in the kitchen alcove.

Flossie shook her head. "We *can't* leave, Violet. We owe Tackett a week's worth of rent. He made it clear he won't be kind about it, and we have no money yet. Besides, where else can we go?"

"You mean we're trapped?"

"Shhh!" Flossie urged, her eyes darting in the direction of Cora's room. "Don't rub it in; she's liable to go mad." Flossie paused. She sighed and put a hand on my shoulder. "For now, we need to *survive*, Violet, until we can think of something better."

I was silent a moment.

"Let Cora alone tonight," Flossie said finally, patting my shoulder. She sighed again, looking tired and discouraged herself. "I'll come check on you before I go to bed."

With that, she disappeared back into Cora's room. The door clattered shut. I stared after her, my mind reeling.

I went back downstairs, anxious for something to do. The sun would come up soon, and I decided to peel and dice potatoes for breakfast; if I was clever, I could combine them with yesterday's corned beef and make a hash.

I stood at the kitchen counter, peeling until I was lost in a trance.

In the front parlor the men's voices thundered over the music of the piano.

We can't *leave*, Flossie had said. *Besides, where else can we go?*

I felt a warm, slippery moisture forming in my palm. I looked down and, to my astonishment, realized I had not only picked up one of the kitchen carving knives but was squeezing it by the blade. I had felt nothing as the blade bit into my skin.

I gasped and yelped, throwing the knife down immediately. It clattered against the dingy tile, and I cast about desperately for something to clean and bind my hand.

"Violet!"

Flossie had come to check on me as promised. Upon hearing my yelp, she rushed in.

"Oh, Violet," she said. "You're bleeding!"

Still trembling, I was making a mess. Flossie took over. She led me back to the counter and began to rummage for supplies. She found a bottle of whiskey and doused my wound. I winced.

"What happened?" she asked, cinching a scrap of cloth into a bandage and snipping away the excess with a pair of sewing scissors.

I stared at my hand in disbelief and took a breath but couldn't find any words.

"It was one of your spells," Flossie quietly deduced.

She looked my bandage over one last time, gave it a gentle pat, then led me to my alcove and helped me crawl into bed. "This isn't exactly what any of us imagined. But for now, Violet, just rest."

She remained for a moment, stroking my brow, until eventually I closed my eyes. I was amazed how Flossie never seemed to worry for herself, only others. Eventually she sighed and I heard her soft steps moving away. She was likely going to check on Cora yet again.

Just rest. I knew I should be grateful; at the very least, I hadn't been separated from Cora and Flossie. I loved them. I cared for them more than I had ever cared for myself.

But there are those who say that three is an unlucky number, and unluckier still when it comes to groups of young girls. *Triangles make for poor allegiances*, people will say. After all, a triangle—what is that?

The blade of a knife, coming to a point.

2

found out later that Cora had been reprimanded for dancing with
some men while turning others away. Evidently it was not her place to
discriminate.

How foolish we were! The Barbary Coast was teeming with houses
hung with red signs—the signal that "good-time gals" would offer a
weary sailor or lucky gambler a warm welcome. Tackett did not hang a
red sign on the door, but, truth be told, he did not have to. Everyone
knew the girls who lived in his boardinghouse also worked in his
dancehall, performing the old can-can or dancing the Bunny Hug
with sweaty patrons who slipped Tackett some coin. It was a short
walk from the dancehall to our boardinghouse, and Tackett's greed
knew no bounds.

We vowed to one another that our stay was temporary, a stepping-
stone to something better. Flossie hid her despair, but when it came to
Cora, I never saw a girl more like a cat in a burlap sack: even when she

was able to keep her smooth, charming composure on the surface, beneath it she was full of hellfire. We *would* leave, Cora determined. Flossie insisted we just needed to hit upon the right plan.

Routine soon shaped our days. While the other girls rested and bickered over clothes, I laundered the sheets, scrubbed the floors, peeled potatoes, and boiled cabbage. It was lowly labor, to be sure, but I preferred it to what I imagined their work to be like. I'd watched the occasional man staggering in, clutching a girl under his arm like a crutch, sweating and drooling and roaring with laughter. I'd smelled their booze and indigestion. I'd heard the thumping against the wall, the grunts, even the shrieks and howls and guttural profanities. My blood curdled to imagine what little romance these encounters offered.

We each found a way to forge forward. Flossie plodded along with her usual stalwart pragmatism. Cora discovered that, with her great beauty and sharp tongue, she was able to manipulate most men, and was minorly appeased by the small measure of control this afforded her. She also found distraction in collecting showy, frilly dresses, and flipping through society magazines while dreaming of a life beyond. But as the days went by and the glossy pages turned, I noticed a new and vaguely strained note in Cora's disposition towards me.

"She thinks you might feel you're better than us," Flossie confided to me one day.

My heart seized in protest, as though stabbed to believe Cora felt I was putting on airs.

"I'm the maid," I pointed out. "I scrub the privy she sits on!"

"Still," Flossie insisted, nodding, "you're the lucky one."

Long ago—as far back as my earliest days in the orphanage—I had cultivated a talent for invisibility, to the point where I could complete my chores in front of the sisters without them remembering I had ever entered the room. (*Have you tidied my study, Violet? Oh—I see you already did!*) When I ran errands that sent me tripping along the city streets, I noticed that passersby looked right through me; I was a common urchin, an unremarkable piece of urban scenery.

On nights when the girls found themselves obliged to entertain "suitors," I gave silent thanks for my ability to go unnoticed. I cranked the player piano and watered the whiskey, all without a second glance from the men who leered at the other girls in their loosely laced corsets and rolled stockings.

It wasn't all gloom. We had the company of some of the other girls—Henrietta, Mary, and Opal—and it is an incredible fact that when a group of women is cast into a situation bounded by less-than-desirable circumstances, they still find ways to laugh together, to find sisterhood and solace in one another. This was true of Tackett's boardinghouse, especially during the mornings and afternoons—stolen hours, free of male visitors.

The pact we'd made to someday leave the boardinghouse kept hope alive—for a time. But one day turned into seven, one week into twelve months, and twelve months into two and a half years. With little knowledge of the world, there was no way to leave, and nowhere for us to go.

One evening, just after I'd turned sixteen, I found it difficult to keep away from their rowdy, dazzling primping. Despite varying wildly in stature and shape, they treated their dancehall dresses like communal property, and preparations to go out always took on the enthusiastic, bickering tone of a horse-swap. I watched Henrietta wiggle and jiggle her way into a corset.

"Oof! I reckon I better lay off the sausages down at the beer hall! I kin barely squeeze into this infernal contraption!"

I was fond of Henrietta. She was red-cheeked and full of lewd jokes and merriment, with lively blue eyes that twinkled like Father Christmas's when she laughed. She was bawdy and sensual and was always going on about "getting the pleasure out of life." When she gave impromptu lectures about getting the pleasure out of life, it always called to mind the way she sucked the marrow out of chicken bones (very thoroughly).

"Lace me up, will ya, Mary?" Henrietta asked.

Mary—in many ways Henrietta's gaunt-faced opposite—crossed the room and commenced her dutiful best. As Mary's long, bony fingers were working hard at the laces, a loud fart sounded. Mary tsked and made a face.

"Henrietta!"

"Just makin' room, dearie!"

Henrietta looked at me and winked.

"When you get to be an ol' lady like me, you take it where you kin git it."

At thirty, Henrietta was the oldest "girl" in the house—and the one with the biggest heart. While she bore no love at all for Tackett, she seemed the least sorry for herself. Once, I asked her how she managed to keep a merry face all the time. She shrugged.

Ain't much else a woman can do, she'd said. *The world only needs so many schoolmarms! Not that I woulda had the learnin' for such anyhow. No . . . there are only two professions on offer, I'm afraid. A wife, or the kinda trouble that drives wives crazy.*

Now, as I watched Henrietta struggle into the corset, I let out a giggle. Mary continued tugging away, clearly hoping not to be downwind of another fit of flatulence. Despite her profession, Mary was fond of praying the rosary and had a talent for stern looks. She shot one at me now and I took my cue.

I left and poked my head into the next room, where Flossie was helping shy, round-faced Opal pile and pin her glossy black hair. Every time Opal locked eyes in the mirror with Flossie, she offered a sweet, timid smile. Flossie barely noticed. She was working hard, a mouthful of hairpins gripped tightly between her thin lips. That was Flossie's way: caring, but efficient.

Flossie glanced up and noticed me.

"Violet—don't you have a roast in the oven?"

During my two years at the boardinghouse, I had proved to be an efficient maid but a mediocre cook. Bread burned, gravy lumped, meat came out rubbery.

"You're right," I sighed. "I'll go check on it now."

I continued down the hallway, but when I passed Cora's room, the sight of her stopped me in my tracks. She sat at a rickety old vanity, putting the finishing touches on her makeup. I didn't mean to stare, but it was hard not to. As she carefully daubed rouge on her lips, her green eyes bright and her hair piled in a shapely bouffant, she made a perfect picture—a flame-haired Gibson girl in the flesh.

Her eyes met mine in the mirror. "Well, don't just stand there . . . Come in, Violet."

I stepped inside. She turned to get a better look at me, and I suddenly felt very aware of my plain brown hair and dull gray calico dress.

Over the past two years Cora had further cultivated her haughty, imperious air. She might have been forced into a life of dancing for coins, but to talk to her, you would think she was Marie Antoinette. This air ought to have repelled others. But on Cora it didn't; it rendered her even more magnetic.

"I'm curious, Little Mouse," she said, squinting at my features. "Let's put some rouge on you . . . I want to see how it looks."

I sat in her chair as she went to work, powdering and rubbing rouge into the apples of my cheeks, then dipping a brush into a little pot of red lip paint to trace the curves of my mouth. When she was done, she nodded with satisfaction.

"Why, Violet, I never noticed: your eyes are quite an unusual shade of gray!"

I turned to the mirror and gasped. Like Flossie, I looked a bit clownish. But . . . surprisingly, a clown with a few fetching features. There was a certain prettiness to my face I had never noticed before.

"My, my, Violet, it appears as though you like it," Cora commented flirtatiously. She gave a sly smile and winked at my reflection in the mirror.

I am ashamed to admit, I would have stared longer. However, a loud rapping sounded downstairs, making me jump to attention.

"Oh! The back door! I forgot to unlock it!"

I rushed out of the room, down the stairs, and through the kitchen. It wasn't until I had pulled the bolt back and thrown open the door that I realized I had not taken a moment to wipe the makeup off my face.

·"Jasper! Did you get everything on the list?"

Jasper stood there, blinking at me with surprise. He looked twice at my painted face, then cast his eyes to the ground, his tanned cheeks flushing red.

"Just as you wrote it," Jasper replied. "Down to the last."

A year older than myself, Jasper's main duty was to stand outside the dancehall and collect admission fees at the men's entrance. (Ladies entered free of charge.) But Tackett sometimes also put Jasper to work running the odd errand; in this case, he had picked up our month's supply of dry goods from the general store.

He began to lift sacks of rice and flour from a cart in the alley, carrying them in through the kitchen door. As he hefted the bags over his shoulder and stepped past me, he stole little glances at my made-up face. I knew all the girls down at the dancehall fawned over Jasper but found it impossible to ruffle him with their lewd flirtations. And yet, around me he sometimes took on a youthful softness that put me in mind of a puppy. The problem was he was eager and handsome—too eager and handsome to be anything but trouble.

With his errand unloaded, he handed me the list I'd scrawled on a little scrap of paper.

"You've a beautiful hand for writing, Miss Violet."

I have never been someone who knew much what to do with a compliment. I busied myself with the groceries.

"I'd like someone to learn me to make letters as nice as you do. But I'm guessin' you had a natural talent for it."

"You seem to do well enough with what you know," I reminded him.

"I do . . . all right . . . I suppose."

Footsteps thundered down the stairs and giggles and shrieks came from the sitting room. Jasper glanced curiously in the direction of the noise.

"Thank you, Jasper. I reckon you ought to be getting down to the dancehall."

"Oh, but I could stay, Miss Violet, and help you put these sundries away . . ."

"Nonsense," I said. "I won't keep you another second."

I ushered Jasper out the door where he rejoined his now-empty cart in the alleyway. He smiled at me, disappointed but not offended. I closed the door only to hear a loud tittering behind me. I whirled about to face Henrietta and Opal.

"Well, ain't he awful sweet on you!" Henrietta cackled.

I tried to deflect their jibes. "Don't be silly. He likes to hang about the house when he knows you girls are getting dressed. I'd wager he merely wanted to get a glimpse of Cora primping."

Opal shook her head. "He's the only one who *doesn't* stare at her, actually . . ."

I felt a little color rise to my cheeks. I said a silent prayer that they would let the subject drop. In the next second Henrietta sniffed at the air.

"What's that I smell burning?" she asked.

"Oh!" I cried, rushing to the oven and yanking the door open, only to encounter a blast of hot smoke. "Oh, no!" I pulled out a burnt roast. "Not again!" My eyes welled up with tears—partly from the smoke, but also from having reduced yet another dinner to inedible cinders.

"He's going to have my hide!" I whispered.

Hearing my distress, Flossie came downstairs, swooping in to my rescue.

"We'll fix it," she promised. She rooted in a drawer for a butter knife and set to scraping the burnt matter off the roast, then off each piece of diced carrot and celery.

While Flossie worked, she directed me to boil and mash some potatoes we found in the larder. We then arranged a pair of plates, using the mashed potatoes to mask any remaining evidence of char.

"There!" Flossie said. "Good as new. Now hurry and take it in to him. Don't forget a plate for Blanche . . . She's on her high horse today."

"Thank you, Flossie," I replied, reaching for her cool hand and giving it a squeeze. "Again. Truly."

"Hurry!"

I obeyed and lifted the tray, carrying it upstairs until the hallway ended at a closed door. I reached up to knock and held my breath.

After a moment, the door flew open.

"Well?" Blanche snapped. "Bring it in."

Her mouth pursed irritably. At twenty-nine, Blanche was one year younger than Henrietta, but since Tackett's favor had fallen upon her, she had taken to acting as though she were a forty-year-old madam. In years past, Blanche must have had a sultry, pert-nosed, blonde appeal, but in the years since, her face had hardened around the mouth. Her eyes were sunken and her poorly dyed hair had taken on a brassy, canary-yellow hue.

"Hurry up." She snapped her fingers.

I carried the tray into the dimly lit room, trying not to peer in the direction of the rumpled, unmade bed. I set the tray on a small table by the bay window, where Mr. Tackett sat expectantly. The curtains were drawn against the lingering day, but even under the yellow gaslight the black dye in his hair glowed blue.

They were a pair, Blanche and Tackett: two strange and unnatural pigments on a painter's palette.

To my surprise, Tackett smiled at me as I approached.

"And what has our little chef prepared?" he inquired, his tone as dark and slick as his hair.

Blanche frowned at this, and I felt her watching me.

"A . . . it's a rump roast, Mr. Tackett," I replied.

"Indeed."

Tackett almost never spoke to me. More often than not, if he did, it was in reproach. Suddenly I realized: I was still wearing the rouge Cora had so carefully painted on my face. I felt my stomach flutter. I hurried to deposit the tray, but as I leaned over, Mr. Tackett's eyes roved over my shape until his gaze came to rest upon my posterior. He gave it a long, leering look.

Blanche's scowl deepened.

I recoiled and managed to scurry out of the room, but I felt the telltale draft of someone just behind me, and in the next instant Blanche's viselike grip landed on my shoulder. She whirled me about so that my back was up against the wall. A moment passed wherein neither of us spoke. Then, finally, she lifted a hand to my cheek and swiped at the rouge, inspecting her fingertips.

"You'd be wise to clean that off straightaway."

It could have been a warning—or a threat. With Blanche, it was hard to tell.

"Ye—yes, ma'am."

I held my breath as she squinted at me for a long moment. Finally, she released my shoulder and sighed with disgust. She turned on her heel and strode back into Tackett's room.

I stood frozen, shivering in the warm, humid hall. The memory of her fingertips swiping my cheek chilled me.

3

Two days later, Henrietta came into the kitchen wrapped in her dressing gown. I caught sight of an eggplant-hued bruise blooming beneath one of her merry blue eyes.

"What happened?" I blurted, alarmed.

Henrietta waved a dismissive hand.

"Don't worry yerself over me, dearie," she said. "I had a li'l difference of opinion with one o' my regular dancehall Romeos is all."

"Here? Last night?"

Henrietta nodded.

"I didn't hear. I must've slept right through it. Did Tackett put a stop to it?"

My blood curdled as Henrietta's usually warm chuckle betrayed a bitter edge.

"Well, he got to the fella all right—eventually. Tackett demanded to be paid an extra two dollars for 'damages done to his property.'"

Henrietta paused and grunted. "Think if Tackett could find a way to collect that extra cash every night, he would, even if it meant we was all wearin' shiners."

I recoiled. I knew I ought to have been accustomed to such goings-on, but even after two years in the boardinghouse I still found myself shaken and outraged. Henrietta's constant gaiety was part of her thick skin, but for once I could sense her working to keep herself from despair.

I made up a plate of breakfast for her in silence, putting an indulgent pat of extra butter on her grits.

She thanked me and left the kitchen, but I was still thinking of her a full hour later as I was gathering the dishes. My eyes fell upon a row of empty milk bottles.

I had an idea.

Once I'd finished putting the plates away, I paid a visit to the butcher. This much was routine. But I had already made up my mind that, on my way back, I would take a small detour. I hiked up to a pretty little park atop Russian Hill. As it was April in San Francisco, the flowers were already in full bloom. The hill was covered in a hardy smattering of different wildflowers, but there were also a few rosebushes and daffodils—all of it a bit haphazard and unkempt. It was still early, and for the most part I was alone. I took a tiny pair of sewing scissors from my pocket and snipped the stems of as many flowers as I could without attracting attention, carefully folding my curated bundle into my tattered cardigan.

Back at the boardinghouse, I rounded up every empty bottle I could find, cleaned them, tied hair ribbons around each, and filled them with several inches of water pumped from out back. Next, I turned to the flowers I'd pilfered from the park and set about lovingly bundling and rebundling them until I had crafted six individual arrangements. The bulk of my plunder was smaller stock: lavender and orange poppies, woolly blue curls and tidy tips. But I'd managed to collect a couple of irises and tea roses, too. The biggest and most colorful bunch was intended for Henrietta, but there was also one each for Flossie, Cora, Opal, and Mary. I even made one for Blanche.

When all six were ready, I crept stealthily about the boardinghouse to put an arrangement in each of the girls' rooms. I hoped the flowers would serve as a small beacon of cheer. Everything in our lives was at pains to prove otherwise, but I wanted to remind the girls there was beauty, too, in our world.

With my mission completed, I resumed my regular duties: boiling the laundry, beating the feather beds, scrubbing the floors. Two hours into my chores I felt a shadow hovering over my shoulder. I looked up to see Opal smiling shyly at me.

"That was awfully nice of you," she said.

I grinned but played along. "What was?"

Opal laughed. "I know you're the one behind those flowers. They're very pretty. Thank you, Violet."

"It was nothing," I insisted, but Opal just shook her head and smiled wider.

As late morning gave way to early afternoon, each of the girls sought me out in turn. I felt my heart swelling with satisfaction. I had put the prettiest arrangement in Henrietta's room; it contained a particularly voluminous iris, its purple and white frilly petals bursting from the stem like a tiny but luxurious lavender waterfall.

"Them's the prettiest flowers I ever been given," Henrietta said. She paused and chuckled. "Well, truth be told, they're the *only* flowers I ever been given. Still, though . . . the prettiest!"

Even though I knew life in the boardinghouse lacked true romance, I was nonetheless surprised to hear this. It made me gladder than ever that I had taken the trouble.

It wasn't until I was out back, scrubbing the privy, that I heard the terrible commotion. First came the sound of smashing glass, then Tackett's tobacco-hoarse voice shouting. I realized he was yelling my name. I threw down the wire brush and hurried back inside, alarmed.

"YOU!" Tackett bellowed. "I hired you to cook and clean—not to waste your time."

The flowers. I was surprised he'd noticed them—and more surprised still that they had raised his ire. I recognized the once-magnificent iris among the broken bits of glass and flora in a wet heap on the wooden plank floor. The arrangement Tackett had confiscated and dashed to the ground had been Henrietta's. My heart twisted indignantly in my chest, but I couldn't find my tongue. He would happily beat me for anything I might say.

To my great surprise, Blanche stepped in.

"Horace," she said soothingly, "I rather like the notion of flowers in all the rooms. You might say they give this place an elegant touch. Maybe with a few little improvements like this you could even charge the fellas more. Why, just down the street Madame Elodie put in electricity and velvet curtains and was able to raise her price by a whole dollar apiece."

Ordinarily, talking business mollified Tackett, but I could see right away that Blanche had miscalculated. Tackett turned to glare at her, his face filling up with rage.

"*Electricity and velvet curtains?*" he spat at her. "You're as big an idiot as the rest of these greedy cows!"

Blanche flinched as if slapped. She may have earnestly liked the flowers, but coming to my defense had just cost her dearly. Tackett would not soon forget—and neither would she.

Tackett followed her gaze back to me.

"Clean this up." He pointed to the murky puddle. "And get rid of the rest of that nonsense. Don't let me catch you squandering time on such foolishness again. This is *my* boardinghouse, and I ain't runnin' no highfalutin parlor! Do you understand me?"

"Yes, sir."

My voice was trembling—with fear, but with outrage, too. Yet I did as I was told. I cleaned up the shattered glass and rounded up the remaining arrangements still lingering in the girls' rooms. I set about dismantling my gifts.

Flossie and Cora came to check on me as I toiled in the kitchen.

"I'm sorry, Violet," Flossie lamented.

"Your arrangements were pretty—very stylish, in fact," Cora said, perhaps hoping a compliment might make me feel better.

"I despise him," was all I could manage, removing the flowers from the bottles and dumping them in a pile. My throat was thick with angry sobs. I refused to let them out, but Cora and Flossie knew me.

"You can always put ipecac in his food," Cora joked, referring to the small bottle of expectorant we kept to remedy the girls' coughs and colds. Too much made a person vomit. Her face brightened. She gave a wink and flounced upstairs.

"She's never serious," I said.

"I don't know about that," Flossie replied. "I believe Cora *would* like someone to slip ipecac into Tackett's dinner." She caught my surprised expression and quickly corrected herself. "Oh, but ignore her, of course!"

"Of course."

Flossie patted my shoulder sympathetically and followed Cora upstairs. Alone, I resumed my work. When I had finished dismantling my modest arrangements, I threw the flowers into the alley to wilt.

I stood staring at them for a moment, watching their colorful, crisp petals as they grew limp and rubbery, abandoning their cheerfulness to the muck.

4

wondered if I had not yet seen the worst of Tackett's wrath, but the next day Blanche told us he was under the weather and laid up in bed.

"Is he suffering from a hangover?" I asked Flossie.

She shrugged.

"Perhaps. Blanche says he looks a little green around the gills. He's not much for breakfast, so you needn't bother."

Tackett didn't emerge from his room all day. His office remained dark and empty. Truth be told, all of us enjoyed a reprieve from his presence—even Blanche. The mood around the boardinghouse became lighter, contented, almost lackadaisical.

By the time evening rolled around, the storm clouds of yesterday's emotions had lifted—mostly. Cora and Flossie were dressed and ready for the dancehall early and sat lounging around Cora's bedroom, thumbing the well-worn pages of the ladies' magazines that Cora collected.

I wandered in and lingered. Truth be told, I didn't care much for society pages, but it was always mesmerizing to watch the expressions that flitted over Cora's pretty face as she absorbed their contents, dazzled.

"Tackett still sick?" Cora asked when she noticed me hovering by the door.

"Reckon so."

Cora chuckled. "You didn't take my little suggestion to *heart*, did you, Violet?"

"Which suggestion?"

"About the ipecac."

"No!" I said, shocked.

"Now, Cora," Flossie chastised from her chair. "You know Violet would never." Then she cocked her head at me. "Although you're not still upset about what Tackett did to your flowers, are you?" She waved me in and patted the bed beside her.

I shrugged and came over to sit.

Flossie gave me a sad, solemn stare.

"Of course, you know *why* he did it, don't you?"

I frowned. I hadn't given it much thought; I'd been too angry.

"Tackett can't have us putting on airs, thinking we're worth more than the scraps he gives us," Flossie explained.

"That's awful lousy of him."

"I didn't say it wasn't. But that's Tackett. It's how he's earned his fortune."

Cora's head snapped to attention at the word "fortune."

"He's an absolute miser. And I heard his safe is packed to the gills. He's got more gold than Midas himself!"

"Maybe it is, and maybe it isn't," Flossie said. "But you know as well as I do it won't change anything for us."

Cora looked at Flossie for a long moment, then sighed. Tackett was a skinflint; if he were as wealthy as the rumors insisted, we'd be the last to know. Cora turned back to her magazines. I watched her trail a wistful finger over a socialite dressed up for a masquerade ball.

"If I were rich," Cora mused, "all my clothes would be tailor-made. I'd have more hats than Alva Vanderbilt and more dresses than Evelyn Nesbit!"

Flossie laughed and exchanged a look with me, raising one eyebrow.

"And you'd 'let them all eat cake,' I suppose."

Cora snorted, little interested in history.

"I'd let them all *eat their hearts out!* That's what I'd do," Cora retorted. She paused, then looked up at Flossie. "Why? What would you do?"

"With money?" Flossie pondered this, chewing her bottom lip. Her face took on the angular birdlike expression she got when she was adding sums in her head.

"Enroll in typing school," she finally answered. "That way, if I ever lost my fortune, I'd have a skill . . . something to help me live as a modern woman and avoid . . . well, *this*." Flossie waved a hand about the room.

"*Ugh!* Practical, indeed—*too* practical!" Cora said, dissatisfied that Flossie wouldn't play the game the way she preferred. Cora turned to me.

"What about you, Violet?"

I blushed.

"I don't know . . ." I stammered. "I wouldn't know what to do with a great fortune."

Realizing I was even more hopeless than Flossie, Cora sighed and turned back to the society pages.

"I like what Flossie said, though," I admitted. "It *would* be nice to have some independence. And there are girls managing it now. I'd work as a shop-girl, perhaps . . ."

Cora's head snapped up again. She snorted loudly.

"Hah! You, Violet? There's nothing 'modern' about you—not a stitch! You've always got your nose in a book. If you were a shop-girl, you'd moon about, always lonely, dreaming of the kind of gentleman suitor that you and Flossie are always reading about in your silly, boring books!"

"That's not so!" I protested, annoyed. "Flossie?"

Flossie gave me an apologetic look but nodded in agreement.

"I can imagine you as an independent shop-girl, but I have to admit, you *do* seem the type to pine for a Rochester or Heathcliff of your own, Violet."

I fell silent. Was this true? Did I secretly dream of love? In the orphanage, love had taken the form of yearning for parents who only existed in our fantasies. And in Tackett's boardinghouse . . . well, love was a dangerous proposition, to say the least. But I realized they were *partly* right: I dreamed of love, but, more than that, I dreamed of having a family. My parents were but a faint specter in my memory; yet, I could still feel the warmth of their hands as they tucked me in at night, turning down the oil lamp and planting a cool kiss on my forehead. The knowing smile they exchanged when they believed I'd drifted off to sleep. I wanted to live in that memory and remake it for my own family someday . . . but I knew, of course, I was destined to do no such thing; I'd been forfeited to the orphanage for a reason.

The door suddenly flew open, and Blanche materialized. She was clearly in an irascible mood, and both Flossie and I snapped to attention.

But Cora refused to be ruffled. She continued to recline on her bed, as serene as ever. She flipped a magazine page as though bored. Blanche stared at her.

"Hello, Blanche," Cora said in a pleasant tone.

"Tackett wants to see you," Blanche responded. She paused, then added, "In his room."

"Me?" Cora blinked, surprised. Then she covered the surprise with a lazy yawn.

"Yes. Lord knows why. Hurry up, now!"

Blanche's whole body had stiffened as she delivered this summons. Flossie and I exchanged a quick, wary glance. Blanche had long since established herself as Tackett's "favorite," but Cora's beauty was unparalleled, and Blanche knew it.

She clapped her hands as if to hurry Cora along, and after a belabored moment Cora rose and smoothed her skirts. Then she sighed and strode out of the room.

As the staccato of Cora's heeled boots faded down the hall, I ventured, "I take it Tackett is feeling better?"

Blanche's head swiveled until her gaze fell on me. She ignored my question.

"Shouldn't you be busy?" she snapped. "If you've nothing to do, there's a pile of stockings that need darning in my room. Don't dawdle."

With that, she stamped down the hall, leaving the door ajar so I might follow her. I rose reluctantly to my feet.

"And, Flossie," Blanche called over her shoulder, "have the girls line up for inspection! Tackett and I will be along soon."

Some minutes later I sat at the kitchen table darning stockings while Flossie corralled the girls at the bottom of the stairs. I peeped at them through a crack in the swinging door. Blanche came down and conducted a preliminary inspection as though she were in charge. Eventually, another door slammed upstairs and Cora and Tackett descended. Though she remained silent, I could see Blanche's mouth twisting; it was plain she was fuming, wondering if she might soon be replaced.

But Cora hadn't been in Tackett's quarters for very long, I reasoned to myself. And besides, she detested Tackett more than anyone. I watched her take her place in the line.

Tackett moved along the row, looking each girl over as a merchant might evaluate his wares. I felt hot bile rise in the back of my throat. Tackett made small comments about Henrietta's appearance, then Opal's. He only grunted at Flossie and Mary. When he got to Cora, he smiled. Tackett never smiled unless he wanted something or was about to be handed some coin.

Watching this interaction, Blanche piped up.

"That's a lovely brooch she's wearing, isn't it?" Blanche remarked.

All eyes moved to the brooch pinned near Cora's décolletage. It was small but pretty—a rosette of opals and amethyst.

Blanche addressed Cora directly. "Tell him where you got it."

"It was a gift," Cora said in a dry voice, leery of Blanche's intentions.

"Who from?" Blanche prodded.

"Young MacCready."

"Young MacCready . . ." Blanche repeated, pretending to muse upon the name. She turned back to Tackett. "Isn't that the same Mac-Cready who owes you quite a gambling debt?"

Tackett looked at Blanche for a moment. Slowly, his eyes lit up.

"So it is, Blanche."

"Seems to me that brooch should go towards the debt he owes you."

"Why, you've a point," Tackett agreed, eyes bright. "I believe it should."

"Well?" Blanche said to Cora. "Turn it over."

Tackett held out his hand. Cora gave Blanche a long, hard stare, then unpinned the brooch and placed it on Tackett's open palm. He smiled a second time, gaze lingering on Cora's bosom.

"There are ways to earn it back, my dear," he said.

At this, Cora's eyes flashed with hatred, while Blanche appeared freshly worried. *Had she miscalculated again?* I held my breath.

But before Cora could reply, Tackett suddenly went pale and he lurched away. I believe he meant to bolt to the privy. He didn't make it: a wretched stream of yellow vomit spilled from his mouth and onto the floor of the hall.

"Horace!" Blanche fussed. "Oh, Horace, you're still ill. Let me help you to your room!"

Tackett trembled with humiliation, but it was plain he was in no condition to decline.

"Get 'em down to the dancehall," he muttered as Blanche helped him back up the stairs. "It's still a workin' day. And tell the girl to clean that up."

"You heard him!" Blanche shouted over her shoulder.

Everyone—Cora, Flossie, Mary, Opal, and Henrietta—scrambled out the front door.

I went to fetch the mop and bucket. If I was quick about it, I could get the job done before Blanche came back downstairs. I hardly wanted to cross paths with her; I could only imagine her dark mood.

Later that night I recalled the picture of Tackett doubled over in pain, vomiting onto the floor . . . and I smiled. *He deserves it*, I thought to myself. I remembered what Cora had said about putting ipecac in his food and almost wished I *had* done it. As far as I could tell, there wasn't enough justice in the world for Tackett.

When I readied my bed in the kitchen alcove and went to change into my nightshirt, something fell from the pocket of my smock. It fell with a small, empty thump onto the floor. I picked it up and examined it: it was a bottle. I was both shocked and puzzled.

I looked at it more closely, and saw that it was empty.

5

The empty bottle had me rattled. It couldn't be mine.

I'd never seen it before—I was sure.

Wasn't I?

Unable to sleep, I comforted myself with the one distraction that had always soothed me: reading a book. Books were hard to come by— a definite luxury—but Flossie somehow managed to keep me in good supply. She was no great beauty like Cora, but when she put her mind to it, she could get anything she wanted. Luckily for me, Flossie wanted books, and she was willing to share.

During our days in the orphanage, a mutual love of reading had formed the basis of our friendship. Some of the other girls, like Cora, could barely read the letters stamped on a sack of flour. I knew it wasn't Cora's fault; she had trouble with the written word. When the sisters made her read aloud, she became instantly flustered, tossing her hair and declaring that books were for boring people. The only words Cora willingly read were printed in gossip columns and on face cream advertisements.

But Flossie and I read ravenously, despite the limited selection available, and eventually found a way to borrow any and every kind of novel we wanted. Or, rather, *Flossie* found a way and was kind enough to share her secret.

It began when she spied me reading one day and nodded at the book clutched in my hands, asking what it was.

"Thomas Aquinas," I answered.

Flossie rolled her eyes. Admittedly, it was dry.

"Sister Louise loans me her books," I said. "But . . . what are *you* reading?"

Flossie's lips curled into a smile. It was a curious expression for her. Like the cat that caught the canary, it bore a hint of a devilish secret.

"A story called 'The Turn of the Screw,'" she said. "It's by Henry James. It's very modern, I think."

"'The Turn of the Screw'?" I repeated the title aloud. "Where did you get that?"

"The library. I heard people talking about it."

"I don't understand," I stammered.

Flossie scampered over to perch on the edge of my cot. She leaned towards me and whispered the full story: She had ingratiated herself to Sister Edwina; she said Sister Edwina even considered her an unofficial novice of sorts. And sometimes . . . Sister Edwina wished to have access to a book here and there that none of the local convents owned. In these cases Flossie was sent with a handwritten note to the big new public library, and the librarians there almost always found a way to procure them.

"But . . . Sister Edwina reads books like *that*?" I pointed.

Flossie shook her head and gave that tight-lipped smile again, explaining her true secret: over time, she had learned to mimic Sister Edwina's penmanship so perfectly that now she could write a note asking for any book she wanted—any book at all! And so Flossie had gained access to an entirely new world of treasures.

"I'll share them with you," Flossie promised. "You aren't like the other girls here."

I grinned. But then Flossie's face suddenly crumpled, and she looked forlorn.

"Do you think me very wicked? For imitating Sister Edwina's script?"

I quickly shook my head. "No," I decided aloud.

Flossie smiled, relieved.

"I'm so glad you feel that way, Violet. I'll share: I'll borrow books for the *both* of us. It'll be our secret, so long as you never give me away. You won't—will you?"

"I won't," I promised.

And I didn't.

Our pact made, Flossie regularly snuck off to the library, eavesdropping on the librarians as they whispered about new titles. When we wound up in Tackett's boardinghouse, Flossie continued to find ways to borrow or buy books, and our secret continued. During dry spells, we reread early favorites—and even chilling tales like "The Turn of the Screw" grew to be a comfort to me.

I was grateful to Flossie for this, and especially grateful that night as Tackett snored upstairs, waking only to make terrible retching sounds. I methodically turned the pages and lost myself in the young governess's plight, momentarily putting aside my anxious wonderings.

6

Despite its regular ruckus of hilarity, Tackett's boardinghouse was a place full of silent sorrows. Perhaps this was to be expected; perhaps most brothels are full of such things, no matter how famous their "good-time gals."

But in April of 1906, I felt a new darkness creeping into the house—something truly ominous. This feeling was persistent yet frustratingly vague. If I tried to close my eyes and envision the source of my unease, it was as if an evil shadow stood just out of sight.

It could not have been the impending earthquake, for while it would soon be upon us, how could anybody have imagined such a thing? There are those who insist that animals—horses and dogs and cats and such—can sense earthquakes beforehand, but I don't credit it. When I think back to the week that led up to the earthquake, I remember the stray cats in the alley getting up to all their regular tricks, scrabbling and hissing over fish-heads, just as they always did.

No, we had no warning of the "Big One," nor the terrible fires yet to come, and in any case the darkness I sensed presaged a different kind of evil—something that had nothing to do with the whims of Mother Nature.

Tackett vomited nearly two days straight, but eventually, he recovered from his terrible stomach ailments. One week later it seemed as though life had returned to normal, and I awoke early to begin my usual ritual of boiling coffee and grits and frying up eggs and bacon.

I enjoyed these morning hours. I liked filling the cool kitchen with the humid scents of coffee and hot food. When the smell reached the upstairs hall, it lured the girls, one by one, from their rooms. Once the house was full of giggling and teasing and gossip, the day truly began.

Flossie was almost always the first downstairs, and more often than not she was kind enough to lend me a hand in my work. Next came Henrietta, followed by Opal and Mary, then Cora, who—rather like a cat—liked to luxuriate in bed as long as possible. Blanche typically came down last. She and Tackett did not sit to eat with the rest of us. Instead, she expected me to ready a tray that she would bring up.

That morning, when Cora entered the kitchen, she eyed me preparing their tray.

"I shouldn't bother with that if I were you," she said. "Evidently he's sick again."

I stopped and stared at her. I still hadn't told anyone about the empty bottle I'd found. The night I found it, I thought of tossing it into the alley, but wound up stuffing it under my bedroll, like a guilty secret.

"It was impossible to ignore his retching," Cora continued. "Not to mention Blanche's grousing. I'd wager she'll be down here any moment, hollering at you to clean his mess and bring up a sick-pail."

Sure enough, no sooner had Cora spoken than we all heard Blanche's boots on the stairs. I gestured to Flossie to take over a frying pan of eggs and clambered to fetch the pail and a mop. By the time Blanche swooped into the kitchen, I was nervous, but ready.

The second her gaze fastened upon me, her frown deepened.

"I heard Tackett's fallen ill again," I said.

"Indeed." She observed the pail and mop with narrowed eyes.

"Would you like me to take care of matters upstairs?" I asked haltingly.

"Well, I hardly want you to just stand there, now, do I?" Blanche sniped before finally turning away.

Upstairs, Tackett was sleeping, and I saw that he had vomited onto the floor beside his bed. He looked extraordinarily pale, his face shiny with perspiration. Even if someone *had* put something in his food . . . well, I had never seen ipecac take a body so violently. He was racked with trembling convulsions as his stomach turned out all its contents. He could do little more than sweat and sleep.

The acid bite of bile filled my nostrils until my senses dulled and I could detect the terrible odors no more. Once the floor was clean, I placed a sick-pail near Tackett's head. Blanche stalked in just as I was finishing, and I hurried out. I spent the remainder of the morning ducking in and out to change the pail and trying to avoid notice.

Sometime in the late afternoon, as I attempted to cook supper, Blanche returned to the kitchen, and I was trapped. I'd burned the evening meal again, overcooking a pot of stew. She entered the kitchen just in time to catch me in a state of chaos and distress.

Blanche surveyed the job I'd just botched. Her yellow hair had been curled with tongs, and her rouge was painted onto her cheeks in two pink circles. I thought for a foolish moment that she was considering helping me, but finally she sighed with what I took to be disgust.

"Ugh. You hopeless idiot!"

I cringed, but this had a funny effect on Blanche; it was as if I'd waved a red cape in front of a bull. She twitched like an enraged animal and stared me down. At first, neither of us spoke, but suddenly, as though filled with a fresh wave of vitriol, she snapped, shoving me into a corner and pointing a finger in my face.

"*Don't* think I haven't noticed that you never get it right; one night you burn the dinner and the next you barely cook it!" she hissed. "Why, who's to say *you're* not the one to blame for his getting sick?"

My eyes widened. Blanche's own gaze narrowed.

"*It had better not be something you're doing on purpose!*"

I felt the blood leave my face. Blanche stared me down further, leaning in until our noses were almost touching.

"But no . . . you're too dull to be that conniving, aren't you? I'm telling you: dim-witted or not, you had better watch out. He's already realized he'd do well to move you down to the dancehall and hire a *real* cook."

The kitchen began to spin around me until all I could see were different colored streaks. Ignoring my distress, Blanche continued berating me. I heard her voice dimly, as if from far away . . .

Such was my state of terror, I cannot recall Blanche leaving the room. The next thing I was aware of, I blinked my eyes and found myself standing in the cellar, clutching the body of a dead rat. The moment I felt its coarse, matted, flea-bitten fur in my fingers, I screamed and threw it away from me. It gave a gruesome, wet thump against the cellar wall, then slid to the ground. I stared at it, horrified.

My heart was racing, and I waited for my pulse to slow. There had to be a reasonable explanation for my present state; and of course, as I thought about it, there was. It had long been my task to lay the rat bait in the cellar, not to mention to collect and dispose of the carcasses. After Blanche's dressing-down, I must have had a spell. Surely I'd come down here to escape, my trance leading me to the comfort of my regular duties.

"*Violet?*" I heard a voice call, thin with concern.

"Flossie?"

I watched the familiar hem of her skirts come down the cellar stairs. When she saw me, she gasped. The rat had left a stain of brownish blood on my hands. Flossie walked towards me with a handkerchief and wiped at my palms roughly, worried.

"Are you all right?"

I nodded weakly in the dim light.

"Your spells? What set it off this time?"

Fragments of Blanche's words drifted back to me. *He's already realized he'd do well to move you down to the dancehall . . .* Tears sprang to my eyes, and I trembled with a mixture of fear and shame.

"I was upset," I choked out. "Blanche . . . she caught me burning tonight's stew and she laid into me."

A wave of emotion I'd been holding back suddenly crested and broke. Tears spilled down my cheeks and I crumpled to the ground. Flossie sank down next to me and attempted to soothe me.

"That's her way; you know that, Violet. She's angrier than a hornet most days. The pretty little fool thought she'd be running this place by now. But when Tackett's not vomiting into a pail, he's busy making eyes at Cora, and Blanche can't stand it."

I felt a sob catch in my throat.

"She . . . means . . . to have me moved . . . to the dancehall . . ."

Flossie froze. She knew I was hoping she would say it wasn't true, that Blanche was bluffing. But she appeared uncertain, and reluctant to lie.

"I'm sorry, Violet . . ." she said quietly.

At this, I felt my chest tighten. I wanted badly to keep a stiff upper lip, but the room had begun to spin again.

"Oh, dear—*breathe!*" she ordered.

Flossie gripped my upper arms and bid me to concentrate on the rise and fall of my chest, gently stroking my hand. After several minutes I managed to slow my heart. By then something in Flossie's face had hardened.

"This can't go on," she said. "I have a solution, I think. But you must come with me—and be very, very quiet."

Once I was stable on my feet, Flossie led the way back upstairs and, to my surprise, to Tackett's empty office. Tackett was still sick upstairs, and Blanche was presumably busy tending to him. Flossie quietly pushed the office door open and turned to me.

"I need you to keep a lookout. Can you do that, Violet?"

My heart began pounding again, but I nodded and positioned myself carefully inside the doorway, poking my head innocuously into the hall. Behind me, Flossie nimbly crossed the room. I suffered yet another shock to realize that she was bound for Tackett's safe.

To my astonishment, Flossie knelt and dialed the combination. The safe door swung open, and she darted a hand inside to retrieve something.

"But . . . Flossie!" I whispered at her. "How on earth . . . ?"

Flossie shook her head and put a finger to her lips. In another flash she had closed the door and spun the dial.

"Quickly," she hissed, "before someone sees us!"

She shooed me out and back along the hallway.

Once we'd returned safely to the kitchen, Flossie produced a tiny brown bottle from her skirt pocket. Slowly I began to comprehend: she'd filched a bottle of laudanum.

"Sister Louise used to administer that when my spells got especially bad," I murmured, remembering.

Flossie offered a gentle smile and nodded.

"I know. I remembered it helped," she said.

She bid me sit at the kitchen table while she started boiling water and making a weak mug of tea. Once it was ready, she pulled the stopper from the little brown bottle and shook in three simple drops. She handed the mug to me.

"But, Flossie, how did you learn Tackett's combination?" I asked, accepting the mug and staring at it in disbelief.

"Cora got it out of him. Don't ask me to tell you how—I doubt she would want you to know."

"You mean to say that Cora . . . allowed Tackett in her bed?" I didn't want to believe it; Cora had grown into an accomplished coquette, but she was also proud. While it was true that she was ambitious, sometimes even ruthless, I preferred to believe that she had her limits.

"Shhhh . . ." Flossie urged. She gestured to the mug cupped in my hands. "There, now. Drink that to calm your nerves. I think you ought to lie down for a while."

She paused, eyeing the burnt mess of the meal I'd abandoned when my spell struck.

"I'll see what I can do about fixing the stew," Flossie said.

I sipped the tea as I was bid.

After a moment, I asked, "What if Blanche comes looking for me?"

"I'll keep her away. Or, at the very least, I'll put Cora up to the task. There's no one to keep Blanche preoccupied like Cora."

We shared a weak smile.

Once I finished my tea, Flossie helped me into my alcove. I let her cover me with the blankets. I was warm, already feeling the effects of the laudanum. The last image I remembered was Flossie leaning over me with a concerned expression, trying to soothe my worries. Her lank blonde hair caught the light, making a halo around her head as she stroked my brow with a cool hand.

Just rest, Violet . . . she was saying. *Just rest now. All will be better soon . . .*

I shut my eyes, and all went black.

7

\\\||||///

"*V iolet? . . . Violet? Are you awake?*"

I struggled to force my eyes open; my eyelids felt as though they were weighted.

When I finally came to, I rolled to my side to see Cora.

"Violet?" she said. "Are you all right?"

Beside her stood Henrietta.

"The hour's growing late, dearie," Henrietta urged gently. "We're off to the dancehall and wanted to see that you were feelin' awright before we left."

My throat was dry as paper as I swallowed. I slowly blinked and surveyed the scene before me. Someone had not only fixed the evening meal but also put the kitchen back into immaculate order. *Flossie*, I thought gratefully.

The kitchen had been set in order, and yet . . . something felt amiss. Still groggy, I struggled to sit up.

"I napped longer than I meant to," I murmured.

Cora gestured that I should lie back down.

"Flossie said you needed the rest. Go back to sleep! I didn't mean to rouse you . . . We only wanted to make certain you were all right and to say good night."

"But . . . Tackett?" I said, worried.

"The last we heard, he was sick, drunk, and shittin' up a storm," Henrietta said. "Or should I say, the last we *smelled*—hah! Can't keep his food down, yet still demandin' his whiskey, o' course. Oh, but you ain't gotta worry yerself. Cora brought the two of 'em a fresh bottle, and Blanche is stayin' in with 'im. They oughtn't give you much trouble."

Cora rolled her eyes.

"Her *Royal Highness* had the nerve to order me to carry a fresh bottle of whiskey and two glasses in to them on a little tray! Can you imagine? The nerve."

Of course, I could imagine. Henrietta shrugged this off. "The p'int is, the sooner they get in their cups the better, and you can just rest your weary head."

Cora tucked my quilt back around me, a kind gesture from her. While Flossie was quite maternal, Cora was usually too busy being glamorous. But at the moment she appeared genuinely concerned.

"Sleep," she urged. "We're off now, and we only wanted to tell you."

The two of them left the kitchen. I knew they were headed through the sitting room to the front hallway. The clatter of boots shook the ceiling above my alcove. It was the familiar sound of the other girls trooping down. Their footsteps sounded jaunty, merry. Tonight there would be no inspection; I knew from the happy staccato that everyone was relieved.

I listened as, one by one, their boots tapped along the front hallway, over the threshold, and down the porch stairs. I tried not to think that I was now alone with Tackett and Blanche. An eerie sense of quiet filled the house. I strained to listen harder.

Nothing.

I stared at the sloped ceiling and willed myself to go back to sleep. But the drowsiness I had felt only minutes earlier moved further and further away, like a receding tide. I finally gave up.

I knew I ought to be glad for the peace and quiet, for the fact that, whatever she was doing, Blanche wasn't storming into the kitchen. But that night I could not enjoy the silence. There was something peculiar about it; it was somehow too immense. The more I tried to ignore it, the more I was gripped by a queer, unsettled feeling. Something was wrong. I rose from bed and quietly padded around the boardinghouse, peering into empty rooms, unnerved. The pit in my stomach tightened as I neared the door at the end of the second-floor hall. Tackett's room. I took a breath and held it, then leaned in close, eventually resting my ear against the thin wood.

Nothing.

I felt a sudden shiver of icy fear. I jumped back as though stung and hurried downstairs to where I'd always felt safest: the kitchen. Once there, I lit a fire in the stove and admonished myself. I was being foolish, of course, allowing my imagination to get the better of me.

I spent the next two hours doing every chore I could think up. I scrubbed the stains out of the laundry. I scoured the privy, usually my least favorite task. Then I wandered the house, feeling lost, until I finally set to work wiping the grease and smoke from the glass shades of the gas-lamps.

But when all this was done, I was again left empty-handed. I felt my gaze move as if by its own volition to Tackett's room above. Eventually, my body followed, and I found myself once again standing in the hallway outside his door, holding an oil lamp.

My hand was trembling when I reached up to knock. The sound echoed menacingly.

I waited.

Nothing.

I knocked a second time and waited.

Still nothing.

"Mr. Tackett, sir?" I called. "Miss Blanche?"

Still nothing.

Finally, I gripped the doorknob. I remember my knuckles were white. I pushed the door open and released the handle. The hinges gave a plaintive groan.

All was dark and quiet within. I worried that they might be sleeping, but in my gut I already knew this wasn't possible. The terrible smell in the room hit me like an anvil. A smell of bile again, but something else, something metal—like *iron*, perhaps, and a third odor, too . . . a rotten scent I couldn't quite place. The trembling in my hands began to move through my body—a cloud of black fear widening and tightening, buzzing until every inch of me quivered.

"Mr. Tackett? Miss Blanche?" I repeated. I carried the oil lamp across the black room, its circle of light blooming into the darkness like a terrible flower. I set the lamp down on the nightstand beside the two figures and—after taking a breath—reached a hand towards the bed.

I steeled myself as I drew back the sheet.

Tackett stared at me with milky, sightless eyes. His mouth was slightly ajar, the corners crusted with foamy saliva gone dry.

The greater shock was Blanche. She lay next to Tackett, her body contorted into a most unnatural position, her pink silk dress soiled with her own excrement. There were other signs of disarray, too: when I pulled back the sheets further I spied pools of vomit and urine, and the bed-clothes beneath both of them were rumpled as though given a good thrashing. I do not know how much time passed as I stood staring; I could not look away. It struck me all at once that not only were Tackett and Blanche dead but they had died a most *violent* death. The trembling in my hand became uncontrollable. I uttered an involuntary shriek and let the sheet drop, cringing at the volume of my own voice. But of course there was no one to hear. My next realization stopped me cold. I was alone in a house with two corpses.

Cora. Flossie.

I found myself in motion. I fled the room, stumbling down the stairs and out the front door without so much as stopping for my shawl.

8

There was a damp chill in the air—as there so often is when evening arrives in San Francisco—but I barely noticed. My blood pumped furiously, and I stumbled over my feet as I ran. The streets were loud and busy, filled with a cacophony of horses whinnying and drivers scolding one another in brash voices. The overpowering odor of manure moldering in the gutters was an unexpected relief: alive and earthy after the putrid scent of death I'd just encountered. My ears filled with the frenzied *plinkety-plonk* of a dozen player pianos, their tinny notes spilling out from the saloons. I rushed past a man urinating against the side of a building. He gave a lecherous laugh as I glanced at him but I barely took notice. I continued on, passing other Barbary Coast revelers and breathing in the wafting odors of ale and tobacco and the floral spice of opium.

When I arrived in front of the dancehall, I was sweaty from running, and the city's steep, sloping streets had knocked the wind out of me. I looked between the two entrances; the one closest to me was a paying entrance for men, and a short distance away was a free entrance marked LADIES, though it was well-known that nary a true "lady" had ever graced this door.

"Violet!"

Jasper had spied me from his post where he collected coins at the men's door. He jumped down from his soapbox, a hank of sandy hair tumbling across his forehead. It grazed his cheekbone as he stared at me, wide-eyed, excited. I desperately waved him off. I was flustered, and there were only two people in the world I trusted enough to tell my secret.

"Violet!" he called again.

"Not now, Jasper—I've . . ." I fumbled. "I've important business."

Jasper frowned at me, stung, but ultimately obeyed. I felt a prickle of guilt, but if I dallied, Jasper might inquire after Tackett, whereupon I would have to either lie or tell the awful truth.

I crossed over to the women's free door. A steady stream of young women were entering, some merely poking their heads in to see if the action inside was worth their while. They were very much alike in appearance: colorfully dressed, their cheeks rouged, and their necks doused in cheap toilet water that did its best to imitate the perfumes of Paris. A few of the girls eyed me, clearly wondering what I was doing there, dressed as I was. I felt myself grow self-conscious and I hesitated. I rarely visited the hall, and the couple of times I'd been sent to deliver messages I'd quickly learned it was never easy to get any of the girls alone; their dance-cards filled up quickly and stayed full. I hadn't the faintest idea how I would draw Flossie and Cora away. Intimidated, I felt shyness curling over me in a familiar wave.

But then I remembered the two lifeless figures back at the boardinghouse, and I gulped down a breath and plunged inside.

The dancehall was an echoing, humid space. It was as though even the walls themselves perspired. Countless couples thronged the wooden floor, which was badly scuffed and stained with tobacco expectorate. I knew most of society had declared scenes like this indecent: bodies touching bodies as they wiggled through the Bunny Hug, or the Grizzly Bear, or whatever other dance steps the irreverent citizens of San Francisco might've dreamed up and declared to be in fashion. Tables ringed the room, occupied by exhausted dancers resting their feet and voyeurs with no intention of joining. A stage sat at the far end, bathed in the brilliant beams of the calcium lights. Down below it a small, sweaty band cranked out one ragtime hit after another, flanked by dilapidated red curtains that had seen better days. A row of girls danced upon the stage, but Cora and Flossie were not among them, which meant they were likely ferrying customers about on the dance floor below.

I skirted the edge of the crowd. Unbridled shrieks of hilarity bounced off the windowless walls. A drunk man tried to pull me into his lap, roaring with laughter at my plain calico dress.

"Lookit this one! You've done 'scaped the convent, ain't ye, darlin'?" he slurred, playing the comedian to his friends.

My cheeks flushed and I pried myself out of his clutches. My eyes searched the dance floor pleadingly, desperate for any sign of my friends.

"Violet? What are you doing down here?"

The voice came from over my shoulder. I spun around and saw Flossie, her pale coloring overwritten with bold rouge and lipstick. I was so relieved, I felt tears spring to my eyes. I was even more relieved to see she didn't have a customer in tow.

"Flossie!" I clutched her outstretched arms to steady myself. "Flossie, you have to help me! I shouldn't have gone in, but the silence in the house . . . it was deafening!"

Flossie puzzled over this, trying to guess what lay behind my cryptic words.

"You mean . . . Tackett?" she finally asked, catching on.

"They were so very quiet . . . I thought perhaps they were just sleeping . . . but, oh, Flossie . . . when I finally went to check, he was . . . oh, Flossie, they *both* were . . ."

Before I could finish the sentence, Flossie gripped my wrists and squeezed hard.

"Shhhh," she said. She nodded, her lips pressed in a tight line, and I knew she understood. She glanced around with caution, but the people packed nearest us were lost in their own merriment. I didn't see any of the other girls.

"I'll fetch Cora. We'll come see to it," she said.

A short time later the three of us stood around Tackett's bed. Flossie bravely pulled back the sheet and we stared dumbly at the corpses.

A leathery, overly groomed man in life, Tackett was profoundly grotesque in death. His muscles and tendons appeared ropy and strained, and his pirate's face was nearly purple. Blanche was equally ugly; her pale skin was peppered with greenish-looking splotches, presumably where her veins had burst. Her eyes were also open, her swollen tongue lolling between her thin white lips.

"My word," Cora murmured. "That stench is truly terrible."

She suppressed a gag and brought the back of her hand to her nose.

"Yes," I agreed miserably. "Whatever happened to them . . . it seems it took them violently."

"It could only have been one thing," Flossie said.

Her tone was flat, unemotional, certain. Cora and I turned to look at her. Flossie glanced at us, then back at the bodies.

"Poison."

The image of the empty bottle I'd found in my pocket instantly sprang to mind, and I felt my brow bead with icy-cold sweat. But . . . that couldn't be—could it? Ipecac didn't kill a body; it only made him vomit for everything he's worth.

I looked again at the contorted corpses. No. This was something more than simple ipecac. An image drifted into my mind unbidden—of the rats I regularly removed from the cellar, their stiff paws frozen mid-spasm, their spines curled backwards into commas. Blanche and Tackett were frozen in convincing imitation.

But . . . Tackett had been sick. *Repeatedly* sick. Had that been no coincidence? I looked automatically around the room, and my gaze landed upon a tray laden with two half-eaten bowls of stew.

You rest . . . I'll fix the stew . . . Flossie had instructed only hours earlier.

On the bedside table stood the bottle of whiskey—a good third of it gone now—and two glasses, just the slightest ring of caramel-colored liquid left at the bottom of each. I thought of Cora's indignation when Blanche had pointed out her brooch and Tackett confiscated it.

Her Royal Highness *had the nerve to order me to carry a fresh bottle and two glasses in to them on a little tray!*

Was it possible? But no. Tackett had so many enemies. These were girls I'd always trusted and loved. And yet, I looked between my two dearest friends and felt a brief flicker of doubt. To my further shock, I saw that they were also peering back at me. I made a quick inventory of the reasons they had to wonder about me: I had been alone with Tackett and Blanche in the house. I had been the one to find them. And, yes, Tackett had repeatedly fallen ill . . . and I had been the one to cook all of his meals.

For a moment, the air between us grew thick.

But we were a family. And we were standing together. I could feel that we were united; we would decide between the three of us what actions to take.

Flossie spoke first.

"I suppose we ought to send for someone . . . a constable, a coroner," she said, weighing the options.

Another moment of silence passed. Then, to my surprise, Cora clenched her jaw and shook her head.

"NO."

Her voice splashed into the room like cool water, abrupt and resolute. Flossie and I turned to look at her.

"No," she repeated. "If we call for the law, they will want to know exactly what happened. They'll make trouble for all of us—*us*, who have trouble enough already! And even if they don't wind up labeling one of us a murderess . . . then, what are we left with?"

"What do you mean?" Flossie asked.

"With Tackett dead, the dancehall is likely to close. We'll be homeless, or we'll land right back somewhere like this while another *man* holds our purse strings, doling out barely enough for us to eke by!"

Flossie blinked at Cora, flabbergasted.

"But . . . what do you suggest?"

Cora's indignation had energized her, and she practically thrummed with new determination.

"Tackett's dead," she replied. "We're likely to be blamed. But . . . we know the combination to his safe! I say we *take* our independence. We've earned it."

Flossie cocked her head, calmly calculating the risks.

"You mean . . . *steal* some of his money?" I asked, my voice quivering with a mixture of excitement, fear, and disbelief.

"No," Cora answered coolly. "I don't mean *some* of his money. I mean we should take it *all*. Tackett's entire fortune. There's no record of his riches—only rumors. And, truly, that money *should* be ours. We take it and we leave town. We finally live how *we* like, each of us—on our own terms."

She fell quiet, waiting for her words to sink in.

"Cora's right," Flossie finally said.

"What?" I stammered, caught off guard.

Flossie turned to me.

"It's a chance to have our freedom. And besides, the alternatives . . ." Flossie paused. She gave me a grave look. "Don't forget, Violet, with the police will come questions."

I stood stock-still, absorbing this.

Flossie pressed onward.

"Cora is right, Violet . . . but if we are to act on this, then we haven't much time. Quite frankly, it's a miracle none of the others have returned from the dancehall already."

After a minute I relented, miserable and terrorized by the sightless eyes of the two corpses. I was ready to run—anywhere, really, as long as I would still be with Flossie and Cora.

And so it was decided. Flossie snapped the white sheet in the air and let it float down over the bed, concealing all. I remember watching Tackett's and Blanche's distorted faces disappear once again, Tackett's empty, milky eyes vanishing from view.

The bodies would not stay hidden long. The smell alone was enough to give them away. Flossie was right: we would need to act quickly.

I allowed Flossie to usher me downstairs to Tackett's office while Cora went looking for something to contain our spoils. She returned with a beat-up carpetbag and two old saddlebags that, while weathered, would serve. Flossie bid me to stand guard outside the office door for the second time that day. And yet again, I watched her tiptoe across the room, kneel down beside Tackett's safe, and twirl the dial with confidence.

A strange shiver came over me: we were about to *steal*—and no small amount. But then I remembered the two corpses lying upstairs. I felt certain that none of us had done that. Moreover, I felt certain that all three of us deserved a life beyond the boardinghouse. Here was our chance—perhaps our *only* chance.

In the next moment Flossie had depressed the handle of the safe, then she and Cora began to extract stacks of bills, gold bars, gold nuggets—even precious gems. It was staggering to see: a veritable treasure chest, like something from a book.

Cora caught me gaping. She grinned and winked.

"Stingy as he was, hard to believe he was sitting on all this, eh? He was the worst kind of miser!"

I was shocked to witness her delight. A stray echo drifted back to me then—something Flossie had mentioned. She had said that *Cora* had been the one to wheedle the safe's combination out of Tackett. Was it possible she had planned for this?

But before I could finish my thought, a strange, loud rumbling filled the room. We froze. The walls began to shake, and the three of us looked to one another with wild alarm. After a handful of seconds, as suddenly as the rumble had begun, it ceased. Frightened, baffled, we all held our breath.

A moment passed. Nothing.

Then a louder, more violent rumbling ripped through the room. We were shaken up and down as if an enormous wagon were passing by outside. The vertical motion was joined by a side-to-side swaying that made my knees go weak as I staggered and struggled to remain upright.

"What's happening?" I screamed.

The air filled with the sounds of wood splintering and glass shattering.

"*Grab what you can and get out!*" Flossie screamed. "*It's an earthquake!*"

If I had thought Flossie was the picture of organized determination earlier, now she turned feverishly efficient. She frantically stuffed piles of bills into the saddlebags and proceeded to hurl one to Cora and the other to me.

Clutching our new, ill-gotten fortune, we raced out of the boardinghouse, which had begun to toss like a ship on rough seas.

Outside, we stood panting, clutching one another in terror, unsure where to turn for help. We were joined by countless neighbors, a mix of both familiar and strange faces, some sleepy, some irritated or panicked. We all wobbled together on unsteady sea legs, a great mass huddled on the shaking ground.

Soon, Henrietta, Opal, and Mary came running up the lane. They joined the huddled mass; I remember feeling Mary's bony fingers gripping my upper arm like a cold vise. She sucked in a breath.

"Pure evil!" Mary hissed, her tone both awed and offended.

Henrietta cried, "Lord in Heaven Almighty!" with a religious fervor I'd never heard from her before.

The cracking grew louder, and I realized it came from the wooden frames of the buildings breaking, snapping like twigs underfoot in a forest. Our dilapidated abode did not stand a chance against the shaking's tremendous vigor. The old clapboard house swayed and twisted and sagged.

In a matter of seconds, the floor caved in, and the entire boardinghouse was instantly reduced to rubble, filling up the cellar like liquid poured into a cup.

9

stood weak-kneed as though the bones in my legs were two quivering molds of calf's-foot jelly. Heavy dust filled the air. The rumbling of the earth, the screams of terror, and the din of structures crumbling deafened our ears. There were explosions—from what, I can only guess: factories, gasworks, power plants. In the distance, flames leaped into the sky, a sickening display of fireworks.

While the 'quake eventually died down, the explosions and rumblings of collapsing buildings lasted long after. I felt a nudge and turned to see Flossie. She silently urged me to hide the saddlebag between the folds of my skirt.

She was being cautious, of course, but her worry was unnecessary: no one was paying us any mind. The other girls were mesmerized by the pile of rubble where our home had once stood, cowed by the continuing sounds of explosions.

I don't know how long we cowered together in shock. Finally, after what could have been minutes or hours, the dust began to settle.

"Did . . . everyone make it out all right?" a shy voice piped up.

We turned to see Opal, her warm brown mare's eyes full of genuine concern. I exchanged a look with Flossie, then Cora.

My head was spinning again. But slowly, I began to comprehend. In the space of mere seconds, the earthquake had buried the bodies of Tackett and Blanche. The fact of their violent deaths was now our secret alone: we were three very lucky girls indeed.

A final look passed between the three of us. In that moment it was decided. Our pact was made.

Tell no one.

"No," Cora said, answering Opal's question. Her voice was firm. "Tackett and Blanche didn't. We ran out when we felt the first tremor, but they . . . they didn't leave."

Opal's eyes widened, but she nodded somberly, accepting the grim news.

Much later, we learned that the first jolt we'd felt was merely a "foreshock." The 'quake itself lasted only about a minute, but its destruction cut a widening trail of ruin through the city like the wake behind a great ship. The buildings all around town were honeycombed with wood and coal stoves, and the city quickly ignited like a powder keg. Once lit, the fires were the worst of all. Blazes soon raged in all directions. The exhausted firemen in their rubber burnout clothes scurried between them as though the entire city were an anthill stomped into total chaos. The fire was hungry and ruthless.

The town burned for three days.

We—the newly homeless citizens of San Francisco—found ourselves clustered like so many flocks of lost sheep dotted about the city in a series of makeshift shelters. Whether by virtue of bravery or ignorance, some survivors stubbornly returned home, though all were advised against it. In the days after the earthquake, I have a vivid recollection of peering into the gaping maw of a second-story building and watching a woman hang sheets where there had once been walls, her children playing around her on a plank floor that had become more steeply pitched than a listing ship's deck. Some lived in cable cars that the Army had requisitioned and quickly converted into "housing," bedding down on cramped bunks within the cars at night, a sleeper train to nowhere. There were also those who dug holes in the mud in Dolores Park, like rabbits living in burrows. And still others who erected slapdash wooden shacks amid the rubble in the streets.

The group of us from the boardinghouse—Flossie, Cora, Henrietta, Opal, Mary, and myself—took shelter in the tent city erected in Golden Gate Park by the U.S. Army, and waited. The camp had little to offer other than camaraderie and the safety of military patrol. There wasn't much in the way of hygiene or comfort. The tents were little more than bedsheets—not at all waterproof; they collected the morning fog and dripped a steady tattoo upon their occupants. The ground was soggy, turning to muck under the tread of so many feet. Only if you had the coin to spare was it possible to get a proper cot. Strictly speaking, Cora, Flossie, and I did: we had Tackett's fortune—or at least the portion we'd smuggled outside before the worst of the earthquake struck. But, wary, we agreed not to spend a cent. During the first few nights we diligently sewed bills and coins and even gold nuggets into our clothes, working by touch, feeling about blindly in the dark.

In the light of day, all was concealed, but every time a man in uniform came clop-clop-clopping astride his horse, my pulse quickened and my brow grew cold with sudden sweat. We were, after all, guarding a secret. The cavalry soldiers never guessed as much, of course; they were only there to keep the peace. I knew perfectly well that if they looked our way twice, it was likely on account of Cora's fetching figure and scarlet hair. But this did little to keep me calm.

The temporary residents of the camp were a mixed lot: spinsters and grifters, families and lovers, friends and strangers, all jumbled together, rubbing elbows in the breadline. In the evenings, people gathered around the oilcan fires and took turns telling their stories, everyone eager to recount the events that had led up to the terrible rumbling that shattered so many lives. It made a certain kind of sense that each person might want to add his memories to the greater patchwork that was steadily taking shape as memories eventually formed the scalpel that history used to autopsy the great 'quake.

Flossie, Cora, and I often sat listening to these stories, but we never told our own. Fortunately, no one bothered to ask us about our memories of that final day before the 'quake struck; after all, there was plenty of sensational material to go round without our contribution.

The city continued to burn. We spent our days helping to peel potatoes or hang laundry, and when that wasn't enough to keep us occupied, we took restless walks, watching dumbfounded as the flames licked up block after block, making an audible sucking sound as they gobbled the air.

It seemed, for a time, that the city would burn forever. But eventually the fires were extinguished, and life began to take on a strange new routine. Word of the chaos had spread, and sightseers began to visit. We watched jobless locals begin pandering to these voyeuristic hoards, setting up slap-dash shacks with signs proclaiming "RESTAURANT!" to feed them. Others collected and laid out remnants of the devastation along the broken sidewalks—everything for sale, all scavenged. One could buy a music box or a mantel clock that had miraculously survived, or if the tourist was in a morbid mood, there were broken bits of plaster crenellations or fragments of stained-glass windows to be had. The impromptu "shopkeepers" shouted: *Objects of the great calamity! Buy one, and place it near yer hearth! I promise ye years of storytelling!*

"Well, you must admire their resourcefulness, if nothing else," Cora said with a shrug.

While hardly noble, these profiteers were the first sign of San Francisco's recovery. Bit by bit, the city poked its head up from the ashes, rising shyly at first, curling into the air like a seedling sending its first green shoots up from the soil, feeling for sunlight. Folks began to rebuild.

California is like a woman, Henrietta used to preach back at the boardinghouse, her hands upon her wide, maternal hips. *She's forever reconfigurin' herself. She's about as likely to stop rearrangin' things as fashion itself is to stand still!*

She meant, of course: not likely at all. This seemed truer than ever in the weeks that followed the earthquake. Because there was no denying: California really *had* reconfigured herself. It was as though God had split an invisible seam that ran the length of the mountains along the coast, shifting the earth like two pieces of cloth pulled in opposite directions. Entire towns folded like card-houses. I recall reading about the Salinas River in the newspaper and how the earthquake diverted its course to the sea near Monterey by six whole miles.

We changed, too—diverted course, like that river.

There were free omnibuses carrying folks to Fresno, to Los Angeles, even to faraway Nevada and Oregon. The eternal question in the camps: To stay and resettle? Or to go?

Opal was the first to leave. She'd heard of a job picking fruit on an orchard in the Sierra Nevada foothills.

Mary disappeared without saying goodbye. One morning she was simply gone, along with her rosaries and sad, worried eyes.

It was down to Henrietta and the three of us. But when Henrietta began to take regular walks with a shy, handsome young man named Liam, I sensed she might be thinking of a new life, too. Sure enough, as the camp in Golden Gate Park began to break up for good, Henrietta announced that she had fallen head over heels. It turned out, Liam was a greengrocer ten years her junior, and she intended to marry him and help him rebuild his shop—a surprising new existence for Henrietta, but one I felt she might genuinely enjoy.

"Come and visit as soon as you can, dearie," Henrietta ordered as she hugged me goodbye. "I'll miss you."

"I will," I gave my word, hoping to keep it.

"I'll be a-worryin' about you—I know it in my bones." She drew away from me and held me at arm's length, her hands clamped on my shoulders. "Mind ye keep yer eye out for that one," Henrietta added, lowering her voice. She tipped her chin discreetly to where Cora stood next to Flossie.

"I know the three of you are thick," Henrietta continued, "but three ain't ever lucky for friends, and that one there's a little too regal for her own good. Best to know when to keep close and when to steer clear, ye hear?"

I nodded. Henrietta dropped the subject and brightened.

"Goodbye!" she announced. She squeezed me against her bosom one last time, then blew kisses to Cora and Flossie. "Watch yerselves, ladies, and don't accept any tin pennies, ye hear?"

We watched her march away, her ample rear end twitching side to side. I felt the first inklings of emptiness. There were very few Henriettas in this world.

The day after Henrietta left, I woke early in the morning with a start. I grabbed for the sleeve of my dress to pat at my sweating brow, hoping to hide the evidence.

"Another dream, Violet?" Flossie asked gently.

I looked at her, willing myself to lie, but my shoulders sagged and I nodded. She came to my side and kissed my cheek sympathetically. She knew the nightmare I'd suffered without my having to utter a word. It was always the same: Tackett and Blanche, staring at me with vacant, milky eyes, their bodies contorted.

"You won't have those dreams once we leave camp, I reckon," Flossie promised. "Your mind just needs to focus on something fresh . . . and there's nothing fresh here."

We'd come to the camp in April . . . and now the end of summer loomed. The light leaned long and golden in the afternoons; soon it would turn brittle on the breeze. We knew we needed to make up our minds soon about where to go and what to do.

Cora woke up, oblivious to my tortured sleep. She and Flossie went to stand in line for a crust of bread and some hot coffee. Still feeling troubled, I remained behind, tidying our tent.

But as I shook out my bedroll, something unexpected fluttered free and fell to the ground. It was a slip of newsprint, folded in half and inscribed with a message in lead pencil. Two words were printed on the outside.

I KNOW, it read.

Puzzled, I unfolded the paper. There was more within.

ABOUT THE ARSENIC.

My veins ran cold. Five simple words. There was nothing else written, no signatory. I broke out in an icy sweat and the hairs on the back of my neck pricked to attention. I stared, motionless, until the paper began to shake in my hand like a leaf ruffled by the wind.

For a moment, I thought I might scream, but I choked back the cry and instead sprang to my feet. I had to find Flossie and Cora. They needed to see.

They were still waiting in the breadline. I motioned to them urgently.

"Please—I've something to show you . . . something *private*."

Cora looked annoyed. They were nearly at the head of the line, which meant Cora was close to a tin mug of hot coffee, and she was not inclined to delay its receipt. But Flossie nudged her, and eventually both conceded, following me away from the cluster of shuffling bodies.

"What the blazes is it, Violet?" Cora demanded.

I said nothing, only held out the scrap of newspaper, displaying the words scrawled outside, then opened it to reveal what was written within. Flossie choked on a gasp. Cora's mouth hardened.

I tried to hold my hand steady but I couldn't master the tremble.

"I found it," I explained in a low, quavering voice. ". . . in my bedroll."

Cora's pink cheeks turned an uncharacteristic white.

"You *found* it?"

"I was tidying up. And it was just . . . *there*."

"You mean someone put it there," Cora said, comprehending.

The three of us exchanged troubled looks.

"Someone knows about Tackett and Blanche," I said, suddenly convinced.

"Shhh!" Flossie urged, darting a glance around. "We'll talk about this later. For now, we must all think what to do . . . and we definitely need to rid ourselves of *this*."

Flossie took the note from my shaking hand, strode to one of the oilcan fires, and tossed it in. I watched the paper blacken around the eerie words until it all turned to gray and the slip of paper crumpled into ash.

Flossie dropped her voice to a husky whisper. "Until we can decide what this means and what's to be done, we must all three of us act as normal as possible." She turned to look at me. "Can you do that?"

There were only a handful of occupations to keep one busy in the camp. Flossie said she wanted to clear her head and went for a walk. Cora went on a hunt for new magazines. I made up my mind that it was better to keep my hands busy and volunteered to help boil the camp's laundry. I thought the sweaty, intense labor might be good for me. For an hour or so, as my arms strained to churn the heavy paddle, the distraction worked.

But eventually my mind wandered back to the shock I'd felt upon reading that note. I think the *true* shock came from the realization that, while I was frightened by the note's appearance, I was not altogether surprised; it was as if I had been half-expecting it. Tackett and Blanche were never far from my mind; in my dreams, their corpses stared up at me, lifeless and yet somehow full of accusation. And then there was the empty bottle I'd found that first night after Tackett had fallen sick. I had yet to tell another soul about that bottle; I was too afraid of what someone—even someone as loyal as Flossie—might say.

I KNOW ABOUT THE ARSENIC, the note had said.

Anxious, I glanced up from the pot of boiling laundry to see one of the Army patrolmen looking at me with a frown. I'd been hot and tired, but now my nerves quivered with new intensity. I turned back to the laundry, but it was no use: my heart hammered in my chest. I felt a familiar tingling in my extremities, and soon my vision was crowded with black blotches, a sign that a spell was coming.

"Violet!" I heard someone call softly behind me.

It was Flossie, returning from her walk.

"Violet, you're swooning. Quick, take my arm," she said quietly, so no one else would hear.

I did as instructed, and she helped me away.

"She's not feeling well. Someone else will have to finish up," Flossie said to one of the women hanging sheets on a line, tipping her chin to the boiling pot I'd abandoned.

As we hurried past the Army patrolman, I kept my head down.

Flossie led me back to the relative safety of our tent and bid me to lie down. She covered me with a blanket to stop my chill and stroked my forehead.

"Well, that wasn't exactly what I meant by 'acting normal,'" she teased.

"I'm sorry, Flossie," I said, feeling awful.

"No, no—don't apologize. I know you can't help your spells, Violet. I'm just glad I found you before . . . well, before anything *happened*."

She was referring to the times I'd lashed out with odd behaviors, all while in a trance.

"Was it the note that set you off?" she asked now.

"I feel like someone is watching us," I confessed.

She studied my face for a moment. "Do you?" she asked.

I nodded. "Someone knows," I said. "About Blanche and Tackett."

Flossie regarded me with an unfamiliar flicker of wariness. "The note said 'arsenic,' but it did not name Blanche and Tackett specifically."

"Flossie, surely you think the same," I insisted. "Someone *knows*."

"Violet . . . you're certain you *found* those bodies that way, and that's all—right?"

I blinked. "Of course!"

She studied me a moment longer, then drew a shaky breath and let out a sigh.

"I suppose I oughtn't listen to Cora, anyway. After all—between the two of you, I'd believe *she* was capable of such a thing, not you."

"What are you talking about, Flossie?" I asked, piecing together the meaning behind her words. But she only shook her head.

"Don't trouble yourself, Violet. Just rest."

She sat on the ground beside my bedroll and took my hand. Her touch was cool but comforting, and little by little, I finally slowed my breathing and fell asleep.

When I woke up, it was dark. I sensed movement in our tent. I blinked into the darkness and saw the silhouettes of my friends.

"Flossie? Cora?"

"*She's awake*," I heard Cora whisper.

"What's going on?" I asked. I felt Flossie return to my side and take my hand again. I began to make out the dim moons of their faces.

"We're deciding what to do," Cora answered.

I felt Flossie give my hand a compassionate squeeze. "Cora agrees with me," she said. "We've decided that we must leave the camp." She paused, then added in a softer, apologetic whisper, "Leave, and split up."

A tight feeling of panic gripped my throat. To think they had discussed this without me!

"*Split up?*"

"That note . . . we're not safe."

"We've no choice now," Cora added bitterly.

"We need to leave, one by one . . . starting tomorrow, and with you, Violet."

"Me?" I whispered, blinking into the dark, dumbfounded.

"You found the note in *your* bedroll. We have to get you away from here."

My stomach dropped. I tried to picture myself living without Cora and Flossie, and tears instantly sprang to my eyes.

"But . . . where will I go?"

"You've money now," Flossie reminded me. "If you're careful, you can go wherever you like! You certainly don't have to wind up at a place like Tackett's, or be anyone's maid. You'll find your way, Violet. You're stronger than you think."

I wanted to protest, but something held me back. The truth was, I *did* feel like we were in danger. And as frightened as I was for myself, I was more frightened still for the friends I loved. I thought again of the empty bottle I'd never told them about. Blanche's and Tackett's milky, sightless eyes flashed in my mind again, and I shivered.

"Where will each of *you* go?" I asked.

"I don't know," Flossie answered, hesitating. "The best idea might be to leave the city altogether. But who knows—perhaps it's possible to start over here; the earthquake has changed the city so."

"Flossie . . ." I said, my stomach churning with fresh panic to picture my friends leaving town without a trace. "I can't bear the thought of never seeing either of you again. I simply can't."

"I can't either," Flossie replied, forlorn.

"How about this," Cora said. "If all seems safe, then exactly one year from now we can all meet in this very park—let's say, exactly one year from today, at noon, by the bridge at Stow Lake."

"A whole year?" I repeated, daunted. "Won't a month or two be enough?"

Flossie shook her head, resolute. "Tackett and Blanche . . . that happened in April. Now it's August. Whoever sent that note knows how to be patient. We have to wait a year, at *minimum*."

"So, are we agreed?" Cora asked.

"Violet?" Flossie prodded.

A year. One full year. Alone. I opened my mouth, then closed it again. I couldn't quite speak the words.

Finally, however, I nodded. I felt the lump in my throat give a lurch and choked back a soft sob of surrender.

10

Only a few hours later, as dawn heralded the day, I rose and did exactly as I had been bid: I hugged Cora and Flossie goodbye, and trudged away through the muddy lanes of the tent city. My eyes were raw and tender from crying, and the air was damp with ocean mist and the scent of boiling coffee mingled with the odors of the latrine. My worldly possessions fit neatly into one of the saddlebags. As I walked, I felt my skirts swinging heavily, my share of Tackett's fortune lightly bruising my ankles where it was sewn into the hem. I felt laden with gold and secrets, and at the same time I felt completely empty, knowing that I was leaving behind the only two people I'd ever loved.

That first day, I wandered the chaotic streets aimlessly. Every inch of San Francisco was alive with the hustle and bustle of rebuilding. I saw masons laying bricks. I watched men hoist a freshly painted sign above a brand-new general store. Automobiles honked at one another in the streets in a language of jolly, casual curses.

The cable cars were running again, trundling people up and down the hills. I paused in the street near Union Square to let one pass. It gave a cheerful ding, but after it was gone, I stepped over the tracks and glanced down, into the narrow trench where the cable sang a steady, faintly high-pitched *whirrrr*. I found myself suddenly overwhelmed. There was something awful about the fact that the cables ran twenty-four hours a day, never stopping; I was reminded of the relentless march of time. Time was marching on for me, too, and with a tremor of dread, I realized it would carry me farther and farther away from Cora and Flossie.

A new panic gripped me, and I felt my breathing grow ragged and a familiar cold sweat gathering upon my brow. I worried that I might soon have one of my spells, right there in public—without Flossie to come to my rescue. I cast about in desperation and noticed a women's apparel store where I might take refuge. I remembered the small fortune sewn into my dress. Once I'd discreetly ripped a few bills from the hem of my left sleeve, I took a breath to steady myself and pushed through the door.

The store was small but well-appointed, complete with displays featuring lifelike mannequins. At first, I prodded timidly at the racks, pretending to admire, while attempting to quietly slow my racing heart. Luckily, the shop-girls weren't paying me much attention, busy chattering to one another instead. There were two younger girls—not much older than myself—and a more matronly woman. I shyly eavesdropped as the girls chatted about a fancy tearoom they hoped to visit. I gathered that it was being constructed within the new Palace Hotel.

"Who knows, Effie," one girl said. "Maybe Bert will take you there when he proposes!"

Effie rolled her eyes. "Are you pullin' my leg? Rebuilding the Palace'll take at least a year or two, Annabelle—I should like to be wed long before that!"

I was intrigued. I lingered, listening. But my presence eventually—and unavoidably—incurred the notice of the older attendant. She cleared her throat and came out from behind the counter.

"May I help you . . . miss?" Her tone was polite, but rote. Her expression betrayed her misgivings as she took in my filthy smock.

Under ordinary circumstances, looking as I did, I might have been thrown out without so much as a greeting. But the earthquake had changed everything, jumbling together the rich and the poor.

"Are you seeking something in particular?" the woman pressed.

The two younger girls ceased their chatter and turned to look me over with curious expressions.

"Yes," I answered at last. I pointed to the girl on the left. "I want a ladies' suit exactly like hers."

The matron turned and looked at the young shop-girl I'd heard them call Annabelle, then returned her gaze to me for a long lingering moment, as if struggling to picture the same suit on me. It was a light gray two-piece suit, with a nipped waist and what was popularly known as a "walking skirt"—a very straight, ankle-length skirt with just enough give to allow for all the modern pursuits: bicycling, walking . . . even working as a shop-girl.

"Well, you're in luck," she said. "We still sell that model." She eyed me again. "We can fit you, but it will need alterations, which—*as I'm sure you're aware*—require a corset."

"Oh, yes. I mean to buy one of those as well," I said, feeling foolish that I had not thought of this. I had never owned one. "I . . . I lost everything in the fire. It was so sudden."

The matron appeared skeptical.

"We've been in the camps," I embellished. "Waiting for our home to be rebuilt."

She humored my lie with a mechanical nod, then her appraising eye took quick account of my slight frame. "Well, once we've found you a corset, I can take the measurements and you can pick up the suit tomorrow."

"No," I replied. She sighed, as though her original guess had been correct: she had wasted her time. "Take the measurements," I continued, "but I'll wait here for the alterations. I plan to wear it out."

At this, her mouth twitched. She clearly found my desperation unsettling.

"Alterations done in such a hurry . . ." she said, hesitant, "will cost extra."

I produced the bills I'd ripped from my sleeve and handed them to her.

"I'll be wanting to keep the dress I'm wearing, too, of course," I added. "For sentimental reasons."

Either the corset was pure pain, or the matronly attendant had taken a severe disliking to me. As she laced me up, I tried to hide what a shock it was—how would I ever walk the steep hills of San Francisco in something like this? Once the measurements had been taken, the matron sent for the seamstress. She warned me that the alterations would take all day—and they did. While I waited, I picked out four more suits. These, I assured them, I could retrieve another day. As I was finally changing into my new clothes, a plan was taking shape in my head. There were other items I would need as well: extra shirtwaists, stockings, gloves, and an everyday purse with a drawstring for carrying upon my wrist. The shop-matron's disdain for me lessened with each purchase, though she still regarded my soiled smock with suspicion as I folded it carefully into the shopping box along with everything else, a very poor cousin to my new acquisitions.

At last, newly attired from head to toe, I left the shop. I stood outside on the street, feeling reborn and marveling at my confidence. I'd staved off one of my spells all by myself, and I'd transformed myself into a fashionable young lady, to boot. *You're stronger than you think*, Flossie had said. With a pang, I wished I could return to the camp and find Flossie and Cora. I doubted Cora would call me "Little Mouse" if she could see me now!

Proud as I was, I didn't have time to relish the emotion; the sun was already slumping low in the sky, and a cool wind had picked up over the Bay, heralding a chilly San Francisco night. I decided to capitalize on my newfound confidence and make the most of it while it lasted. I wandered westward, to a newer area of the city, where I'd heard several women's hotels were establishing themselves. I found my way to the Fulton Arms, a modest-yet-respectable new building, surrounded on all four sides by a small yet tidy green lawn.

After rummaging through my packages and ripping several more greenbacks from the lining of my old smock, I entered and inquired at the front desk. The appointed landlady and "den mother" was a middle-aged woman with a chaotic halo of frowsy auburn hair busily escaping from a hasty bun. She introduced herself as Mrs. Campbell, and made a point of telling me she was widowed with three children, as if to warn me that I oughtn't compete when it came to sympathetic hardships. I sensed right away that she hated her fellow residents, if for no other reason than they were young and optimistic.

"Occupation?" Mrs. Campbell demanded as she signed my information into the register.

I didn't answer right away, still summoning my nerve. Her bloodshot, hooded eyes lifted to my face, stern and indifferent.

"Shop-girl," I said, willing my voice to convey a sense of surety.

Mrs. Campbell looked at me for a long moment.

"And *where* are you employed?"

"Oh . . . I mean, I was, before the earthquake," I said, relenting.

"We only accept *employed* ladies of good reputation who can guarantee the weekly rent," Mrs. Campbell informed me.

I pictured what Flossie would do to convince her.

"I'm confident I will find another post soon enough. How about eight weeks' rent in advance? Would that serve as a sufficient guarantee?"

I produced the sum in question—along with a token for Mrs. Campbell to keep, should she be so inclined—and quietly slid the bills across the desk.

Mrs. Campbell arched an eyebrow. Her eyes went to my freshly acquired packages, then back to me, her mouth puckered sourly. Finally, she sighed and reached for the bills.

"Fine," she grumbled. "But if you don't have a letter of employment in seven weeks' time, then I'll have nothin' more to do with ya—is that clear?"

I nodded. She grunted and dug through a drawer to produce a key. And with that, I was officially a resident.

Once I had uttered the lie aloud—that I was a shop-girl—I felt obligated to make it true. The next morning, I dressed and set out early, scouring the shop windows for signs that read ATTENDANT WANTED. I mustered the nerve to inquire at two different shops, but got turned away both times. I felt my new confidence beginning to crumble.

When I passed a bookshop, I ducked inside seeking comfort, and wound up using more of my secret fortune than I intended.

"An educated lady with diverse tastes," the bookshop attendant commented as he peered at the stack I brought to the till. I'd picked up everything from William Cowper's translation of *The Odyssey* to a volume of stories by Edgar Allan Poe.

I smiled awkwardly, hardly wishing to correct him.

"We can deliver if those prove too heavy," the attendant added.

"No, no—I'm capable," I promised.

If only he knew; despite my slight frame, I'd performed plenty of physical labor.

Later, when I returned to the apartment house, I adjourned to my room and snuggled in bed with my new treasures, reading until the last remnants of purple dusk waned in the window, and my eyelids drooped.

The next morning, I woke and set about dressing and tidying my room. But when I lifted my pillow to make the bed, I glimpsed a slip of folded paper. I froze, startled. It took me a moment to recover myself. When I did, I reached a trembling hand to retrieve the paper, thinking all the while of the eerie note I'd found in my bedroll back at the camp.

But this time, when I unfolded the paper, there was nothing written within. Well, that is to say, there was nothing *handwritten*. My eyes scanned the typeset words and I realized it must have come from the book I was reading. Sure enough, I found the book on the floor beside my bed, and upon closer inspection, was able to match the slip of paper to a torn page from "The Tell-Tale Heart."

I blinked at my discovery, feeling a mixture of emotions: relief there had been no threatening message inside, yet unsettled by the fact that the page had not only been torn but *folded* and lost under my pillow. There was no evidence that anyone but me had been in my room, so it followed that I must have managed to rip and fold the page myself—but I had no memory of doing so. I was alarmed to think perhaps I'd had one of my spells again, without even knowing. Was it possible?

I tucked the paper back into the book and did my best to shake off my doubts, and yet, I felt deeply uneasy.

A handful of days passed, and I began to establish a routine: rising early, dressing, and leaving the apartment house when all the other girls did, as though I had a job to go to. But instead of going to a dress-shop or a glove counter, I shyly roamed the streets until eventually, a bookshop or library lured me inside. In the evenings, when all the girls gathered in the common room downstairs, pinning each other's hair and telling stories about their customers and beaux, I retreated to a corner with one of my books, pretending to read while secretly eavesdropping.

In some ways, the excitable buzz of their camaraderie reminded me of Cora and Flossie—and all the other girls in the boardinghouse. But in other ways, they were different from any girls I'd ever known. Several worked as shop-girls, and this new, modern life meant they occupied a curiously ambiguous social position, floating somewhere between the classes. With neither lordly husband nor lowly pimp to answer to, once they left their shop counters for the day, they were free to gossip and gad about, tittering over the occasional handsome man who'd winked at them in the streets. I listened in, excited to observe this emerging class of young women, but never truly feeling like one of their number.

A week passed, and the jolt of fear I'd experienced upon finding the folded, torn page under my pillow faded. But my doubts piqued again a few days later, when my old nightmare returned to me. This time, as the grotesque image of Blanche and Tackett haunted my dreams, the nightmare took on a new, horrifying twist. The two corpses stared up at me with their cold, milky eyes—eyes that had always been distinctly vacant—when all at once a new sharpness filled them; their macabre faces were frowning at me. I winced. I thought, for a moment, on what to do, but before I could decide, both of their right arms rose in unison from the bed, their hands like two spastic claws, their bones cracking as they closed their fists and pointed a finger each. I realized: they were pointing at *me*.

I woke up with a scream.

The window showed signs of early dawn. My white cotton night-gown was soaked through with sweat. Flossie's worried, dubious face floated back to me: *Violet . . . you're certain you* found *those bodies that way, and that's all—right?* I'd reassured her that, of course, that was all. But I hadn't told her about the empty bottle I'd found. I hadn't told anyone about that.

As I calmed myself and dressed for the day, it occurred to me that the nightmare was a symptom of guilt. I firmly refused to believe I had anything to do with Blanche's and Tackett's deaths . . . Nonetheless, the truth remained: I hadn't gone to the police when I found them, and when Cora suggested the three of us rob the contents of Tackett's safe and run away, I hadn't put up much of a protest. Now here I was, living off the spoils.

That morning, I made up my mind: I would redouble my efforts to procure a position as a shop-girl. If the other girls in the apartment house could do it, so could I. With any luck, I could eke out my own living and hide Tackett's money away until I could think of something better to do in order to alleviate my guilt.

I continued to study the other girls in the apartment house—now with a more specific purpose. I listened carefully to their chatter, taking notes. I copied their style, their mannerisms, even their gestures. When I came upon a HELP WANTED sign, I pretended I was *not* Violet, the "Little Mouse," but rather one of these modern, fashionable, independent girls.

After a few days spent making relentless inquiries, I finally got the job.

It was a small store that specialized in women's shoes. I was hired to be one of two attendants, while an elderly Italian cobbler lived in a small apartment in the back room crafting special orders and repairing soles. I earned an hourly wage. Though it was modest, I would be a real "shop-girl."

I was paid by the week, and by the end of the month I was relieved to discover I could indeed make ends meet out of my own earnings. I took what was left of my share of the money we'd stolen—still a considerable sum—to one of the newly rebuilt banks downtown and acquired a safety-deposit box. If she knew, Cora would laugh at me for refusing to spend Tackett's money, but I didn't care.

However, I *did* wonder what Flossie and Cora might say if they could see me in my new routine. In fact, I wondered about Flossie and Cora all the time. Where were they? What were they doing? I counted the days until our reunion, filled with a sense of waiting.

11

I was overjoyed to call myself a real shop-girl, and yet, I soon learned that daily life at the cobbler's was rather dull. While the process of taking measurements and helping customers order new shoes could be quite involved, the shop received only a handful of visitors each day, and there was only so much dusting and ordering that could be done. As several more months passed, my life—the life I had worked so hard to carve out for myself—began to grate on me. I couldn't help but notice how socially confined I'd become. My only regular company, Nell, had a snide, priggish disposition. The elderly Italian cobbler spoke English but preferred not to.

One morning, I passed a bakery and was tempted by the window display. I bought three flaky pastries dusted with sugar, thinking to give one each to my fellow workers. But when I showed them to Nell, she turned up her nose and said, *You know, of course, you aren't allowed to eat on the job.* The elderly Italian accepted my offering, but after taking one bite, only gave a gruff *Hrmph.*

Another day, catching sight of a book I was carrying when I arrived in the morning, Nell reminded me that, much like eating, reading would not be tolerated on the job. I knew the other girls at the women's hotel did not have such a dull time at their posts. Most of them came home tired but bright-eyed and full of stories about all the outrageous customers they'd encountered! Many flouted the rules while on duty, trying on merchandise or reading fashion magazines under the counter. I admired their boldness. If Cora were in my place, I knew she would likely ignore Nell's admonishments and do just as she pleased.

The year moved slowly at first. But eventually the days passed, then weeks, and even months. Finally . . . at long last, when the white and pink blossoms dropped from the trees and spring turned into summer, the one-year anniversary of my parting with Cora and Flossie arrived— I had made it!

Despite Nell's grumbling, I had arranged to take a few days' holiday, and on the appointed morning I woke up feeling festive indeed. I dressed myself in my finest clothes, and arranged my hair carefully, hoping to impress Cora and Flossie with my new patina of sophistication. Cora had named noon as the hour for our meeting, but I couldn't wait: I hurried to Golden Gate Park and made my way to Stow Lake by ten o'clock.

It was a warm August day—unusual for San Francisco, whose "summer" days typically occurred during October or April. At first, I sat on a bench and tried my best to be patient. I could feel the morning sun warming my cheeks, infusing them with color. The park was full of people who had been lured outdoors on account of the good weather. I watched couples promenade. Governesses supervised young children as they launched sailboats on the pond, prodding them along with sticks. A large yellow dog splashed into the lake, chasing a ball. A soft breeze carried the scent of the ocean through the eucalyptus leaves. I tingled with excitement. I waited, at first happily, then expectantly.

But as the noon hour came and went, my waiting turned frazzled, panicked. The warmth of the day that had seemed so pleasant now felt like a torture; I felt myself sweating through the stiff fabric of my corset and into my shirtwaist. The tendrils that had escaped my pinned-up bun pasted themselves against the sticky sides of my face.

By three o'clock, with a sinking heart, I was forced to admit it was unlikely Cora and Flossie were going to come. Nonetheless, I waited four hours more, until the sun sunk low in the sky, and returned the very next day.

Perhaps they had deemed it unsafe.

Perhaps, after our parting, they had left the city entirely—one or both of them. I'd always known there was a possibility our parting had been permanent, but had never truly believed it would be so.

In the days after I'd given up waiting in the park, a strange mood settled over me. My disappointment buzzed around in my head like an angry wasp I couldn't fan away. I was tempted to go find Henrietta, but the fact that Cora and Flossie had not turned up in the park reignited the worry that perhaps we were being watched by someone seeking to do us harm. The last thing I wanted to do was bring trouble to Henrietta's door.

When I returned to work at the shoe shop, the peeling wallpaper and battered wooden counters looked dingier than ever, and Nell's uppity disposition felt personal, intolerable.

I was desperate for friends, I realized, and not only was Nell a far cry from Flossie and Cora but she made it clear that she *disdained* the idea of being my friend. She already had her own friends, I learned, for one of them in particular was in the habit of coming around the shop in the evenings to collect Nell and entice her to the beer hall. For all her goody-goody posturing, Nell evidently had a capacity for gossip and booze with which I was unacquainted.

"Would you like to come with us, Violet?" Nell's friend asked one evening as we were tidying up the shop.

I turned from the display shelves I was ordering. I realized I very much *did* wish to go. But before a single word escaped my lips, Nell piped up to answer for me.

"No, no," she hurried to insist. She turned to me. "We actually aren't going anywhere at all tonight. She's mistaken; we're only walking together. It's straight home for the both of us!"

An awkward pause passed as Nell's obvious lie hung in the air.

"But next time we do go, I'll be sure to tell you," she fibbed.

I nodded and returned to the shelves. "You can go on," I said after a moment. "I'll finish this without you."

Nell required no further urging. She gathered her shawl and her day-purse and looped her arm through her friend's. Once they were out on the street, she either forgot that much could be heard through the glass windows—or else she didn't care.

"What were you thinking?" she scolded her friend with a laugh. "Inviting her along? She's a bore, and an oddball besides!"

More shocking than overhearing straitlaced Nell's damning assessment of my "boring" character was the realization that her words genuinely stung. They were oblivious of me as I stood there, watching through the window at the two of them laughing.

My heart ached for Flossie and Cora.

My eyes drifted to the coatrack near the door, and I noticed Nell's beautiful blue bonnet still hanging on the hook. Nell loved that bonnet; it was by far the finest thing she owned, and she wore it every day. She must've left it behind by accident, desperate to hurry her well-meaning friend away from me.

I stared at the bonnet. I knew I could run after them and bring it to Nell. She might like that. But as I continued to stare, I began to lose sense of all time. *Oddball. Bore.* I recall seeing the fabric of the bonnet up close: a lovely, deep-sapphire velvet.

The next thing I became cognizant of, I was holding the bonnet in my hands . . . but it was dripping wet and covered in some kind of ink. As I glanced around, I knew I was in the cobbler's workshop, and I must have dunked the bonnet in the vat of tanning dye he used to tint shoe leather.

I gasped, feeling like a criminal. I cast a wild look around, but it appeared I was alone. The workshop was empty, and there was no crack of light under the door to the cobbler's little one-room apartment. Frightened by the fact I could not recall having perpetrated the act of vandalism, I threw the bonnet down and ran from the workshop, and then from the shop altogether.

My hands stung from the dye and were still stained purplish-black. I tried desperately to rub them on my skirt as I hurried along. I knew two things: my spells had gotten the best of me, and I couldn't go back to the shoe shop ever again.

In the weeks that followed, I hardly knew what to do with myself. I began roaming the streets during the days I ought to have been at the shoe shop. Walking became an addiction. I soon became dimly aware that I was searching the crowds . . . for Cora and Flossie. Anytime I saw a wispy blonde head gleaming in the sun, or scarlet ringlets bouncing below the nape of a bonnet, my heart leapt. But, of course, none of these false sightings ever turned out to be my friends.

Walking and not working was taking a toll in more ways than one. I was forced to visit the safety-deposit box and retrieve a bit more of Tackett's stolen cash. I decided that, as my repentance, I would start the process anew and look for employment yet again. I made up my mind that this time I would hold out for a post at one of the big new department stores. I was certain that, at one of those behemoths, I could watch the whole world go by; if Cora and Flossie were still in San Francisco, sooner or later I'd know.

As luck would have it, the Emporium—that great institution of fashionable consumerism—was set to reopen its doors. By then, two whole years had passed since the earthquake. Dressed in my most respectable ladies' suit, I took myself over to Market Street to inquire about a position. The store was closed but bustling with workers preparing the lovely displays.

The mood around the store was so incredibly opposite of that I had known in the shoe shop, the merry buzz of activity left me nearly dizzy. I was shown to a back waiting room, where I sat patiently until I was quizzed by a grim-faced drill sergeant of a woman who never quite introduced herself. Instead, she strode up to where I sat and required me to quickly add and subtract sums in my head. A short while later I was shown to another back office, where a middle-aged man with a pencil moustache introduced himself as Mr. Larchfield.

"Well, aren't you the dapper daisy!" he chuckled from across his desk. "Though I suppose I ought to call you a 'dapper violet,' eh?"

I mustered a weakly appreciative smile.

"Hmm. Yes. Doesn't quite have the same ring to it," he lamented, annoyed that I was not more amused.

"No, no, it's very clever," I conceded, throwing in a little laugh for good measure.

We sat in silence for a moment as Mr. Larchfield peered into a file folder and slid his finger down some kind of list.

"Well, Violet . . . I believe we may in fact have an availability for you. We still need to fill the post at the millinery counter!" He punctuated his conclusion with a smile full of teeth that were startlingly long for his small mouth.

"Oh, why, yes . . . wonderful," I said.

The truth was, I wasn't terribly fond of hats. I'd always assumed I might never afford one. Hats seemed to exist only to make me feel my inferiority. And after my time in the hotel, I'd come to think they weren't very modern. But I wanted the position so badly, I went on nodding and grinning.

"Report to the store at nine o'clock tomorrow morning. Miss Addison will show you the ropes," Mr. Larchfield said.

He scribbled several notes down onto a form. Then he tore off the bottom portion and handed it to me.

"Here's your employment slip; Miss Addison will want to see that. Congratulations, dapper Violet."

12

had, in some ways, made only a slight adjustment, trading shoes for hats. But during those first few weeks, the Emporium provided exactly what I hungered for. It was enough to watch the customers flooding the aisles: rich people, poor people, mothers pushing babies in lacy buggies, elderly couples squabbling, adolescent girls pestering their fathers for the latest fashions. Locals, tourists, and immigrants freshly arrived from the docks. Chinese families. Negro families. Everyone's eyes swept over the mirrored shelves and glass displays, hungrily searching. It was just as I had hoped: if you stood still in the Emporium, the whole world passed by.

I worked six days per week, with one short break in the afternoons. I was beginning to learn that all shops had their routines, and that, for all its impressive size and flashy displays, the Emporium was no different. Most customers made nearly identical small talk. They asked to try on the hats from my display. I handed over the requested model and held up a little hand-mirror for the customer to admire herself. Less than half of those who tried on a hat bought one; my job was to smile either way.

For more serious patrons, I took down custom orders. In these cases, the customer would describe everything she wanted, and—in one week's time—our milliner would have ready any hat a person could imagine. We received very few of these demands, but when I did get one, I wasn't half-bad at them; I found I was good at guessing and transcribing each customer's desires. I had, in fact, something of a gift for helping customers find just the thing they wanted. Most were young women, not much older than myself. We'd make friends, but only for the duration of our exchange. In truth, while I was adept at my job, I found it a challenge to make a more lasting bond.

This was true, too, of my interactions with the other shop-girls who lodged in my women's hotel. Over time they began to strike me as shallow, fickle creatures. Most of them changed their minds daily as to which fellow they fancied. None of them had the smallest fraction of Cora's panache, and certainly none had picked up as many books as Flossie.

Before long, loneliness—that familiar anguish—began to nibble at my edges yet again.

Then, as I sat sipping coffee on my Sunday off, I finally gave in to temptation.

I set out in the early afternoon, picking my way across the city, nervous that Henrietta might have forgotten me. But I felt a sense of relief as soon as I spied the green-and-white-striped awnings. The stalls outside the store were stacked high with the ruffled heads of cabbage and lettuce, mingled with jewel-toned fruits, each red or green apple shined to a mirror-like polish. There was something friendly and welcoming in this sidewalk display that assured me that Henrietta had not changed one whit.

I walked past the stalls and poked my head in cautiously. I heard Henrietta before I saw her.

I blinked, my eyes adjusting from the bright day outside. There she was, sitting on a stool in front of the cash-box and holding court, telling stories to a small group of very rapt customers. When she spied me, however, she shrieked and shot to her feet.

"Violet!" She ran to embrace me. "Are my eyes deceivin' me?" she exclaimed, squeezing me tight. "Ain't that something—my own dear Violet strollin' into the shop like it was jus' any regular day!"

Any worries I'd had evaporated in that hug. I squeezed her back, then we released each other. She stepped back to take in the sight of me once more, and I felt proud to think she was noting my new sophistication.

"Come, come!" Henrietta insisted. She pulled up a stool next to her own. "Help me mind the till; we can gossip and catch up on everything that's happened! Why, I ain't seen you since that soggy tent city!"

"The shop looks wonderful," I said. "Everything has gone well for you, I take it?"

Henrietta grinned and nodded. "I hate to say it, but it turns out I'm awful fond of selling produce," she said. "The world's a brighter place! I *like* helpin' folks squeeze a good melon, much more than I ever liked lettin' them pay to squeeze the two I got right here—hah!"

She shook her bosom with her hands as if to demonstrate. I laughed while glancing about uncomfortably. But it was plain that she couldn't care less who heard her. If anyone was going to be embarrassed about the life she'd been forced to lead before the earthquake, it wasn't going to be Henrietta; I had to admire her for that much.

Now she took a closer look at me, cocking her head and narrowing her eyes.

"Why, you look as though you've somethin' more pressing than our reunion on yer mind," she assessed.

I nodded.

She turned and shouted over her shoulder, "Liam! I'm fixin' to take Violet upstairs for a spot of tea. Mind the shop now, will ya?"

Her husband, who had been stacking cans in the opposite corner, crossed the room and tipped his cap to me. Henrietta grasped my hand and led me up a narrow flight of stairs to the apartment she kept above.

Unsurprisingly, Henrietta's apartment proved to be a warm, magical place. She'd had it wired for electricity and furnished it with lots of cozy, soft furniture. Every window overflowed with potted plants. Henrietta had a weakness, too, for strays, and showed me how she had collected a parakeet, a sweet old hound, and a full litter of kittens playing in a large wooden crate. The kittens were a recent addition in more ways than one, she explained with an affectionate chortle.

It was soon plain that Henrietta had no intention of boiling tea. Instead, she poured a pair of flower-patterned teacups full to their brims with whiskey, then scooped up one of the homeliest orphans and handed him to me. The scraggly little tabby promptly curled up near my neck and purred with drooping eyelids. I snuggled the warm, furry body and enjoyed the thrumming purr at my throat. As I sipped at the fiery whiskey, Henrietta and I talked a bit. I asked her about the greengrocery. Before long, she saw right through to the heart of me.

"What's on yer mind, Violet?"

"Well . . . you haven't heard anything about where Cora or Flossie might be, have you?"

She blinked, surprised.

"Can't say that I have. I never pictured you losin' track yerself. You three were thick, and pardon me for sayin' so, but you seemed like you'd be a little lost without them."

"I am," I sighed.

"Why'd you part in the first place?" she asked.

I was seized by a sudden panic. How stupid of me! It was a natural question to ask, and I had no answer—no *honest* answer, that is. As I tried to think of what to say, the kitten nuzzling my neck grew restless. I set him back down among his brothers and sisters.

"We . . . had a falling-out," I said. I felt my face flush.

"All three o' ya?"

I nodded, but the way Henrietta looked at me, I could tell she knew there was far more to the story than that. She fell silent. I squirmed.

But, generous soul that she was, she let the subject drop.

"Well, you don't seem so lost to me—tell me about that fancy department store you work in nowadays."

I happily embraced the opportunity, and the two of us caught up on the more mundane details of our new lives, swapping funny stories about our respective customers. We spent over an hour like that, until we'd laughed ourselves hoarse and our bellies were warm with whiskey.

13

Though she'd had no news of Cora or Flossie, seeing Henrietta restored a measure of joy to my heart. After our visit, I began to harbor a tiny friendly feeling towards the world again.

Then, one day, as I was walking to work, a ragamuffin boy selling newspapers just outside the Emporium caught my attention. A great many boys sold newspapers, and most of them looked a bit underfed. But this particular boy was so very skinny, it appeared he was held together by his suspenders. More pressingly: I noticed he was also being stalked by a band of larger, mischievous boys, ready to pounce.

It was all over in a flash. Before I could blink, the bullies had relieved him of his stack of papers and the boy was on the ground. He struggled valiantly and even managed to topple one of the bullies by grabbing his leg. But this victory was short-lived, and they rained blows on him with the sort of cannibalistic vitriol only young boys can exhibit. Before I could blink a second time, I had rushed towards them, flailing my arms and shouting, "Hey! Leave him alone! *Leave him alone at once!*"

I had no idea what I was doing, but it seemed to work. The boys took one look at me—oh, the picture I must have made, neatly dressed in my ladies' suit and necktie, yet charging after them like a bull!—and the whole group turned tail and ran. When they had vanished, I approached their bedraggled victim and helped him over to a nearby stoop. He didn't thank me; he merely continued to cry, snot pouring down his face and an unappealing black eye rapidly blooming under his left socket.

"That was the entire day's earnin's," he sobbed.

"But you've lived to tell the tale," I said, trying a cheery tack.

"Aw, that gang's just a bunch of rotten thieves," he insisted. "It's my pa who'll do the real killin'."

He would not be consoled. The fount of salt water and snot continued to pour. I put my arm around him but the gesture had no effect.

"Pardon me," came an unexpected deep voice. I looked up to see a well-groomed middle-aged gentleman peering down at us. At first, I assumed he wished to enter the shop behind us, so I made a move to help the young lad out of the man's way. But he waved a hand to stop us. Instead—and to my great surprise—he knelt down so he was at eye-level.

"I saw it all. Six against one. You fought very bravely, lad."

"Much good it did me," the boy lamented.

"What is your name?" the man inquired.

"Joe," the boy said sullenly, then added, "Joseph," as though to give himself a faintly better shine.

I snuck a closer look at the gentleman. He was a striking man—in his late forties, perhaps, his fair hair laced with silver, with blue eyes, and a stern-set jaw. He must have felt my gaze on him, for he glanced in my direction and caught me looking. He winked. It was a quick, deft gesture. In the next flash he had returned his attention fully to the child.

"Well, Joe-Joseph," he said, "I witnessed your misfortune. Most unfair of those lads! But it also seems you've managed to win the sympathies of this beautiful young lady."

The man nodded in my direction, and I felt my cheeks redden. Cora was the beautiful one; I'd always been plain.

"Never undervalue a woman who picks you up after you've fallen on rough times."

Joe only stared, dazzled and bewildered by the man's vocabulary and accent, both of which suggested a world far out of Joe's orbit.

"I'll tell you what I'm going to do," the man continued. "I'm going to help you. But it'll have to be our secret."

The man reached into his pocket and produced a sum of money. Joe's eyes went wide to see paper and not coin, his blue irises suddenly surrounded by white.

"I'm going to give you the money for the newspapers that those boys stole from you," the man concluded. "But—and I hope you are listening, Joe-Joseph—I *don't* want you to go out and buy another stack, do you understand? I want you to tell your parents you sold them all, and here are the earnings. And today . . . today I want you to spend the day doing something you like." The man paused and leveled a very serious look in Joe's direction. "Can you do that for me?"

Joe's eyes were still enormous. He glanced at me, silently asking if this stroke of luck was true. I nodded. Then he glanced again at the gray-green bills gripped delicately in the gentleman's hand.

"All right. I have your solemn oath that you'll spend the day playing?"

Joe nodded.

"You'll, say, spend the day fishing down by the pier?"

Joe nodded.

"Do you know how to dig for worms?"

By then Joe was nodding so vigorously, I worried his head might topple off.

"Fine. You've given your word and I shall place my trust in it. Here you are," the man said. He released the money into Joe's custody.

"Th-thanks!" Joe stammered. He pocketed the money with a furtive air and scrambled up from the stoop as if anxious the gentleman might change his mind. "Can I go?"

"Of course. Run along. Remember: fishing! Or stickball! No selling papers today."

The stranger and I exchanged a happy chuckle as we watched Joe scamper off.

"Your compensation far exceeded the value of those newspapers," I commented with a smile. "I'll wager his pa will want to know how he managed such a boon. Hopefully he won't demand the boy earn that much every day."

"Let's hope he spends some of it, then," the gentleman said, smiling in return. "Perhaps he'll buy a nice candied apple or a mitt for playing ball. But handing him money isn't anything, really. Your bizarre performance is what caught my eye. It's not every day you see an otherwise polite-looking young woman tearing down the street, hooting and hollering like a crazed fishwife!"

His smile turned into a warm grin, but I felt my face grow hot. I knew I'd made a fool of myself; I'd simply been counting on anonymity.

"It was a superb performance, by the way. When I first laid eyes on you, I believed you truly mad!" The man laughed. "More importantly, though: without it, our poor Joe might have been much worse for the wear."

I brightened ever so slightly to think this might be true. I smiled at the stranger, and for a moment our eyes remained locked.

Somewhere a clock struck ten and I jolted to attention. *Ten!* The Emporium doors were now open! I'd lost track of the time. I stood up and brushed off my skirts.

"Oh! The hour!" I said. "I'll be late to my post!"

"Your post?"

I nodded, already hurrying away.

"There'll be no one to mind the counter! I am sorry; I must run."

I scurried off, much the way Joe had only minutes earlier. I cast one look over my shoulder. The handsome stranger stared after me, a mixture of surprise and remorse on his face.

I felt a flicker of sorrow. I would have liked to stay with him longer.

14

A few days later, around two or three o'clock, a pair of ladies departed my counter, sadly—and predictably—without purchasing anything. They had tried on just about every hat we offered, and in the wake of their visit I occupied myself with setting everything back in proper order. I lifted each hat onto its corresponding stand and carefully cocked it this way or that. After I had set all thirty-three hats back in their rightful places, all that was left on the glass countertop before me was the little hand-mirror I used to help ladies admire themselves.

I was feeling idle, bored. When I lifted the mirror, I caught a flash of a woman's face, and with a start I realized that woman was me. On the morning of the 'quake itself, I had been a mere girl of sixteen. Now—suddenly, it seemed—I was eighteen, a grown woman working in a modern department store. Who was this person I had become? I paused to examine her. In the glass I saw my light brown hair and pale gray eyes. My hair was still rather plain in color, although I had learned to sweep it into a becoming chignon. My heart-shaped face was still somewhat childish, although some of the baby fat had begun to melt away, sharpening my cheekbones. My eyes had always been my most distinctive feature—an irony, I felt, as they lacked an emphatic color. But there they were, staring at me—those gray eyes. There was something new in them, something haunting. I was surprised by their worldliness, their new aura of allure.

I'm ashamed to say I was entranced for a full minute or two, until I was interrupted by a man clearing his throat.

"Oh!" As quickly as I could, I slapped the mirror against the counter, then winced as it hit the glass with a violent *CRACK*.

"Beg your pardon, sir!" I rushed to apologize, but when I looked up, I froze. The man stared at me, a hint of an amused smile lifting the corners of his distinguished features.

"Oh—it's you!" I blurted, before I could stop myself.

"I don't mean to interrupt."

"Not at all!" I felt myself choking on my own humiliation and covered it with a delicate cough. "May I help you with something? Would you care to have a look at one of our hats?"

He didn't speak for a moment, and I finally dared myself to meet his eye. His blue gaze fastened on my gray one as it had on our first encounter, until eventually he spoke.

"It was such a kind gesture—helping that young lad," the gentleman said.

"That's thoughtful of you to say," I replied. "But I did very little. I believe your own generosity made a great deal more difference."

"I am ashamed to say I never would have noticed the boy," he admitted. "I would have looked right through him, even in his state—miserable as it was—if it had not been for you. I have been meditating upon that fact a great deal, and it weighs on me."

His humility was sincere, but I found myself uncomfortable and blushing.

"Either way, I suppose it's a coincidence," I said, "our meeting twice in one week."

"Coincidence . . ." he repeated in a low murmur, as though baffled.

I'd forgotten how handsome he was. I could not, for the life of me, guess what he was doing at my counter. Any thought that he had come to seek me out on purpose felt too impossible, too vain, to consider.

"Can I help you find a hat, sir?" I prompted. "I should be quite happy to assist you."

His expression twitched. "Ah . . . yes . . . a hat," he said. He took a breath and looked around my counter. "Do you like hats?"

"Certainly," I lied. "All ladies love hats. As a matter of fact, I hold one of the most popular posts in all of the Emporium." The latter bit, at least, was true.

He cleared his throat again and composed himself.

"Well, then. Let's see, now . . ."

His eyes moved to the shelves behind my shoulder.

"Hmm," he said appraisingly. "I'm afraid none of those will do."

"Oh," I murmured in an apologetic tone.

"Those are lovely but ordinary," he continued. "And I'm looking for something special."

"We do take custom orders, sir," I replied, my rote instincts taking over.

He smiled, his lips twisting with a subtle, enigmatic expression.

"Yes," he said. "That will be just the thing. Will you guide me through the acquisition?"

"Of course," I replied. I took out the pad of order forms and extracted a pencil from a deftly concealed drawer. Before I could stop myself, I had licked it like a crass schoolgirl. I blushed but he did not seem to notice. Instead, he shot me an earnest look.

"I'm very grateful for your help, Miss . . . ?"

"Violet," I replied, idiotically blushing again. "Management prefers us to offer our given names," I added, trying to explain away the familiarity.

"Miss Violet," he said, retaining a hint of politesse. His handsome face lit up. "My name is Harry."

He briefly took my fingertips in his hand and I felt light-headed.

"Now . . . where do we start?"

"Well, let's begin with forms," I said. I began to lay out for him the many shapes that a hat might take.

"Which do you advise?" he asked.

"Advise?" I echoed. "Well, I suppose it depends on the lady."

"The lady is unique," he asserted. "I've the feeling that I've never seen nor met anyone quite like her."

"Ah," I said, as though I knew. That was an old sales trick: that perfect tone of comprehension, no matter what the customer should say. In truth, I was slightly irritated by his adulation of this mystery woman. I found myself falling into a cheeky mood, and before I knew it, I'd helped him to order the most *unique* hat I could possibly imagine. By the end of our time together, the poor gentleman and I had managed to design the greatest monstrosity the millinery world might ever know.

The hat, a disaster in lavender silk, was slated to have an enormous brim, an equally huge and complicated pale blue satin bow, a terrible mess of ermine, and a large enough pile of black and white feathers to make it appear as though a medium-sized Dalmatian had curled up to nap on top. I thought of the woman destined to wear it and pitied her the neck cramps she was likely to experience.

I couldn't understand what sort of mischievous devil had gotten into me: I had always been a light touch with the custom orders, someone who listened and prescribed a tasteful and exacting gift. But I had to admit: I'd developed a schoolgirl crush. And, sadly, I was expressing it exactly as a schoolgirl would.

As I wrote up the slip for the gentleman to sign, I silently chastised myself for my rude and reckless behavior. The woman was sure to hate the gift, the gentleman was sure to return it with (justifiable!) complaint, and I was sure to come under great reprimand.

"Here you are," I said, holding out the claim slip. "We'll have it ready for you this time one week from today."

"Thank you," Harry replied.

He accepted the slip but lingered.

"Is there anything else?" I prompted, nervous again.

"I suppose . . . not."

His blue gaze was locked on my own once more, and I felt my cheeks grow warm. Eventually, he inclined ever so slightly at the waist to bid me farewell, and turned to leave. As he strode away, I noticed a pair of servants trailing in his wake, their arms burdened with packages. They had been standing some distance away, all the while I'd been taking the gentleman's order, and I had been too blind—too busy making mischief—to notice.

The presence of manservants could only mean that Harry surely came from great wealth. I groaned inwardly. As kind as he had been to that little newsboy in the street, everything was bound to change when he got a glimpse of the custom hat; he would not be so forgiving if he thought I was having a laugh at his expense. Rich men were sure to make trouble over poor service.

What had possessed me?

15

I pushed the incident from my mind, knowing there was nothing I could do—not until the hat was ready, anyway. Once the gentleman claimed it . . . well, then I supposed I'd have to deal with whatever came next. I let a few scenarios play out in my head, imagining myself apologizing, offering to pay for the hat's replacement. Then I commanded myself to stop fretting. Fretting, I had learned, was a useless occupation.

One week later, the hat was ready. The box alone was unwieldy. I peeked inside; it was every bit as ugly as I'd imagined. I sighed. It would not be a peaceful day. From the moment I'd stepped through the doors that morning, I'd felt terribly jumpy—I was dreading the inevitable. I caught myself searching the crowd for the gentleman's tall, familiar shape. Twice I thought I saw a flash of his silver-threaded fair hair, but both times the head belonged to someone else.

Then, finally, when I was arranging hats with my back to the counter, a man rang my bell.

"May I help you?" I said pleasantly, turning. He held out the claim-ticket that corresponded to the custom hat. He was an older man, white-haired, with rather hollow cheeks. I winced and looked again, recognizing him as one of the two manservants.

"Something wrong, miss?" the man inquired.

"Not at all," I said, recovering.

"I've come for the order," the man reminded me.

"Of course." I shook myself. "Here it is." I handed over the enormous hatbox that had been giving me the evil eye all day. I hesitated for a moment, debating. Then I forced myself to do my job. "Would you care to have a look at it?" I touched the box as though to lift the lid.

"None of my business," he replied. He scooped up the box with a mechanical air and turned to go. "Thank you kindly."

I watched him leave and cringed, very certain that he—or, worse, his master—would be back soon to complain.

The day wore on, but the hat and its purchaser didn't return. I found myself rather worried. What if the gentleman—like so many men—couldn't tell a good hat from a bad one? Oh, but he would have to be *blind* not to see this hat's particular awfulness.

What if . . . what if he gave it to the lady of whom he spoke so highly—"she" of the unparalleled uniqueness? Would he dare? I shuddered to think.

When I arrived home that evening—after nine hours on my feet—I was surprised to discover my landlady, Mrs. Campbell, in a snit.

"I'm not a post office, I'll have you know!" she fired at me the second I stepped into the common room. I had the distinct feeling she had been lying in wait.

"Do you hear me?" she said now, as I had been too baffled to reply. "Not a post office! If you're going to be accepting gifts from all manner of strangers, you'll not be doing it through me. This is the first and the last! I've got better things to do."

The other girls lounging around stared at me, but I was still too stymied to muster a reply. With a great heave, Mrs. Campbell thrust something at me and stomped away. A door slammed.

I blinked at the object in my arms. It looked rather familiar. Could it be? And if so, what an odd way to lodge his complaint: returning it to my personal residence!

Self-consciously, I carried the box upstairs and unlocked the door of my little room. Once inside, I put the box on the table and carefully pulled at the satin ribbons, untying the bow.

After a moment, I lifted the lid.

Sure enough, inside was the hat. Pinned to its brim was a card.

> *Your kindness deserves to be acknowledged with a gesture*
> *of generosity in return. I would be ever so honored if you would*
> *accept this token of my admiration, and wear it to the Palm Court*
> *to take tea with me at a time and date that suits your convenience.*
> *Yours truly,*
> *Mr. Harold Leland Carlyle*

I was flabbergasted. I read the note twice over, and then again a third time, until its meaning finally began to sink in. My mind summoned the image of the man I'd met—his intense gaze, his polished demeanor, his good looks, and his kind, dignified face. My heart fluttered a little to picture him sitting across from me, those blue eyes burning into me over the distance of something so simple as a tea-table.

But then I reread the part about how I should oblige him by wearing the hat. I peeked again in the box. The monstrosity and I proceeded to stare each other down. If it was a contest, the hat was winning. It glared smugly at me, ugly as sin.

"Aw, *cripes*," I finally muttered aloud, with a mixture of horror and amusement.

16

Mr. Harold Leland Carlyle's invitation was accompanied by a courtesy card marked *"Répondez s'il vous plaît,"* which I was to send back with my reply. There were two categories to choose from. One simply stated "Sincerest regrets," while the other gave the address of the tearoom at the Palace Hotel, along with a blank space for me to fill in the date and time.

The Palm Court at the Palace! I thought back to the day I'd eavesdropped on those two shop-girls. They'd dreamed that someday their beaux might take them. I reminded myself that Harry Carlyle's interest was likely not romantic. His note had indicated that he believed my act of kindness ought to be rewarded. It was merely an act of charity. Still . . . an invitation from a stranger. Even if it was only charity, it was incredibly forward. The note made no mention of a chaperone.

My pen hovered briefly over the line marked "Sincerest regrets." My better sense dictated that I ought to decline. But then I asked myself:

What would Cora do? I was suddenly possessed by a passionate, impulsive spirit. Perhaps it was the same mischief that had possessed me when designing the hat. Before I could stop myself, I'd scribbled in three o'clock for the following Sunday.

With my selection settled, the only matter of concern was . . . what to wear with *that hat*.

When the appointed day arrived, I opted for the dignified blue ladies' suit I'd worn when I'd first inquired about employment at the Emporium. I piled my hair high. Then I lifted the hat out of its box and placed it atop my head. Using every hairpin in my possession, I attempted to pin it into place. It was, as I'd imagined, very heavy and not at all persuaded to stay put.

My neck was already throbbing before the hansom cab I'd hired pulled up to the Palace Hotel. The driver helped me down, making little effort to mask his annoyance at my cumbersome apparel. After I paid him, I listened to the horse's hooves clop-clopping away with a wave of queasiness. I glimpsed myself in one of the hotel's plate-glass windows and paused. The pile of ermine and feathers quivered and listed, as though ready to topple. The rest of my costume was so practical as to render the note of contrast utterly comical.

I entered the hotel and found my way to the tearoom, teetering a little with each step. Once there, a maître d' looked twice at the ridiculous picture I made, a deep crease appearing between his eyebrows. But he quickly recovered himself. As I gave him my name, a renewed flicker of self-consciousness flashed into my mind: What was he thinking of me—an unchaperoned woman meeting a man for tea?

"Your cousin has already arrived, miss, and is waiting for you at the table," the maître d' announced. "Please follow me."

Aha, I thought, *so my host has told the establishment a little white lie.*

I followed the maître d' as he stepped through the yawning entrance into the dining room. Its glorious diffused light startled me. *That* must be why people said the tearoom at the Palace was among the best. While its marble pillars, potted ferns, and chandeliers were all very nice, the true showstopper was the enormous glass dome that capped the cavernous room. It was spectacular, Victorian and yet somehow modern—like something Tiffany might create. It gave one the impression you were still outdoors but had just wandered into some incandescent alcove where light bounced the way sound echoes. It was beautiful.

I let my awed gaze drop and all at once I saw him: "Mr. Harold Leland Carlyle." His patrician profile was slightly inclined over a menu; he was even more handsome than I remembered. He glanced up and we locked eyes. I felt my heart quicken.

As I followed the maître d' across the room, my self-consciousness grew with each step. The hushed murmur of conversation and the delicate clinking of fine china and silverware gave off a dignified din; my ladies' suit seemed like a dull rock in a sea full of shining silks and satins.

As we neared the table, Mr. Carlyle rose from his seat and gave a dignified bow. As I attempted to curtsy in return, I felt the hat wobble. I briefly considered making a mad dash and letting it fall as I bolted.

But it was too late. Already Mr. Carlyle was circling the tea-table, pulling out my chair and holding it for me with a polite air of consideration. I obediently sank into the seat and allowed myself to be gently pushed in. The maître d' bustled away.

"Thank you for accepting my invitation, Violet," my host said, once we were alone. "May I call you Violet here?"

"Of course, if you wish," I replied. "We are, after all, *cousins*—or so I hear," I added. "Although I suspect I am your poorest relation."

Mr. Carlyle laughed. "Yes. As I have no relations to speak of, in fact, I will have to allow you to keep that dubious distinction—though I must insist that poverty itself can be quite subjective; glimpsing your bright face from across the room just now, I felt my spirits suddenly enriched."

I blushed again. "That is too kind of you to say, Mr. Carlyle."

"I insist you call me Harry," he concluded. "It's only fair, if I'm to call you Violet."

The request turned back upon me was almost too much.

"Fair enough," I conceded, and then, with a little spurt of courage, added, "Harry."

He nodded in approval. Then he reached for the teapot.

"Does Earl Grey suit you?"

"It does indeed."

He poured and offered cream and sugar. I was not used to having a man prepare my tea for me. It was vaguely thrilling. He handed me my cup, then lifted his own. Together we took a few tentative sips. I snuck a second look around the room. That dome was really quite something, although it gave one the curious impression of being underwater. However, I winced when I saw a table of ladies looking at me. They might have been staring at my hat, but I felt certain they could tell I didn't belong. My cheeks colored with the discomfort of knowing I was a foreigner in a strange land.

"Have you visited the Palm Court before?" Harry asked, as though reading my thoughts.

I shook my head.

"This is a bit beyond my reach, I'm afraid. I'm certain you've guessed that I'm not quite equal to your station. If not, and I have somehow misled you, well . . . I apologize."

"No," he said in a decided tone. "You did not mislead me. It is *you* who I wanted to take to tea today, exactly as you are. And I can assure you, I have glimpsed your kindness. You are *more* than equal to my station."

My mind flickered back to the earthquake and to the events that had just preceded it. Harry couldn't know the awful complications in which I'd become entangled. Perhaps his well-mannered mind couldn't even conceive of them.

I pressed my lips into a polite smile, then cast my gaze about, hoping to change the subject. A waiter arrived and promptly deposited a tiered tray of prettily prepared morsels.

"Please," Harry urged, waving a hand to suggest I go first.

I glanced at the tray, trying to pick out the most proper item with which to start.

"Are those . . . cucumber sandwiches?"

"I'm sure they are," Harry replied. "But I can already tell it's not the cucumber sandwiches that interest you the most."

I couldn't help but smile. He was right. I reached a hesitant hand for a delicate-looking pastry layered with chocolate and vanilla.

Harry chuckled, and reached for one himself.

After that, we talked and ate as we pleased, eating the most appealing things first and ignoring the more routine staples. I would have expected a man of Harry's status to be the type to hold court, and I was surprised to learn nothing could be further from the truth. He seemed genuinely interested as he asked me questions about myself—and he had quite a lot of thoughtful questions indeed. I had to navigate my way carefully through the conversation. I knew it wouldn't do to tell him about my previous life in the boardinghouse, much less explain how I'd managed to come up a bit in the world.

To my relief, Harry changed tack to ask me about my passions and pastimes.

"Books," I blurted, without hesitation.

Harry grinned at me. "Tell me, what are some of your favorites?"

The answer took me quite a long time to relay; there were so many. I began with the most recent ones I'd loved and worked my way backwards. After ten minutes of chattering happily on, I realized I had not let Harry get a word in edgewise.

"Oh!" I said, embarrassed. "You said 'some,' not 'all'! Here I am, going on and on. You must be on the verge of passing out!"

"Not at all," Harry replied. He was smiling at me with a fresh twinkle in his eyes, looking rather amused. "I must say, though, you are impressively well-read. It would be quite something to read something together someday."

A new heat rushed to my cheeks; for some reason it was an intimate thought. I'd only ever read books "together" with Flossie. I gazed at Harry, realizing I very much wanted to take him up on his suggestion. But anytime I cleared my throat to say as much, I felt my voice fail me, and could only muster a shy smile.

I tried to turn the tables a bit, hungry to know more about my host. Harry's past was so unlike my own; his family history stretched back to America's colonial days and was full of landowners and prudent businessmen, men who'd bestowed the Carlyle name upon schools and libraries on both coasts.

"I know I've been lucky," Harry admitted, "inheriting the fortunes of those who came before me. Of course, along with inherited wealth comes various inherited occupations—ones that don't always suit exactly."

He went on to explain that he'd inherited several logging operations and timber mills in Oregon; his ships traveled down the coast with regular cargos of lumber, which were dispatched at a solid profit. This was his duty but not his passion. He still wanted to make a contribution, he explained, one that went beyond industry.

"I'm passionate about the arts," Harry continued. "I believe the city of San Francisco *could be* one of the great cities of all civilization."

He explained that he hoped to patronize the eventual formation of a city symphony and a city opera. He dreamed that San Francisco might one day possess a grand art gallery that included some of the world's greatest masterpieces.

I listened to him talk, moved, but also leery of his practical intent. After all, not so long ago, San Francisco had proved she was capable of incredible destruction. It seemed plain to me that Mother Nature was the true artist in this city, and those who brought mankind's finer works to reside here were only tempting fate. Harry seemed to read these thoughts in my expression.

"It's true," he admitted. "The earthquake showed us that we are at the mercy of any act of God. But now . . . after all that was lost, the city is more full of energy and dynamism than she was before." He paused. "Perhaps a taste of destruction reminds us why we create."

I turned this observation over in my mind, weighing the truth therein. I had to admit: I, myself, had created my new life specifically so the old might be destroyed.

"Either way, in recent years I've devoted myself to helping Alma Spreckels. She's crusading for San Francisco to build a museum rivaling the very collections in Europe!"

His countenance had lit up; it was touching to see.

"You harbor such passion for the arts," I observed. "They absorb you. I daresay if you had a wife, she'd be jealous—and perhaps with good reason!"

I meant the remark in good humor, but as the words left my lips, Harry stiffened. His jaw clenched, and an eerie silence settled between us.

After a few awkward seconds, he reached into his vest and produced a pocket watch. "My goodness," he commented. "I'm afraid I've kept you here longer than my due, Violet. You were very kind to meet me."

The sudden chill of his demeanor cowed me. I attempted to return to our old joke.

"Anything for a dear cousin," I said, smiling and giving a pleasant shrug. But my humor didn't quite hit its mark. He looked at me with a slightly pained expression.

"Yes. We can keep up the pretense if you like," he said.

He nodded as he spoke. Then a hesitant expression passed over his features. He cleared his throat.

"But either way, I should like to see you again—nothing untoward.

A simple walk in the park, perhaps, or a symphony concert. I could even procure a chaperone to accompany us, if that would make you feel safer."

I stared at him, surprised and secretly delighted. I'd assumed our acquaintance would end with the meal, as our incompatible social stations dictated it ought. I studied Harry for a moment; he seemed a miracle to me. I'd never held the attentions of any man save Jasper. Before me sat a handsome, distinguished gentleman who'd not only read the books I loved, but who seemed to love them, too.

"Are you sure?" I asked. "You have, after all, completed your act of charity. It was a lovely tea, and I am very grateful."

"The only act of charity was on your part, Violet," he replied, frowning. I wondered if I hadn't confused him. "But you're quite within your rights if you'd like to decline," he added when I continued to sit in silence, staring wide-eyed at him. "I hadn't thought how broaching the subject might put you on the spot. You have my sincerest apologies."

"No—I'd like it," I finally managed. I blushed, and tried again. "I'd like to take a walk in the park."

His face brightened. The warmth returned to his bearing. We sat smiling at each other until a hint of shyness settled over the table.

"Well, now," Harry said with an air of finality. "I only have one more question for you, Violet . . ."

His voice had again turned grave, as had his expression. I felt a flicker of worry.

"Yes?"

Harry leaned forward over the tea-table, his brow creased with concern.

"What are we to do about your terrible taste in hats?"

I was dumbstruck at first, slow to catch the joke. His eyes moved from my face upwards, to the terrible monstrosity. For all its ungainly weight, I'd forgotten I was wearing it.

"Is that truly the latest in ladies' fashions?" Harry asked. "And are you earnestly fond of it?"

I abruptly burst out laughing. "No," I said.

"Oh, thank heavens," Harry said, grinning.

"I actually don't like hats at all," I confessed.

"I think the hats know it," Harry joked.

I blushed madly, but he did not seem angry—quite the contrary, in fact. He joined in my laughter, and together our giddiness grew like a snowball rolling downhill, picking up speed. The other tables were looking at us, but the more we tried to tamp down our laughter, the more irrepressible it became.

"I thought perhaps I was hopelessly out of touch."

"You're not out of touch," I told him. "It *is* truly terrible! I'm very sorry to say so, and I'm even sorrier I am the one responsible for its creation. I've cost you the expense, and I apologize."

"No apologies." He shook his head and smirked. "It was entirely worth it to see you sitting here, wearing it now."

"I don't know what the devil got into me. I've never helped a customer design a worse hat." I hesitated, daring myself to go on. "I admit I may have given in to a spark of jealousy . . . thinking of the woman you intended to give it to."

At this, Harry looked genuinely pleased. He struggled to suppress a smile.

"Let's throw it into the Bay—the two of us. Perhaps the winds will sail it to Alcatraz."

"It will sink straight to the bottom, I am sure of it," I said. By now I was laughing so hard, I felt tears coming to my eyes. "You can't imagine how much it weighs!"

It should have been embarrassing. The two of us were struggling to keep from attracting the entire room's attention. But I was not embarrassed one whit. I felt for the first time in a long time that I was in the company of a true friend.

17

\\\||///

Loneliness is a paradoxical beast. Oftentimes it is only when one has had a recent taste of good company that one feels the needling dagger of solitude most acutely. Working at the Emporium, I regularly spoke to customers, but I'd forgotten how much I enjoyed passing time *with* someone. Waiting on a person is quite a different thing from sitting together as companions. I had not shared such camaraderie with anyone since I'd been parted from Cora and Flossie. The lovely hours I'd spent with Harry had reawakened my deeper feelings of isolation and the grief I felt for my absent friends. I knew that if he made good on his promise to extend a second invitation, I would accept.

Almost two weeks passed, and I'd begun to despair, when I came home to find my landlady again in a snit. Evidently, Harry did not do anything by half-measures, and he had sent his manservant to deliver another formal invitation. It included another gift, and this time I opened the long, narrow box to discover a beautiful silk parasol accompanied by a card engraved with Harry's initials. *Please do me the honor of joining me for a stroll in Golden Gate Park*, the note read. The parasol was intended for my comfort during this stroll, and Harry promised we would be accompanied by a chaperone.

I deliberated for a brief moment. My misgivings did not have to do with the chaperone or the notion of taking a stroll—and it certainly wasn't Harry, for I was longing to see him again. I only thought of the last time I had visited Golden Gate Park, when I waited for Cora and Flossie. But no sooner had this sad shadow cast its pall than I shook it off. I seized the R.S.V.P. card, sent it back, and began counting the hours.

When the appointed Sunday afternoon finally arrived, I was overcome with excited, jittery apprehension. I donned my nicest dress, a purchase from the Emporium: a white, summery frock with subtly puffed sleeves, the sort of thing I pictured well-mannered ladies wearing to a picnic. I made my way to the park, full of nerves, trying to think up interesting conversation to make. It was as if Harry's attention was an exotic butterfly that had landed on me quite by mistake, and any minute now, I expected it to flutter away; I wanted to memorize the pattern on his wings before he was gone.

When I first spied Harry standing beside the little boathouse at Stow Lake, I was granted a moment to observe him from afar. He was admittedly quite dashing, and I found myself surprised all over again that he was waiting for *me*. A tall man, he stood with an extremely upright posture. He was middle-aged, but in a distinguished manner, rendering him all the more handsome for his years. As he awaited my arrival, I noticed his jaw clenching and his hands fidgeting idly with his pocket watch. Was he also nervous? It didn't seem possible.

As I pondered this, his eyes suddenly flicked in my direction. He smiled, and I, smiling in return, strode towards him.

"Hello, Violet. This is Miss Weber," Harry said, introducing an older woman standing a few paces away. I was slightly taken off guard; I hadn't noticed the woman as I'd approached. "She's agreed to be our chaperone for the day."

Shyly, I took her in. She was one of those flinty women who appear to be cast of iron. The features of her face were wide yet chiseled, defined mainly by a carved cheek and square jaw. Her dark hair was threaded with gray—a flat gray that, unlike Harry's glinting silver, refused to catch the sun. She may have been beautiful once, but now she gave the impression of a rock shaped by an unrelenting tide.

"A pleasure to meet you," I lied, giving a rote bow of my head.

"Ma'am," Miss Weber replied inscrutably, nodding.

"So many boaters out today," I remarked. "I can hardly blame them. What beautiful weather!"

"Would you care to be rowed about the lake?" Harry asked, his blue eyes sincere. "The parasol should keep the sun off your face, Miss Weber will ensure our good conduct, and I can think of no finer way to spend this pleasant afternoon."

I laughed softly, making an effort to tamp down my nerves. "Who can say no to that?"

Harry arranged to rent one of the little boats tied to the dock. Then he helped the two of us climb in—Miss Weber and me. He had the limber jauntiness of a young man, and it was difficult not to admire his graceful physique.

Miss Weber sat in the prow, allowing Harry and I to face each other in the stern. Harry's back was to her as he rowed. I believe she intended to be polite, but unfortunately it meant that whenever I looked in Harry's direction, I could not avoid catching Miss Weber's eyes over his shoulder. Every time I smiled at Harry, Miss Weber appeared to scowl back at me. This caused me to cringe just slightly, which in turn made Harry frown in puzzlement.

"That's a lovely dress," Harry remarked as he rowed. "White is angelic; it suits you." His kind compliment elicited a skeptical twitch of Miss Weber's thin lips. I swore I even heard a soft tsk, but Harry, for his part, appeared not to hear it. As we chatted on, I summoned my nerve, curious and slightly unsettled.

"It was very kind of Miss Weber to agree to be our chaperone," I said. "Tell me, how are the two of you acquainted?"

I addressed the question to both of them—I had no wish to be so rude as to talk about Miss Weber as though she weren't present—but the elderly woman simply stared off into the middle-distance, leaving Harry to explain.

"I've known Miss Weber all my life," Harry said. "We were children together—weren't we?"

Miss Weber nodded.

"Her mother was my governess, some many, many years ago."

"Oh!" I exclaimed. I immediately struggled to hide my surprise. I had not pictured the two of them as contemporaries; Harry was so handsome, so dapper, while Miss Weber so colorless and severe.

"Yes," Harry continued. "She was made to play with me—though I'm sure it held little allure for her; she was eight years my senior and far more mature! And yet, she tolerated me all the same."

At this, Miss Weber finally smiled—the first expression of its kind to genuinely grace her face—and cast her eyes shyly upon the green surface of the water beyond our rowboat.

"Now Miss Weber serves as the head of my household staff," Harry continued. "And a miraculous thing, too—I'd be lost without her!"

"It's awfully nice that you've remained so close to the family for all these years," I said. But Miss Weber still refused to engage me.

"At this point, Miss Weber isn't simply *with* the family; she is part of the family!" Harry agreed. "And as I'm the only Carlyle left, the poor creature must endure me all on her own. I suppose you could say Miss Weber and I are family of a different kind."

At this pronouncement, Miss Weber's smile widened, and something about it changed. It was . . . *smug*.

I felt a strange twinge. She had lived with Harry all his life and clearly commanded a deep degree of his respect. I couldn't help but be a little jealous. And though it will perhaps make me sound crazy, I could swear Miss Weber detected my jealousy—and *enjoyed* it.

The lake itself was a man-made reservoir, a ring-shaped body of water dug out around a tall island—a chunk of land dubbed "Strawberry Hill" after the many wild berries that grew there. Once we completed a handful of circuits around the island, Harry rowed us back to the dock.

"Miss Weber was kind enough to pack a few provisions for us," Harry announced, helping me out of the boat. "Shall we have them"— he paused, his eyes scanning our surroundings—"over there?"

He pointed to an expanse of green beneath a tidily trimmed weeping willow. I nodded happily.

As it turned out, Miss Weber had packed an impressive picnic. She reached into a basket and produced a cold duck salad, truffled potatoes, a batch of delicate cheese puffs, and a flask of fresh lemonade. She had also brought cutlery, plates, and glasses. The entire production was very civilized.

Yet, the dance of lunch was rather awkward. Miss Weber prepared and served us our plates but refused to take anything for herself—despite Harry's many urgings.

"Wouldn't be proper," Miss Weber insisted with a resolute shake of her head. Instead, she retreated several paces away and sat glowering at us from a dark pocket of dense shade under the willow tree. *If she believes she's doing us a favor*, I thought, *she would've made things so much easier by joining in.* But of course I had the strong suspicion that Miss Weber harbored no intention of doing us a favor in the first place. It was plain that I had not won her fancy, and that she disapproved of the interest her master had taken in me.

"You haven't eaten very much," Harry observed, watching me push food around my plate. "Perhaps you still need to work up an appetite." He paused and tipped his head back in the direction of the lake. "Would you care to stretch your legs, and feed the birds with me?"

I agreed, and Miss Weber immediately offered up a bag of what I presumed were bread crusts. Together, Harry and I set off to feed the waterfowl.

I was relieved to see that Miss Weber did not intend to join us. She remained seated under the willow, and once we were out of earshot, I began to relax. Harry offered me some jumbled crusts, and I took them, intending to toss them to a nearby flock of mallards. But as I looked at the crusts, I gasped and laughed.

"What is this?" I exclaimed, inspecting the bread more closely.

"A *croissant*," Harry answered, very matter-of-factly. He examined the flaky, artfully rolled exterior and shrugged, unfazed.

"Yes, I think I recognize it from the spread at the Palm Court," I said. "That's awfully fancy feed for a flock of ducks. Are you certain it won't be too rich for them?"

Harry laughed in return. "Hmm," he said, and looked through the bag. "It appears it's all pastries," he concluded. I peeked inside and glimpsed a wide variety of gourmet creations.

"Whatever happened to a few stale bits of old bread?" I teased.

Harry shook his head. "Miss Weber probably hasn't served a plain loaf of bread in all her life, I'm afraid."

"Ha! Just imagine!"

"Imagine what?" Harry asked.

For a fleeting moment, I was confused. I didn't immediately realize I'd uttered this aloud. "Well . . ." I began cautiously. "I suppose what I mean to say is that there are people who would find this bread quite a luxury . . . and here we are, tossing it away to quacking ducks."

I glanced at him, suddenly nervous. Part of me desperately wanted to explain *why* I found the pastries so luxurious—that, back in the orphanage, there had been girls who would have shaved off all their hair, walked on cut glass, or yanked out a tooth just to eat such a prized morsel.

But the wiser part of me shied away from this. Telling Harry about my past represented a dangerous game; he could only ever know so much. What would he think about my time in the orphanage? What would he make of the years I'd spent in the boardinghouse, working for

Mr. Tackett—pouring whiskey and cranking up the player piano while drunken, amorous men thud-thud-thudded against the walls?

Remembering such sounds, I cringed. Surely Harry would be disgusted. I couldn't bear the thought of how he might see me, knowing where I'd once lived.

And yet, I still felt driven to tell him *something* about my past. I pinched my arm for a dash of courage.

"Harry . . . at tea I brought up the differences between us . . ."

"Differences?"

"I mean that we are not equal in station. You are kind to act as though this is of little consequence, but I fear you might feel differently if you knew more about my life, my upbringing."

Harry held me steady in his blue stare, then shook his head.

"Violet . . . there is more than one way to know a person. I would enjoy your company and ask you no questions . . . if only . . . if only you can promise me you would do the same." He paused and looked more deeply into my eyes. "Can you do the same in return, Violet?"

I looked at him in surprise. I thought of the questions I hadn't asked him, and wondered if I might be content never to. Harry seemed to read my distress and let out a warm, friendly chuckle. Somehow, it eased me.

"Just wait until you figure out that it is *I* who am not worthy of *you*, Violet," he said. "If it's all right with you, let us only go forward. I mean it: forward, starting here in the present, and into the future."

What a curious windfall! I looked at him, and felt my eyes shining with unexpected contentment. When he held out his hand, I offered him my own—and realized, in that moment, that my hands had not felt so cool and clean in a very long time.

"You know something, I thought I would be sad today, being here in the park," I admitted, surprised at how easily my new memories with Harry had made me forget that day I'd waited for two friends who never came.

"Oh?" Harry asked, concerned.

I laughed, touched that he should care. "Yes. After the earthquake, so many of us wound up in this park."

"I had not thought of that," Harry said, mortified. "I'm sorry."

"Don't be sorry!" I protested. "You caused nothing. And in a way . . . perhaps that event has made me who I am."

Harry gave me a solemn, meaningful look. "Yes. Perhaps it has made all of us who we are," he said, his voice suddenly cryptic. "And still, I don't like to think of it." To my surprise, he shuddered lightly.

"Are you all right?" I asked.

Harry looked at me, seemingly surprised that I had noticed.

"Yes," he said. He paused again, then cleared his throat. "Tell me, Violet, what is the one thing you crave most in life? Besides an endless library, that is."

He smiled, and waited.

"Besides an endless library?" I laughed, but I saw that he was quite serious. I pondered the question for a moment or two. "I'm not sure . . ." I began to say, but then halted. "No. I *am* sure; I've just never said it aloud. Truthfully, my dream has always been a dream of *family*." No sooner had I uttered the words than I felt the weight of their truth. This basic comprehension staggered me. "I *do* love books—you're quite right—but I love them for their unflagging companionship. I suppose I dream of having a favorite person as I do a favorite book. Or make that a few favorite persons—*plural*, as families so often are."

I blushed, realizing I had just indirectly brought up the subject of children, but Harry only gazed at me, an awed expression on his face.

"Have I said something wrong?"

"Quite the opposite."

We stood staring at each other for another moment until he turned to the waterbirds again before changing the subject.

"Have you worked up an appetite yet?" he inquired.

"Indeed."

He led me back to where our picnic was still spread upon the grass.

"Oh, dear," I let slip, as soon as I took another look at the contents of our plates. It was the duck salad that had caught my eye. "But . . . we just fed these poor creatures! And now . . . to think of them on our plates!"

Harry squinted at his own portion, as if putting two and two together. Like me, he appeared dismayed.

"I suppose it *is* a bit barbarous, isn't it?" Harry mused, pushing the duck salad around with his fork. "An oversight on my part, I suppose."

We laughed again, but it was an uneasy laughter. It was safe to say both our appetites had vanished. I glanced over to where Miss Weber sat, and I swore I saw the strangest little smile playing about her lips. Was it possible? Had she done it on purpose?

18

few days later, I finished my work-day and stepped outside to walk
home. The city had begun to sink into an early, mellow twilight,
hastened on by a thick bank of fog. It was well past six, and the foghorns
sighed in syncopation, three different notes of deep bass. I could smell
the salt in the air, mixed with the tang of exotic foods—San Francisco's
regular perfume. The gas-lamps along Market Street were lit. I was
strolling along, tired from a long day, when a familiar face caught my
attention. She appeared to see me as well, for her pale blue eyes widened
and she marched directly up to me, peering into my face with her keen,
birdlike features.

"Flossie?" I stammered.

"Violet!" she exclaimed.

As we drew up to each other under the lamplight, a familiar halo
shone upon her pale, straw-colored hair. My heart seized and leapt. I

couldn't believe it. Hearing her utter my name, a small dam of emotion broke within me. I fought back tears as she beamed and threw her wiry arms about my neck.

"Violet!" she continued to exclaim. "Oh, how happy I am to see you!"

"Flossie . . . where have you been?"

I could barely choke the words out. Perhaps she worried that the hug itself was to blame for my breathless state, for her embrace eased immediately.

"Are you all right, Violet?"

"How long have you been back in San Francisco?"

"Oh . . ." She hesitated. Her eyes darted towards the street, where nattering automobiles navigated around clop-clopping horses. "For quite a while."

She trailed off and smiled mutely. I wasn't sure what to make of this. Perhaps she was still nervous to discuss our past in public. But her next remark surprised me all the more.

"Well . . . the truth of it is, Violet, Cora and I never left."

"What do you mean?" I asked. I felt a headache coming on and pressed my fingers to my temples. "If you and Cora never left town . . . why didn't either of you show up that day? I waited. I waited the next day, too, just in case."

Flossie squirmed. She bit her lip and made a few false starts at explanation. Finally, she gave a great sigh.

"You may as well know, Violet."

"Know what?"

"Cora was against it. I think she was still worried about that note you found."

"The note?"

"Yes. After you left, we never received another message. So Cora thought, perhaps, it had something to do with you . . . and only you." Flossie paused.

My head reeled. A bitter taste formed in my mouth and a pit opened up in my stomach.

"Do you mean to say that the two of you never lost touch?" I asked.

"We planned to split up," Flossie insisted, "but Cora convinced me that it wasn't necessary." She looked at me haltingly. "I'm sorry, Violet."

I suddenly felt sick with betrayal.

"But now fate itself has reunited us!" Flossie quickly added, smiling again. "And I am overjoyed to see you, Violet—truly I am!"

I didn't know what to reply, but a nearby clock tower saved me the trouble by chiming seven o'clock.

"Oh!" Flossie exclaimed. "It's already seven—I'm late!"

I looked at her, still stung, but at the same time, utterly panicked to imagine Flossie leaving. Would I ever see her again? But to my relief she continued.

"I'm actually meant to be seeing Cora right now. Come with me!" she urged. "She'll be so surprised to see you!"

"It doesn't sound as if she would welcome it," I said.

"No, no, no," Flossie lamented. "You oughtn't feel she doesn't care for you—she does! Please, come with me, and we can all three of us be reconciled. Enough time has surely passed. We'd been hoping we would find you soon!"

I dithered, but already I felt my resistance was feigned.

"Where are you meeting her?"

"At her hotel apartment—you ought to see it; it's quite posh! She's having some dresses made, and she invited me to keep her company so she doesn't get bored. You remember how Cora is . . . She likes to make a party out of everything!"

"A dressmaker?" I repeated. "Calling at such a late hour?"

Flossie gave me a sympathetic smile and shrugged.

"Yes. It didn't take Cora long to figure out that dressmakers will come at any hour—*if* you've got the money to make it worth their while."

She paused again and read the look of surprise on my face as I began to comprehend the staggering ease with which Cora had set about spending Tackett's fortune.

"Come on," Flossie urged. "Cora has always been *Cora*; you know this. But let's go see her together now. Let's have a proper reunion, Violet. It's fate! Please?"

19

During our walk to Cora's hotel, Flossie delineated Cora's new life for me. Somehow, Cora had managed to install herself as a novel fixture on the society scene, claiming to be an heiress from some small town in Nevada no one had ever heard of. She'd made up a yarn about a spinster aunt who'd died, leaving her several silver mines.

"Mind you, I'm not convinced anyone believes Cora's story so much as they are content to let sleeping dogs lie," Flossie confided. "Most folks—male *and* female—are simply tickled to be in her company. She still has that effect."

I asked Flossie what Cora did to keep busy, and she told me that Cora spent the majority of her time running an informal salon for artists and dancers, and enjoyed the courtship of several *nouveau riche* bachelors who competed for her attention with deep pockets and thrilling gusto. So far, she had committed herself to no one; all were welcome in Cora's life, so long as they never bored her. When she needed to appear respectable, Cora employed a hefty, dour-looking woman named Mrs. Barnes to pretend to be her chaperone. Mrs. Barnes was only for appearances' sake, of course, and did very little to rein in Cora's behavior. Mostly she sat in corners like a potted plant and sipped brandy.

"Cora's worked out how to keep amused and still pass herself off as respectable when she needs to," Flossie said.

"Cora always *was* good at getting whatever she wanted," I replied.

Flossie laughed her agreement, and continued to lead the way to the top of Nob Hill. She drew up short outside an enormous hotel with a beautiful white stone façade.

"Cora lives *here*?" I stammered, shocked.

Flossie shrugged.

"She has one of the hotel's finest suites, in fact. Exactly what you'd expect of Cora."

I followed Flossie into the cavernous lobby; it echoed like a cathedral, the clusters of Persian rugs and silk sofas like little plush islands adrift on a marble sea. Flossie nodded at a clerk at the front desk and made her way to the elevator, where a young bellhop awaited, hand poised on the brass levers. The gilded cage closed and we went up, up, up—to what seemed like the top floor. Flossie thanked the boy as we stepped off and proceeded along a wide hallway punctuated with paintings and mirrors in ornate gold frames.

I watched Flossie with awe, surprised to see her at ease in our opulent surroundings. Cora had always taken luxury in stride—it was no surprise she had elected to live here—but Flossie and I were cut from the same cloth. Yet, now she appeared unruffled; she must have paid Cora many visits during the past year.

Cora let out a shriek as she threw open the door.

"Violet! Heavens to Betsy! What are you doing here?"

"I bumped into her on Market Street!" Flossie explained. "Isn't it a surprise?"

"I'll say!" Cora agreed. "Oh . . . but let's not just stand gaping at each other!"

She threw her arms about me and I inhaled a light cloud of perfume. Her grip was surprisingly tight. After a moment, she released me.

"Well, come on! Both of you!" She waved us in and shut the door. "I thought I might never set eyes on you again, Violet!"

"Flossie mentioned as much," I said. "She told me about what's happened since we parted."

Cora frowned. There was an unavoidable bitterness in my voice. I couldn't help it; I was still wounded.

"Why didn't you show up in the park?" I demanded. "I waited. I waited a second day, too."

Cora blinked rapidly. "You mean . . . the bridge at Stow Lake?"

"Yes," I said.

She darted a look at Flossie. "It was . . . well, impossible, Violet."

I waited, but she did not offer further explanation.

"Never mind that business now," Flossie said, in an attempt to restore an amicable mood. "Cora! You ought to show Violet your lovely apartment!"

Cora obliged and took me from room to room, bustling around her palatial apartment with pride. Her silk dressing gown was trimmed with ermine, and her scarlet curls glowed like hot embers under the warm yellow light of electric chandeliers. Her luxurious suite was utterly dazzling, sporting red velvet rugs, curtains, and curvaceous sofas with plump, inviting cushions. There were four rooms, each with an impressive chandelier, and two with fireplaces, their mantels carved of exotic, emerald-colored marble.

As the tour concluded, Cora paused. Her face lit up.

"I know! I'll call down and have them send a boy for a bottle of champagne and some ice from the icehouse!"

I was staggered by the modern luxury to think that one might have a personal telephone in her very own room! But Cora looked quite breezy and indifferent as she lifted the earpiece. She spoke into the mouthpiece, relaying her requests.

"There!" she said, sighing with happiness as she set the earpiece back upon its hook. "Now we shall celebrate in style! Wait—have you ever had champagne before, Violet?"

I thought the answer would be obvious, but I shook my head anyway. Cora clapped in delight. Just then, a knock sounded at the door.

"Hmm, well, that would be awfully fast, indeed," Cora remarked.

At Cora's command an elderly dressmaker entered the room.

"Mrs. Larson!" Cora greeted her guest. "In all the excitement, I nearly forgot!"

The newcomer toddled into the room and regarded the three of us through her spectacles. She had a haughty air about her, and clearly thought we could not possibly be up to any good. But she grimaced and began to unpack her sewing kit, intent on doing her job.

I watched while she set up shop, curious. It was a strange thing, having dresses made in your own home: you paid a woman to boss you about, ordering you to stand uncomfortably as she stuck you with pins like a pin-cushion. The rich have funny ideas about what constitutes luxury. Cora continued to chat with Flossie and me as the dressmaker compelled Cora to stand on an ottoman so she might be measured. While this was transpiring, another knock sounded and the champagne and the ice were delivered in turn.

"Oh, there it is!" Cora exclaimed.

The boy who delivered it kindly dislodged the cork; it let off a pop like the report of a gun.

"Violet, dear—would you pour everyone a glass?"

I found myself vaguely annoyed; it was as if Cora was under the impression that I was still the designated maid. But I bit my tongue and set about distributing the cut-crystal coupes. I even offered one to Mrs. Larson, but she declined, twitching her head no, an army of pins gripped tight in the vise of her lips.

"Well? Go on, then, Violet!" Cora goaded, watching me sniff cautiously at the glass.

As I lifted the coupe to my lips, the champagne tickled my nose with a fine spray. I took a sip; the taste was crisp and lemony and metallic—pleasant enough, but I sputtered at the first swallow, making Cora laugh.

"Why, she's still our dear, sweet, naïve Violet, isn't she?" Cora said to Flossie. "I'm so glad nothing's changed!"

"I don't know about that," Flossie said. "I hardly recognized her on the street! And did you know, Violet has secured a position at the millinery counter at the Emporium!"

"Violet!" Cora exclaimed. "You're a shop-girl now? Oh, we've all done just like we said! Flossie, too, with her dreadfully boring typing courses."

Cora paused, and looked me over anew.

"I still can't quite picture you as a shop-girl," she decreed.

"I think it suits me."

"If you say so, Violet. But I still say you're not the modern-gal type."

It did not sound like a compliment. I told myself I was just being sensitive and pushed the prickly feeling aside. Cora looked at me in the mirror. She cocked her head as though she had just remembered something.

"You know, Violet," she said. "I thought I spied you the other day. At the time, I thought it couldn't be you . . . because the girl I saw was leaving the Palm Court at the Palace Hotel. And the gentleman she was with . . . well, I recognized who *he* was, but it didn't make sense! I was sure it couldn't be you. But . . . was it?"

I glanced at her.

"I . . . was invited to take tea with . . . someone . . ." I said timidly.

"Someone?" Flossie prodded. She, too, peered at me with curiosity.

"Well, yes . . . a gentleman named Harry Carlyle," I answered.

"*Harry Carlyle!* Oh, my word, it *was* you, Violet!" Cora gasped.

The name appeared to strike a chord, and it was plain that—if nothing else—she knew he was a wealthy, important man-about-town. She stared at me for several minutes, and as she did so, her expression darkened, as though she was deciding whether or not to say more. Abruptly, she turned to Mrs. Larson.

"Thank you, Mrs. Larson," Cora said. "I've grown quite tired, I'm afraid. I trust you have everything you need for the dresses?"

We all held our tongues carefully as Cora finished her business and saw the old woman to the door. Once Mrs. Larson had left, Cora whirled about and demanded that I explain how I'd come to have tea with Harry Carlyle.

"How enchanting," Flossie declared, once I'd told the story.

But Cora bit her lip. She still wore a funny expression; it was as if she were having a silent argument with herself.

"You'll be careful—won't you, Violet? Not to get too caught up by his dashing looks and fancy name?"

"I doubt he thinks of me . . . like that," I said, blushing.

"It sounds as though he spends an awful lot of time on you," Flossie pointed out.

"But he's always very upright and proper," I quickly replied. "I'm certain it's merely his sense of charity driving him, nothing more."

"Good," Cora replied, her voice firm.

I was stung. What business was it of hers? And what if Harry *did* take an interest in me that went beyond pity? Why did Cora find it so objectionable?

I thought again of the things Flossie had confided in me. That Cora had talked her out of reuniting in Golden Gate Park. I looked again at Cora's beautiful face, admiring those lovely features as I had done countless times in the past . . . but now I also wondered if they didn't also conceal something a bit uglier, too.

"Let's not forget!" Flossie declared, interrupting my thoughts. "Our reunion! The three of us found our way back to one another. We have cause to celebrate!"

"Yes," I agreed, with one last unsure glance at Cora.

For her part, Cora appeared oblivious to my leery looks. She lifted her coupe of champagne in the air and clinked it against mine with a charming grin.

20

〜||||〜

As San Francisco slowly slid into its "summer" days of September and then October, Harry and I continued our polite strolls, until one day he surprised me with a very novel invitation. His formal request included another gift—in this case, a pair of kid leather gloves and tinted goggles. The goggles in particular left me frowning in puzzlement until I read the card. He owned an automobile, his card explained, and he wished to participate in the big motor parade that the city was hosting in honor of the Portola Festival. I'd heard of the Portola Festival, of course: it was all the talk, a five-day celebration that city politicians had organized to prove to the world that San Francisco had indeed fully recovered from the Great Quake and was ready to dazzle tourists again. There were to be exhibits and food, cultural attractions from the Japanese and Chinese communities, and, most prestigious of all: a motor parade.

I read the invitation twice over. *An automobile!* I had seen plenty puttering about the streets in recent years, but I had never imagined actually knowing someone who owned one, much less going for a ride myself. In his letter Harry explained that the automobile he owned was a Maxwell Runabout model with an open car, a perfect specimen for the parade—however, there were only two seats.

Two seats. *There would be no room for a chaperone.* Thus far, Harry and I had not been left alone together since that initial tea we had taken together as "cousins." During all of our subsequent outings, Miss Weber hovered some short distance away.

My pulse quickened involuntarily to picture being alone with Harry in the car.

On the day of the parade, Harry was to fetch me directly from my apartment house for the very first time. I was nervous, wondering how shabby my women's hotel might look to him. I doubted he would come inside, but even the exterior troubled me.

I was dressed and ready when Harry arrived, though my hands were trembling. I saw him through the window and hurried out. Once on the pavement, we traded shy smiles as he took my hand, folding it into the crook of his elbow.

I felt Mrs. Campbell spying from her window. She'd grown insatiably nosy about my suitor, and now here he was—in an automobile, no less! Some of the other young women were likely peeping out the windows, too; I felt more than one pair of eyes on us as Harry led me to the car.

"Here we are," he said. The sun broke through the morning fog and shone brilliantly down upon the contraption's fresh paint, polished brass, and leather seats. He had left the engine running, and the car shook steadily like a teakettle that had just reached a happy boil. It's an understatement to say I was impressed.

"Up you go!" Harry's cheer matched the weather. With his help, I climbed up onto the polished leather seat, carefully tucking my dress around me. The engine rumbled and I felt my heart speed up as if to keep time. Once we were properly settled in and I had struggled into the goggles—so much for my carefully pinned-up hair—Harry released a lever and the automobile sprang forward. With a lurch, we were off!

It was curious to look straight ahead and not see a horse pulling us. *What an amazing contraption*, I marveled. I must admit, however, the automobile *did* have a little trouble on some of the city's steeper hills.

"There is no city like ours," Harry said almost apologetically as the vehicle struggled. "Engines aren't put to the test elsewhere as they are here!"

Harry steered us along the streets until we met up with a group of motorists gathered near the ferry building. We joined the rattling, vibrating herd, watching as countless automobiles fell in and out of formation, drivers and passengers alike hooting and hollering.

When it came time for the parade to begin, a gun was fired—as at a race—and the whole set sputtered off along Market Street, one giant mass of jittering technology. We bumped and lurched and braked and—ultimately—made our uncertain way along the wide thoroughfare. It was exhilarating, and at the same time, it was a wonder we didn't all collide. I heard my own voice bubbling out of my throat, erupting in a kind of childish laughter.

Harry smiled, pleased by my enthusiasm, furiously working the gears all the while, speeding up and slowing down, tamping his foot on the brake and trying not to bump any of the other drivers. It seemed an awful lot of work, driving. Crowds thronged the sides of the streets, cheering us on, their cries drowned out by the hum of so many engines. Children sat perched upon their fathers' shoulders, waving the red-and-gold flag of the Portola Festival. Pretty girls blew us kisses. A handful of spendthrift spectators sprayed us with champagne. I found myself waving automatically to all of them, as though I were a queen in a royal procession. It was a mad spectacle, a powerful denial of all the devastation the Great Quake had wrought.

We motored along for the better part of a half hour, but before we reached the end, Harry's Runabout began to sputter and cough.

"Is everything all right?" I asked as the car jerked.

To my great surprise, he blushed.

"To be honest . . . I haven't the faintest . . ." he said. "My servant, Davies, is in charge of all the maintenance, and I'm afraid he's still learning."

I laughed in a good-natured way, but just as I did, the Runabout heaved one last lurch and died. Harry steered us to the curb with the last of the momentum.

"Violet—I'm so sorry! Please accept my apologies."

By now his face was beet red. It was a startling sight on a man as distinguished as Harry Carlyle, and my heart went out to him.

"Don't give it another thought, Harry!" I exclaimed, trying but failing to repress a few more soft chuckles. "I don't know any better than you what makes this magical contraption go, but even if we never finish this parade, the day has been just that—magical."

Harry smiled softly, then climbed out and tried to crank the car. The engine simply refused to restart, no matter how many times he turned it over. The parade rolled on, a trail of spectators following behind. As the crowd slowly began to clear, I saw that we had broken down in front of a livery. A young man stood out front, watching the final remnants of the parade putter along the street.

With a jolt, I realized I was looking at Jasper—Tackett's former errand boy.

He grinned and waved when he spotted me, but then frowned as he took in my situation. Jasper moved as though to approach us, and my heart began thumping nervously.

"Miss Violet!" he called. "Why, what are you doin' here? I haven't seen ya in . . . well, I don't *know* how long—I guess since the Big One hit!"

"Hello, Jasper. It's good to see you."

Jasper stopped to stand on the curb, and I said a silent prayer that he would not mention Tackett's boardinghouse.

"I take it you're in the parade?"

"Well, we *were* in the parade," Harry replied. "I'm afraid we've hit a snag."

Harry stood from where he'd been crouching in front of the car. I held my breath as the two men took each other in: Jasper young and eager and handsome but born to the gutter; Harry tall and very debonair in his suit but old enough to be Jasper's father. I climbed out of the Runabout and stood awkwardly between them.

"Harry—this is Jasper," I said. I had a rote impulse to explain more about how we knew each other, but I fought against it. No good could come of that. "And, Jasper . . . this is Mr. Harry Carlyle."

Harry politely offered his hand, and Jasper took it. There was a palpable tension in the air.

"Do ya need a hand?" Jasper inquired.

"Do you know how to fix an engine?" Harry asked.

Jasper laughed and shook his head.

"No, but I work at the livery there." He pointed at the stable behind him. "Just started last month," he added with a proud grin, for my benefit. "We can push 'er in there and offer you a cab home, and you can send your man to see about fixin' the car when it suits."

Harry frowned, thinking this over. He glanced at me with an apologetic expression.

"All right," he said. "Thank you—yes. And I insist on paying for the livery cab."

"That's real good," Jasper replied, laughing. "Because your driver will insist on collecting his fare."

Harry laughed, too, but I thought perhaps it sounded a bit stilted.

I stood aside as Jasper and Harry rolled up their sleeves, pushed the automobile into the stable, and set the brake. It was dim within, like a cave: clean, but thick with the scent of hay and freshly mucked manure. Jasper went to see about securing us a cab and came running back less than a minute later.

"Bishop'll take ya," he informed us. "Lucky, too—he's got the nicest covered carriage in all the livery."

A carriage drawn by a team of horses pulled around, and Jasper paused for a few fleeting seconds before opening the door. Once he did, he gave a little bow.

"You sure look well, Miss Violet," he said. "I still can't believe I'm seein' ya! Thought I might never set eyes on ya again."

I was acutely aware of Harry watching Jasper watch me.

"You, too, Jasper—thank you for your assistance," I replied, and allowed him to help me up.

"Yes, thank you, Jasper. I am much obliged to you," Harry said politely.

He climbed in, Jasper closed the door, and the driver whipped the horses.

Harry and I were alone. It was pleasant inside, with pale blue button-back leather seats and curtained windows—although I was certain that Harry was accustomed to even finer.

We rode for several minutes in silence. Harry did not meet my eye; he only stared out the window with what I took to be an air of disappointment.

His silence felt different somehow—ominous, even. I slowly became sure that, in meeting Jasper, Harry had seen the truth of my lowly station. I was convinced: he was now repulsed by me. When I could no longer take the silence, I cleared my throat to speak—but to my surprise, Harry beat me to it.

"I believe I am keeping you from your rightful friends, Violet," he said.

"What?" I demanded, alarmed. "'Rightful'?"

"I only mean that the lad is very handsome, and far closer to your own age than I am. I'm keeping you from having the full, rich life you deserve."

"Is that what you think?" I said, with a mixture of amusement and outrage.

Harry shrugged. "It is the most logical conclusion. I'm an old man, Violet." He paused and shook his head. "I've been foolish to think our love can be anything besides a very hopeful, well-intended illusion."

Harry had just used the word *love*. I remained perfectly still as these words passed over me, but it took all of my concentration; each word was like a tiny bomb. *Our love . . . very hopeful . . . illusion.* Of course, if I am being perfectly honest, I had harbored my own hopeful illusions. But I had never dared name them—not even in my head.

"Harry," I said, suddenly very sure of myself. "You're being ridiculous."

"I know it," he replied.

But I laughed and shook my head. "Not about that. About Jasper. I don't love Jasper—he's nice, of course . . . an old friend . . . but I don't love him; I never could. I love *you*, Harry. I've wanted you all my life! Only—I didn't know it until the day we met. And then, I never dreamed I would be worthy of you."

"Worthy? Of me?" Harry echoed, as if startled and dazed.

"Yes."

"Violet . . . *I* am the one who is not worthy of *you*."

As he said this, I felt him inclining towards me, until his breath was warm upon my face. I had never been so close to a man. I felt my heart speed up, pounding more and more heavily, unnerving me. Was I about to have a kiss, or an attack of the heart?

As our lips almost touched, I could feel the heat radiating between our mouths.

But then he pulled away.

I felt the cold air rush back in, a chilly tide between us.

"Harry . . ." I said. "Why did you stop?"

"I don't want to take undue advantage of you."

"You *aren't*," I insisted.

He said nothing, only looked out the window again. I hardly knew what to do. The joy I had felt only seconds before now turned to the worst kind of black despair. I was utterly confused. I felt my cheeks with my hands and found tears there; I'd begun softly crying. Harry noticed and turned back to me. To my surprise, he pulled me into his arms, tucking his forehead against mine.

"Violet—I mean it when I say I am not worthy of you," he repeated. "But I cannot bear to see you sad. Please . . . there is nothing I would like more than to kiss you. It is not for lack of loving you."

"Then, why?" I demanded.

He lifted his head from our embrace, and I took the opportunity to peer up at him, straight into his eyes. There was something cool but thoughtful there; I could faintly discern that he wanted to tell me something.

But in the next second, the warmth returned to his eyes and his face moved so close to mine, it blurred into a lovely shapeless form. I felt his lips on my own. It was an intimate kiss, conveying a million meanings, filled to the brim with contradiction: passionate and urgent, yet careful, kind, and gentle.

When he drew away again, he sighed, a soft smile playing at the corners of his mouth.

A glance out the window told me we were nearing my building. The driver pulled the cab over and the carriage shook as he climbed down to open the door.

Harry got out and took my hand to help me down. "Violet," he said, "I'd like to ask you to take a stroll with me—say, a week from today, on your next Sunday off, in Alamo Square? I would ask Miss Weber to chaperone, but . . . I think there are some matters we need to discuss . . . privately. I want you to feel free to say whatever you need. I promise you'll be in plain sight all the while, but we can have a discussion unto ourselves. Will you meet me?"

"Of course," I quickly agreed.

He named a time. Then he walked me the short distance to the front door of my women's hotel.

He bowed very stiffly, taking care not to touch me or show that we had shared any intimacy. This was for my reputation, I knew.

"I look forward to our next meeting," Harry said.

"As do I."

He turned and strode back towards the carriage. I watched the livery cab drive away with a strange, dizzy sensation. My lips still tingled with the memory of Harry's kiss. How long, I wondered, could I make this feeling last?

Already, I wanted more.

21

I was so excited to see Harry again that time stretched infinite, the seconds moving at a maddeningly sluggish pace. During the days I was occupied at the Emporium, but in the evenings I had little to anchor me.

Since our reunion, I'd visited Cora and Flossie a handful of times. I'd taken tea with Flossie at her apartment—a beautiful, well-furnished residence that was quite nice but, of course, not so splendid as Cora's. Flossie had recently taken up mah jong, and she tried to teach me, but it turned out I was hopeless at it.

"Best for you to stay away from the gambling rooms in Chinatown, Violet," Flossie teased as she gathered up the beautiful painted ivory tiles and put them away.

"Ha," I laughed. "You don't go there yourself, do you?" I asked.

"I've been once or twice," Flossie replied.

"What? That's no place for a lady!" I felt genuinely shocked.

"No. But it can be fun—if you *win*, of course."

She looked at me from under her lashes and gave a sly smile. I shook my head, still laughing. It was difficult to picture straitlaced Flossie, with her lank blonde hair and small, puritanical features, sitting at a gambling table.

The week dragged on. I was grateful when Friday rolled around, for Flossie and I had plans to visit Cora again at her lavish hotel apartment.

Once the Emporium doors were closed for the night and I'd tidied up my millinery counter, I hurried over to Cora's hotel. I found the two of them sitting on a blanket spread out on the beautiful Persian rug, eating cold chicken as though on a picnic.

"Violet! Come join us," Cora called.

"I hope you have an appetite," Flossie added.

"Yes," Cora agreed. "She could certainly do with some fattening up, couldn't she, Flossie? Hardly any meat at all on those bones!"

Yet again, I was stung, and couldn't tell if Cora's jibes were meant to be so mean. Flossie read my expression.

"Well, I'm not one to talk," Flossie said, trying to redirect Cora's critical eye.

"I suppose you could do with some fattening up, too," Cora agreed.

Flossie waved me over and I pushed aside my grievance to join them on the rug. It was a queer sort of picnic. The chicken was greasy and delicious; the plates were bone china with real gold edging. A bottle of champagne rested next to us on the floor, in a silver bucket filled with ice. I watched the beads of condensation slowly roll down the sides of the bucket and drip onto the ornate rug, marveling at how Cora could treat such nice things as though they were of no more consequence than a flour sack.

We ate, and I listened as Flossie asked Cora about her many beaux—who, evidently, had contributed to much of the opulence I now saw around me.

"They love to spoil me," Cora reported. "And who am I to deny them that pleasure?"

Flossie turned to me. "But we're forgetting! Violet has snared the attentions of San Francisco's most famous bachelor of all." She gave me a wink.

Cora bristled slightly.

"Yes, but you said yourself, Violet—you haven't any romantic sentiments between you . . . Isn't that right?"

I'd been keeping my kiss with Harry a secret, but at the same time, ever since it happened, I'd been bursting to share the news with them. I took a breath and cast my eyes down at the rug sheepishly.

"As a matter of fact . . ." I began, trying to steady my quivering voice, "I think I might be in love with Harry. And, even more miraculous, I think he might be in love with me, too."

Flossie looked surprised, but smiled kindly. Cora, on the other hand, recoiled and frowned as though disturbed.

"And . . . what makes you think he might requite your love, Violet?" she asked. Her tone was not friendly, and I stiffened.

"We shared a kiss," I said defiantly.

Cora fell quiet for a moment, her brow furrowed. Finally, she cleared her throat.

"Violet . . . I don't know how wise it is, getting entangled with Harry Carlyle."

By now, my whole body was tensed. I doubted Cora would restrain herself in the slightest degree if *she* had the chance to charm someone like Harry Carlyle.

"You think I'm a poor match for Harry," I blurted bluntly. The champagne had begun to fill my head with a soft, dizzy buzzing, and I recklessly continued. "Perhaps you think he better belongs among your suite of admirers."

"No!" Cora protested, looking genuinely shocked. "It's not that, Violet! Please don't misunderstand. It's more a question of . . . well, you know I've always kept an ear out for the latest gossip, and . . . there's quite a bit of gossip about Mr. Harry Carlyle. There are . . . *rumors*."

"Are rumors really to be trusted?" I challenged, uneasy.

Cora exchanged a look with Flossie. "You ought to know what's been said."

"All right. Go on," I finally answered.

"It has to do with his wife."

I felt myself pale. "His *what*?"

"Violet . . . you ought to know . . . Harry Carlyle was *married*," Cora said.

I was taken aback, somewhat crestfallen in spite of myself. I was stunned to realize I had never contemplated Harry's marital status, previous or otherwise. As he had not mentioned a wife, I had unthinkingly assumed none had ever existed. Perhaps, I had unconsciously avoided asking. But it bothered me to realize I had ignored the possibility that Harry had lived—and *loved*—long before I'd bumped into him.

Now, as Cora described what she knew of Harry's wife—a celebrated beauty, famed for her perfect breeding and elegant taste, and an accomplished pianist with the voice of an angel, to top all—I found myself squirming. Having been married to such a lady, how could Harry possibly feel anything for me? Cora continued, despite my pallor.

"But you say he's not married *presently*, correct?" I interrupted, before I could help myself.

"No," Cora agreed, shaking her head. "But, Violet . . . *that's* the scandal."

"What do you mean?"

"Harry's first wife *died*."

I did not register this revelation with the same intensity. Where was the big fuss in his being a widower? This was a relief; a divorce would be far more scandalous.

But Cora could see I did not comprehend her meaning, not wholly.

"His wife *died*, Violet," Cora said, her voice very careful and deliberate. "In a very mysterious manner, during the earthquake."

I looked at her for a long moment.

"Plenty of people were injured during that awful earthquake, Cora. Many of them fatally," I reminded her.

"Yes. And you know as well as I do, it wasn't as simple as that—for *some*." Her voice was heavy with meaning.

I said nothing. How on earth could she compare Tackett's death to that of Harry's wife?

"There was quite a lot of gossip after the earthquake, Violet," Cora went on. "They say the wife had been cuckolding him, and everyone in San Francisco's high society knew he'd been possessive, wild with jealousy—she was *so* very beautiful, I'm told. There were rumors that she'd been talking about leaving him . . . And then, well, the earthquake happened, and somehow Harry and all the house servants made it out of his mansion with nary a scratch, while not a soul ever saw *her* alive again."

Cora's voice dropped to a softer, more confiding octave.

"Evidently he has a temper not to be trifled with."

I sat very still, absorbing her words, the glass of champagne fizzing in my hand. I felt as though she had bashed me over the head with a club. But after a few moments, I shook myself back to life.

"No," I said finally. "It's simply not Harry. It's impossible."

Cora looked me up and down carefully. She turned to Flossie.

"Flossie? Don't you think you ought to talk some sense into her?"

Flossie had been silent up to this point, watching the two of us with trepidation.

"You've given Violet so much to think about; I'm sure she'll take it into consideration. I don't like to see her upset . . ." Flossie said, biting her lip.

Cora huffed and turned back to me.

"Of course, you aren't to be *blamed*, Violet," she said. "It's only natural to want some company . . . and a man like Harry Carlyle! Why, I can only imagine meeting him left a big impression."

I had had enough. I stood up and smoothed my skirt. The champagne raced to my forehead, just behind my eyes, and I steadied myself.

"Where are you going?" Cora demanded. "Don't be cross with me, Violet—I'm only trying to look out for you!"

I did not wait to hear the rest. Instead, I quickly crossed the room, strode through the foyer, and let myself out the front door. Cora called after me but I was too angry to listen.

It wasn't until I was on the street that I heard footsteps running up behind me. I whirled about, thinking Cora had come to apologize, but I found myself staring into Flossie's eyes instead.

"Violet, please don't be angry!" she begged. "Cora means well. I think she might be feeling a little jealous."

I didn't say anything.

"You can't realize how you've grown into a fine young woman, Violet."

"Flossie," I said, "*why* did you let Cora talk you out of reuniting with me in Golden Gate Park that day?"

Flossie paused, chewing the inside of her cheek.

"It came down to the blackmail note," she replied finally.

"You mean she convinced you that I was the main target, and that you two would be better off steering clear?"

"Well, yes and no. Cora pointed something out . . . something I hadn't noticed at first."

I blinked, utterly confused.

"What?"

"It was about the penmanship," Flossie said. "It . . . well, it looked an awful lot like *your* handwriting, Violet. And, well . . . *you* found it, after all."

At this, I felt light-headed.

"Oh!" Flossie rushed to say. "I'm not accusing you of anything, Violet—*never!* But when Cora pointed that out, I suppose I naturally . . . *wondered*. I nursed you through so many episodes back at St. Hilda's. And then at the boardinghouse, you remember, you'd begun to have . . . spells again."

My heart sunk. A sharp pain shot through my head and I put my hands to my temples, wincing.

"I'm sorry, Violet," Flossie said. "I didn't mean to upset you."

"No," I replied. "I . . . I'm tired. I think I ought to go home."

Flossie looked at me.

"Honestly, Violet—ignore Cora. I'm sure it's merely jealousy. I, for one, am sublimely happy for you."

She threw her arms around my neck once again. When she released me, I smiled and bid her good night, turning to walk home along the vertiginous, foggy streets of San Francisco.

22

W ere Cora and Flossie right? *Had* the writing on the blackmail note looked like mine?

I pondered this as I walked home that night, trying to summon the memory of that note and the shape of the letters on the paper. I suppose it *had* resembled my own penmanship . . .

I shivered and recalled something Flossie had said while we were in the camp. She'd asked me if I was certain I'd found only Blanche's and Tackett's bodies and nothing more. The question startled and befuddled me, and I remember insisting to Flossie that of course there had been nothing more. But then Flossie went on to say something cryptic about how she "oughtn't listen to Cora anyway." It dawned on me now: Cora must have made insinuations about me. Insinuations that I'd done more than just discover the bodies.

I felt sick with betrayal: Cora was one of the two people I loved most in the world. But when the sensation of betrayal passed, it was supplanted by a strange new inkling of suspicion. I had to admit I could not be *entirely* certain I had nothing to do with the note. My mind flitted back to the torn book page I'd found under my pillow only days later when I was undoubtedly alone. And I could not deny the fact of my spells. But the funny thing about the bizarre behavior I got up to while having my spells was that often the results favored *Cora*.

I began to remember a long list: in the girls' home, for instance, Sister Edwina called Cora's red hair "the devil's work" and found reasons to cane Cora at every opportunity. One afternoon, Cora came charging out of Sister Edwina's study just as I was entering the room to clean it. Her green eyes flashed with angry tears, and I knew without having to ask that Sister Edwina had just performed one of her disciplinarian "holy humblings." I had never seen such a look of rage, but before I could voice my concern, Cora stormed off, and Sister Edwina called me into the room.

Then I was left alone to tidy her study.

The next thing I was aware of, Flossie was shaking me gently. I'd been asleep on my cot in the sleeping hall.

"Violet . . . Violet!" she admonished. "What did you do?"

I blinked, focusing my eyes on her face, then down to the floor beside my cot. Sister Edwina's beloved cane was laying there, broken in two pieces.

"I didn't," I murmured weakly in protest. "I *couldn't* have . . . I'm not strong enough."

But Flossie gestured, and as I looked closer, I saw two piles of books, stacked a short distance apart from each other. The answer came at me in a rush: I must have placed the cane on top of the stacks, and stepped with all my weight.

However, all these years later, I wondered: *Why* was Flossie so certain I had been the one to snap Sister Edwina's cane? Cora could have just as easily stolen the cane, and she had far more reason to destroy it. With my spells, it would be impossible to tell the difference between what I'd done . . . and *what it only looked like I'd done.*

As I retraced my steps from Cora's luxurious hotel to my own small room in the women's hotel, I ventured to think back to even darker, graver events.

It was no secret that Cora used to talk about wanting to burn the orphanage down. *I'd be doing everyone a favor, burning this wretched place to the ground,* she once joked. So it struck me as uncanny when exactly that happened.

Flossie and Cora had woken me in a panic the morning the fire broke out, and we'd quickly made up our minds to run away together. Afterwards, the papers said it was arson, and I passively wondered briefly if it wasn't out of the question that perhaps Cora had had something to do with it.

But, then . . . there was also a reason I had *ceased* to wonder about Cora.

It wasn't until we'd been on the street for a day that I reached into my pocket and found the charred remains of several burnt matches. I recoiled as if stung, shocked and frightened at the sight.

What is it? Flossie asked at the time, concerned by my sudden spasm.

Nothing, I'd insisted, dropping the remains of the matches and quickly rubbing the powdery black stains from my fingers. *Nothing.*

_____

Like the empty bottle I'd found in my pocket, I'd never told anyone about those charred matches.

Perhaps it wasn't so terrible of Cora to question my potential guilt, after all—perhaps Cora was not being spiteful, but cautious and concerned. Yet . . . I was absolutely *certain* that I'd had nothing to do with Blanche's and Tackett's deaths.

Wasn't I?

23

While Flossie's revelation about the note had me preoccupied . . . I
was surprised to discover that I was far more concerned with Cora's
gossip about Harry, and more specifically the fact that he had been
married before—and to a beautiful, elegant, worldly lady.

Madeleine Carlyle.

My interest went well beyond simple curiosity. I found myself
thinking about this mystery woman with every passing minute. Sitting
around the common room of my women's hotel, I couldn't help but fish
for details from the other girls. When I mentioned Madeleine Carlyle's
name, they practically lit up with delight.

Oh, of course! they all exclaimed with breathless excitement. *Why,
she was one of the greatest beauties San Francisco has ever seen! And remember the headlines!*

I pretended indifference as I listened, but my stomach churned
with every word. Some of the girls prattled on about the darker rumors

surrounding Madeleine—the same gossip Cora had repeated about Harry's jealous temper, and about how they were rumored to have had a terrible fight on the night of the earthquake—but I paid little mind to these ominous insinuations. I knew they couldn't be true. Harry was too patient, too kind—I could already see as much from the time we'd spent together.

No, I was far more caught up in the fact of Madeleine herself . . . the fact that she'd existed. The fact that Harry had loved her. By all accounts, she was a dazzling, impressive woman. I became convinced that *this* was the reason Harry had maintained such a restrained distance from me, that evening in the livery cab. I'd practically thrown myself at him, and told him I *loved* him—and poor Harry had been forced to be polite about it. The differences between Madeleine and myself must have been too stark for him to endure. The memory of our kiss reshaped itself in my mind: I'd foolishly pressed him for the kiss, he'd obliged me . . . and, in doing so, he'd realized that despite whatever mild affection he felt for me, I could never hold a candle to his late wife.

Now Harry's invitation to take an unchaperoned stroll "so we might discuss matters in private" took on a new light. Undoubtedly, Harry intended to finally tell me about Madeleine, as a way of explaining why he did not wish for our attraction to go any further.

I was so convinced this was the intention behind Harry's invitation that, when Sunday rolled around, I felt like I was marching off to the guillotine. After much fussing with my hair and my dress, I made my way over to Alamo Square. I was early, but Harry was already waiting for me. Our greeting was awkward; somehow the memory of the kiss we'd shared had wedged itself between us, leaving us both shy. But my shyness was tinged with sorrow—if only I hadn't pressed for the kiss!

Perhaps Harry would not be about to deliver his bad news now, and we might have been able to spend more time together.

Composing himself, Harry offered his arm.

"Will you walk with me?"

"Of course."

We began our promenade. As far as parks went, Alamo Square was large and open, sloping up a great hill.

"Were you able to retrieve your automobile from the livery?" I inquired politely.

"Yes—I used it to travel here, as a matter of fact." He pointed to the street, where I recognized the Runabout parked curbside.

"Did you discover what the trouble was?"

"Ah, yes," Harry said, laughing softly. "Lack of gasoline."

I looked at him. He shrugged.

"I wasn't lying when I said I truly know nothing about automobiles. And while Davies is trying his earnest best, he is still learning."

We laughed together, then fell into another nervous silence. We walked until we came upon a pretty bench and sat down. The awkwardness between us had softened but had not yet completely dissolved. I glanced around and saw several other pairings of men and women, some strolling, some sitting over picnics spread on the grass. A little grove of cypress trees leaned as though in memory of a strong wind. Seagulls cackled at the pigeons, and somewhere over the hump of the hill a dog barked.

"Once upon a time, this was naught but a watering hole," Harry explained. "A place to tie up one's horse."

I looked at him, and he turned and laughed.

"I'm not claiming to be so old as to remember all that, mind you!"

he said, and I blushed. "I understand that was quite some years ago," he continued. "There was only one tree in the middle of the grassy knoll— one great, ancient-looking cottonwood. But I'm told that's why they've built around this little patch of green as they have, making it into a proper square, and that's where this park gets its name."

"Alamo?" I asked, not certain I understood.

He pointed at a large tree. "Something to do with the Spanish word for cottonwood, I believe."

"Oh." My thoughts rushed back to Madeleine. I'd learned that she was fluent in the three major romance languages: French, Italian, and Spanish. Was Harry repeating some fun tidbit of information his late wife had once used to charm him? The thought disturbed me. I shoved the specter of Madeleine Carlyle out of my mind.

"I warned you that there was a matter I wanted to discuss in private, Violet," Harry said. "You can likely guess what it is."

"I can," I replied, nodding. "And please allow me to apologize for my behavior during our last meeting. I see now that my affections were likely unwanted."

Harry frowned. "Unwanted?"

"Yes—I was very forward, and you were only being polite. I see that now."

Harry's eyes moved over my shoulder, to something just beyond. He flinched, and I paused, mid-apology.

"Harry?"

It took me a moment to realize that Harry had grown very still.

"Harry?" I repeated.

He had gone utterly pale. His complexion was sickly, white as a sheet, and his brow was beaded with sudden perspiration.

"Are you quite all right? You're not looking well."

I tried to follow his gaze. All I could make out was another couple. The woman had dark hair and was quite beautiful, but other than that, the pair appeared unremarkable. I saw no reason for Harry's discomfort.

"Harry?" I repeated once more.

Finally, he shook himself. "Forgive me . . ."

"Not at all," I said. "But has something upset you? I don't understand. You look as though you've seen a ghost."

"A *ghost*?" he repeated, as though appalled by the very word.

"A cliché expression," I said. "But I could find no other way to describe how pale and surprised you looked just now!"

"No, no," he said. "Hardly a ghost. Just a stranger who looked familiar is all." He took a deep breath and turned with a small, apologetic smile, composing himself. "Violet, I haven't a clue what you've been going on about. You were *not* being forward, and you are far from unwanted."

"I . . . I . . . oh!" I stammered, surprised.

Harry grinned affectionately. "In fact, the matter I'd like to discuss points in the opposite direction. But first, how about some lemonade?" he said brightly, producing a flask and two cups. He laid his wares out on the bench between us and proceeded to pour.

I gratefully accepted a cup. The turn of events had me flustered and dry-mouthed. The sunshine was getting a little hot, and the cool, sweet-and-sour bite was welcome on my tongue.

"You're very thoughtful."

"Miss Weber takes excellent care of me, as you can see."

I felt a surprising shiver of jealousy, and silently scolded myself for it. I'd spent the past two days consumed with thoughts of Harry's late wife. And now I was green with envy over his affection for his head servant? What sort of creature was I turning into?

"She is a marvel," he went on. "Everyone says so!" A fond smile appeared on his face. "Why, as a matter of fact, Miss Weber personally oversaw the rebuilding of my home. Every detail! She supervised it all, quite literally from the ground up. Miss Weber . . . well, she has helped me through some very hard times. I am as devoted to her as she is to me, I tell you."

"She is a very impressive individual, indeed," I forced myself to say.

Another lull settled over us and we continued to sip our lemonade.

Harry cleared his throat.

"As to the question—or questions, really—that I'd like to ask you, Violet . . ." Harry began.

"Yes?"

"I can't tell you what an effect you had, that day I met you on the street—but it wasn't just that little newsboy you saved." He paused. "And I apologize if what I'm about to say seems too sudden . . . but I've already come to feel very strongly about you."

He looked into the distance, and I waited for him to continue. But Harry's brow abruptly furrowed, and he stiffened again. This time, I followed his gaze and saw a man crossing the lawn, heading towards us. I looked on with curiosity.

"Mr. Carlyle!" the man cried in a familiar tone. He was dressed in a brown suit, his hair parted in the middle and slicked down with oil. He looked respectable enough, but not quite the class of person I'd expect Harry to know. I glanced at Harry again, and to my surprise, I saw a dark shadow of anger settling there.

"Stay back: I've no comments for the press today!" Harry's voice was firm, irritable.

The press. Well, then, that solved the mystery; the man was hardly a welcome associate.

And yet, it was clear Harry was quite disturbed by the man. In an uncharacteristic gesture, he took my cup of lemonade and tossed its contents onto the grass, briskly packing up.

"Mr. Carlyle!" the reporter repeated. "I thought I saw your motorcar in the Portola Festival parade last week!"

Harry offered the man nothing but a frown, but he barreled on.

"Our readers will want to know, Mr. Carlyle—what is the name of your charming companion? How are you acquainted?"

With a jolt, I realized the reporter meant *me*. His notepad was out and a pencil hovered, ready to take down my name. Panicked, I looked desperately between the two men. I was not prepared for this. To my relief, Harry said nothing. Instead, he waved a hand at me to follow him out of the park. I complied.

Harry cranked up the Runabout's engine and hurried back into the driver's seat. But the man followed us, a dog with a bone.

"Mr. Carlyle! Please! Surely your mystery woman has a name? Are the two of you courting?"

As his desperation increased, the man's disposition shifted from canine to that of a mosquito; he buzzed this way and that, eventually standing directly in front of the vehicle while continuing his questions.

"Give way!" Harry ordered, but the man didn't relent.

"FOR GOD'S SAKE, GIVE WAY, MAN!" Harry shouted again, clearly losing his patience.

Still, the man refused, and to my surprise, Harry clenched his jaw and released the hand-brake. The reporter jumped back, and Harry hit the gas pedal, wrangling the steering wheel to swerve around him.

Though unhurt, the man screamed, but we were already speeding away.

"My . . . goodness!" I managed to choke out, several blocks later. My jaw had dropped at how close we had come to mowing him over.

"Don't feel sorry for *him*," Harry replied. "He's the worst kind of parasite. A blight on mankind. I ought to know: I had to deal with him, and plenty more like him, back when—"

Suddenly, Harry broke off. Had he been about to say, *Back when my wife was alive?*

"Please . . . you have too kind a heart to waste your sympathy on the likes of *him*, Violet—you must trust me in this," Harry concluded.

I agreed, but I felt empty. I didn't know what to think. I became dimly aware that Harry was driving in the direction of my women's hotel. Our outing was drawing to a close already, and the moment felt premature. Everything was going amiss. My mind drifted back to the dark-haired woman in the park. Had she reminded him of Madeleine? And if so . . . why did he look so haunted? My mind flicked back, yet again, to the gossip Cora had repeated. *Foolish gossip*, I told myself.

No matter how hard I tried, my mind could not stop returning to Madeleine. I'd begun to realize that whatever matter Harry had wished to discuss privately today, he might not have intended to mention her at all.

We reached my women's hotel, and Harry pulled alongside the curb and put the hand-brake on again. He twisted in his seat to address me face-to-face.

"I'm sorry that awful reporter interrupted our day."

"Thank you for not telling that man my name," I said.

Harry gave a genteel nod.

My heart had not left my throat since the reporter posed the question. In that instant I pictured the whole truth coming out—the truth I'd already narrowly escaped once, when Harry met Jasper.

I shook myself now, and rubbed my arms, warding off an involuntary shiver.

"Harry," I said, still wondering what he had originally brought me to the park to talk about. "Is the day already over? Surely we could go somewhere else to finish our conversation."

Harry looked at me a long moment. Finally, his smile returned and he inclined his head in affirmation. He lingered there for a moment, and I felt my heart speed up to think he might kiss me again.

His face sunk closer, and closer . . . There were plenty of unanswered questions between us, and I would have been wise to ask any one of them, save the one that came tumbling unbidden out of my mouth.

"Why have you never mentioned your wife to me?"

As soon as the words burst forth, I regretted them. The dark shadow of anger returned to Harry's face. His face emptied and his jaw clenched.

Time stood still as he said nothing.

"Harry?" I said now in a small voice.

"Yes," he replied. His voice was now ice-cold. "I had a wife. She died on the night of the earthquake. I never mentioned her because you are worlds apart, the two of you, and until now, I had rather preferred to keep it that way."

A stiff silence fell between us.

"I'll help you out of the car."

"Harry . . . I'm sorry . . ." My chest filled with disappointed dread as I realized he meant for us to part on this sour note. "That was out of place," I apologized. "It's none of my business."

Harry remained silent as we approached my door. Once at the stoop, he touched his hat in a mechanical way and turned on his heel without another word.

"Harry," I called to the blank, unfriendly canvas of his receding back. "I am truly sorry. Please . . . accept my apology."

He paused, then gave me a small nod from over his shoulder.

"Fine. I accept it," was all he said. Or, at least, I *believe* that was what he said. All the while, the engine of his automobile had been idling at the curb, sending up a steady rattle-rattle-rattle. He climbed into the open car and, with businesslike efficiency, dropped the hand-brake and motored away.

I watched his Maxwell Runabout move into the distance and turn a corner, my heart sinking as he vanished from sight. I knew I had made a fatal misstep.

24

Days passed. Before long, a week. I heard nothing from Harry.

It felt as though I'd been tricked. Once I'd heard Cora's gossip, there was no un-hearing it. It was only natural I would eventually ask Harry about Madeleine . . . although it was a surprise nonetheless to witness his reaction. What could it mean?

One day at work, I became aware of a pair of eyes on me. I jolted to attention and found myself staring at Flossie.

"Oh!" I exclaimed.

"Why, look at you at your official post, Violet!" Flossie said, smiling. "You look so glamorous, I might even be tempted to buy a hat!"

I smiled and blushed.

"I'm afraid you caught me daydreaming, Flossie," I rushed to apologize, embarrassed that she'd seen me slouched over the counter, staring into the middle-distance.

"No, but I mean every word!" Flossie insisted. "And you shouldn't listen to Cora," she continued, as though confiding in me. "Putting you down for wanting to work as a shop-girl . . ."

Flossie noticed my expression sour and gathered herself.

"Never mind about her. My visit to see you here was long overdue."

"I'm happy you came, Flossie."

"Also . . ." she began tentatively. "I read in the society pages . . . Mr. Harry Carlyle was reported to have had an unnamed female companion alongside him during the Portola Festival's automobile parade, and was seen again with that same young woman a week later—*alone*, in Alamo Square."

I blushed, and glanced quickly about to determine whether anyone else might be listening. "It was me," I admitted.

Flossie brightened.

"Good for you! It's true what I said the other day: I do believe Cora is jealous. Harry Carlyle is rumored to be one of the wealthiest bachelors in all of San Francisco!" she said with fresh enthusiasm. "Do you . . . perhaps . . . have any *news* to give me?"

A wave of misery overtook me. I shook my head.

"It's . . . it's not to be, Flossie. I'm afraid I've gone and scared him off—and for good, I think."

Flossie's smile fell.

"Oh, dear," she said.

She reached out to pat my hand where it lay on the counter between us. Then her eyes flicked to the clock on the wall. She glanced around the sweeping showroom floor.

"Am I right to think that the store closes soon?" she asked.

I looked at the clock. The store was meant to close in ten minutes, and I told Flossie this was so. Her face brightened again.

"Well, then, meet me outside when you're all through. I'm taking you to supper. We'll dine out somewhere nice, somewhere that's bound to cheer you up!"

"You don't have to do all that, Flossie," I protested, but she waved an insistent hand.

"What are sisters for, if not times like this?" she said.

I relented. The truth was, I wanted her company anyway. If you were in the mood to talk or wanted to unburden yourself, there was no one like Flossie to make you feel better.

"I'll wait for you outside," she said, and turned to go.

Flossie had been in earnest when she'd proposed to take me to dine out "somewhere nice." We walked from the streets surrounding the Emporium north through Union Square and then upwards, to the crowning peak of Nob Hill, where she selected an extremely fancy—and impressively expensive—restaurant in one of the palatial hotels there.

I protested at first, convinced that two middle-class young women would stand out in such a place; but, much as she had done earlier, Flossie waved away my concerns.

"The world is changing, Violet!" she scolded. "If we behave like we know what we're about, no one will question us."

Flossie's dictum proved to be true. The maître d' showed us to a pleasant table for two, and a waiter promptly took our order. The dining room was gorgeous, with soaring ceilings, fine linen tablecloths, and gold-plated silverware that shone a rosy-yellow hue, catching the glow from the chandeliers. The only place I'd ever been that was nearly as nice was the Palm Court. Given the awful hat, one might think I'd have felt more out of place during my tea with Harry, but as I darted a glance around the dining room now, I felt exceedingly self-conscious. The men and women were all dressed in the kind of finery that, at the Emporium, would cost an arm and a leg. Meanwhile, I was still wearing one of my modest brown dress suits, a suit that clearly marked me as a shop-girl.

"Stop fidgeting and hold your head higher!" Flossie commanded with a smile, noticing my intimidation. "No one will care about your station—so long as you don't!"

Flossie was wearing the kind of suit she likely wore to work as a typist: no finer than my own. But, since entering the restaurant, she'd undergone a significant change. It was difficult to pin down exactly what had altered—something in her carriage and demeanor. Her timid, frowsy impression had vanished completely, and had been replaced by a regality equal to Cora's. Her birdlike air had not dissipated, but now she resembled a majestic eagle as opposed to a frightened sparrow.

Between the three of us, Cora had always gotten all the attention. Now I realized Flossie was a much more intriguing specimen than most people credited.

"Well?" Flossie said with a gentle expression. "Shall we discuss what happened? Why are you so sure you've frightened off Harry Carlyle for good?"

I told her everything. How I'd asked about his late wife. How he'd gone so stiff, and clearly disdained me by the time we parted.

"I suppose Cora baited you into that particular trap, didn't she?"

I was surprised by her insight. I'd suspected much the same, but never would have voiced it.

"Violet," Flossie said, leaning closer. "You must be cautious with Cora . . . especially if you've got something she might want for herself."

I mulled this over, shocked that Flossie had considered this, too.

The waiter arrived with a slip of paper on a silver tray. Flossie reached for her beaded purse.

"Is it very expensive, Flossie?" I asked, suddenly anxious.

She waved me off.

"I told you," she insisted. "Don't mention it. It was my wish to cheer you up."

I smiled, and she sent me a shy glance in return.

"Do you have much left?" she asked.

"Much?" I replied. "Of what?"

"You know . . ."

"Oh," I stammered.

It took me a moment to regain my bearing and answer.

"I spent a bit when I left the camp. I needed proper clothing, and my room at the women's hotel."

"Of course," Flossie hurriedly agreed, embarrassed to have brought the matter up.

"But once I found some employment, I put it in a safety-deposit box. It . . . it just didn't feel right to spend it."

"The nightmares again?"

I nodded. An awkward beat passed. For a fleeting moment, I thought to finally tell Flossie about the empty bottle I'd found. But in the next second, Flossie's face brightened.

"Shall we go?"

As we stood and made ready to leave, Flossie changed the subject back to Harry one last time.

"If I were you, Violet, I wouldn't let one foolish mistake ruin what could possibly be a lifetime of happiness."

"But how can I change what has already come to pass?"

"You ought to go to Harry, and tell him how sorry you are! Admit your misstep, and promise never to broach the subject of his late wife again—he will see that you are in earnest; I'm sure of it!"

"I don't know," I said, shaking my head doubtfully.

"Oh, but you must!" Flossie said. "Do it for me. You've always said that we are just like sisters, haven't you?"

I nodded my head in agreement.

"In that case, I am your *elder* sister, and it is my job to look to your happiness."

I dithered, biting my lip.

"Please?"

Flossie looked at me, her big eyes so sincere. I wanted to say yes just to please her, but I already knew I would not dare approach Harry again, not even with an apology, not after what I'd done.

"He was so cold, Flossie. You ought to have seen him."

Flossie sighed. "Well, just so long as you consider it," she said, and took my arm.

Together we made our way out of the restaurant and back onto the street, where we bid each other goodbye. The night was cool and slightly damp from the sea. We clasped hands under the new electric glow of the streetlamps.

"You *did* lift my spirits, Flossie. Thank you."

She grinned. "As I said, Violet—we're sisters."

25

Two more weeks passed with no sign of Harry. I began drafting apology letters. I didn't send any of them; I hadn't the nerve. Harry hadn't made me any promises. It was a gauche thing to bring up a man's deceased wife, much less demand he explain himself in the same breath.

I came home one day to find my landlady once again buzzing about the entrance hall.

"You must put a stop to this tomfoolery, or I'll be forced to ask you to leave!" she yelled, in lieu of a hello.

I saw that she held an enormous box papered in silver foil, tied with a white satin bow. My heart jumped into my throat, and I had to swallow it back down just to retain some semblance of calm.

Could it be? My fingers itched to tear into the box. I was desperate to see the familiar *H.C.* monogram on its card.

"It's indecent of you! Treating me like a filthy servant!" Mrs. Camp-bell thrust the box into my outstretched arms. "And entertaining gifts from a man! I shudder to imagine what you do to encourage his in-terest!"

She huffed away.

I hurried upstairs, looking at the box as I scrambled along. It was not a hatbox. The shape was wrong. It was not a glove box either. Too large. No. Instead, it was . . . I couldn't think! What could it be?

My heart was pounding as I unlocked the door to my room and carried the parcel inside. Once I had untied the ribbon and lifted the lid, I gasped with absolute surprise. Inside was the most beautiful dress I'd ever seen. I reached out to touch it: it was gray, almost iridescent silk. I lifted it out for inspection. It had an Empire waist, all the latest rage. The collar and sleeves were trimmed with tiny pearls and handmade lace.

My mind raced to guess at the beautiful garment's meaning. I lifted the dress higher, and as if to answer me, the calling card fluttered out, like a butterfly dropping from the heavens. I grabbed for it.

> I am attending a small symphony concert and would be
> extremely pleased if you would honor me with your presence.
> Eternally yours,
> Harry

Written at the bottom of the note was a time and date, his customary R.S.V.P. card, and instructions to wear the dress, if I should be so in-clined. I read it once, twice, and a third time. There was no mention of our previous conversation, of our awkward exchange . . . or of my rudeness. Was I forgiven?

On the evening of the concert, I was giddy with a mixture of nerves and excitement. Once again, I dressed myself with the maximum amount of care, donning the beautiful gown, and doing my best to match it with a carefully pinned bun. Once my toilet was complete, I sat waiting near the window, compulsively patting my hair with gloved hands.

At exactly half past six, a beautiful carriage came down my street, drawn by a pair of purebred mares. My heart gave a spastic contraction.

I glimpsed Harry's face in the paned window and hurried down to the street outside. No matter how shy I felt to see him again, I couldn't wait an instant longer.

"Violet," Harry said with surprise as I rushed from my building, catching him on his way up the path.

Despite my best efforts to keep my composure, I began to grin like a maniac. But just as I stepped from the small porch, my foot caught on the stonework, and I pitched forward.

I panicked; I was sure to land flat on my face.

But Harry lunged to catch me. I laughed, and the sound danced on the night air. Harry joined in, and whatever sour note still lingered from our last meeting utterly evaporated. We walked together towards the carriage, where the driver waited, holding the door open. I climbed in nimbly enough and settled myself on the sumptuous velvet upholstery. Harry sat across from me. In seconds we had set off, the driver urging the horses on at a gentle clip.

Like a pair of shy children, Harry and I traded smiles.

"I am glad to see you tonight," he said finally.

My smile widened into an unabashed grin; I could not help it. All the while, my head was swimming with questions—questions that I was too afraid to ask. He had sent such a lovely dress, which I now wore with pride. He had offered his arm to me, and I had taken it. I hadn't the faintest idea where we were going—to a concert, presumably, but I had not demanded a single detail beyond that. We were alone, unchaperoned save for the driver. I was glad that, whatever we had to say to each other, we would not be forced to say it while withering under Miss Weber's gargoyle stare.

We rode up and down the steep inclines of the city streets, until we wound our way into a newer area called Pacific Heights. It was a rare clear evening in San Francisco, without a trace of chilly fog. Nearly every block possessed stunning views of the Bay and the blue sea beyond. The houses were large and impressive, some of them new and modern, coated in fresh plaster, while others boasted the ornate scrollwork of the Victorian decades. Everything was bright and clean; the buildings were rowed up like vertebrae, glowing in the long-leaning rays of the setting sun like bleached whalebone.

Eventually, we came to our destination: a newly built mansion belonging to the Spreckels family. The mansion was large and rectangular, pristinely white, with Greek columns. All at once, it dawned on me what we were heading into. I had been so overjoyed to receive any invitation at all from Harry . . . I hadn't pictured the specifics.

As we climbed out of the carriage, Harry offered his arm to me. He noticed that I had begun to tremble and paused.

"Is something the matter, Violet?"

Other couples milled about, drifting past us, up the stairs and into the mansion. They were elegantly attired—and well above my station. I eyed them with caution. This evening was sure to change Harry's mind against me again, and possibly for good.

"I'm not certain I belong with the company you keep," I admitted in a quiet voice.

"I'll admit, they *can* be tedious," he joked. "But consider this: your presence will certainly elevate the room." He patted my gloved hand where it rested in the crook of his arm while I tried to swallow down my reluctance.

We strolled up the stairs, mingling with the other concert-goers. Once inside, we entered an echoing marble hall and were greeted by a butler holding a tray of delicate glasses filled with champagne. Harry lifted two and handed one to me. This was only the third time I'd ever had champagne. I thought briefly of Cora and tightened my hold on Harry's arm, vowing not to cough and sputter again.

It soon became clear Harry was friendly with all of the other guests—or, at the very least, *they* were eager to claim a friendship with *him*, as Harry was one of the wealthiest, most powerful men in the room. Paired off in couples, each floated over in turn to pay their respects to Harry, while inspecting me out of the sides of their eyes. Each time, Harry introduced me in a loud, forceful voice, as though to impress upon them that I was not to be discounted or ignored.

He introduced me to one guest—Millicent Abbott, wife of Theodore Abbott—with particular zeal.

"Why, you and Milly ought to go to tea sometime, Violet," Harry said, upon making the introductions. "Violet's read everything on the face of the earth, Milly. And I understand you're quite fond of Dickens."

"Ye-ess," Mrs. Abbott replied, looking me over dubiously. "It's a wonder we haven't crossed paths before."

I knew this last remark was meant to point out the fact I had never entered society before, and hardly belonged.

"She's an awful tyrant," Harry whispered under his breath to me, once the Abbotts were walking away. "But she runs things, among the women. If you get in good with her, you'd have a much easier time of it."

I wanted to ask him, *An easier time of what?*—but before I could, the concert was announced. Everyone moved in the direction of the ballroom. It was, as Harry had promised, most grand. Cushioned chairs had been laid out in rows. Once the milling crowd was seated, the discordant sounds of the musicians tuning their instruments slowly died down. A conductor stepped out, bowed, then rapped his baton against a music stand. The musicians began to play.

"This is one of my favorites—a powerful piece from Vivaldi," Harry whispered. It was indeed powerful—very vigorous and very beautiful. But it was also difficult to concentrate. I felt the eyes of the other guests perpetually darting in our direction, taking inventory of my person. It occurred to me that they might be comparing me to Madeleine, and the simple thought alone was overwhelming. I forced it from my mind.

The musicians played themselves to a frenzied climax, and the concert drew to a close. The men stood to give an ovation, the women clapping where they sat, their gloves making a muffled pattering.

Once the conductor made his final exit, Harry helped me to my feet. I glanced around, reluctant to return to socializing. I saw the Abbotts, returning to talk to Harry—likely to inquire how we had enjoyed the concert—and I felt a familiar rush of blood to my head, followed by a cold prickling break out all over my skin . . . the feeling I often got just before I had one of my spells.

A terrible dread gripped me.

Harry, noticing, asked, "Are you ill, Violet?"

"I think I need some air."

"Of course. Let's get you some. I was going to suggest a drive in the carriage tonight, anyway. Would that suit?"

I nodded and took his arm. We left the Abbotts still struggling to make their way across the room through all the milling bodies, frowning after us.

The night air rushed at me like a cool balm. Gratitude flooded my body, and I felt my spell receding. The gauzy sleeves of my gray dress fluttered in the evening breeze as we climbed into the carriage and Harry gave orders to the driver. The horses whinnied, the whip snapped smartly, and the coach lurched gently forward. For the first few moments we rode in silence. Outside the window the last rays of light drained from the evening sky while the city began to twinkle with gas and electric lamps.

The coach carried us westward, to the cliffs overlooking the point where the Bay began to meet the sea. People were building houses there now, dubbing the neighborhood "Sea Cliff" after its spectacular views. Still, the houses were fewer and farther between than in the heart of the city. There was a sense of ruggedness and isolation.

Eventually, the driver maneuvered us to a pretty spot that overlooked the rolling waves. He pulled at the horses' reins and the carriage stopped.

"The view here is incredible, if you're willing to step out," Harry said.

I hesitated for the briefest of seconds. I knew we were quite near the bluffs, and I felt a tiny chill of fear. Harry read my expression deftly.

"I'll keep you safe. I promise."

I blushed.

"Of course," I replied.

We climbed out and picked our way over the rocky land to where the eucalyptus and cypress trees gave out to reveal a steep drop and a thrilling view of the crashing Pacific below. Harry's figure was silver in the moonlight as he pointed to a large, flat boulder near the edge. "Let us sit for a minute or two."

We sat in silence, listening to the sounds of the wind, the water, and the gulls. It was terribly dark, but quite lovely. The water stretched out like an enormous roll of unfurled black velvet. Occasionally, the lights of a passing ship winked at us.

"I know you mightn't want to talk about it," I ventured timidly, "but I hope you know I'm awfully sorry . . . about the questions I asked, last time we met."

"You're mistaken, Violet," he insisted. "It is my turn to apologize, and I'm sorry I didn't say as much on the card I sent—it didn't seem an adequate space for the magnitude of apology I owe you."

I was dumbfounded. "These past weeks . . . I assumed your silence meant you were finding it difficult to forgive me. You were . . ." I trailed off, momentarily unsure. "Well, you seemed quite angry that day— understandably!" I finished.

But Harry only shook his head. "Not understandably, but I *was* in a terrible mood. That reporter brought out the worst in me." He paused, then continued more carefully. "I don't mean to make excuses for my behavior. There's no excuse, and the truth is, you were quite right to ask about my wife."

"It was not my place," I said.

"Well, Violet, I suppose that's what I want to talk to you about now. It *is* your place—or, at least, it might be."

I blinked at him, waiting for further explanation.

"I had hoped to skip over certain parts of my history entirely, but I see now how improper that was, how selfish, and how rude to you—especially given the specific matter I'd hoped to discuss with you that day."

"Matter?" I echoed.

He nodded. "I will tell you about my wife, Violet," he said. "In fact, I will tell you *all* about her. You're right in guessing that it is a subject that pains me . . . though not in the manner you may think. I don't relish the conversation, but I understand we must have it, if we are to proceed."

"Proceed?"

"Yes. I will tell you the story of the last night I saw Madeleine, and then I never wish to speak of this again."

Madeleine. It was strange hearing Harry finally speak her name aloud. I didn't reply, and instead waited for him to continue.

"When I first met Madeleine, I admit, I was utterly enchanted," he said.

I felt a prickle of jealousy return yet again.

"We courted, we married, and for at least a year or two, we were happy. I wanted for nothing. Madeleine was the perfect wife. All who met her were instantly charmed and agreed that I was a very lucky man indeed."

Suddenly, I wasn't so sure I wanted to hear this story anymore. I gritted my teeth and swallowed, willing my stomach to steady itself.

"Over time, however, she changed," Harry said. "Perhaps she grew bored with our life together . . . She began to behave in an increasingly erratic manner. I would find her doing strange things—say, gardening in the middle of the night, by candlelight. Then she began to act out in public, vamping for attention. She took up with seedy characters."

He paused, and a sharp flicker of discomfort passed over his features. He made an effort to force it away.

"Eventually, our relations grew stormy. Madeleine and I had reached an impasse. She insisted she'd fallen in love with one of her paramours— a foreigner, who even claimed to hold some sort of noble title back in Italy."

Harry paused a second time. The flicker returned. His face twisted in the moonlight as though he had tasted something sour. I listened to the thunderous crashing of the sea below us and felt a second chill. Harry heaved a great sigh.

"Surely you've already heard some of this from the gossips. We were fighting. Everyone knew it. And then . . . we stopped."

I ventured a quiet breath. I could remember all too well Cora's awful insinuations.

"Busybodies had glimpsed my fury," Harry continued. "But none of them ever glimpsed what came after. It was all rather anticlimactic, I'm afraid. The gossips prefer the sensational—and *fictional*—version of events. But the truth is, my marriage dissolved very quickly in the end. Madeleine announced that she had made plans to join her European lover in Italy, and put an end to our arguing by simply leaving.

"I had not yet decided how to tell others. Though she intended to spend the rest of her days with her lover, Madeleine told me she had no intention of helping me arrange for a divorce or easing the scandal one would likely create; the effort and shame would be mine alone. The day Madeleine packed her bags and left, I told no one. I thought I was postponing the inevitable.

"But then . . . the earthquake struck. Everything in San Francisco was turned upon its head. Miss Weber persuaded me to cover Madeleine's scandalous departure by claiming Madeleine had perished in the earthquake. After all, the mansion had been left in utter ruin."

He paused and smiled sadly.

"I believe she meant to protect both of our reputations—Madeleine's as well as my own—for Miss Weber truly loved her mistress. She never quite got over the cruel manner in which Madeleine left; though the death is a lie, I think Miss Weber is happier memorializing Madeleine than ruining her good name.

"In time, I came to appreciate the wisdom of Miss Weber's tactic, for it allowed me to mourn the dissolution of my marriage in peace. People are merciless on the subject of divorce, but they do not question grief."

But people are *talking*, I thought to myself. *Even now, years later.*

As if reading my mind, Harry gave a stiff nod.

"I know there are plenty of rumors. I know the gossips have made ominous insinuations. I am not a fool."

I stared at him. He went on.

"I am not a fool," he repeated, "but the gossips are. They look to add some macabre glamor to their hum-drum lives. I only care what *you* have heard, Violet, and what *you* think of me."

"Me?" I echoed, bewildered. "I know in my heart none of that gossip is true; you are too good a man. But I'm not sure my opinion much matters—I am a nobody."

"You are *not* a nobody," Harry said firmly. "You have the kindest soul of anyone I have ever met. And if you will have me, I should like for you to be my wife."

Now that the moment had finally arrived, I gasped. I suddenly felt very dizzy, as if the pitch-black night and the salty sea air had turned into a kind of opium, intoxicating me.

"Wife?" I said.

"Yes, Violet," Harry said. "I had been living in a kind of hell, brokenhearted and disenchanted, until I met you. You make me believe in the goodness of people again. I cherish the feeling I have when I am around you. When I asked you what you most wanted in life, you said you wanted a favorite person, the way you'd always had favorite books. You said you wanted a sense of *family*. I should very much like to give that to you."

I could see he wished me to speak, but I was incapable. The idea of marrying Harry, and of having a family—a *real* family—was too much. Though I'd hardly been aware of such, I'd always taken some measure of security from the notion that such things were out of my reach. Now, presented with what I wanted most, I couldn't help but think of my spells, my dark, fatal flaw—a curse. One that kept me in a constant state of terror, worried that they might spill over, splashing out and staining someone I loved. Or, worse still, that they might be handed down from one generation to the next, a cross for any potential children to bear.

How could I possibly offer myself to Harry as a wife and mother?

I couldn't.

I made up my mind I would say so.

But as Harry waited for my reply, he misread my hesitation.

"I understand my history is complicated, Violet," he conceded. "It's far from the story you may have dreamed your future husband would have. I hope . . . well, I hope it is not the macabre gossip that is giving you pause . . ."

"Oh, no—Harry! I would never think that of you!"

He brightened slightly.

"I can't tell you how grateful I am that you are too sensible a girl to listen to such things," he said.

"It's not that," I confirmed.

"If it's not that, then there is nothing standing in our way, is there?" Harry said, hope gleaming in his eyes. "Only the fact that I love you, and the question of whether you love me. I don't mean to press you, Violet, but do you know your answer?"

I attempted to speak, but my mouth only opened and closed stupidly, like a fish's. For the slenderest of seconds, the strange shiver of vertiginous fear I'd felt upon getting out of the coach returned to me, though I could not say why.

"Violet?"

I blinked.

"Yes," I said. "Yes."

I loved him; it was the only answer I could give.

26

We were married by a judge, and with two simple words—"I do"—I became Mrs. Carlyle. Harry felt that—given his secret—to marry in a church would be disrespectful. I had to agree; after all, his wife was still living.

I realize how irregular our situation was. The fact that I can say "his wife was still living" sounds so much worse than what the circumstances truly were. Harry was no bigamist. Our intentions were those of an honorable, monogamous match—the kind of match Harry had wished for in his first marriage. It wasn't his fault he'd been forced to declare Madeleine dead and gone. She'd given him no other choice. The newspapers would have eaten it up if he'd gone chasing after her, and demanding a divorce in her absence would have meant double the humiliation. When Madeleine left his life for good, he felt she might as well have died . . . for she was dead *to him*.

As we discussed all this yet again during the days leading up to the wedding, Harry couldn't help but read the worry on my face. He made one promise to me—a crucial promise, in my eyes, for I did not relish the thought of a sudden annulment.

She will never return, he vowed. *For better or worse, I know her mind. I can promise you: I will never see nor hear from Madeleine again, as long as I live.*

I accepted his promise. Besides, as I kept reminding myself: there were unpleasant matters in my own past that I, too, should like to close the door on, once and for all. Harry and I would make new lives together.

Marriage meant more plans. I gave my notice at the Emporium, forfeiting my coveted post at the millinery counter. Harry wanted us to honeymoon, after which I would take up residence in his mansion. Time was flying by quickly; we were to leave in three days' time, setting sail to the U.S. territory of Hawai'i—a destination Harry had picked. Europe was out of the question, for obvious reasons. Harry had heard no news of Madeleine on the Italian social scene. *But you can be sure she's gadding about the Continent*, he said with glum disdain. *I'd rather never know about it.* He'd read about Hawai'i, he said; he'd always liked the travelogue Mark Twain had written on the subject, and, if nothing else, the landscape sounded quite beautiful.

I didn't care where we were headed. Once the judge uttered the words "I now pronounce you husband and wife" and Harry kissed me delicately on the lips, I knew: *I was a wife!* Of all the things I'd ever allowed myself to imagine, I had never imagined this. I was determined to push my self-doubts aside.

Before we sailed, I went to tell Cora and Flossie my joyful news.

"Oh, Violet!" Flossie gasped, when I told them. "Congratulations! How extraordinary! Think back to our days in the girls' home, to the boardinghouse—who would have imagined you'd one day marry Harry Carlyle!"

At this, Cora turned to Flossie with an alarmed expression, and I realized: Cora had expected Flossie to scold me.

"You aren't worried, Flossie?" Cora demanded. "Wait until the society pages get ahold of the story . . . Why, they'll demand to know everything about Violet!" She paused, shifting her gaze to look me square in the face. "And I do mean *everything*, Violet."

I shook my head, resolute.

"Harry has promised to shield me from them. He knows that I . . . well, only that my life was different before this marriage. He believes in privacy."

Cora snorted.

"And he has secrets of *his own*, no doubt, that he would like to keep hidden, I imagine," she replied.

I bit my lip.

"Well, there is some truth to that, but it's not what you think," I said.

"Not what I think? I'll be plain about what *I* think," Cora replied. "I think they fought on the night of the earthquake, and he had something to do with her death!"

"He didn't!" I protested.

Cora raised a skeptical eyebrow. Even Flossie looked dubious.

"He *couldn't* have had anything to do with her death, because, well . . . she's not dead," I blurted out, before I could restrain myself.

Now they both stared at me, eyes agog.

"She left town with her lover, in the middle of the night, a day before the earthquake struck," I said.

I may as well tell them all of it now, I figured. I turned to Cora.

"What you heard about Harry and Madeleine having discord is true—or partly true, I should say," I told her. "She turned rather erratic, running around on him. Eventually, she ran off altogether. The timing was coincidental. Harry was frustrated that she refused to give him a divorce—he would have to take pains to acquire one at his own public and social expense. A trusted servant suggested he save both their reputations and wash his hands of the scandal by having her declared dead."

Neither Cora nor Flossie had moved. They both sat, still staring at me, their mouths slightly open. Cora shook herself first.

"And . . . this is what you believe, Violet?"

"Yes," I replied.

"And you've still gone and married him?"

"Yes."

They continued to stare at me, silent. Cora's eyes were boring into me.

"What if Madeleine Carlyle comes back? What then?"

"She won't," I said. "Harry says he knows beyond a doubt that she won't return."

Cora cocked her head, wary.

"I don't believe it," she said, after thinking it over.

"What do you mean?" I asked.

Cora shook her head. "I don't believe it. It's too fantastical."

Now it was my turn to stare.

"Either she's alive and one day your marriage will be ruined," Cora insisted. "Or else . . ." She hesitated briefly. "Or else, Violet, *Harry is lying.*"

I felt my throat tighten.

"Fine," I said. "Believe what you wish." I began to gather up my things. "For once, Cora, I had merely hoped you might be happy for me."

"Violet—please don't go!" Flossie pleaded. But I was already halfway to the door. "We honestly do wish you all the best! You know we love you like a sister!"

I was willing to believe Flossie. I looked at Cora and arched one eyebrow.

"It's only that I'm worried about you," Cora said.

"I see," I replied. I was surprised by the cold note in my own voice. "I'm so very deeply touched by your concern."

And with that, I left for my honeymoon.

It was not the send-off I'd hoped for. And when we departed, at first, all I wanted was to turn back. The ocean voyage was rough, as I did not take kindly to the motion of the ship. It reminded me, I think, of the earthquake. But Harry proved his husbandly devotion, holding my sick-pail and reading novels aloud by my bedside.

When I began to feel better, we took a tour of the ship. It was a 3,000-ton iron steamer, and we were personal guests of the Spreckels family, which accorded us accommodations far grander than anything I'd ever known: our cabin was the largest on board. I remember being afraid to touch the taps in the bathroom: everything was plated in real gold.

We did not consummate the marriage at sea. Perhaps this was on account of my being so ill. Instead, we lived as a pair of passengers, keeping company with each other and slowly growing accustomed to each other's small habits and nocturnal noises as our ship chugged away across the Pacific. Unexpectedly, I found the experience intimate in a different way, for I soon knew the sound of Harry breathing at night, and the warm smell of his skin in the morning. I grew used to him glimpsing me in my nightgown, my hair cascading in a long tangle down my back. Even at my most ill, he gently touched my flushed cheeks and called me beautiful.

After a few days, I found my sea-legs, and we began to stroll the open deck.

At first, the view was all the same: blue, blue, blue, and more blue. Choppy blue, calm blue, blue with foamy white caps. The ocean stretched on longer than I ever imagined it could; the horizon was so empty it terrified me. Eventually, I noticed that, slowly but surely, the exact *shade* of blue was changing. Then, after a while, I realized I no longer needed my shawl to keep me warm while we were above deck. The trail churned up by the ship's propellers transformed from navy to vibrant turquoise. Finally, jagged teeth of land sprang from the horizon, emerald green and astonishing.

When at last we steamed into the bay near Honolulu, I was already enchanted. The sand was punctuated by tall, waving palm trees, and farther in the distance were those jungle-green mountains we had sighted from sea. A warm breeze caressed everything like a happy sigh.

The clouds moved idly overhead, puffs of cotton without a care in the world.

Once our ship had docked, we were brought by a motorized limousine to the Moana Hotel, a lovely white-columned palace with a short circular drive. A flock of bellhops took our bags, and once inside, I was awed by the hotel's gracious interior, its lovely rugs and furnishings as stately as anything I could imagine we'd have encountered in Europe. A courtyard revealed an enormous banyan tree, its roots hanging down from its canopy in ropey vines.

The air smelled sweet and strange—a scent almost like jasmine mixed with lemons and brown sugar. During the days, we read books and swam in the sea, visited plantations and were chauffeured to breathtaking vistas. I tasted a pineapple for the first time. We also drank a watery kind of milk directly from the hairy hull of a coconut shell. At night, we slept with all the windows of our suite thrown wide, breathing the perfumed air. The sea played us a symphony of softly crashing waves.

It was there, in Hawai'i, that Harry and I reached for each other for the first time. An enormous moon shone through the open windows, and we removed our clothes slowly, until our bare skin glowed silver, strange and otherworldly in the blue moonlight. Harry's mouth on my body was nearly the same temperature as the balmy Hawai'ian night air, giving the touch of it a delicious, delicate subtlety—like a feather.

Later, when the act was complete, Harry held me, and I could feel my mind reeling.

"What are you thinking?" he asked.

I hesitated, unsure if I ought to say.

"Please?" he asked.

"I am thinking . . . I *was* a child," I said. "But all at once, everything has changed—in the most wonderful way. And now . . ."

"Now what?"

Up until that moment, my life had been nothing but a testament of surviving my own childhood. I had long assumed that providing another creature a childhood of its own was a luxury I could not afford. I'd managed to overcome all the rest of it; all of a sudden, I no longer wished to be a slave to my spells or let them hold me back.

"I'm thinking of how much I *would like* to have a child," I finally confessed.

"Is that all?" Harry asked, laughing happily. "Well, then, I shall try my best."

He tipped my face to his own and I felt as though I were happily drowning in a warm tide of love. I never wanted to stop reaching for Harry. I had always guessed wives were many things, but now I knew that they could be happy, greedy, beloved creatures—for this is what I had so suddenly become.

27

E ventually, after three weeks of utter bliss, our honeymoon drew to a close. We boarded the steamship that chugged its way back across the Pacific, bringing us home to San Francisco. It was sad to leave a paradise such as Hawai'i was, but I knew there were still many new things in store for our future together. First on that list was my relocation to Harry's mansion. I would live there now as "Mrs. Carlyle," an experience nearly as exotic to me as the Hawai'ian Islands.

The Bay was cool and foggy as we arrived. After wearing so many light silks and linens, I felt quite buttoned up in my traveling suit. In our absence, Harry had had Mr. Davies acquire a larger automobile, and he came dressed in a chauffeur's suit and cap to fetch us from the pier. As he drove us from the pier to Harry's mansion, people stopped to stare, and I began to feel nerves stirring in my stomach and fluttering up to my chest. I realized I was apprehensive about my new life—or, rather, about my ability to live up to my new role.

In Hawai'i, hearing my new name had been a novelty. The first few times a bellhop or a maître d' said it, Harry and I had exchanged a look, and I had giggled, as though we'd just shared a secret joke. The name sounded like a delicious treat—something to drink in along with all those funny fruit juices. Now that we were back in San Francisco, the sound of "Mrs. Carlyle" had an unexpected weight to it. The name seemed *more* than me somehow—more mature, perhaps. It caused me to feel a little foolish, like a girl playing dress-up in her mother's clothes. I wondered how long it would take for me to settle in properly.

I had never before set foot inside Harry's house. When we pulled up out front, I stared, bowled over by its size. It looked less like a house and more like a small hotel—the kind of luxurious hotel I could never have imagined setting foot in when I was Tackett's maid.

"Nothing to be nervous about, my pet," Harry said, noticing my sudden trembling.

He offered me his arm, and together we strode up the walkway and entered the grand foyer. As we stepped inside, my eyes swept the gracious room. I took my first look at the place Harry had meticulously rebuilt in the wake of the earthquake—the place that was now to be my home.

I gasped.

Two staircases ascended either side of the foyer. But it wasn't the grandiosity of the room that struck me; it was the large oil portrait that hung at the top of the stairs. A beautiful, dark-haired woman with brooding brown eyes. In an emerald green dress, she sat angled away, looking back towards the viewer with an air that was simultaneously seductive and guarded, as though she might be hiding a secret. As my eyes met the dark eyes of the portrait, my heart leapt into my throat.

I knew exactly who I was looking at: *Madeleine.*

What was she doing here? If what Harry had told me was true, it pained him to talk about her, and one would think he would be equally pained to see her image every day. Was it for appearances, to keep up the lie he had told when he'd had her declared dead?

As I pondered this, the first Mrs. Carlyle gazed back at me, cruelly indifferent to my arrival. I had to shake myself to turn away. There were other matters to attend to. A short row of servants stood there, waiting to receive us. And there, among them, stood Miss Weber.

Miss Weber! I received my second unpleasant jolt of the day. How could I have forgotten? Living with Harry also meant living with Miss Weber. He had told me on no less than half a dozen occasions how treasured she was, how indispensable to him in his everyday existence. And now here she was, frowning at me.

I smiled, hoping to ease the tension, but she refused to smile back. She was making no effort to hide her displeasure at receiving me, and especially unenthusiastic to receive me as the new Mrs. Carlyle. I recalled what Harry had said the night of his proposal: that Miss Weber had loved Madeleine—so much so that, despite Madeleine's betrayal, she would rather memorialize the woman than rue her name. Perhaps my arrival was more difficult for Miss Weber than I could imagine.

Harry, for his part, was utterly blind to her disapproval. He chattered on, filling Miss Weber in on our recent journey (the scenery was heaven, he told her, but the food could never compare to her cooking). Miss Weber said nothing to me—not a single word of welcome—nor did she even glance in my direction. Harry absorbed the entirety of her attention; I do believe she enjoyed pretending I didn't exist.

Once their brief reunion had run its course, Harry went down the line, saying hello to each servant and introducing me in turn. Mr.

Davies acted as a sort of butler and chauffeur to Harry, and was senior to all the other servants save for Miss Weber. Mabel, a young yellow-haired girl, was the head maid, and Bess—a girl who I guessed might be Mabel's sister—was the under maid. A dark, Slavic-looking woman named Velma did much of the cooking. Otis and George tended the grounds, and a young lad named Percy served as an all-around errand boy. I shook each hand in turn. When I got to Percy, I broke into a grin, remembering the little newsboy from the day Harry and I first met.

"I should like to give you a proper tour of your new home, if you would like one, Violet," Harry said, and I agreed with embarrassing desperation. I could not imagine poking around that posh mansion on my own. Harry began to show me.

"We were able to salvage many of the furnishings, personal treasures, antiques, and such after the earthquake," Harry said, "but the structure of the mansion itself sustained too much damage. The whole shell had to be razed and rebuilt. Luckily, Miss Weber was able to recall where every last stick of furniture belonged. She put this house back in order exactly as it had been, down to the smallest bit of bric-a-brac."

I found this slightly puzzling, but held my tongue.

We proceeded to roam about. With Harry as my guide, I discovered several rooms that absolutely stunned me: a mirrored dining room fit for a king and queen; a music room with a grand piano so beautiful that I was full of regret I didn't know how to play it; and—my favorite of all—a rich wood-paneled library with so many books filling its tall shelves that a helpful ladder on rails had been installed. The rails ran around the perimeter of the room, and Harry demonstrated how to roll the ladder about so I might have access to any book I wished. There was also an enormous stone fireplace ("Miss Weber will have one of the kitchen maids lay a fire for you anytime you wish") and tufted leather armchairs so deep, one might get lost in them. My eyes greedily searched the spines of books for the titles of novels I had not already read.

Each time we passed the portrait at the top of the stairs, Harry made no comment.

"And this hallway here," Harry said as we neared the conclusion of his tour, "leads off to Miss Weber's section of the house."

"The servants' quarters?"

"Yes," Harry replied, nodding, "although the turn of phrase is a bit misleading, as it solely belongs to Miss Weber now."

I was perplexed. "What do you mean?"

Harry smiled. "Miss Weber is the only one who lives in now."

"The only one who lives in?"

"Yes. The other servants go to their own homes at night. After the earthquake, it was one of Miss Weber's requests, and as she was doing so much, I was happy to oblige."

I hesitated before finally confiding in him. "I find that rather odd."

Harry's eyebrows shot up. "What exactly do you find odd?"

I hesitated. The corners of his mouth were twitching; it was the first frown he'd given me since before our wedding vows. I made a resolution to tread very carefully.

"Merely that . . . well . . . no other servants sleep in the mansion?"

"Miss Weber is the only one."

"Typically, houses of this size keep more servants living in, no?"

"I suppose," Harry admitted. "Are you worried your needs won't be attended to properly? I assure you, that won't be the case. During the day, there is plenty of help on hand. And besides, Miss Weber is a magician at anticipating my every need. I'm sure she will do the same for you."

I blushed.

"No—I wasn't worried about that," I said. "I'm not accustomed to having my needs attended to at all, if I'm perfectly honest."

"No, I don't suppose you would be," Harry agreed. His voice had grown distant. I cringed to hear the chill in it.

"Harry," I said, in a softer tone, "you've told me many times how grateful you are to Miss Weber for helping you to rebuild your home. But . . . *why* remake it exactly as it was before? It doesn't make sense. I should think you might want something more modern, something . . . *different*." I hesitated, gathering my courage. "And then . . . there's the portrait . . ."

I halted. Harry had grown absolutely silent. His face had darkened. He was quiet for several minutes. Inside, I squirmed. When he finally broke the silence, he confirmed my fears.

"The painting is a portrait of Madeleine, if that's what you're asking. Miss Weber insisted on a reproduction of the original, hung where it had always been. She . . . has her reasons. I've obliged her in this."

"Miss Weber insisted?" I repeated, baffled.

"Violet . . . I know it's unorthodox, and this detail must be strange for you. Please do your best to tolerate it for now. I asked you once, Violet, not to bring up my life before the earthquake, and I ask you now to honor your promise. If for any reason you feel like your needs here are not being met, you've only to let me know."

With that, he turned on his heel and strode in the direction of the master bedroom—the bedroom that we were now to share for the rest of our lives. Left alone, I wandered back to the landing and gazed again upon the portrait, uneasy.

28

t is a well-known old saw: If the painter is competent and has done his job properly, the portrait's eyes should follow you. Unfortunately for me, Madeleine's portrait had been executed with impressive skill. Those dark brown eyes—so dark they were almost black, really—followed me whenever I traversed the room, no matter which stairway I elected to climb. I was all too aware that they were beautiful eyes, heavily fringed with dark lashes. And then there was her expression: sometimes coquettish, sometimes reticent, but always—always—full of mockery.

I was determined to ignore this unexpected houseguest, but this proved no simple task. There was something deeply disconcerting about the portrait. I still couldn't understand: *Why was it here?*

I could not help but notice that Madeleine bore more than a passing likeness to the woman who had caught Harry's attention in Alamo Square. He'd gone white as a sheet when he laid eyes on that woman;

perhaps he'd believed it actually *was* Madeleine, returned from Italy? He'd promised me she would never return.

I began to wonder, though . . . How could Harry be so absolutely *certain*? What if Madeleine *did* return? Within days of moving into Harry's mansion, this possibility began to obsess me. It was my own fault: I had agreed to strike a most curious deal in my marriage. If Madeleine returned, it wouldn't even be considered a marriage: it would be instantly demoted to a tawdry, adulterous affair.

Once my fixation had taken root, the mansion that had been rebuilt to resemble its original, brick for brick, began to give off the impression that it was *waiting* for something. *Could it be?* I wondered. *Could this house be waiting for its mistress to come home?* Did Harry perhaps—even in some small way—secretly wish for Madeleine to return to him? He had confessed how deeply she'd wounded him; a man didn't feel that much agony unless he had also felt deep love, too.

Besides the woman in Alamo Square, the portrait also bore a faint, curious resemblance to Miss Weber. They differed in beauty, of course: Miss Weber was old and gray—prematurely so, in fact—whereas Madeleine was sensuous and beautiful, with hair like a glossy raven's wing. And yet . . . it was as if Miss Weber might have been a distant relation. I nearly plucked up the courage to ask, but Miss Weber continued to make it clear that she did not care for me. She was coldly mute; as I attempted to settle in, it was as though she made a concerted effort to speak as few words to me as possible.

Even so, the first week in the mansion was pleasant, for I had Harry as my constant companion. We slept late and began our mornings in the library, drinking milky tea and reading books—sometimes aloud to each other. In the afternoons, he took me to call on various friends, who greeted us with sherry and more tea, and sometimes even the amusement of parlor games.

But by the second week, Harry was obligated to attend to his work once more, and this meant that he was gone for a good portion of the day. We took our breakfast in the formal dining room, early in the morning, and afterwards, he trekked down to his dockside office, where he oversaw the import and export of his logging operations up north. Once he left, it was as if the whole day stretched long before me, and I was at pains to fill it.

"Perhaps you might like to call upon some of the people I introduced you to," Harry suggested.

I shook my head. I'd made one attempt to call upon Milly Abbott—just as Harry had originally advised—and the result had been disastrous. When her maid spilled tea everywhere, I had sprung into action, hoping to help clean it up. Milly made her disapproval plain.

"You could take up the running of the house," Harry said, "but you certainly don't have to. Presently, Miss Weber sees to it all, and I don't think she would mind either way."

"I would like to help," I said. "It would be nice to feel useful."

Harry was correct that Miss Weber reigned over the affairs of the mansion. But he was wrong when he supposed she wouldn't mind my involvement. In fact, shortly after that conversation with Harry, Miss Weber and I began to play an unspoken game of tug-of-war.

It began when I saw a desk I admired in one of the guest rooms, and ordered it to be moved to the library, where I might make use of it as my personal desk. I reasoned that a good desk would help me in my efforts to oversee the management of the household. When I approached Mr. Davies, he received my request with an air of cool obliging. The desk was made from a beautiful, very solid single piece of deep-red mahogany that proved to be quite heavy. Mr. Davies arranged for two of the younger, more muscular gardeners to move it, carrying it down a flight of stairs. Once it was nestled into the little bay of beautiful leaded-glass windows in the library, I cheerfully set about filling it with brand-new stationery: a diary, embossed letterhead and cards, and several lovely fountain pens. I went to bed that night excited to rise the next morning and sit down to my happy little workstation.

I woke up the next morning, dressed, and joined Harry for breakfast, making the most of our time together before he left for his office. Once he had departed, I made my way to the library, intending to spend a couple of hours at my desk looking over the various household accounts. When I walked in, however, I froze. The desk was gone. Everything had been moved back to the way it had been before. There was no sign at all that the desk had ever graced the room.

I scratched my head, confused.

Eventually, I made my way upstairs to the guest room where the desk had previously resided. And there it was! I could hardly believe my eyes. It had resumed its original position so seamlessly, I began to wonder if my efforts to move it and set it up had all been a vivid dream. But . . . *no*. I knew in my bones that it had not been a dream. I went in search of Mr. Davies.

"The gardeners returned the desk to the guest room," Mr. Davies informed me, his voice flat with disinterest. "As ordered, ma'am."

I was baffled.

"*Whose* orders?" I demanded.

He blinked at me, confused, and faintly annoyed.

"Why, yours, of course," he answered. "Miss Weber came to relay the order. Said the mistress of the house wanted it returned to its proper place."

I shook my head. "I wanted no such thing."

I turned and left Mr. Davies alone. I felt my cheeks growing warm with a flood of emotion—emotion I couldn't quite put a name to. Why had Miss Weber ordered the desk to be moved back, and why in my name?

And then, all at once, it hit me: Miss Weber had not ordered it returned in *my* name.

Mr. Davies had said only that she'd relayed to him that "the mistress of the house" had wanted it moved back.

I found Miss Weber in the kitchen, overseeing the grocery delivery. When she saw me, her pinched face tightened further, and I knew I had guessed correctly.

"Miss Weber," I said. "I had a desk moved from upstairs into the library yesterday. Mr. Davies tells me you ordered him to move it back."

She looked at me with a stern, blank expression and issued no apology.

"Why did you do that?" I prompted, when she refused to reply.

She continued to stare at me wordlessly, and I grew uncomfortably hot. If she was going to be stubborn about this, so was I, I decided. We were at a stalemate.

Finally, Miss Weber gave a little shrug of her shoulders—almost as though to suggest she couldn't be bothered to care about such trifles.

"I was simply restoring things to order," she said. "That is where the desk has always belonged."

"Well, I thank you for that, Miss Weber, but I wanted it in the library so I might use it if I'm to take over the household accounts."

Before she could help herself, Miss Weber gave a little snort. The sound of it left me feeling stung. Angry, I frowned at her, and her prissy scowl vanished. She seemed to sense she had gone too far.

"Yes, ma'am," she said in a neutral voice. But she made no move to see about relocating the desk. I cleared my throat and tried a new tack.

"Mr. Davies mentioned you'd said that 'the mistress of the house' wanted it returned to its proper place."

"Yes, ma'am," Miss Weber said.

"Why did you say that to him?" I demanded.

She looked at me blankly.

"Why did you say that to him?" I repeated.

"Because that's where *she* always kept it," Miss Weber finally answered.

Without a further word, Miss Weber turned on her heel and left the room.

I was shocked by Miss Weber's behavior, but there was nothing to be done. Harry deeply valued her and I had no desire to upset him so soon after moving in.

It bothered me, however. It bothered me that, when Miss Weber said, *That's where* she *always kept it*, I knew exactly who the "she" in question was.

Miss Weber's loyalty to Madeleine puzzled me. Harry and Madeleine had suffered through a terrible marriage. Madeleine had wounded Harry and ultimately jilted him, and it seemed to me that Miss Weber owed her greater loyalty to Harry. Why, then, was Miss Weber so devoted to Madeleine? And why did Harry not only allow it, but cater to it?

What a curious and uncomfortable arrangement I'd unwittingly gotten myself into! What was it going to be like, constantly doing battle with Miss Weber over things like the simple rearranging of a desk? I wondered if I'd made the right decision in rushing into a marriage with Harry. But as soon as these doubts came to me, I shook them off. No. I loved Harry. And he loved me.

I found Mr. Davies and asked him to once again move the desk to the library. He gave me a look of pure annoyance but politely agreed.

"The gardeners will be here in two hours' time," Mr. Davies informed me. "I shall have it done then."

I thanked him. Feeling a bit at loose ends, I wandered upstairs to where the desk waited. It was a pleasant enough room, with lavender-colored wallpaper and an enormous four-poster bed. I crossed to where the desk nestled next to a wardrobe, pulled out the chair, and sat down.

After a moment, I opened the desk drawer, expecting to see all the items I had so carefully arranged the day prior—the fountain pens, the special embossed stationery—but the drawer was empty. I wondered where the items could have gone. Slowly, I leaned to one side and peered down into an ornate, tin-stamped wastebasket on the floor to the left.

There they all were: all of the lovely accessories I'd purchased. And, very likely according to Miss Weber, they had been "returned to their correct order."

I felt my cheeks grow hot with anger once more.

29

I regularly received the silent treatment from Miss Weber, until one day . . . I didn't. It was as if her stubborn silences had melted away in the night, like snow washed away by a warm rain. However—and unfortunately for me—they were replaced by a sort of constant idle monologue that centered only upon one subject: Madeleine Carlyle.

Miss Weber was not so much talking *to* me as *at* me. She could not have cared less whether or not I responded; the only thing that piqued her interest were questions about Madeleine—which, of course, she was happy to answer. She could go on and on, in that flat droning voice of hers, rhapsodizing about Madeleine's way of doing *anything*.

I suppose it was very clever, in a way—a tactic aimed at keeping me in my place, which, in her opinion, was *not* as the lady of the house. According to Miss Weber, Madeleine had been an exquisite host, a connoisseur of fine cuisine, an expert on cordials and brandies, an accomplished linguist, a gifted musician, a talented seamstress . . . and so many other things that I lost track—possibly on purpose. It was truly infuriating. Even when I wasn't in the same room, Miss Weber's comments echoed in my head like taunts.

It got so that Miss Weber did not have to say Madeleine's name; she would simply begin and end sentences with "*she*," and I was meant to understand.

Given all this, Madeleine was never very far from my mind. I had promised Harry I would not ask questions, yet secretly, I found myself eager to collect every scrap of information I could. I began a little ledger, writing down all the facts about Madeleine that Miss Weber let slip. Soon I was hungry for more; I began to hunt down old newspapers and clip any mention of Madeleine Carlyle from the society pages. I kept this project concealed from Harry, of course.

It dawned on me one day that perhaps Miss Weber was planting a sort of bait to precipitate my failure. If Harry ever caught me nosing around in Madeleine's past, I would lose his trust. Could Miss Weber be so conniving? Was I being played for a fool?

I was unsettled. I badly needed to talk to another person, someone outside of my new home.

There were only two people on the planet I'd ever confided in, but this time I did not want to consult Cora and Flossie. Cora's vehement opinions about Harry's marriage to Madeleine—and how it ended— were still prickly in my memory. It wasn't easy to think of someone else I could talk to.

I closed my eyes, and the obvious answer dawned on me.

Henrietta threw her arms in the air the second I poked my head shyly through the greengrocery doorway.

"Violet!" she hollered at me. "I was just thinking o' ya, and here ya are!"

She was seated in her usual spot, minding the till. A handful of customers milled about.

"Come over here and let me hug ya!"

I grinned and crossed the shop, aware of the customers' eyes on me. They were regulars, I presumed, for they seemed familiar with Henrietta's loud antics.

After a moment, Henrietta released me.

"What is it?" she asked.

"I . . . well, I have news," I said. "Rather a lot of news, to tell the truth."

"Any of it good news?"

"Some of it."

"Hmm. I suppose we'll be needin' a tipple of whiskey, one way or another," Henrietta replied.

I smiled, grateful.

Just as she had on my previous visit, Henrietta called her handsome young husband to take over the till and we proceeded upstairs.

I was glad to see her cozy apartment again. Its warm, muggy air and cheery atmosphere welcomed me. Henrietta gestured to a fluffy armchair and once again poured two teacups to the brim with whiskey.

"I oughter be direct with you," Henrietta announced, catching me off guard. "I might know some of yer news already. Cora came to see me the other day. Of all people!"

"Cora?" I said, freshly alert.

"I was as surprised as you," Henrietta said. "Never thought she cared enough to track me down. But she did, and we actually had a hell of a time drinkin' and gossipin'!"

Henrietta paused and looked at me with an apologetic expression, then added, "While she was here, she told me you've a highfalutin beau now—that you went and got yerself hitched. I hope I ain't takin' the wind outta yer sails none to tell ya I already know. Congratulations to ya!"

"Thank you." The words issued automatically from my lips, but I was already lost in thought, mulling over the implications of Cora's visit. Had she sought Henrietta out just to gossip about my marriage? What else might she have mentioned? And why? My head was spinning.

"Did Cora . . . say anything about Harry, specifically?"

Henrietta sighed. "I think she mighta been worried for ya. She told me he's a widower, and, well, that she had a few doubts about how he ended up that way."

I stared at Henrietta, unsurprised and yet mildly horrified.

"She said he'd told you some tall tale about how his wife had run off on him in secret, but that she didn't believe it." She searched my face cautiously. Henrietta could be crude, but she was a sensitive soul, and never wished to hurt anyone. I could feel she was treading carefully now.

"Cora is . . . *Cora*," I said, frowning. "There's another side to it."

"Of course, dearie," Henrietta cooed, sensing my agitation. She reached over and patted my hand. "Of course. How's about I give us both another tipple?"

She refilled our teacups. I took a sip and felt the warmth spread throughout my chest. I began to tell her in detail how I had met and married Harry, how Cora had hurt my feelings by repeating the rumors she'd heard, and how—if I was being brutally honest—I thought Cora was very likely jealous.

"I hate to say it, but I think Cora might be happy to see my marriage fail."

"I'm surprised to hear ya goin' on like this, Violet—you always trusted Cora before. Sometimes . . . well, sometimes I thought of it as yer weakness."

I tipped my chin up defiantly. "Cora's trying to make me hysterical over nothing, though! I have no reason to believe that Madeleine Carlyle didn't simply walk out the front door," I insisted.

I waited for Henrietta to agree with me, but she was silent. I prodded her.

"What is it, Henrietta?"

"It's only that . . . well, I think you've got that part backwards, dearie. You say you have no reason to believe she didn't simply walk out the front door. But if you ask me, you have no reason to believe she *did.*"

A chill ran down my spine.

"You mean, you think . . . Madeleine Carlyle didn't run off to Italy?" I asked, stunned.

Henrietta shrugged apologetically.

"Honest, Violet—I'm just repeatin' what I'm hearing *you* say. It sounds to me like it ain't all Cora; you have doubts yerself. If Madeleine Carlyle was as fancy and as brash as everyone is makin' her out to be, then it don't seem like she would be able to remain offstage for long—not even if she was clear all the way in Europe. The gossips and the newspapers woulda caught wind o' her by now, and they woulda been scandalized to think Harry was lyin' about her death."

I was shocked to realize that Henrietta was right. These were *my* doubts—doubts I didn't want to have, but couldn't completely ignore.

I switched tack and started telling Henrietta about Miss Weber. I told her about the little battles we'd been waging against each other, starting with the incident of the desk.

"Miss Weber's probably the strangest piece of this whole puzzle . . . It's as if she's expecting Madeleine to return someday and she's intent on keeping the mansion exactly as Madeleine left it," I explained.

"Hmm." Henrietta pondered. "That's an awful funny way to behave."

"Surely that suggests that Madeleine is still alive?"

"And might someday return—don't think ye would want that to happen either," Henrietta pointed out.

"No . . . I don't suppose I would," I agreed. "But it would put these other questions to rest."

Henrietta's eyes snapped to my face, twinkling with a new idea.

"Maybe there are ways for you to get some answers!"

"What do you mean?"

"Is there a grave? If there is a grave, surely the coroner collected a body. Ain't that the way it works? If Madeleine Carlyle is off gallivanting around Europe, then what did they put in the ground the day they buried her?"

What a macabre conversation we were having now! I shuddered, picturing this imaginary grave, this imaginary funeral. How had I never wondered about this? When Harry told me that he'd "had Madeleine declared dead," I imagined a very bureaucratic act had taken place, and that was all. But now I had to wonder: How far had Harry gone to convince people of Madeleine's death?

And even worse: *What if she* had *died the night of the earthquake?*

"I reckon there's an official record on file somewhere," Henrietta said.

I imagined going to the city morgue and gleaning what information I could. But then, I imagined Harry finding out that I had done as much.

"Are ya cold, dear?" Henrietta asked.

"No, why?"

"You shivered."

I mulled over everything Henrietta had said, long after I bid her farewell and walked home.

That night, as I brushed my hair before the vanity and Harry dressed for bed, I studied him in the mirror, suddenly aware of how little we knew about each other.

He caught me watching him as he unbuttoned his well-tailored dress shirt and I immediately turned away, blushing. To my surprise, Harry chuckled.

"I suppose I'm not as fair a sight as you," he said, reaching for his silk pajamas. "I promise you, I was much more handsome as a lad—it's a pity you didn't know me then!"

I've found that, more often than not, the people who make these kinds of derogatory remarks about themselves are the ones who can take comfort in the utter sanctuary of knowing it is absolutely untrue. Harry was quite attractive for a man of any age—so much so, that the society pages frequently commented on his "devilish good looks." I was embarrassed to admit, even while pondering the dark secrets he might be keeping, I was admiring his form—in particular, his broad torso. He had the body of an older man, but one of robust, athletic physicality. Time had worn lines into his face, especially around his eyes, but these, too, had a becoming effect, giving him the aura of a deep, knowing kindness. His gaze held an alertness that was almost unsettling; it was thrilling to be looked at by such a man. I even loved the silver that threaded his hair, glittering in the light like the actual precious metal itself.

He came over behind me now and gazed over my shoulder, studying my reflection in the mirror.

"You may be onto something," he said. "I'm afraid the view from my vantage is far superior to the view from yours."

His lips twisted into a charmingly roguish smile.

"Surely you aren't fishing for a compliment," I teased.

"You've caught me out," he replied. "I am guilty."

He paused and ran his fingers up the back of my neck as though admiring it. His touch sent a pleasurable shiver down my spine. He craned his neck and kissed me.

"To be perfectly frank, though, Violet, the highest compliment you can give me is your love. I'm moved every time I look at you, and I cannot know what I did to find myself so lucky."

He drew me to him, and we moved to our marital bed.

30

Shortly after my visit to Henrietta's, things began happening around the mansion that I couldn't explain—eerie things.

It began when I awoke with a stomachache very late one night, in the hours before morning. My stomach was full of fire, it seemed, and—not wanting to wake Harry—I made up my mind to see what I might find in the kitchen to soothe it. Peppermint tea, I thought, or perhaps some boiled ginger might do the trick.

All was dark as I crept downstairs, and I carried a small oil lamp with me to light the way. The mansion had been wired for electricity, but only in a limited fashion. I knew that pushing one of the buttons poised and waiting on any of the switches would have filled the cavernous rooms with a blast of cool yellow, but I much preferred the enchanted glow of my oil lamp. In my dressing gown and slippers, I padded my way through the maze of hallways that led to the kitchen.

Once there, I found a second oil lamp and lit that, too. I dialed the second lamp up to its brightest illumination and placed it on the table in the middle of the room, then took the first lamp into the pantry to rummage around the shelves.

It was while I was deep in the pantry that I heard a curious noise. It sounded like a door swinging open on creaking hinges. I froze, and held my breath. Only two people besides myself slept overnight in the mansion: Harry and Miss Weber. I worried I had disturbed one of them. I waited, listening . . . and after a moment, I heard what sounded like a soft footfall. It was too light to be Harry. It was drawing nearer to the pantry. My heart fluttered: Was I afraid of Miss Weber? I suppose I was a little. I knew I would have to apologize profusely for having woken her, and even though she would be obligated to accept this apology, Miss Weber would nonetheless make it clear that she thought me a rube.

The steps were drawing nearer and nearer; now they were almost to the pantry doorway. I swallowed, and gathered my courage. But just as I was about to call out "Miss Weber?" the door to the pantry swung shut in my face with a violent *CRACK!*

I jumped back, my heart racing, and stared at the closed door. Had someone meant to shut me in here? My oil lamp was still burning, but it felt too bright now. I wished to open the door, but I didn't want whatever was beyond to see *me* before I saw *it*. I hesitated for a brief moment, too frightened to do anything at all. Eventually, I dialed the gas lamp down to its lowest setting and reached with a trembling hand for the doorknob.

It didn't turn.

Panicked, I began to wrench the knob in one direction and then the other. Finally, I felt a click, and the pantry door sprang open. I gulped down a breath of relief and poked my head cautiously into the kitchen.

All was dark. The air was thick with the scent of paraffin, and I realized that the lamp must have fallen from the kitchen table and was dashed to pieces on the marble-tiled floor. Or . . . had it been knocked over on purpose? I felt certain that the pantry door had been slammed shut by a human hand. My eyes searched the room by the light of the remaining lamp clutched tightly in my grip. I found the other smashed on the tile, a puddle of glistening oil pooling around it. But there was no sign of another person . . . or even that anyone had recently been in the room. I moved slowly around, taking care not to step in glass or oil. When I had skirted the periphery of the kitchen and drawn up to the hinged door to the dining room, I put my hand out for the light switch. The electric fixtures clicked on, flooding the room with their artificial light.

Once my eyes adjusted, they fell immediately upon the door that led out to the kitchen garden. It was just slightly but noticeably ajar. Did this account for the creaking hinges I'd heard? A cool night breeze was whistling through the open crack, causing the door to yawn open and shut like a wave lapping at the shore. Had a draft caused the pantry door to slam and also caused the lamp to tumble off the table?

But why was the door to the kitchen garden open in the first place? This door was meant to be shut, the bolt across it drawn tight. Could Miss Weber have overlooked it? I moved to close it . . . but just before I pushed it all the way shut, I stopped and drew the door open again. I poked my head out into the chilly night air. My cheeks tensed on feeling the icy wind, and I could smell a hint of sea salt in the air. I was still holding the oil lamp, and I lifted it above my head to survey the garden.

I am not certain what I expected to see. My senses were all heightened. But there was no one. The garden was surrounded on all sides by topiary hedges, and the light from my lamp glimmered upon neatly trimmed leaves, revealing nothing save for a few tomato vines, row upon endless row of root vegetables, and several overgrown herb bushes.

No intruder, I thought, with a sigh of relief. *Or, if there was an intruder, he has run off.*

I had just begun to breathe more easily, when my eyes caught upon a bright flickering through the leaves. I turned down my own lamp to take a better look. To my surprise, light was indeed coming from another source. Someone *else* was carrying a lamp, or possibly a candle, just on the other side of the hedges.

I have always considered myself a coward, so I cannot explain why I did what I did next. Reason compelled me to retreat behind the kitchen door, to close it and bolt it, and perhaps even sound the alarm. But I did not do this.

Instead, I stared at the dimly flickering light for several seconds, barely breathing or thinking.

Then, as if animated by some other, outside force, I stepped towards the topiary maze. It was a narrow winding passageway bounded by hedges that I knew would lead me into the rose garden. I turned the dial of the gas lamp in my hand all the way down. This was a gamble: There would be no relighting it quickly now that it was off. But I didn't want whoever was out there to see me coming. I could feel my heart pumping madly, sending blood through my veins so fiercely that I could hear and feel the whoosh of it in my ears.

That rose garden, of course, had always been *Madeleine's*.

The rosebushes had survived the earthquake, and then—more miraculously, perhaps—survived the mansion's razing and rebuilding. I had visited the rose garden on only two or three occasions, and though it was quite lovely and boasted prize-winning roses, I had always felt distinctly unwelcome there. Now I paced silently along the pebbled path that wound back and forth in the dark green topiary, rocking each of my footsteps gently into place in the gravel. The ground instantly chilled my feet through my thin slippers.

I rounded one turn, then another, and finally, I reached an opening between the hedge walls. I turned, emerging into the clearing beyond. The Carlyle mansion was positioned upon a hill, and from the rose garden during the day, one could see all the way to where the Bay met the Pacific. With no moon out, I could still distinctly feel where the ocean surged. The sea had become a vacuous swath of inky blackness. I felt the immensity of the night all around me.

The rosebushes were arranged in concentric circles, with two foot-paths passing through them to mark the four cardinal directions. In the center was a marble pedestal about the size of a small table, inlaid with a large brass compass medallion. I had never paid much mind to this monument, but now it caught my eye. Upon the center of the pedestal, a single candle flickered—the light I had glimpsed through the hedges. The sight of it raised the hairs on the back of my neck. Who had placed it there? I looked around and saw no one. The ground was soft with dew, but I could not make out any trace of footprints. What's more, the night carried with it an ocean breeze—as was almost always the case in San Francisco—and yet, though the candle flickered and guttered, it managed to stay lit . . . as though the flame were supernatural.

I froze, waiting to see if anything else might manifest, or if the candle might surrender to the wind. But no one appeared, and the candle flickered on. All at once, I felt an urgent desire to run back to the house. The panic that had gripped me while I was enclosed in the pantry returned, cresting over my head and crashing down like a wave. My feet were in motion before I truly understood what I was doing. I raced through the topiary maze in reverse, stumbled back through the kitchen garden, and darted back inside the mansion.

"*Harry! Harry!*" I heard myself scream as I half-ran, half-stumbled up the stairs. By that time I was running in the dark. I was liable to trip and knock my teeth out, but I didn't care. When I finally arrived at the door of our bedroom, I wrenched it open and burst into the room.

Already, Harry had switched on the electric lamp on his nightstand and was rubbing the sleep from his eyes.

"Violet!" he exclaimed. "What has gotten into you?"

His voice was chastising, but his touch was gentle as he helped me over to the bed and crouched next to me.

"Take a breath," he instructed, "and tell me what is the matter."

I did as he advised, and once I had regained a modicum of composure, I began to explain about the kitchen, the pantry, the open door to the garden. When I got to the lone candle burning in the rose garden, he frowned.

"And you say this candle was simply left there to burn? With no one to mind it? It's still there now?"

"Yes," I said, relieved to see that the image troubled him as well. "I don't think it's causing any harm, and yet, at the same time . . . there is something terrible about it. Almost like . . . well, almost like someone put it there as a kind of shrine," I finished.

The frown on Harry's face twisted deeper, as though someone had prodded him with a fireplace poker.

"Hmm," he said. "Show me, then; I'd better see to it."

He retrieved the oil lamp that sat on the fireplace mantel in our bedroom and took my hand in his. Together we retraced my steps. With Harry's hand gripping my own, I found I was not afraid.

However, when we reached the kitchen, I felt the hairs on the back of my neck stand on end yet again. The electric lights that I had turned on—and *left* on—were now switched off.

"How . . . how can it be?" I stammered.

Harry turned to look at me. "What is it, my dear?"

I told him—I'd left the lights on. I'd raced upstairs to find him so quickly, I hadn't had time to switch them off, nor had I wanted to.

"Someone else must've been here!" I said in a hushed voice.

"Hmm" was all he replied, reaching out to press the switch. The lights snapped on.

I gasped. It wasn't that anything was amiss; it was, in fact, that *nothing* was amiss. The shattered oil lamp was gone. Whoever had cleaned it up had done an immaculate job, leaving not a single trace. It seemed impossible. I deliberated as to whether I should tell Harry about this part. It might give Harry reason to doubt me.

As it was, Harry seemed to be studying my reactions closely. I turned to see him looking at me with a very odd expression. His annoyance at having been woken up in the middle of the night had vanished. Now he was frowning with concern.

"And you say the door to the garden was ajar?" he asked.

I thought the answer was obvious until I saw that the door was, in fact, bolted shut.

"Are you certain? It looks as though it's been locked all night, Violet," Harry said.

"No," I insisted. "It can't be. No! It might be shut now, but it *was* open. I never would have set foot in the gardens, except for the fact that door was open."

"Well, there's nothing now but to see for ourselves . . ." Harry mumbled as he fussed with the door. The bolt was stiff; he had to wrestle with it to ease it open—which only cast further doubt on my already shadowy claims. It was also quite noisy, the metal shrieking as Harry seesawed it from the latch. Once he had drawn it back, he turned the knob and swung the door open.

"Follow if you must, but stay behind me," he whispered over his shoulder.

I was grateful he still believed an intruder might be lurking just outside. He stepped into the night air and I followed. Holding the oil lamp aloft, he made his way to the rose garden. My stomach sunk with every step, for before we had even made the last turn through the hedges, I could already plainly see: the candle was gone.

I stood off to one side as Harry paced in a careful loop, holding the oil lamp low to the ground to search for footprints in the mud. After a thorough inspection, he heaved a weary sigh and turned to me.

"Violet . . . are you certain you weren't merely dreaming?"

I recoiled and shook my head.

"But . . . you *heard* me. It was my shrieks on the stairs that roused you from sleep. It's not as if I never left my bed!"

"True," Harry replied, as though weighing his doubts. "But . . . is it possible that you may have been sleepwalking? It's a rare affliction, but not unheard-of."

I looked at him, appalled. He did not believe any of the things I had told him about: the unbolted door, the candle . . . But as I thought them over, I began to doubt my own mind. I hadn't yet mustered the nerve to tell Harry about my spells, and now I began to sweat, wondering if I hadn't just accidentally allowed him to witness one.

And yet . . . I *knew* the feeling of having had a spell, even if I didn't always recall my actions. I'd felt none of my usual sensations that evening. I hadn't grown short of breath or clammy; I hadn't seen black spots in my vision; there was no sense of lost time, no frustrating blank space in my memory. This had been nothing like that.

Harry led me back inside the house, whereupon he bolted the door. He gave the knob a firm tug as though to demonstrate that it was securely sealed.

"If it will make you feel better, in the morning I'll ask Miss Weber about this door . . ." He hesitated, then added, "And about the candle, too, if you think it wise."

"No!" I said, just a little too quickly. "I mean—no, thank you," I corrected myself. "I'll talk to Miss Weber myself."

"All right," Harry agreed. It was plain he was relieved to let the matter drop. "Let's return to bed, my darling." He urged me back in the direction of the stairs. "I am tired, and I'm sure you are as well. We could both use a good night's sleep. If you are still troubled by any of this in the morning, I will help you to seek a resolution."

It was a gallant offer, considering the doubts written on his face. I knew he had quietly accepted his own explanation: that I'd had a nightmare and gone sleepwalking. Perhaps, if I told him about my spells, he wouldn't be shocked or disgusted. But I knew that if I told him about my spells, I might have to tell him more about my past— about St. Hilda's, and, worse . . . about Tackett and Blanche.

Reluctantly, I followed him back to our room, and we tucked ourselves in under the heavy down quilt that graced our marital bed. The thick bedding still held some warm remnant of our body heat from more than a quarter of an hour before. And yet, huddle as I might, I couldn't quite shake off the chill I'd acquired when I stood in the rose garden, staring at that candle.

31

O ver the next few days, I slept very little. Instead, I lay awake in bed, straining to hear all the stirring sounds of the mansion. I could feel the muscles in my eyelids rigidly tensed; I could not have forced them shut if I'd wished.

It wasn't as if I expected dusk to bring pure silence. I understood that all houses, large and small, are given to a symphony of little noises in the night. Each house is a living, breathing creature in its own right, and makes the sighs and grumblings and groanings that are only natural to its animal state. *That's just the house's bones settling,* say some. There is something of bones, to be sure, but also of a kind of digestion—as though it were possible that a house might need to work through the events of the day like a heavy meal.

And so, in the weeks that followed my midnight misadventure in the rose garden, I listened to the taps and the creaks and the groans of my new home, memorizing them as best I could. But I was also listening for something more: I was listening for evidence of a *human rustling*.

I became convinced that some of the sounds I was hearing—a distinct footfall, for instance, that moved through the hallways—could not be chalked up to the usual milieu of nocturnal sounds.

"Are you absolutely certain that Miss Weber is the only servant who spends the night on the premises?" I asked Harry one day.

He looked at me with a surprised frown.

"Of course," he replied. "Why do you ask?"

I dithered.

"You aren't still upset by that nightmare, are you?" he asked. "I know your sleep has been troubled as of late, my pet."

"Troubled?" I asked, surprised. As far as I knew, it was only I who lay awake at night.

"Yes—I'd say so," Harry insisted. "You've been mumbling in your sleep . . . thrashing about. You rarely wake in full, but it is clear you are far from being at peace. It is all I can do sometimes to hold you and soothe you."

I looked at him, incredulous. It didn't seem possible. I couldn't remember sleeping very much in recent days, and I couldn't recall any nightmares. I had grown accustomed to watching over the house while listening to Harry snore; it baffled me to imagine our roles reversed.

I was certain that he was wrong. Or at least that he was exaggerating or else misinterpreting. But between the two of us, I let the matter go.

I did, however, wish to confront Miss Weber. The trick was how to approach her. I did not want her to feel that I was accusing her of anything, but at the same time, I hoped to catch her off guard. If I could only get a glimpse of her reaction, I might better know if she had anything to do with the noises I'd been hearing.

"Miss Weber," I said one afternoon, while she was polishing the silver, "I was wondering if I might ask about something . . ."

Two beady blue eyes found my face, and Miss Weber arched an eyebrow in a mixture of inquiry and skepticism. "Yes?"

"Well . . . I know you keep the tapers for the dining room here, but I was wondering where you keep the others?"

"Others?" She frowned.

"Yes, other candles," I said. "Like the one I found burning the other night in the rose garden. It was thicker than a taper and a bit more squat. Where do you keep *those* candles?"

To my surprise, Miss Weber froze, and her already gray complexion paled and turned waxen.

"Did you say you found a candle *burning in the rose garden*?" she demanded with a slight gasp.

Her lips trembled. I had expected a reaction, but nothing so severe as this. I felt a chill down my spine.

"After dark? In . . . *Mrs. Carlyle's* rose garden?" Miss Weber repeated, her eyes wide.

"Yes," I said matter-of-factly. I did not correct her misapplication of the name "Mrs. Carlyle."

But Miss Weber seemed unable to find proper words. Her mouth opened and closed in a series of flustered motions.

"Oh . . . !"

"Miss Weber!" I said, half-chastising, half-concerned. "What has gotten into you?"

I had never once spoken to Miss Weber in such a tone. Despite our roles as mistress and servant, I was often more like a schoolgirl, and she a schoolmarm. But Miss Weber did not appear to notice my rudeness. Instead, she very abruptly reached out and clamped my arm in her iron grip.

I winced.

"Please!" Miss Weber said. "You cannot know what it is you saw. You would do well to be cautious!"

She was gripping me tightly enough to make her own hand tremble, and my arm began to hurt. Finally, I allowed a passive "*Ow!*" to escape my lips, and, upon hearing it, Miss Weber immediately released me. She closed her eyes and shook her head emphatically, then composed herself once more.

"I'm sorry, ma'am," she said. "Please forgive me."

I rubbed my arm, frowning in confusion. Her theatrics had left me discombobulated.

"If I take your meaning correctly, you know about the candle. Are you the one who placed it in the rose garden?" I asked. "Is it some sort of . . . memorial token?"

But Miss Weber wouldn't answer. She only looked at me, her lips pressed in a flat line. I tried a different tack.

"You are the only member of the household staff who resides on the premises, Miss Weber," I said. "At night, you are the only other person here besides Mr. Carlyle and myself—isn't that so?"

She looked at me warily, but gave a stiff nod. I pressed further.

"I'm awfully surprised by the hours you keep," I said.

"Hours?"

"Yes. I've been hearing someone walking around—quite late; sometimes just before dawn. I must assume it is you."

"No, ma'am," Miss Weber said. "That would not be me."

I frowned. "Are you certain?"

"I promise you, ma'am, I go to bed at quarter to nine every night, and I never stir."

I gave her a sideways glance. "But you recognized my story about finding the candle in the rose garden—how could you know, if you're never up and about after hours?"

A shadow fell over Miss Weber's face.

"The other servants," she answered.

"The other servants?"

"When they all lived in, ma'am. They reported seeing things . . . strange occurrences, like what you mentioned. Some of the maids became downright hysterical. They were constantly gossiping. I thought their hysterics might upset Mr. Carlyle. Some had to be dismissed."

A slow comprehension seeped in.

"*That's* why you insisted on being the only servant to live in-house?"

"Indeed, ma'am," Miss Weber said.

I thought back to the night I'd seen the candle burning, and the deep frown on Harry's face. I had to admit . . . he had looked relieved when we didn't find anything out of place downstairs, and almost happy to chalk my story up to a bad dream.

"It has been difficult for him, living here . . . with *her* gone," Miss Weber said. "He remade the house exactly as it was, down to every detail. He can't seem to let her go. If he'd ever known about the strange sightings that the other servants reported . . . well, it might drive him mad . . . mad enough to believe she *isn't* gone after all . . ."

"What do you mean?"

Miss Weber looked oddly helpless.

"Only that . . ." she began, but hesitated. "Only that I do believe he lives in a state of constant terror that she may someday come back—which, of course, isn't possible. But they say fear knows no logic."

"Yes, it would be very bad for him if she *did* come back," I said, half to myself.

Miss Weber was staring at me oddly.

"Ma'am?" Miss Weber said. "Are you feeling quite all right?"

"I am—why?"

Miss Weber shook her head in an embarrassed way. "It's only that it's a very odd thing to say. I can't pretend I know what you mean."

She hesitated, then continued.

"I know that the night the earthquake struck was . . . very difficult for him, and I do not believe he was to blame for what happened."

"Not to blame for what happened?—Miss Weber, what exactly *did* happen? Were you present that night?"

Miss Weber only pressed her lips together and shook her head, refusing to answer this.

"Please," she finally said. "I beg of you: Leave the house and all the things in it exactly as they are. This house . . . has a way of making its unhappiness felt if you change anything in it. Earlier, I spoke of the other servants seeing things, but I confess: I've seen things . . . inexplicable things . . . myself, too."

I stared at her.

"Miss Weber, you can't possibly expect me to believe that it is the *house* that lit the candle . . . Why, the idea is ludicrous!"

But Miss Weber had finished polishing the silver and was retreating from the room. As I watched her go, she looked back once, shaking her head and holding a finger to her lips. She had shared her most guarded secret with me—or part of it, at least—and I wasn't at all sure what any of it meant.

32

C ora's gossip. The eerie candle in the garden. Miss Weber's reaction, and her insistence that it wasn't possible for Madeleine to return. My mind circled back again and again to the point Henrietta had made: If there had been a funeral, there surely had been a burial. And if a burial had occurred, then *someone or something* must have been put into the ground, and there had to be a record . . . somewhere.

I itched to investigate. I knew Harry would likely see it as a betrayal, but how could I ignore the possibility that he'd lied to me? Poking my nose any further into the matter was risky and unwise. But then, the next day, an opportunity landed in my lap.

"I need to travel up the coast to Oregon, my love," he announced over breakfast. "To see to the logging operations there."

"Oh," I murmured, partly dismayed, and partly caught off guard.

"I've made arrangements to take a steamer this afternoon, but I promise you, I'll return by early next week."

"I see." Suddenly, the opportunity struck me. I felt a surprising tingle of anticipation.

"Is that all right, my dear?"

"I'll eagerly await your return—that's certain. But I understand."

"Oh, darling, I am sorry to leave you at all. You are indeed an angel."

I felt a tiny tremor of guilt, as the truth was: my mind was already racing ahead. I turned to him with a bright smile, hoping I wasn't completely transparent.

"I shall miss you," I said. In spite of the plan forming in my brain, I did mean it.

Later that morning, Miss Weber assisted Harry as he packed a small suitcase. After he bid both of us farewell, I lingered around the mansion for a half an hour to ensure that he was truly gone—then could wait no more.

I was tugging a pair of gloves on and padding softly down the stairs, when I ran into Miss Weber. I expected her to pass me like a silent but chilly breeze. Ordinarily, she did not speak to me unless spoken to— and even then, she was often incredibly terse. So I was quite surprised when she paused to ask me where my errand would take me.

"Oh!" I blurted. "I . . . I thought it might be a nice day to take a walk to the flower market."

Miss Weber took this in with a dubious expression. I'm not sure why I picked that particular lie, other than the fact that I was headed to City Hall, and the flower market was nearby. I could buy an armful of flowers on my way home as proof.

"If that is the case, you ought to know that the only arrangements we keep in the house are composed of lilies," Miss Weber said meaning-fully.

Well, then, I mused. *Madeleine had a fondness for lilies.*

As for myself, I had always abhorred them. They had likely in-grained themselves in my earliest memories, from the time my mother and father had passed away.

Clearly, Miss Weber believed I might trigger another wave of strange happenings. I stared after her receding back and shivered.

She paused at the top of the stairs and turned to address me one last time.

"I shall see to it that lunch is ready upon your return."

"I might . . . be a while," I added, biting my lip. "I had thought to do some shopping downtown."

"I see . . . I assume you'll be wanting to pay your respects, then," she said.

A jolt of alarm ran through me.

"My *respects*?" I repeated, panicked.

But she only offered a cold nod of her head.

"To your old post at the Emporium?"

"Oh! Why . . . yes, of course. I suppose I will."

Relieved, I wished her a good day. She no doubt wondered how to interpret my flustered demeanor, but she had no way to pursue it further. I took my leave quickly.

There was a great deal of rebuilding still going on in San Francisco's civic center. A magnificent new city hall was under construction, promising to rival the beautiful buildings of Europe. In the meantime, the various offices of city bureaucracy had been haphazardly honeycombed among several nearby buildings.

I began my inquiries and was volleyed back and forth from one bureau to another. Finally, a clerk indicated I'd come to the right place.

"If the death certificate was issued around the time of the earthquake, as you say, the details might be rather limited," the clerk warned me. "So many folks that died in the Great Quake had to be buried in a hurry." He paused. "What's the name of the deceased?"

"Madeleine Carlyle."

The clerk looked at me twice quickly.

"Hmm. Well, why not say so in the first place? There's likely to be a better record of that, to be sure."

He began to search a logbook, keeping a wary eye on me. I knew that most of the people who had come asking after Madeleine had likely been reporters. As I was a woman, the clerk was trying to puzzle out exactly what I could be. The papers had announced Harry's remarriage, of course, but Harry had forbidden them from running any likeness of me, or even describing my particulars. I knew that, dressed in one of my shop-girl suits, I hardly looked like a candidate for the new Mrs. Carlyle.

There were no restrictions on public records, the clerk informed me, but I would have to register my name. He handed me a list to sign.

I bit my lip. I couldn't bring myself to sign my maiden name, and my new surname, Carlyle, wouldn't do. I pictured Harry discovering that I'd requested to see Madeleine's death certificate, and cringed.

My hand hovered over the page, fountain pen gripped neatly between my fingers. A strange impulse came over me.

As I handed the list back, the clerk only glanced at my signature in a perfunctory way. I breathed a sigh of relief. He gathered up the forms I'd signed and bustled out of sight.

"You may as well have a seat, Miss Weber," he called to me as he headed into the back room.

More than a quarter of an hour passed before the clerk reemerged, a single piece of paper in hand.

"Here it is," he announced. "The death certificate in question. Complete with a coroner's report, in fact. You can have a look, but we don't transcribe copies, and all originals must remain here."

A coroner's report meant that there *had* been a body . . . or that someone had attested as much. I sucked in a breath, suddenly jittery. I stood and approached the counter once more. The clerk handed over the sheet of paper and I studied it.

My eyes ran up and down the document, then up and down again. The death certificate claimed that Madeleine had died as a result of being struck on the head by falling debris. This was a familiar cause of death for victims of the earthquake. The certificate was dated two days after the disaster—presumably the day the corpse had been found. After a very brief autopsy, the body had been committed to the Laurel Hill Cemetery.

I blinked, dumbstruck. I don't know what I had been expecting. I'd certainly imagined something much more detached and purely logistical. A report attesting that Madeleine had died in the earthquake but no body. A token memorial stone but no grave dug. A bureaucratic death, a death on paper—one that would fit Harry's explanation. I cleared my throat and addressed the clerk once more.

"Sir, if I am reading this document correctly, then . . . Madeleine Carlyle—she was interred at Laurel Hill, and has a headstone?"

The clerk peered at the paper and nodded.

"That's what it says," he concurred. "The city's puttin' an end to burials in town—runnin' out of room. Most folks will have to go down to Colma. But the Carlyle estate appears to still have rights to a number of plots in the Laurel Hill Cemetery, and it says here, that's where Harry Carlyle buried his late wife, just next to a plot reserved in his own name."

The words struck me with all the softness of a hammer.

"Miss? Are you all right?"

I looked up and blinked. It was obvious from his expression I had grown quite pale.

It was inevitable, then, that curiosity drove me on.

As promised by its name, the Laurel Hill Cemetery wound around a hill, with a zig-zagging path that meandered between its many mausoleums and graves. It was an older cemetery, and reflected all the changing fashions in mourning the dead: Roman obelisks mingled with Gothic Victorian monuments, and marble benches sat in semi-circles around stone angels.

The weather was fresh and fair, a stark contrast to the morbid nature of my errand, and to the many tombs around me. I had no map, of course, and there was no one to give directions. I wandered the grounds, my eyes scouring each stone.

I finally found what I was looking for atop the cemetery's highest peak.

CARLYLE.

I was surprised to see the scale of the monument. A mausoleum had been built around the twin plots; a tall Gothic turret mimicked the exterior of the Carlyle mansion itself. Several well-cared-for rosebushes were planted in a wide horseshoe. The expense must have been colossal.

Once again, it struck me as odd that Harry would go to such great lengths for a woman who had wounded him and was still alive. Was this, too, the result of Miss Weber's influence?

I poked my head inside the structure. Within, there were two marble tombs and benches along two sides. I decided to enter. Feeling like an utter trespasser, I timidly crept in and sat on one of the benches.

As I studied my environment, my mind went blank. *How strange it is*, I thought, *to secure plots at the top of the hill, with the best view, and then to build a mausoleum that shut it all out.* A great length of time must have passed, for when I snapped back to attention, I noticed the light had moved from one end of the mausoleum to the other.

But it wasn't until I stood to leave that I noted something even stranger: the words carved into Madeleine Carlyle's marble tomb.

NEVER FORGOTTEN.
HER SPIRIT LIVES ON.

I wavered, reading the words over and over again. Was it a message, cryptically intended?

After leaving the cemetery, I hurried downtown to make a few small purchases—a hat and a little coin-purse—so as to have some proof to show Miss Weber. But when I approached the mansion, the door flew open before I had made my way up the walk. I blinked at the dark shape of the doorway and made out her figure. Still paranoid that she had discovered the truth about my day's errand, I braced myself for her chilly chastisement.

I realized: I had forgotten to buy flowers.

"Were the lilies all gone? Had they run out?" she said. From anyone else, it might have been a friendly inquiry, a routine bit of small talk, but, coming from Miss Weber, I knew better.

"Oh . . . I didn't see any I liked," I lied. I could see straightaway that Miss Weber didn't believe me. Her mouth twisted into a knowing sneer.

"I suppose it was not for lack of looking," she said, as though playing along. "You were gone a good length of time."

"Yes," I cautiously agreed. "I did some other shopping." I held up my alibi, but, to my surprise, Miss Weber seemed little interested. She waved a hand, gesturing for me to hurry up.

"I didn't know when you were expected to return—and told them as much—but they insisted on waiting," Miss Weber said, while I stared at her, puzzled. "I've shown them to the conservatory and given them tea. They await you there."

"I'm sorry . . . *Who* awaits me?"

Miss Weber looked at me coolly. Whoever these guests were, I could see: she did not approve of them. I tried to think of who would possibly come to see me. Cora and Flossie? I suppose Miss Weber would regard any friends from my more impoverished past as degenerates. However, she had one more surprise for me.

"They gave their names as *a Mr. Horace Tackett and a Miss Blanche Bernard*," Miss Weber informed me.

I felt my stomach drop and my knees go weak.

Tackett and Blanche? It wasn't possible. I *knew* beyond a shadow of a doubt it wasn't possible. And yet . . . I couldn't understand it.

"Are you quite all right, ma'am?" Miss Weber asked. Her voice did not reveal concern so much as curious suspicion, tinged with a smug satisfaction at seeing me rattled.

"I . . . I'll go upstairs and put my things away," I said.

"I shall inform them of your imminent arrival," Miss Weber said gleefully.

33

was trembling when I came back downstairs. I picked my way through the echoing hallways towards the conservatory. With each step, my dread mounted. I wondered who my assailant might be—for surely, these two individuals hoped to intimidate me. Perhaps I would finally learn the identity of my long-ago blackmailer. Faced with the immediate possibility, I wasn't certain I wanted to make this particular discovery after all.

But as I approached the glass-walled, plant-filled room, I heard a very familiar sound. It was laughter. But not just any laughter: the musical tinkle of *Cora's* laughter. My heart began to beat faster, and I hastened my pace. As I descended the stairs into the sunken room, I instantly recognized them both—despite the fact that they appeared to be dressed as clowns.

"Jasper! Cora!" I uttered, before I could stop myself. "What are you doing here?" As soon as the words had left my lips, I darted a glance over my shoulder. I did not want Miss Weber to catch on to their lie. I was in luck: she had disappeared into the kitchen, presumably to tell the maid to bring a fresh pot of tea.

"Violet!"

Jasper greeted me eagerly. He leapt to his feet, grinning, then seemed to catch and correct himself. He straightened up, suddenly more formal.

"I mean . . . *Mrs. Carlyle*," he said, and gave a small deferential bow.

I couldn't tell if he was mocking me.

I heard Cora's laughter again: bright, beautiful peals.

"Yes! Why, hullo, *Mrs. Carlyle*!" Cora called from across the conservatory. Unlike Jasper, she did not bother to rise but sat giggling, as though someone had just told her the most entertaining joke. I smelled a familiar odor, something that mingled strangely with Miss Weber's densely brewed Earl Grey. It was the scent of whiskey, and I realized Cora's pale complexion was quite rosy. She was tipsy.

I looked at them. It was plain they intended an impersonation of sorts. Jasper was dressed in a suit befitting a much older man. His hair was slicked in the fashion that Tackett had always worn. Cora was wearing a blonde wig styled after Blanche's familiar coif, with half of it pinned up and the other half in tight, snakelike coils that slithered about her neck and fell to her shoulders. Her lipstick was garish and her powder had been over-applied; clearly a comment on Blanche's poor complexion. It was a wonder Miss Weber had let them into the house at all.

"*Mr. Tackett . . . Miss Bernard*," I said, speaking their pseudonyms through gritted, smiling teeth and nodding hello to each of them in turn. "What brings the two of you here? It has been some time . . ."

"Well, yes, Violet—it *has* been some time," Cora said. She gave a small, indignant sniffle. "Flossie mentioned you'd been around to see her after you returned from Hawai'i . . . but somehow you failed to call upon me!"

Cora made a jokey show of having been shot with an arrow. I could see that she was genuinely annoyed and perhaps even a touch hurt.

I looked around again. The young kitchen maid, Bess, entered with a fresh tray of tea, but there was no sign of Miss Weber herself. Jasper offered me his arm and escorted me to the small round tea-table, where he pulled out a chair for me.

"Thank you," I said, still recovering from my earlier fright.

He nodded and sat back down in his own chair.

"Of course, I can understand that your *new life* keeps you busy," Cora said.

"It does," I replied. "But it wasn't that, Cora. I . . . I suppose I wasn't entirely sure you were happy for me."

"I *am* happy for you, Violet," Cora said, but her voice was stiff. I found it difficult to wholly believe.

"Me, too, Violet," Jasper chimed in. Then he turned sheepish. "As soon as I heard your news, I been plenty happy for you. I guess I shoulda known that day I saw you ridin' around in an automobile that you were moving up in the world."

He looked around the conservatory, with its glass walls and bubbling fountains, the largest of which was crowned with cherubic young lads forever pouring urns of water. The mansion had a good many more cherubs and gargoyles than I could have ever wished, but I knew that, through Jasper's eyes, it was all very posh, a sign of my new, prestigious husband's great wealth.

"You deserve it, Violet," he said. He gave me an earnest stare. "You really do."

"That's kind. I . . . I don't know what to say," I managed to murmur.

Rough around the edges or not, Jasper was always brimming with good intentions. Now it was my turn to feel sheepish, and we exchanged an awkward look. Cora finally broke the tension.

"See, Violet?—Nothing but happiness, all around!" she crowed.

She hiccupped and clapped a hand to her mouth, then quickly laughed it off. She was indeed drunk. But somehow, she still managed to appear pretty and charming. She was having fun now. She picked up her cup of tea and took a sip with her little finger curled in the air, making fun.

"It's very nice here," she said more sincerely, looking around. "But I'm still trying to imagine you living here, Violet. It's as if you have been reborn a *different person!*"

"Not so different as *some*," I said to her. "For instance, the two of you seem quite changed indeed."

She smiled and swept an arm in the air to show off her handiwork. "Not too poorly done, is it?" she said. She pointed at Jasper. "I think we got the part in his hair just right, don't you?" She fussed and patted at Jasper's head. "Oh! And look: the mole! I drew it on myself," she added. She pointed to a dark brown mark on Jasper's chin.

The truth was, I did not find their joke funny—not one bit. Any minute now, Miss Weber would return. I had a short time to get my answers—if any were to be had. I dropped the pretense, if only for a fleeting moment, and leaned towards Cora to whisper in a low voice.

"*What has possessed you to be so morbid, Cora?*" I demanded. "Dressing up like this? Don't you think it's obscene?"

"See here, now, Violet . . . you ought to know: it wasn't my idea in the first place!"

"What do you mean? I don't understand."

"Flossie put ol' Jasper here up to it a handful of times already. She got Jasper to pass himself off as Tackett and collect on some old debts around town. You'd be surprised, but not everyone knows Tackett went missing. As long as we're careful, the whole business works like a charm!"

I shook my head and frowned. I was trying to piece it all together, but it didn't make sense.

"*Flossie* put Jasper up to this?"

"She did, indeed," Cora replied. "But . . . of course, it was my idea to come *here* to show off our 'mastery of disguise,' as it were." She looked at me, gave a wink, and dissolved into laughter again. "Oh, Violet! You ought to have seen your face! Why, it was priceless! I do believe you entered the room expecting to see Tackett and crummy old Blanche, risen from the grave!"

She cackled terribly, and I tried to shush her, but it was no use.

"You *did* give me a bit of a turn," I admitted. "I can't say I was tickled."

"No, of course," Cora said, frowning and nodding. She paused, then broke out into a giddy grin again. "Oh, but it was so amusing for *us*—wasn't it, Jasper?"

Jasper did not answer. He shot me an apologetic look.

"Aren't you at least a little bit glad to see me, Violet?" Cora prodded now.

I sighed. "Yes."

"I wanted to see you, Violet. And see how you are living. It's lovely here, and I'm glad for you." She paused, then added, "Well, it's lovely . . . with a few exceptions."

"What do you mean?"

"That's quite a portrait, Violet," Cora said. "I mean the large one hanging over the stairs."

She let the comment sink in. She meant *Madeleine*.

"Does he ever talk about her—his late wife?"

"Cora!" I snapped at her. "For goodness' sake, *hush!*"

I was suddenly overcome by a wave of irritation. I threw another quick glance around for Miss Weber. The fact that she had not entered the conservatory under some pretense or another was highly unusual, and I began to wonder if something wasn't amiss in some other part of the mansion.

"We didn't mean to cause ya any misery, Violet!" Jasper said now, looking cautiously between me and Cora. "Would you . . . would ya like us to go?"

He peered into my face intently. That lock of hair permanently intent on falling over his eye came loose from its hold. Jasper smiled his crooked smile. He'd been famous throughout our old neighborhood as a handsome lad. As I gazed back at him, I thought—for the first time— I could begin to see it. He had the well-defined cheekbones and jawline that flattered both men and women alike, and the trim yet muscular physique that only those who are young and naturally athletic possess. I was always a little shocked that his devotion had landed on me, as opposed to a more dazzling girl, like Cora.

"No," I said after a moment. "Of course you're welcome to stay and have some tea." I hesitated, and realized that—despite their grotesque costumes—I actually was *glad* to see them. They represented a familiar past; a much-needed anchor, as lately I'd begun to feel completely lost to myself.

Cora seemed pleased to hear me say this. Her smile put me further at ease—until she winked. When Cora winked, you could never be sure what might happen next.

"Let's talk about merrier things. Did you know? I finally forced Jasper to dance!"

I smiled, entertained. For all the time he'd spent working for Tackett at the dancehall, Jasper had always shyly refused to dance, no matter how many of Tackett's girls asked.

"He can do the waltz now," Cora insisted, triumphant. "And would you believe it? He's not half-bad! Jasper—show her how it's done!"

She prodded him to stand up. Jasper appeared mortified, but Cora appeared equally intent.

"Show Violet how well you waltz, now, Jasper!"

Eventually, Jasper stood up, red in the face, and offered me his arm.

"This isn't the time or place . . ." I began to protest.

"Nonsense!" Cora returned. "We're having a bit of fun now, aren't we? And there's practically enough room in here to throw a ball. Look!"

She pointed to the large open space of the conservatory floor.

"I . . . I'm not sure I know how to waltz, myself," I admitted. This was true. Harry had taken me around the dance floor a couple of times in the course of our honeymoon, and I had proven myself a true novice. I'd managed to step on his feet on at least three occasions.

"Jasper will lead you," Cora insisted.

"Sure," Jasper said. "I think I can lead you through the basic box step . . . Would you like to, Violet?"

I really *didn't* want to dance. Where on earth could Miss Weber be? What if she returned at the wrong moment? I hardly wanted her to come into the conservatory to see me dancing with a man she took to be a suspicious stranger.

"We have no music," I protested.

"Pish!" Cora decreed. "I'll count it out—or, Jasper can. Just let him show you what he's learned!" Cora pleaded.

I could hear the inebriation in her voice. She was in a mood for fun.

"Only a quick showing, then," I relented.

Jasper, still waiting with his arm extended, gave a small bow. I stood up, and allowed myself to be gathered into his arms. He took a moment, making certain we had struck the proper frame, then gave me a nod. Cora began counting time in a sing-song voice, and we stepped in a slow, even tempo.

First we waltzed around the small space beside the fountain, and then in a circle around the fountain itself. Cora's counting became a little slurred, and Jasper took over. We waltzed on. I heard Cora laughing, and soon heard her clapping as well.

"Not bad!" she called. "Not bad at all, you two!"

Before I knew what I was about, I heard my laughter echoing off the walls of the glass conservatory. Jasper grinned at me, and I grinned back. Out of breath, we began to slow down. We were both weak with merriment, leaning into each other.

For the briefest of seconds, the warm skin of my forehead touched Jasper's.

But just as this occurred, I heard Miss Weber clear her throat. I froze immediately. Jasper's hands tensed where he held my waist and my hand. We turned and looked, and to my great shock, I beheld not only Miss Weber but also . . . *Harry.*

"Harry!" I exclaimed, instantly shoving Jasper away. "I . . . I thought . . . Why aren't you in Oregon?"

He stood, looking at me for some time, his spine very stiff and upright. The expression on his face was inscrutable, a stony wall concealing unknowable depths. I did notice, however, the small muscles along his jaw clenching. This was a telltale sign that Harry was displeased. It was an expression I'd seen him wear only once before: when that reporter harassed us in Alamo Square. He'd never aimed it in my direction. To bear its full brunt was surprisingly powerful.

"The matter turned out not to be as pressing as I had thought. I was able to send a clerk in my stead," Harry answered finally. "I hurried home, looking to surprise you and thinking you might be sad at the prospect of being alone." He paused, and gave a stiff but polite nod to Cora. His eyes moved to Jasper, and remained there with a penetrating stare. "But it appears you're not very lonely, after all."

Jasper stumbled forward and put out his hand.

"We met once before . . . at the livery," he said.

Harry said nothing. He allowed Jasper's hand to hang in the air.

I knew I ought to intervene. I bit my lip, realizing that Miss Weber knew them as "Miss Bernard" and "Mr. Tackett."

Before I could say anything, Harry spoke.

"I'm suddenly quite tired." He turned to me. "I will retire upstairs."

He looked coldly at each of us in turn. His eyes lingered on Jasper for a full moment, running up and down the young man. Then he pivoted stiffly on his heel and strode out of the room. I watched him go with an acute sense of shame.

"I don't believe he was very pleased to meet us," Cora remarked.

"Please, Cora," I begged. "I think it would be best if you and Jasper go now."

"Yes," she agreed, standing up and smoothing her dress. "I can see as much for myself."

I called for one of the servants—not Miss Weber, for she, too, had disappeared—and asked that "Mr. Tackett" and "Miss Bernard" be shown out.

When I finally ventured upstairs, Harry was in his dressing room. Miss Weber was attending him, unpacking his bags. When she saw me, her bloodshot blue eyes snapped quickly from my face to Harry's, and then back again. She did not utter a word, instead curtsying and scurrying out of the room.

We were alone. Harry's back was to me, so I guessed I would have to speak first. But as I opened my mouth, he whirled about, and I realized: He was neither cold nor detached. He was red-faced and trembling with anger.

"I'm not even away from our home for one night, and *this* is what you get up to?"

I stared, too shocked to answer.

"What in blazes were they doing in *my house*?"

"They're . . . old friends," I mumbled meekly.

"Indeed!" Harry said. "I saw for myself just how 'friendly' you were."

I didn't say anything.

"Not only that, but Miss Weber says they gave their names as Horace Tackett and Blanche Bernard," Harry spat at me. "And I know for a fact, Violet: that's a lie."

A tremor of panic seized me.

"*Why* are they coming here, dressed in obvious costumes, telling lies? What am I to think, Violet?"

I shook my head, wordless. He grew angrier at my lack of a response.

"I told you on the day I met that young man—the day I saw the way he looks at you—I told you I wouldn't blame you if that's what you wanted: someone your own age. You insisted you had no feelings for him."

"I don't," I insisted.

Harry looked at me with skeptical disbelief, his complexion nearly purple with anger.

After a moment, he sighed.

"Please . . . just leave me be," he said.

Filled with a mixture of apology and self-pity, I hurried from the room.

I spent the evening alone. The sunset was elusive; the golden afternoon vanished in dismal relief into the cold and fog and left no trace of itself behind. I sat by the fireplace in the library and kept myself occupied with a book. Harry had gone into town. It was plain he had left to avoid me. He was not the sort of man to go carousing when angry . . . but perhaps I'd pushed him beyond familiar boundaries.

One by one, the servants departed for the night. I could hear Miss Weber in the kitchen, fixing a pot of chamomile tea for herself, her last ritual of the day.

When the hour grew quite late, I abandoned my novel and retired to bed. Changing into my nightgown, I wondered if and when I would see Harry. This would mark the first time he'd ever chosen to sleep apart from me. The bed felt abnormally empty as I crawled into it. It was a large imperial bed—larger than any I had ever seen. I pulled the thick blankets close around me in a vain attempt to fill the emptiness.

Some time later, I woke from a light doze as Harry crawled in beside me. He lay still for a moment, then rolled over as though to swim the distance across the immense bed. He was warm when he enveloped me, and I instinctively threaded my arms through his own. He held me for some minutes before speaking.

"Anger is a kind of fear, in truth. I haven't been able to call you mine for very long, Violet, but already the thought of losing you frightens me. Seeing that young man earlier . . ."

I did not want to relive the day's events.

"*Shhhh . . .*" I urged.

I did not want to explain. I did not even want an apology. What I really wanted was his mouth on my own. I saw my opportunity, and took it.

As I kissed my husband, echoes of Cora's gossip came back to me unbidden. *He'd been possessive, wild with jealousy*, Cora had warned. *Evidently he has a temper not to be trifled with.*

Perhaps the fury I'd witnessed ought to have set me on edge, but for the first time since I'd moved into the mansion, I began to believe Harry's jealousy wasn't Madeleine's property alone.

34

One night not long after, I swore I heard the gentle tinkle of piano keys. At first I couldn't be sure . . . but when they sounded a second time, I bolted upright in bed and reached for my dressing gown. After making certain Harry was still softly snoring, I padded to the door and slipped out into the hall. There it was again! A single, stray note, very high and tinny. Then another. As though someone were idly resting a finger on this key, then that, in a haphazard manner. I felt my skin bristle with gooseflesh.

I took a breath to steel myself.

I have never given much credence to ghost stories. They had always struck me as too fantastic, impossible, and Sister Maggie's words, urging pity for the haunted, had never left me. Even as I descended the stairs under the watchful eyes of the first Mrs. Carlyle's imperious portrait, I could not quite bring myself to believe I was hearing a ghostly hand.

When I reached the bottom of the staircase, the notes abruptly ceased. In the absence of sound, my heart began to beat faster. Had the intruder heard me coming? I held my breath and listened. Nothing stirred, and a second suspicion came over me. My panic dissolved into a different feeling: doubt. The piano notes I'd heard—the piano notes I was *sure* I had heard—echoed in my head, taunting me. I could play them back in my memory, clear as a bell—almost *too* clear, it seemed—making me wonder if I'd really heard them in the first place.

I passed through the foyer and into a smaller hall. The music room was on the first floor, beside the ballroom. It was a pretty room, with sumptuous burgundy curtains framing an entire wall of glass-paned French doors that opened up onto the rose garden. On a pleasant day, one could have all the doors thrown wide to enjoy the scent of roses mingling with the eucalyptus-tinged salt air. But on a chilly night such as this, the glass doors let in a cold, clammy draft no matter how tightly shut. I shivered and pulled my dressing gown tighter as I neared the doorway.

Everything had grown absolutely silent and still. Armed again with a low-burning lamp, I peered inside.

Nothing.

I'm not certain what I'd expected, but I felt a flood of relief mixed with just the slightest hint of disappointment. As unpleasant as it would be to discover something amiss, it was just as unpleasant to feel my sanity might be failing me. I thought back to the night I'd found the candle burning in the rose garden, and Harry's patronizing dismissal, the way he'd tried to convince me it had just been a vivid nightmare.

Something sparked in my brain. *The rose garden!* I looked to the wall of glass doors and turned down the wick of my oil lamp. Then I tiptoed across the thick Oriental rug and peeked outside. A full moon flooded the garden in silvery light, turning the roses into colorless stone sculptures. There was no flickering glow of a candle.

I let out a sigh and turned my oil lamp back up. But just as I was about to leave, I glimpsed something unexpected from out the corner of my eye and froze. *The piano.* It was a beautiful Bösendorfer, imported from Austria and immaculately maintained. Ordinarily the lid that concealed the keys was kept shut, protecting the ivory from the ravages of dust. But the lid was open now, and the gleaming white keys stared back at me. The notes I'd heard . . . it *wasn't* simply my imagination. I whirled about as though expecting a figure to step out of the shadows, but still I saw no one. I turned back to the piano.

There, perched above the keys, sat several sheets of music. Where had it come from? I was oddly afraid to touch it, but forced myself to lift them. Beethoven's *Moonlight Sonata.* Besides the printed notes, there were additional markings, scrawled in elegant handwriting.

A gifted musician, Miss Weber had said. *Impeccable penmanship.*

But . . . it wasn't possible. *No*, I thought. Perhaps the sheet music had once belonged to Madeleine, but someone else—a very *real* someone— put it here. The question was who. Miss Weber had long been my sole suspect; now I wasn't so certain. Her distress upon hearing my tale of the candle in the rose garden had been so genuine. That only left an intruder, or . . . *Harry?* None of it made any sense.

Shivering, I decided to beat a hasty retreat back upstairs. I took the sheet music with me—my only tangible proof that the nocturnal stir-rings of the house were real.

Once upstairs, I very quietly slid open the drawer of my nightstand, tucking the sheet music safely within. I crawled into bed. I was still uneasy, but held tightly to the notion that I now had physical proof—*real proof!*—to show Harry.

When I slid open the drawer the next morning, the sheet music had vanished. I blinked into the empty drawer, feeling suddenly quite sick.

35

had held that sheet music in my own hands; I was sure of it. But even without proof, I had to speak to Harry. I broached the matter in a roundabout way.

"Harry . . . sometimes, I feel I am lacking," I said later that morning as we sat together over breakfast. The morning sun was streaming in from a window just behind him, his shape cut out in silhouette as he leaned to pour cream in his coffee.

"Oh?" he said, frowning.

"Yes," I said. "I have to admit, I am not particularly accomplished in any discipline. Most ladies who preside over prestigious houses such as this are very skilled at a number of things: drawing, painting, poetry and languages, gardening . . ." I hesitated, bit my lip, then added, ". . . *music.*"

"Well, yes," Harry reluctantly agreed. "I suppose that's true. But such things are drilled into them in those dreary finishing schools.

And, honestly, they often all learn the same talents—and perform them with a similar style, even! You are far more rare and unique, Violet. You distinguish yourself in your own way."

As we nibbled at our breakfast, kitchen maids occasionally entered and exited the dining room, bringing dishes and taking them away. Miss Weber stood at attention in the corner, overseeing all, her hands demurely clasped in front of her.

"Yes, but I feel . . . *uncultivated* at times," I insisted.

Harry laughed.

"Why . . . you are quite possibly the most voracious reader I have ever met."

I shook my head. "Reading is hardly an accomplishment," I remarked. My mouth went a little dry to contemplate what I wanted to say next.

I could feel Miss Weber's iron gaze from where she stood at attention near the kitchen door.

"Miss Weber, I put some special honey in the larder," I said. "Would you see to it personally and bring it to the table?"

Miss Weber looked far from thrilled to take orders from me, but in front of Harry she gritted her teeth, curtsied, and disappeared.

I hesitated, then pushed on.

"The library here is so full of books . . . I'm sure Madeleine was far more well-read than I."

I held my breath, having spoken her name aloud, wondering if Harry would rebuke me. But he only gave a grunt.

"She certainly didn't spend much time in that library."

I wondered if that might be the reason the library was the only room in the mansion that truly felt like "mine."

"She didn't care for the library?" I prodded.

"She might've pretended she was well-read, but she didn't want to be caught in the act of *reading*. She had terrible eyesight. In fact, she was nearly blind in one eye, a flaw she liked to keep hidden. In order to read, Madeleine had to wear inch-thick spectacles, and she would rather not anyone see her in them; she was quite vain, I'm afraid."

I took all this in, concealing my shock. Miss Weber had left some things out while singing Madeleine's praises! My head reeled: Madeleine had had a flaw! She suddenly seemed more human. Somehow this muddied my feelings about her.

"No," Harry continued, "Madeleine never let anyone see her in those spectacles. If she was returning correspondence, she locked herself in a room with her writing desk. If she wished to impress people with her musical talents, she would only play pieces she had thoroughly memorized in private."

I thought again of the sheet music I'd found—found and then lost. I was sure now that it was hers. I recalled the tidy penmanship. Now I understood that she'd written those notes, probably in private, and with painstaking deliberation due to her poor eyesight.

I wanted to probe further, but I knew if I told Harry outright about the sheet music, he would only think me mad. I had to find another tack.

"I think . . ." I said, summoning all my nerve, "I think I should like to learn to play." I paused, then added, "At present, the beautiful piano you keep in the music room only collects dust."

Harry put down his fork. He didn't reply right away. I gathered my courage and pressed onward.

"In fact," I said, "there's one piece in particular I should like to learn to play for you: Beethoven's *Moonlight Sonata*."

At this, Harry's head snapped to attention. I'd struck a nerve. A flood of color rushed to his cheeks.

"What made you say that?" he demanded.

I shrunk a little involuntarily.

"I don't know. I just thought . . . I just always thought it was so pretty," I dithered. "Wouldn't you like to hear me play it?"

Miss Weber returned with the honey I'd requested. She put the jar in front of me with a plunk and laid a dipper beside it.

"No. I have heard that piece quite enough in the course of my life," Harry answered me coldly. "I don't care for it."

"Well . . . it was just a silly notion."

"It *was* a silly notion," Harry agreed.

I had worn his patience thin.

I turned back to my breakfast in silence. If there was one thing to be gleaned from this touchy exchange, it was that Madeleine Carlyle had very likely played a memorable rendition of Beethoven's *Moonlight Sonata*.

Harry twisted in his seat. "Miss Weber, would you please boil a fresh pot of coffee? I'm afraid this batch tastes rather stale."

Miss Weber nodded and left the room.

Harry turned back to me. We were alone again.

"It's a shame," he mused. "No matter how many kitchen maids Miss Weber hires or fires, they never can seem to poach an egg properly."

He poked a knife into one of the eggs on his plate to reveal a dry, powdery yolk. I nodded, unaware of the shock Harry was about to deliver.

"I understand you were once a cook," he said, after a pause. "Perhaps you could show them how it's done."

I choked on the bite of toast I'd been chewing, and had to spit it into my napkin. Then I stared at him, my eyes wide with shock. I had never once volunteered that fact.

Either Harry did not notice my shock, or he pretended not to. He calmly took a sip of coffee and continued eating. I cleared my throat.

"I . . . wasn't a very good cook," I said, aware of the blush creeping into my cheeks. "Everyone said so, I'm afraid."

"Well, people can be very difficult to please . . . even those without much breeding."

I had no rejoinder. *Was he confessing that he knew about my past?* I couldn't force myself to finish the thought.

"No matter," he concluded, and from his tone I deduced the subject was temporarily dropped.

I sat perfectly still as we finished our meal, but my heart raced, and I felt the toast I'd just consumed churning in my stomach. Harry, on the other hand, was the picture of calm. He picked up the morning newspaper and was immediately absorbed.

A sudden conviction came over me: *Flossie.* As soon as Harry left to go downtown, I would go see Flossie. She would riddle out the true meaning behind Harry's words. If they were cryptic threats, she would know. She would set me straight.

36

had already gotten halfway to Flossie's Nob Hill apartment house when it dawned on me: Why on earth did I expect her to be home? It was late morning on a weekday.

Had she told me where she was employed? I couldn't recall. *A poor friend I have turned out to be*, I thought. I'd long been wrapped up in my own drama. Having already traveled across town, I decided that if Flossie wasn't home, I would try to find a landlady who might know where she was employed.

However, when I arrived at Flossie's door, I knocked just to be certain. Much to my surprise, it flew open.

"Violet?"

After a momentary pause, Flossie ushered me inside. I ducked in quickly. The light within was dim and almost purplish in color. I realized the curtains—sewn from a lilac-colored silk—were drawn. I looked at Flossie and saw that she was in her dressing gown. Her hair was slicked away from her face in a chignon and her skin appeared shiny, as though she had just applied cold cream.

"I didn't expect you, Violet," Flossie said, absently reaching for the sash of her robe and yanking it tight.

"I know it," I said, "and I'm sorry. It's only that . . . well . . ." I bit my lip, then decided it was likely best to just come out with it. "Harry said something peculiar over breakfast this morning . . . I think he knows I used to work for Tackett, in the boardinghouse."

Flossie froze, taking this in carefully and slowly. "And how can you be sure?"

"He mentioned that he knew I used to work as a cook. There is only *one* place I ever worked as a cook."

Flossie's mouth tightened and she became abruptly businesslike.

"Come in. Let's sit down and talk it over. I'll fetch us some coffee."

She led me to her sitting room. I sat on a chaise longue, feeling slightly dazed. Repeating the morning's events aloud had made them real in a way they hadn't been, only hours earlier.

"All right," Flossie said, returning with the coffee.

I saw that my cup was only half-full. She held up one finger as she crossed the room, opened a cabinet, and retrieved a bottle of whiskey. I listened to the *glug-glug-glug* as she gave each cup a healthy dose. Then she settled into the stuffed chair opposite me.

"Tell me everything."

I did. I tried to repeat my conversation with Harry, word for word. Flossie's eyes lit up with what I took to be fear when I described Harry's remarks.

"Do you think Cora's right, and that I've made a mistake, rushing into this marriage?"

Flossie took a deep, weighty breath. She appeared to contemplate this, her eyes darting about in that peculiar way as she made her mental calculations. Then—again, to my surprise—she softened.

"No. You love Harry," she said. She let out a sigh—this one lighter—and squeezed my hand. "And he loves you. I'm *certain* of it."

She paused before pressing on. "Perhaps he does know *something* about your past, Violet. We can't ignore his comment. But he clearly still holds you dear to his heart and has no intention of leaving you. Shouldn't that be enough?"

"What if . . ." I began to say in a halting voice. "What if Harry is accepting of my past, because . . . because he has a dark secret of his own?"

Flossie was silent. She cocked her head at me.

"You mean the rumors about what happened to Madeleine Carlyle on the night of the earthquake." It was not a question.

I nodded, numb.

"If you ask me, I think you've let Cora meddle with your mind. She set you down this terrible path, making paranoid guesses about Harry's past . . . and now it's only natural that you assume he's been busy doing the same." She squeezed my hand and peered earnestly into my eyes. "Please, Violet . . . please don't let Cora's love of gossip play tricks on you. You deserve so much more than that. You really do."

I took a breath, relieved. It was exactly what I needed to hear.

I blinked and took in the room with a steadier gaze. I noticed it wasn't quite as I remembered. A tall marble statue of Diana poised with her bow and arrow had vanished from the pedestal in the corner of the room. There was a ghostly bleached shadow on one wall where an impressive gold gilt mirror had hung.

"Flossie . . . the statue that used to reside just there . . . It's missing. And the mirror, too. Where have they gone?"

At this, Flossie stiffened. A scrim fell over her bright blue eyes.

"Oh, Flossie—did you sell some of your things?"

She was unwilling to broach a full explanation. She gave a quick, jerky shake of her head and simply said, "No, no; it's no worry. You mustn't trouble yourself."

"Are you certain?"

"Yes," she said. "I assure you—I'm fine." She stood up, cinched her dressing gown tight again, and made as though to show me to the door. I rose and followed her. After a pause, she said, "If you want to fret over someone, fret over Cora."

"Cora?"

Flossie sighed, and her posture drooped. Her expression turned from stiff to sorrow-filled.

"That girl is spending money like water, I'm afraid," she said mournfully. "Alas, I don't need to tell you. *You've* seen how she's been living."

I nodded. Cora's fashion of living was indeed very lavish, and it seemed she was growing more ostentatious by the minute. But I also knew that Cora steadily received gifts from her many suitors, and some of them even invested her money on her behalf in worthy ventures. One of my earlier thoughts returned to me.

"Flossie, I meant to ask you . . . well, it's not yet noon on a weekday. Please don't misunderstand me—I know how blessed I am to have found you at home—but . . . *how* are you home? Oughtn't you be at the typing pool?"

Flossie shrugged. "I've left that position."

"Oh," I murmured, not sure what else to say. But before I could awkwardly fumble about for the right words, Flossie's face lit up with a smile.

"Look at you! I am touched," she said, patting my upper arm with her usual reassuring grace. "Don't worry so much, Violet! I begin new employment next Monday. A better position, in fact."

"Ah," I uttered, relieved. "That's marvelous news, in that case."

Flossie's smile tightened and she bobbed her head.

"Yes. It'll have to do," she said. She gave a small, rough laugh. "For those of us who don't find ourselves married to the likes of Harry Carlyle, this will have to suffice."

I was surprised; it was the kind of remark more fitting of Cora. I wasn't certain how to take it. If it had been Cora, it would have been barbed with jealousy. But Flossie had never displayed a single inkling of envy—not for me or for anyone else. She was the rare sort who never seemed to begrudge others' happiness.

I was certain that Flossie had not intended any ill will. I thanked her for her counsel and bid her farewell. After all, she had very wisely talked me out of my panic about Harry—twice, now. Flossie was right, of course: whatever Harry knew about me, he still loved me. I was lucky.

37

continued to hear strange stirrings at night: the groaning of the floor-boards. The sibilance of a whispered conversation. An occasional clunk of a dropped object, never to be found.

My curiosity and fear began to take on the shape of frustration. Was I mad? Was somebody tormenting me? I could not bring myself to believe in ghosts; the notion was simply too fantastic.

I decided to take matters into my own hands and came up with a plan. Each night, just before bedtime, I would rearrange a handful of small items that, according to Miss Weber, had been particularly dear to Madeleine. I purchased a ball of string and several tiny bells, and tied lines at several strategic locations. My logic ran as follows: Whoever was creeping about the mansion at night was trying to create the impression that Madeleine herself was haunting the house. That person would no doubt endeavor to return the knick-knacks to their original locations. Spirits may be made of ether, but human bodies are thick and clumsy. If the pretender *did* attempt to restore the things I'd moved, he would trigger one of my traps!

Once I had carefully designed my plan, I chose a night to deploy it; it happened to be a Friday. I waited until the servants had gone home, Harry had grown heavy-eyed with sleep, and Miss Weber had long since retired. Then I quickly scurried about, moving objects and stringing up my bells. A thin film of sweat beaded my brow as I worked—a testament to my fervor and haste.

When all was at the ready, I turned the lights out and hurried upstairs. As I neared my bedroom, I wondered if I would find Harry awake or asleep, but he had already turned upon his side and was breathing in deep, even sighs. Once in bed, I turned down my oil lamp and lay on my back in the velvet dark, sleep the furthest thing from my mind. I entered into my usual ritual, staring at the ceiling, not quite seeing anything at all. Instead, I listened, hungry for the smallest tremor of sound.

But, alas . . . hours passed without a single peep. In fact, the mansion was *abnormally* quiet.

I waited. And waited more. Somehow, just as dawn was making its blue-tinged debut in the windowpanes, I unintentionally drifted into a state of slumber. Thirty or so minutes later, I bolted upright, frustrated with my lack of vigilance. I looked over at my husband. Harry was still sleeping, but he was beginning to stir every now and again; he would be fully awake in less than an hour. And Miss Weber! She would likely be stoking the fires soon. My traps hadn't worked, but I wanted to remove all evidence before anyone discovered them. I put on my dressing robe and hurried downstairs. It would be tricky untying them; I would have to do it very carefully to avoid ringing the bells myself.

However, I was in for another surprise. In the drawing room, I had moved a small Egyptian figurine from the mantel to an end table. Now it sat back up on the mantel. Whoever had moved it had avoided the strings entirely. I thought I had done an excellent job: the strings were positioned so as to almost be invisible, the bells only hung in the dark corners. And still, somehow, the intruder had managed to dodge them. This was very lucky, I thought, but not impossible.

In setting my traps, I had moved five of Madeleine's treasures. In each case, I found the objects had been returned to their original places. But it was the fifth and final one that disturbed me the most. I'd saved checking on it for last . . . hoping I had outsmarted my tormentor. The object in question was a small engraved music box I'd found on a shelf in the library, a music box that played—of all things—Beethoven's *Moonlight Sonata*. It was small enough to tuck into a drawer, so I had placed it in the drawer of the desk I'd insisted on keeping in the library. Then I'd had a stroke of brilliance. I'd tied bells to the underside *of the drawer itself.*

And yet, when I entered the library, there was the music box— sitting in plain view on the bookshelf! How had the trespasser known to look in my desk drawer? And how had he managed to retrieve it without disturbing the bells? I knelt down to inspect the drawer and peered up from below, but my eyes found nothing. I cautiously slid the drawer open, and heard . . .

Nothing.

The bells were entirely missing. I closed my eyes to think. *Someone has definitely been here. Someone has touched this very desk*—my *desk.*

But there was little time to linger over this conundrum. The dawn that had glowed blue in the windowpanes now grew increasingly rosy, and I could hear Miss Weber stirring in the kitchen. I crept quickly and quietly back up to my bedroom.

I was too late. As I stepped inside, Harry was sitting up in bed. I couldn't see right away what he was doing. He was holding something in his hands, frowning at it in puzzlement.

"There you are, my dear," he said to me as I entered the room. "What were you about, at this early hour? I woke to find you gone."

"I finished the book I was reading and wanted to put it back in the library," I lied.

He did not seem bothered at all by this explanation. His attention had already been reclaimed by whatever was in his hands. He moved, and I thought I heard a muffled but oddly familiar tinkle.

"I woke and found you gone," he repeated, frowning. "And then, even more baffling, found these resting on your pillow . . ."

He held out his hand. *The missing bells!*

"Resting on my pillow?" I stammered.

"Yes," he replied. His eyes searched my face with mounting concern. "I think you'd better tell me what's been going on, Violet."

We locked eyes. I found myself holding my breath. Then, in the next minute, I exhaled and collapsed on the bed beside him, ready to tell all.

I told Harry everything: all about the phantom piano keys I'd heard in the middle of the night, about the sheet music that had vanished, about my attempts to catch the perpetrator in the act. To his credit, while

Harry bristled at certain parts of my story, he did not interrupt me. But when I had done, the first thing he said to me was "I see how this is all my fault, Violet."

"Why do you say that?" I asked.

"I know now that I haven't been taking proper care of you. That first night . . . when you believed you had seen a candle burning in the rose garden . . . I ought to have called for a doctor. Now I can see how far gone these matters have become."

My mouth dropped open.

"You . . . still don't *believe me*?" I demanded.

"Listen to yourself, Violet," Harry urged. "Sheet music that vanishes by morning . . . noises that no one else has heard. You're setting traps around the house to catch a phantom. *Traps!*"

"But . . . but . . . the bells! The bells you found just now, on my pillow! It is proof!"

Harry looked almost as if he were very, very sorry for me.

"Violet, I don't want to upset you, but it's possible you left them there yourself, don't you think?" he suggested, clearly making an effort to use a gentle tone. "It seems as though your mind has been frazzled lately. In all your laying of traps, perhaps you set some things down and forgot about them . . ."

"On my pillow?"

He didn't reply right away. I grew frustrated. Harry didn't even know of my spells, and yet, it was as though he was suggesting I'd had one. I felt *certain* the events of the night had nothing to do with my affliction. I needed him to believe what I was telling him now.

"It was someone else," I insisted. "Somebody is playing games with me."

"Who?" Harry said, shaking his head. "I know the house is large, but there is no one besides us rattling around this place."

"There is Miss Weber," I said with sudden boldness.

"No," Harry said, his voice firm. "Violet: Miss Weber is not playing tricks on you. Why would she do such a thing?"

I could see I would not make any headway pursuing this line of thinking. I began to feel helpless, and Harry seemed to read as much in my face.

"My darling love," he said. "I am so, so sorry. I haven't been sensitive to it, but I can imagine that this new life hasn't been easy. The house is a reminder of my past."

His mention of the house caused something to click in my head. I seized at the opportunity.

"Yes—why, Harry? *Why?* This house *is* a reminder of your past. *Why* did you rebuild it so? I can't believe this is all Miss Weber's doing, and utterly out of your hands. I have tried not to question your motives, but I truly cannot understand it. If your life with Madeleine was a torture, why relive it? You once said your love for her had turned to hate . . . but . . . I look around, and I can't help but wonder if all this is a shrine to her—that you love her still."

I stopped talking. Harry's face had gone dark, his pallor taking on an angry, sickly, nearly purple hue.

"No," he said. His voice was cold. It looked as though he might be trembling. "Don't speak of matters that you know nothing about," he commanded. "I told you, in the wake of the earthquake, I was a broken man. Miss Weber took care of me, and supervised the rebuilding of this place. She had her reasons for remaking everything as it is."

"But I don't understand . . ." I complained softly.

"*You don't need to!*" His voice was sharp.

We had been sitting on the bed, he in his pajama trousers, bare-chested. Now he stood up and shouldered into a white silk shirt, yanking irritably as he did up the buttons. When the last button was done, he gathered himself and turned to look at me with a cold stare.

"We all have reasons for doing what we do, Violet," he said. "You *must* ask yourself if you can live here and also let the past rest. I can't say I care very much for being forced to revisit the darker corners of my personal history."

He paused, looked me square in the eye, then added: "And since we have now broached the subject, I can't imagine you would care very much for being forced to revisit your *own* history, Violet."

I blanched, and my blood ran icy in my veins.

Before I could reply, he strode away. He hesitated, only for the slenderest moment, and turned back to call over his shoulder: "If I have upset you, I understand that you have old friends from the dancehall who might comfort you. I know you still visit them from time to time."

For the first time in my marriage, the love I bore my husband felt surprisingly like hate.

38

Harry and I fell into a cold stalemate. He had grown distant, and while he was never rude—it was not in his nature to be boorish—he was changed, nonetheless. He only spoke to me if necessary. All intimacies between us ceased—not only those we shared in private, but also the small public displays between husband and wife. Whereas he used to offer his arm as we took strolls together or would sit beside me as I read one of my beloved books, stroking my hand, now he declined to touch me at all.

I was equally reclusive. Sensing his distaste, I dared not linger. My words to him were no more than the occasional functional exchange. I still found myself a little angry, especially whenever I tried to puzzle out *how* he knew about my friendships with Cora and Flossie. Had he followed me? Had he gone so far as to employ some variety of detective? The mere thought left me trembling. I felt he'd proven himself to be something of a hypocrite, telling me to stay out of his past while digging up mine.

Even so, I couldn't ever *hate* him—not truly.

I know some women might live like this forever: stubbornly entrenched in a standoff with their husbands. But I was not then—and am not now—among their number. Beneath it all, I loved Harry. What's more, I still found him profoundly attractive; I loved the odd tuft of hair on his surprisingly muscular chest and the scent of his skin—which, under its top note of soap, smelled a little like olive wood warmed by the sun. I loved the way he listened attentively when I read aloud, cocking his head as though to lean into my words. I loved the way I could hear the timbre and cadence of his voice in the notes he wrote me. I loved that when we went on walks, he took in the world around us with an open heart and was drawn to surprisingly sentimental things, like birds' nests buried among the thickest foliage. He was a careful observer; it was no longer a surprise that he'd seen me in the street on that long-ago day.

A week passed in which we exchanged barely more than a dozen words. I could not bear the thought of going on with such a cold distance between us, and finally I put my mind to the task of thinking up some sort of gesture of apology . . . something to reunite us, something to remind him of the girl he'd married. I thought back to our honeymoon voyage, and was struck by an idea. I couldn't very well transport the two of us back to the islands of Hawai'i, but I could, perhaps, remind him of the memories we had shared.

I began making all the arrangements necessary for an exotic feast. I remembered having some kind of smoky, sweet-candied pork in Hawai'i, garnished with lots of tropical fruits—pineapple, in particular. There had also been mashed taro root, chicken in rice, and a variety of grilled fish. I made arrangements to procure all of this, determined to serve Harry a feast fit for a Hawai'ian king. I arranged to have everything delivered to the mansion and brought in a special cook to oversee the preparations. The coconuts and pineapples alone cost me a small fortune, and—not wanting to spoil the surprise by asking Harry for the money—I had to make a special trip to my safety-deposit box. This would be entirely *my* gift to him.

On the night of my surprise, I warmed the house by lighting every fireplace. I festooned the dining room with candles, orchids, and palm fronds. Then I dressed myself in one of the summery frocks I'd worn during our honeymoon, laid a wreath of orchids around my neck, and waited for Harry to come to dinner. During the course of the previous week, Miss Weber had made it clear that she disapproved and wanted no part of this romantic overture, but neither did she spoil the surprise. When all was ready, she found Harry in his study and informed him that dinner was served, as was her custom.

When Harry came striding into the dining room, his eyes were directed at the ground, but a few paces in, he froze. Slowly, he looked up and glanced about, taking in the spectacle.

"Violet . . . !" he exclaimed softly. "What is all this?"

"The islands of Hawai'i," I answered proudly. "Or . . . the flavors of it, at the very least."

He stared, unable to speak. I hurried over to a banquet and dipped a ladle into a large cut-crystal bowl.

"I had some punch made . . . I'd hoped that it might taste a little like the punch we drank at the Moana."

I offered the drink to Harry. Bits of pineapple and passion fruit bobbed in the pinkish liquid, and the scent of coconut filled the air. It took him a moment to respond, he was so stunned. Eventually, he moved to accept the glass. The outside corners of his eyes betrayed the early crinkles of a smile, and I realized that my plan was working.

"I thought it would do us some good to remember a happier time," I explained. "Won't you please join me?"

"Violet . . ." he said, shaking his head. "This is . . ."

I held my breath.

". . . very kind of you," he finished, and I felt my spirits soar.

"I feel terrible that we quarreled," I said.

Harry made a funny face, and began to laugh.

"What is it?" I asked, worried he was laughing at me.

"Come with me," he said, and took my hand. Still carrying our cups of punch, he led me to the drawing room, where a large easel containing an enormous canvas had been set up. The canvas, however, was blank.

"What is this?" I asked.

"My gesture to you," he said. "I was going to surprise you tomorrow: a painter will be coming, and you're to sit for him."

"Me?"

"Yes." Harry nodded. "I . . . I thought, perhaps, if the house reflected you in some way—that if perhaps *your* portrait hung in it, too—then it would show you how important you are to me."

"What a lovely sentiment," I said weakly. The truth was, I did not relish the thought of sitting for a portrait, nor did I relish the idea of my portrait hanging next to Madeleine's for all the world to compare.

But I said none of this to Harry. I merely threw my arms around his neck and thanked him. It was a lovely sentiment, after all.

"Our argument . . ." I said, hoping to apologize.

"Let's not speak of it," he said.

He took my hand again. Together we retraced our steps to the dining room and took in the sumptuous array of dishes.

"Violet, this *is* quite something. You've gone to a great deal of trouble here."

I offered Harry a necklace of orchids and together we sat down to dinner. A floodgate opened. Harry and I had spent over a week avoiding each other, and now all the talk we had bottled up brimmed over the surface. We had so much we wanted to tell!

We talked, and we ate and we drank. Afterwards, we adjourned to our bedroom upstairs.

I can still remember the blissful feeling that warmed me as I fell asleep that night. Harry and I lay entangled in each other's limbs. When we had finally exhausted ourselves in making amends, when there was nothing more to do with our mouths—no more speech, no more kisses—we simply sighed together happily. He fell asleep first and began to softly snore, while I contemplated the miracle of my good fortune.

As I lay awake meditating on my renewed contentment, I was surprised to realize all was quiet within the house. It was as if the mansion itself had been appeased. *Perhaps there was something to that theory,* I reasoned. Houses have a way of reflecting their occupants' anxieties. When I had first arrived at the Carlyle mansion, I felt like a misfit, and I made no secret of how the house made me feel. Perhaps all the strange things I'd heard and seen had only been a manifestation of my own discomfort. And now that I was ready to embrace my new life in earnest, the so-called "haunting" would cease.

I fell asleep that night with this conclusion securely in mind, feeling drowsy with equal parts exhaustion and happiness.

The next morning, I was awoken by the unsettling sounds of someone in agony.

39

H arry was sick.

He was pale, waxen, and clammy to the touch. When he found words, he complained that his stomach pained him and that his head throbbed. After some time, he began retching, and a pail had to be brought to his bedside. The expensive, exotic feast I had arranged proved a terrible, torturous waste, and I held the pail and rubbed Harry's back as he returned the contents in foul liquid form.

"I don't want you to see me like this," Harry complained between moans.

"I'm afraid you haven't a choice," I replied.

"Fetch Miss Weber!"

"No," I said in a firm voice. "I don't mind it—truly. I should mind it more if you send me away."

Harry was too weak to argue any further.

Between waves of sick, I brought him cool, damp rags. He looked so very miserable. I couldn't understand what had happened, but my heart began to fill with dread as I recognized the same symptoms I'd witnessed so many years ago. I tried not to panic as I played nurse, praying for the feeling of daunting familiarity to dissipate like a dark cloud blowing out to sea.

"You've poisoned him, you know."

I whirled around from where I stood at the sink cleaning out Harry's sick-pail, and saw Miss Weber glowering at me. The blood drained from my face.

"I beg your pardon?" I stammered.

"With that Hawai'ian feast of yours. It was likely too rich, too sweet, too exotic. Mr. Carlyle has a refined constitution and is not accustomed to eating such barbarous things."

"He ate many of the same dishes during our honeymoon," I said automatically. I didn't mean to sound defensive; in truth, I was relieved Miss Weber hadn't meant anything more sinister.

"He appears to have lost his tolerance for such nonsense at sea during your return journey, in that case," Miss Weber sniped. She left me to my cleaning.

I was glad. I didn't want her help; I wanted to be alone to think. I was trapped in a state of quiet terror.

It can't possibly be happening again, I told myself, trying to maintain a sense of calm.

Tackett had been poisoned, and on purpose.

I remembered something Flossie had said to me, in the days that followed Tackett's death, during those moments when my resolve wavered and I wondered aloud if perhaps we oughtn't tip off the police about the harm that had befallen Tackett and Blanche—if only anonymously.

Don't forget, Violet. With the police will come questions. You can't possibly want that, either. After all . . . you were his cook.

But Harry's illness passed the next day. A simple case of the stomach flu, I decided. I'd let my imagination run away with me. I was glad, too, that I had not run off to Flossie and Cora in hysterics.

However, my peace of mind proved short-lived.

Mail was typically delivered to a large iron letter box just outside the mansion gate. Mr. Davies regularly retrieved the post and carried it into the house. Any letters addressed to me were customarily laid upon a silver tray and set atop my desk in the library. I didn't receive a great deal of correspondence; most of the letters addressed to me had to do with running the mansion—minor matters that Harry had forced Miss Weber to turn over to my keeping. Sometimes I received the occasional courteous invitation or note from one of Harry's many high-society friends.

However, one afternoon, almost a week after Harry's recovery, I discovered an unusual envelope mixed in with the usual businesslike communications. My name was typed on the front, but the letter bore no stamp or postmark. Puzzled, I slid my letter opener along its sealed flap. Inside was a single sheaf of paper that appeared almost blank, folded into thirds. I unfurled the letter to see that inside someone had scrawled a single sentence:

I SEE YOU ARE UP TO YOUR OLD TRICKS.

Almost immediately, my hand began to tremble. My mind raced back to that day in the tent city in Golden Gate Park . . . the note I'd found under my pillow. Could it be? Panicking, I remembered that Flossie claimed the handwriting had looked like my own. I squinted at this new note and flinched to find that its script, too, looked familiar. The room began to spin. I felt as though I were falling down a well. I scrambled to keep a grip on my sanity.

"Mr. Davies," I inquired, after hunting him down. He was in Harry's closet, brushing Harry's suits. "This envelope was delivered with no stamp. Did you notice anyone unusual tampering with our mailbox?"

Mr. Davies gave me a strange look. He shook his head.

"I didn't see anyone at all, ma'am. Only the mailman himself."

"Did you notice this letter has no postmark and no stamp?"

I held up the envelope, but he averted his eyes.

"I did not, ma'am," Mr. Davies replied. "I can't recall noticing such a thing. I can only tell you that if it had your name on it, I placed it upon your desk, as instructed."

His tone warned me that he wanted none of my investigation. I thanked him for his time and left. There were only two people I wanted to talk to now.

When no one answered the door at Flossie's apartment, I went to Cora's. To my surprise, I found them both together.

"Come in!" a sing-song voice called when I knocked.

Cora's apartment was exactly how I remembered it: a den of sumptuous iniquity. A nest of silks and velvets, with every lampshade fringed. The air was thick with sinuous curls of cigarette smoke.

It appeared that Cora and Flossie were enjoying a spontaneous holiday, so to speak, and were engaged in much the same manner they had spent their free time long ago: flipping through the pages of popular ladies' magazines, gawking at the latest fashions from Paris, and passing a flask of whiskey. They made a familiar picture. Perched on an overstuffed divan, Flossie sat upright with her lank hair loose, while Cora reclined in a state of semi-undress with a glamorous messy plait cascading down her back. It was as if I had tripped over a wrinkle in time and tumbled back to our earlier years. I felt both reassured and disconcerted.

But then Cora broke the spell, and I remembered why I had come.

"Why, Her Highness Lady Violet has come to call on us!" Cora teased, by way of greeting. "What has lured you away from the Carlyle mansion on this fine day?"

I didn't answer immediately, trying to figure out where and how to begin.

"Violet . . . is something the matter?" Flossie asked. She got up and crossed over to me, taking my arm. "Come, sit down. Cora—perhaps you'd better fetch her a glass of water."

Cora rose to her feet, but instead of fetching water, she held her flask out to me.

"That's bound to treat you better," she promised.

Ordinarily, I might have refused. But that afternoon, I reached for the glinting silver flask and took a deep swill. My hand was visibly trembling as I handed it back.

"My goodness!" Cora remarked, raising an eyebrow and shaking the flask as though to confirm how little was now left within. She exchanged a glance with Flossie. "She really *does* have something serious on her mind!"

"Go on, Violet," Flossie urged in her gentle way. "You can tell us."

I launched into my story. During my previous visits, I had held back from telling them too much about the strange things I'd been seeing and hearing late at night around the mansion, afraid that Cora would seize upon these details as proof of her terrible theories. But now I told them everything. I told them, too, about how Harry and I had quarreled, and how I had tried to make it up to him with my fanciful, tropical-themed meal.

"He fell ill," I said. "He was sick . . . much the way—" I hesitated. It was terrifying to say aloud. But I steeled myself. "—much the way Tackett was often sick, before . . ."

I trailed off. The rest was not necessary.

"But you say Harry is now recovered? Perhaps it *was* only a simple flu," Flossie suggested.

"Those were my thoughts as well—or my hopes, really," I said.

I felt Cora looking at me as I said this.

"But . . ." I took another breath and told them about the letter. "Davies, the butler, said he retrieved it from the letter box, but . . . it held no stamp, no postmark." I shook my head and shuddered. "It must have been delivered by hand."

I showed them.

"Like the note you found in your bedroll," Flossie observed.

"Yes," I agreed. "I can't help but wonder if, perhaps . . . it was sent by the same person."

Cora and Flossie exchanged a look I couldn't quite read.

"Is it a possibility, Violet, that it didn't need a stamp because it hadn't that far to go, anyway?" Cora said.

My head snapped in Cora's direction.

"What do you mean?"

"Well, you're troubled, Violet. Perhaps it *was* written by the same person who 'sent' the first note."

My mouth fell open. I turned to Flossie but she wasn't looking at me. She frowned at Cora and shook her head lightly.

"Oh, don't you two look at me like that!" Cora said. "It isn't as though we haven't discussed it before, Flossie, and I can tell you were thinking the same as me just now."

I turned to Flossie. "Flossie?" I said, bewildered.

She fidgeted, and gave me an apologetic look.

"We never reached the conclusion that you did anything," Flossie insisted. "It was merely that we *wondered* . . . about the coincidence of it all."

I was stunned. I looked between the two of them. Cora gazed back at me with no expression, but Flossie was steadily shaking her head.

"We don't *believe* that you did it, Violet," Flossie continued to insist. "And if you say you didn't do it, then we will continue to stand by you—as we always have. It was only that it seemed such a coincidence. Tackett was thinking about making you work at the dancehall . . . and then, well, you were the one to bring him his meals, his drink . . . everything."

"After all, Violet," Cora added, "you would've been the first person the police would've looked to."

I was so bowled over, I couldn't speak. The room fell silent. Flossie looked at me uncomfortably, while Cora cocked her head as though gauging my reaction.

"I didn't poison anyone," I said, when I finally found my tongue. "I may not have cared for Tackett, but I would never harm anyone. And Harry . . . I *love* Harry. Why on earth would I ever hurt him?"

Flossie nodded her head in sympathy. Cora, however, bit her lip.

"But if Harry Carlyle were to die . . . how much money would you inherit, Violet?"

The cut was unexpected—and surprisingly deep. Cora always did know how to say the one thing that would wound me most. The same cunning that often made her the most charming woman in the room also made her the most lethal.

I felt tears spring to my eyes. I rose from my chair and hurried to the hallway.

"Wait! Violet!" I heard Cora call.

But I did not wait. In the next second, I had slammed the door behind me.

Once more, Flossie alone came running after me. I was three blocks away when I felt her grab my arm and whirl me around.

"How dare she, Flossie!" The tears were now threatening to spill over. "It's a lie," I insisted. "And not only that, it's a *cruel* lie."

"Shhhh," Flossie urged, stroking my arm. "I know, I know . . ."

I took a shaky breath and tried to get ahold of myself.

"Cora's in a queer mood today," Flossie said. "You can't take the things she says to heart; you know as well as I do, she simply says whatever is on her mind."

I knew this was true, but it seemed to me that Flossie hadn't entirely disagreed with Cora.

"Flossie . . . tell me truly: Do you believe I had anything to do with . . . well, with what happened on the night of the earthquake? Have you always thought so?"

Flossie made a face, as though deciding how much to say.

"It's Cora's way of thinking, really," she argued miserably. "Not mine. But . . ." She paused. "But I think, at the root of it, she is worried about you."

"Worried about me?" I retorted. "Worried that I'm a madwoman?"

"Well . . ." Flossie dithered. "It's not that Cora means to condemn you—she cares deeply, I am sure of it. But you've always been cut from a different cloth."

"What do you mean?" I asked, although in my gut, I already knew the answer.

Flossie shrugged. "You're just so sensitive," she said. "And your memory—you know how queer it's always been; it's as if you forget the things you have no wish to remember. Even when you first came to St. Hilda's, your aunt told the nuns you'd done something—something they all agreed was unforgivable! But you swore then—as you do now—that you had no memory of it at all. And then, also . . . strange things seem to happen around you. You were the last girl to have been in Sister Edwina's room, before the fire broke out—"

"You can't possibly think—" I stopped. I thought of the matches and my cheeks grew warm.

But Flossie only held up a hand, shook her head, and continued.

"It could be a coincidence, but Cora believes there are simply *too many* coincidences. You were the one bringing Tackett all his meals.

Blanche threatened you. And now you say Harry fell sick just after you insisted on overseeing the preparation of a fancy meal. You also told us that you had quarreled horribly."

I stared at Flossie in horror, shocked to hear my history laid bare in such a terrible, damning manner.

"I don't believe you are a murderer, Violet," Flossie said, anxious to smooth my ruffled feathers back into place. "But I don't blame Cora, either. You must admit . . . things have a strange way of happening around you, and your memories are . . . well, they're a bit flimsy."

I realized I didn't want to talk any longer. Even more than that, I didn't want to listen to Flossie say another word.

"I must go, Flossie," I said. "I must get home to Harry."

She nodded, and we both took one step back from each other.

"I'm sorry it has come out like this," Flossie said. "And I believe you, even if Cora doesn't."

She meant it to be kind, but it wasn't much help.

I made my way home on foot, believing it might do me some good. I needed to think over all that Flossie had revealed. Was it true that I was always in the wrong place at the wrong time? My mind was struggling like a cat in free fall, trying to figure out which way to twist and turn so that I might land on my feet.

When I arrived home, my certainty eroded even further. As I neared my bedroom door, I heard the familiar, hoarse-throated sounds of a man retching into a pail.

40

The hospital window faced north and its only view gave out over a bustling city street, with the unfortunate effect of rendering the light cold and gray.

"Can't we have him moved?" Miss Weber complained for the fourth time. "This isn't a proper place for Mr. Carlyle. There's no privacy at all, and people are always passing in the hallway; they can see straight in."

Ever since we'd arrived, Miss Weber was having trouble sitting still. She buzzed around Harry's bed like an agitated gnat. But despite the dreary amount of light in the particular room he had been assigned, it was a sanatorium for the very wealthy, with renowned doctors and every variety of wellness cure, a far cry from the charity hospitals named after saints that I had always known.

When Harry's mysterious illness had kept him sweaty and vomiting for over forty-eight hours, I made the decision: a hospital was the only way to be certain that he wouldn't take a turn for the worse.

Harry protested, of course. "You're being too hasty, too extreme," he scolded. "I'm not an invalid."

"Please indulge me," I begged him. "I can't stand to watch you suffer."

While Miss Weber was reluctant at first—claiming that she didn't like the idea of Harry under anyone's care but her own—she eventually agreed it was a necessary measure. Seeing that he was outnumbered, Harry relented. In truth, the hospital brought him some relief. Once installed in his new surroundings, his terrible bouts of sickness slowly subsided. Within twenty-four hours, he stopped retching, and began to get some of his color back. At present, he was snoring in what appeared to be a truly peaceful slumber for the first time in days.

"As soon as he is feeling up to it, I'll have him moved," I promised Miss Weber. "I've already made inquiries, and there is a room closer to the solarium that may become available soon. It's on a lower floor, but with a view of the little courtyard gardens."

Miss Weber's lips twitched with impatience. But I was feeling impatient, too. Since we'd brought Harry to the hospital, Miss Weber had fussed over him so much, the nurses and doctors mistook her for his wife—a mistake, I noticed, that she was very slow to correct.

"As always, you are kind to worry for him, Miss Weber," I said. "But the doctors here are very good, and they will keep him safe."

Safe. Miss Weber arched a skeptical brow; the word struck a nerve. When Harry had fallen ill yet again, we had both grown alarmed . . . and I could sense that Miss Weber shared my panicked worry that Harry's condition was not natural. Hearing our voices, he began to stir.

"Yes, ma'am," she relented, sorry to see we had woken him. She began to fuss again, tucking his blankets more tightly around his feet.

I had not considered how checking Harry into the hospital would bring the three of us together in one small room. With every passing second that Miss Weber and I sat perched at opposite sides of Harry's bed, it became clear we were engaged in yet another contest of wills. We bickered over everything, from which books to bring Harry, to which of us should fluff his pillows.

"Miss Weber, you've already changed the water in that pitcher twice," I remarked now, as I watched Miss Weber carry it towards the open door. She clearly intended to change it a third time.

"No one *else* ever refreshes it."

She meant the nurses, but only in part; I understood this comment was meant to disparage me. I raised an eyebrow but refrained from replying.

"Mr. Carlyle is recovering and needs plenty of cool, clean water," she continued, then darted a begrudging glance in my direction and added a flat-toned "Ma'am."

She left the room, and I returned my attention to Harry.

"Harry, my dear," I said in a soft voice, taking his hand in mine as he began to wake.

"Did Miss Weber leave?" he asked, blinking sleepily.

"Gone to get you more water is all," I said reassuringly.

"That's kind," he remarked.

"Yes," I agreed. "Although . . . sometimes I wonder if she isn't enjoying perpetuating the misconception among the doctors and nurses. They all seem to think *she's* your wife."

As if on cue, a doctor came in, clearly under this false impression.

"Oh," the gentleman said, looking between Harry and myself. "Apologies. I had hoped to speak to Mrs. Carlyle."

"*I'm* Mrs. Carlyle," I offered.

The gentleman frowned.

"I thought . . ." He pivoted his head as Miss Weber drifted back into the room, water pitcher in hand.

"I believe you have mistaken my housekeeper for my wife," Harry informed the man. "Miss Weber can be very devoted, but this is my wife."

I gave a nod, but I felt my cheeks color with humiliation. Miss Weber set the pitcher down on a dresser and turned to look at me with a stony, belligerent expression.

The doctor looked me over with a furrowed brow, not bothering to hide his frown.

"Pleasure to meet you, Mrs. Carlyle," he said.

I had the distinct impression it was *not* a pleasure, though I wasn't sure why he'd taken such an instant disliking to me.

"I'm the head doctor of this ward," he continued. "My name is Dr. Thomas. Forgive me for the confusion." He cleared his throat. "Well, then. I'd like to have a word alone with you, Mrs. Carlyle."

I glanced at Harry; he nodded.

The doctor made a polite gesture in my direction, and after kissing Harry on the forehead, I followed him from the room, down a corridor, and into what I presumed to be his office. He offered me a chair, then settled in behind his desk.

"Do you require anything, Mrs. Carlyle?" he asked. "A glass of water? Some tea?"

I shook my head. He stared at me for a long moment with the same disapproving look he'd given me earlier.

"Forgive me for the mix-up," he repeated. "I did not expect you to be so young."

His disapproving tone compelled me to apologize. But I restrained myself.

"It's . . . perfectly all right," I said instead.

"Of course, Mr. Carlyle had a first wife, didn't he?" Dr. Thomas said. His tone implied a statement, not a question. "I recall seeing her face everywhere—quite a beauty."

"Yes," I said, stiffening. "Sadly, she perished in the Great Quake."

"A tragedy," the doctor agreed. "The gossips insisted the loss left Mr. Carlyle a broken man . . ." He paused, then added, "But also the city's most eligible bachelor. You must consider yourself lucky indeed to have caught his eye."

"In fact, I do. Harry is a kind, loving husband."

"Yes. And . . . from anonymity to the manor, overnight. A heady voyage for a young woman."

I blinked with offended surprise, but Dr. Thomas only turned to a file on his desk and flipped it open.

"Of course, Mr. Carlyle's luck has recently taken a downturn, hasn't it? A lovely young bride, but symptoms of a violent illness. Particularly unlucky, when you consider his spotless medical history."

I cleared my throat and mustered a firm voice; if this doctor had anything worthwhile to tell me, I wanted to know it. "Have you been able to come up with a diagnosis?"

Dr. Thomas sat back in his chair and sighed.

"His symptoms may indicate a long list of afflictions. And the most scientific approach is to rule them out, one by one. There are, unfortunately, a great many cancers of the organs that could be the cause—a very grave problem, indeed. He doesn't appear to be suffering from the phlegmatic respiratory issues that might accompany a case of influenza, but one never knows . . . And, of course, it could just be that Mr. Carlyle ingested something that didn't agree with him—a severe allergic reaction, or something toxic."

"Something toxic?" I repeated.

Dr. Thomas nodded.

"Although we have not come to a final conclusion, we are, in fact, leaning towards this latter diagnosis."

He leaned forward in his chair and looked at me, studying my face.

"That's what I wished to discuss with you, Mrs. Carlyle."

"Yes?"

"I must inform you that we plan to take samples of Mr. Carlyle's hair and blood to inspect them for signs of poisoning."

"Poisoning?"

"Indeed. It is a strong possibility, given his symptoms."

My mouth went dry. I felt my eyelashes fluttering against my cheeks.

"An accidental contamination, perhaps. Something he consumes in the course of his usual activities—something he might never suspect." The doctor paused awkwardly, as if debating how to phrase his next statement. "The other possibility is, of course, that someone has been feeding it to him with malice in mind."

"Malice?"

"Yes." The doctor nodded. He seemed both shy about delivering this information and vaguely irritated to have to make his meaning plain. "Malice. Without his knowledge or permission."

"Yes, I understand," I said. "It's only that . . . I can't imagine it."

Dr. Thomas gave me a skeptical look. But then he offered another possibility.

"He is a strong man, as you say—a strident personality in the business world, I hear. Perhaps he has some enemies?"

My mouth was still dry. It opened and closed wordlessly. Finally, I coughed and found my voice again.

"No. I can't imagine anybody might hate him so," I said. "He is successful, yes—but he has always been very charitable, too."

I paused, trying to picture Harry's office near the shipyards. I'd always had the impression he was well-liked by his employees. Was I wrong?

"In any case, Mrs. Carlyle, we haven't confirmed anything yet. We'll know more once we've run our tests."

I struggled to regain my composure.

"All right . . . yes, then," I said. "Please run your tests."

The doctor gave me a funny look.

"I'm sorry to mislead you, Mrs. Carlyle. We aren't asking for permission; the patient has already given it."

I blinked.

"Then why have you summoned me here to tell me this?"

"The patient wished for you to be warned about the situation, in confidence."

"Harry asked you to *warn* me?" I repeated.

Dr. Thomas shrugged. "As I say . . . he thought it would be best if you were advised, in confidence."

"I see. Thank you, Doctor."

Dr. Thomas rose from his chair and held out a hand. I knew I was meant to shake it. For a moment, I could not move. Finally, I struggled to my feet and forced myself to take his hand. I had that strange sensation of moving in a dream—numbly and with great difficulty—as I departed.

I hurried back to Harry's bedside. Already my thoughts were spinning into a dark, foreboding paranoia. Dr. Thomas had said Harry wanted me to be warned. Was there a double meaning in that? Either way, Harry had been made aware of the possibility that he'd been poisoned, and he'd agreed to let them test for evidence. I couldn't imagine what he might be thinking or how he might be feeling.

"I don't wish to discuss it just now," Harry said as I rushed back into the room, reading my worried frown. "I merely wanted you to know."

"But, Harry—this is quite serious," I began to insist.

"Shhh," he urged, tilting his chin towards the open door. "I'd rather not worry Miss Weber. She's very protective of me, you know. And . . . well, she sometimes has a suspicious mind . . ."

I knew what Harry was implying. I felt that hollow tingle of paranoia return. Miss Weber might think whatever she liked, but at that very moment, I wanted Harry to confess his own suspicions—and reassure me that *he* believed I stood outside of them.

"Harry—"

"Shh!"

Before I could say another word, Miss Weber returned. Harry pretended not to notice as she shot me a menacing look. Then she busied herself by pouring Harry a fresh glass of water. She tipped it to Harry's lips, holding his head in what felt like an intimate gesture.

Suddenly, I couldn't breathe. I straightened up and cleared my throat.

"Harry," I said, "I'm afraid I've a terrible headache. I think I might go back to the mansion for a little while."

"Of course," Harry replied.

"You'll watch over Mr. Carlyle?" I said, addressing Miss Weber, though I was loath to concede to her.

"Ma'am," she replied in her usual dry, flat manner. She gave a nod.

Without lingering further, I turned on my heel and strode away in a daze.

I wasn't lying about the headache. I needed air. I needed a walk. All the things Dr. Thomas had just told me . . . it was too much to fathom. I recalled the note that read *I SEE YOU ARE UP TO YOUR OLD TRICKS*. Had Davies glimpsed the note and said something to Miss Weber?

I walked and walked, passing through the streets but seeing nothing, really. When I became aware of my surroundings, I realized I was standing in front of the Emporium. I stood staring for a moment at the revolving door, its glass panes repeatedly winking at me under the blaring sunshine. Its flash hypnotized me. For the briefest of seconds, time lost all meaning. I began to wonder what would happen if I walked through the door and reported for duty at my old millinery counter.

But then my reverie was shattered by a familiar voice.

"Violet?"

I spun about in surprise. "Cora?"

My eyes strained to focus on the lovely shapes and bright colors of the face before me.

"Cora, what are you doing here?"

"I was buying hats—at your old counter, as a matter of fact. Why, I've been at it all day! I just put in three hours' worth of custom orders, if you can believe it."

"Oh," I murmured, barely registering this.

"Violet, I'm glad to see you," Cora said. "I know you were hurt by the things I said last time I saw you," she said. "I want to make things better between us. Really, I do—I'm sorry, Violet. Earnest."

I gaped at her, still numb. Her eyes were sincere.

Suddenly, without warning, I burst into tears.

"Violet! Violet! What's wrong? I only meant to apologize."

Cora embraced me, but this set me to sobbing even more heavily. I gasped for breath and tried to gather myself together.

"He's ill, Cora—*very ill*. Miss Weber and I took him to the hospital. That's where I've just come from."

Cora shook her head, her lashes fluttered. For almost a full minute, she appeared unable to speak.

"Oh, Violet," she finally mustered. "I'm so sorry. Are you going to be all right?"

"I . . . I just want *him* to be all right."

"I understand," Cora said, nodding. She paused, scrutinizing me. "Is there . . . something else, Violet?"

"Something else?"

"You seem like you have . . . more than just this on your mind."

Her hands were still on my upper arms. I felt myself shrug away.

"Isn't Harry being in the hospital enough?" I said.

"It's only that I know you so well, Violet," Cora insisted. "You have that look on your face . . ."

"'That look'?"

"The way you used to look when you'd just had one of your episodes . . . a look of terror, and also of forgetting."

At this, I felt my entire body recoil.

"I have to be getting home now, Cora," I said.

"Wait—Violet! Are you certain you'll be all right?"

"Don't worry about me," I said, calling over my shoulder, already hurrying away from Cora and her piercing green gaze.

41

It was decided that Harry should stay in the hospital another week as the doctors continued to observe him. I spent my days at Harry's bedside, but my nights . . . my nights were now spent alone at the mansion. It was unsettling to sleep in our bedroom without him, knowing that the only other soul in the house was, supposedly, Miss Weber. I had never once ventured into her wing, wishing to respect her privacy, and thus when she retired for the evenings, that was that. I would fall into a state of solitude—solitude, but without the peace that sometimes being alone can bring.

I slept little at night, straining to listen for unfamiliar sounds.

I went to see Flossie at her apartment, and told her of my newfound misery.

"You *need* your rest," Flossie urged. She had gone to the trouble of procuring a small bottle of laudanum. "Just a drop or two in some milk," she prescribed.

Flossie was wise; it worked. At least for a little while.

But after a week without Harry, even the laudanum could not keep me in a state of slumber. I was awakened one night by an eerie tinkling, a sound I recognized: the piano keys. Drowsy at first, I roused myself and concentrated, wondering if perhaps I might still be dreaming. But no—the sound came again . . . a soft trilling of two or three keys. My heart pounded and my mouth went dry. I wanted to investigate—but what if I found somebody at last? I was acutely aware of the fact that Harry was not in the house to help me.

I ought to bolt my door and stay put, I told myself. But . . .

I quickly donned my robe and slippers and crept downstairs. The tinkling continued as I made my way silently to the music room. Only when I stood in the hallway just outside did it stop.

Experiencing a wave of boldness, I rushed in and snapped on the electric lights. It was all I could do to keep myself from crying out, *I have you!*

But, yet again, the room was empty. How could it be? Only seconds had passed. I was running out of worldly explanations.

Determined, I crossed the room to the grand piano. This time, the cover that rested over the keys was closed. This meant the unseen intruder not only struck the last key, but also managed to shut the cover and slip out with inhuman speed—all without making a sound. It was impossible.

Perhaps I *was* going around the bend, after all.

I suddenly felt overcome. My head was hurting and I moved to sit upon one of the two love seats. *Was I mad?* I couldn't even trust my own eyes or ears anymore. And worse . . . someone I loved was in the hospital. Was it possible I was to blame?

I leaned my face into my open palms, and before I knew it, I was crying. My body shook with soft, muffled sobs, and warm salty tears ran between the cracks of my fingers. I carried on like this for several minutes, until—like a curious tickle to the back of the mind—I sensed I was being watched.

I hastily wiped at my face, blinking my eyes back into focus. As it turned out, I *was* being watched. A familiar figure had appeared in the open doorway.

Miss Weber.

She stood there, not moving. There was a strange aura about her— like a person in a dream . . . a person you recognize and feel you know, yet gives the impression of wearing a mask. I considered for a moment that perhaps I was hallucinating, but then the apparition spoke.

"I heard it, too," she said.

I didn't reply right away.

"The piano keys," Miss Weber said.

"You did?" A wave of relief flooded over me. I was not insane if she'd heard the piano keys, too!

"*You* are to blame," the apparition of Miss Weber said now.

The relief I'd felt rushed away like the tide going back out.

"I never touched the piano," I stammered.

"Not that," Miss Weber said. "I don't mean the piano. I mean for Mr. Carlyle's illness."

I stared at her, feeling my pulse quicken. I suppose in some manner, I had been waiting for this all along.

SUZANNE RINDELL

"I haven't poisoned Mr. Carlyle," I said, attempting to keep my voice firm and even. But Miss Weber only shook her head.

"*You* are to blame," Miss Weber insisted. She remained standing in the doorway, like some strange angel posed in a panel of stained glass. "But your crime is your ignorance. You could not have known how your presence would disturb the house."

"What do you mean? How?"

Unnervingly, Miss Weber did not look at me as she spoke. Instead, she stared at some spot distantly over my head, as though lost in thought.

"Once she has been disturbed . . . all is full of unrest. And, I . . . I knew no good could come of your presence. When you first mentioned the candle in the rose garden . . . I knew then that you had angered her."

"Miss Weber—are you saying you honestly believe this house is *haunted*?"

"I'm saying things have happened in this house that you can know nothing about. I've done everything in my power to keep the peace, to honor the past as required. Yet, the past has been disturbed now, and will not rest."

I was speechless. She finally turned her watery blue eyes in my direction, but it was as if they pierced right through me, to a place far away.

"Mr. Carlyle has been poisoned by this unrest . . . It is what is making him sick, and it is your fault," she continued. "I made a fuss about your silly meal, but there is something else at play, something much darker . . . something intent on revenge. He should have never married her."

I shook my head, chilled and unable to comprehend.

"Miss Weber . . . I don't understand." My voice failed me momen-

322

tarily, and I struggled to regain control. "Are you speaking of *Madeleine*?"

Miss Weber slowly nodded, in an eerie, detached fashion. I felt dumbstruck, and it was several seconds before I could recover my tongue.

"If you are saying all this because you mean to protect him, Miss Weber, you needn't worry. Harry has explained it all to me, and I have pledged to keep his secret."

"I'm sorry, ma'am," Miss Weber said very slowly. "I truly cannot say I know what it is Mr. Carlyle has explained to you."

"Harry told me that Madeleine isn't dead—that she ran off on the night of the earthquake. She wouldn't grant him a divorce, and you felt it might be best to have her declared dead for everyone's sake. Harry told me you and I alone know the truth."

Miss Weber's eyes bulged.

"I tell you, ma'am, I don't know what you're talking about."

"You mean . . . you don't believe Madeleine is in Italy?"

She sucked in a slow breath.

"Of course not. I've never heard such a mad thing. Mrs. Carlyle is where she has always been, ever since her funeral: resting in the Laurel Hill Cemetery."

"But . . . but . . . that *can't* be . . ."

Miss Weber only stared at me. As the ticking of the mantel clock filled the room I understood she had no intention of answering. Without another word, she turned and disappeared into the dark hallway beyond.

I sat for several minutes longer. A mixture of emotions gripped me. Finally! Someone had borne witness to the strange goings-on. And yet . . . *the things she'd just said!* Was she being stubborn to protect Harry?

Even if that were the case, it didn't explain Miss Weber's abject fear of the house. I had assumed she was keeping the mansion at the ready for Madeleine's return, but now it seemed she meant to appease some unseen spirit. Was it possible that Miss Weber truly believed in such things? And . . . how could I reconcile this with everything Harry had told me?

I understood that I would eventually have to make a decision: listen to Miss Weber—fanciful ghost stories and all—or continue to trust in my husband.

I would trust in Harry, of course.

Wouldn't I?

It was late. I was cold. I felt an inexplicable sense of dizziness. The encounter had a strange feeling of unreality about it. I glanced again at the empty doorway, wondering if I had ever really seen or talked to Miss Weber, after all.

42

The next morning I awoke before dawn broke. I knew only one thing: I had to speak to Harry. Alone. My only chance would be to dress quickly and slip out quietly—before Miss Weber could insist on joining me. I needed to ask Harry about the bizarre exchange I'd had with her. I already knew what he would say, of course . . . and yet I desperately *needed* to hear him say it.

When I arrived at the hospital, Harry was sleeping. Ordinarily, I would have let him sleep—sleep being one of the more amazing curealls that mankind will ever know. Seeing him slumber . . . hearing his snores . . . I ought to have taken a seat next to him, and waited.

But—in my state of urgency—I woke him.

"Violet . . ." he groaned groggily, when his eyes opened.

"Harry, forgive me," I said. "I have to talk to you. It can't wait."

Harry struggled to sit up. I helped him stuff a pillow behind his neck.

"What is it, Violet? You don't seem yourself. Your face looks drawn."

"Well . . . it's Miss Weber."

"Miss Weber?"

I felt my insides suddenly twist and churn.

"Yes . . . She made some curious statements last night. Things I couldn't make sense of."

Harry frowned. His already pale complexion turned more ashen.

"What did she say, Violet?"

"Well . . . she seems to believe there is . . . how to put it . . . a malevolence in the mansion, and that's what's to blame for your illness."

Harry studied me, the creases in his brow deepening.

"A *malevolence*? I must say, Violet . . . I thought you were above small-minded superstitions. And I can't picture Miss Weber subscribing to such hogwash, besides."

"It's not just that, Harry . . ."

"Oh?"

"It's . . ." I hesitated, chewing my lip for courage. "She mentioned other things, too. She talked about Madeleine."

Wordless, Harry stared at me.

"Harry, Miss Weber *insisted* that she has never heard the story about Madeleine running off to Italy. I thought she might be protecting you, but, Harry—she seemed so sincere. I think she really does believe that Madeleine is dead and buried under that enormous mausoleum in the Laurel Hill Cemetery."

Harry was silent. I could hear my breath, ragged in my chest. After a moment or so, he spoke.

"How could you have any idea what Madeleine's grave looks like, Violet, unless . . . *you've been there?*"

I froze. I was caught.

"I only wanted to see if—"

Harry held up a hand, cutting me off. Was he . . . angry? He was trembling.

"I don't know why you insist on bringing all of this up, Violet. I'm feeling quite unwell just now. Perhaps you should go . . ."

"Go?"

I was alarmed. Had I driven a final wedge between us, after all? But as I looked at Harry, I realized that he had grown *extremely* pale. His eyes were bloodshot, his forehead beaded with sweat. He was beginning to shiver.

"You should go . . . you should go *now*—" Harry began, but before he could finish his plea, he lurched forward and retched violently over the side of the hospital bed.

"Oh—dear Harry!"

I looked about desperately for some way to help him, some way to soothe his retching or a sick-pail to contain the mess. But we had been utterly caught off guard. I wound up screaming for someone to help us—a doctor, a nurse, an orderly.

When I had managed to attract several nurses and a doctor to the room, I begged for answers.

"It came upon him so suddenly!" I said. "How did he fall so ill, so quickly? I don't understand."

"I'll send a nurse to fetch Dr. Thomas," an unfamiliar doctor said.

When Dr. Thomas arrived, he entered the room with a look of consternation. He leaned over Harry with his stethoscope out, but every time he tried to listen to his patient's heart, Harry unintentionally thwarted him with more spastic vomiting. Dr. Thomas abandoned the stethoscope and reached for Harry's wrist.

"Just as I suspected—his pulse is irregular," Dr. Thomas said. "We'll want to take another sample of his hair. I've been charting the contamination."

He glanced around the room to determine which nurse to assign to the task. When his gaze fell upon me, he flinched. It was plain he had not expected me to be there, visiting at such an early hour. His frown deepened.

"Mrs. Carlyle," he said, "I think it would be best if you were to leave us for the time being. There is a waiting room down the hall."

"I'd rather remain with my husband."

"I insist."

I did as I was told, and sat patiently in the waiting room Dr. Thomas had indicated. When I first sat down, I trusted that someone would be along shortly to keep me apprised of Harry's developing condition. I even had a notion that Dr. Thomas himself would come to explain all.

But as the minutes turned to hours, and the hours doubled, my patience grew as thin as an onionskin. When it finally dissolved altogether, I rose to my feet, intent on looking in on Harry. However, a nurse and an orderly intercepted me, hurrying to block my path before I reached the door to Harry's room.

"Mrs. Carlyle?"

"What's the matter? What's happened to Harry?" I demanded.

The pair exchanged an uncomfortable look.

"I think you had better have a word with Dr. Thomas in his office, Mrs. Carlyle," the young nurse urged me gently.

"Is Harry all right?"

Neither of them said anything. I demanded again, "Is Mr. Carlyle all right?"

"If you would just go see Dr. Thomas," the nurse urged. She ushered me in the direction of the office. "He's expecting you."

I allowed myself to be herded like a docile sheep to Dr. Thomas's stenciled door. The nurse leaned around me, rapped lightly on the glass, and twisted the knob.

"Come in, Mrs. Carlyle," Dr. Thomas greeted me.

He waved one hand at the chair opposite his desk. I sat. Then, not knowing what else to do, I simply waited. Dr. Thomas sighed, shuffling the paperwork on his desk. Once he had tapped the stack he'd been working on into neat alignment, he cleared his throat and finally looked up.

"Sometimes, we doctors hate to be proven right, but I knew it the second I saw it," Dr. Thomas decreed. "The fingernails, you see," he continued. He held up a hand, wiggling his fingers in a backwards wave. "The tales they tell, with those little white lines."

I was no medical expert. All I knew was that Dr. Thomas had news for me, and if he danced around the subject one second longer, I might scream.

"Please—what is it? Have you uncovered the cause of Harry's illness?"

He dropped his hand back to his desk.

"We have," he said.

He stared at me over the expanse of his desk, until finally he cleared his throat.

"*Arsenic.*"

I paled. "I beg your pardon?"

"Mr. Carlyle appears to be suffering from arsenic poisoning. We believe he has been ingesting a small amount very regularly over the past few weeks."

The breath in my lungs suddenly left my chest.

"Arsenic?" I stammered. "But . . . how would Harry not have any inkling of this? Wouldn't he have noticed a funny taste, or . . . well, something *amiss*?"

"Arsenic itself has no flavor or odor," the doctor replied. "His reaction may have been masked early on, especially if he was eating unusual foods."

He paused, then pressed on.

"I'm told that you prepared an exotic meal recently?"

All the blood drained from my face. I swallowed, and felt a woolly lump in my throat.

"Those dishes were just a nostalgic lark from our honeymoon. I would never knowingly give him anything that might make him ill."

The doctor raised an eyebrow.

"I was merely pointing out that your Hawai'ian meal appears to have been served around the same time as the initial dose. It might have inadvertently masked his illness as an unexpected stomach upset."

I sat absolutely still, trying to take this all in. There were very few people who'd have the chance to poison Harry—the servants, of course; the special cook I'd hired to prepare the Hawai'ian feast—but Harry had gotten sick a second time long after she'd left. The two people who had the most direct access to Harry were, of course, Miss Weber and myself.

Things have a strange way of happening around you, Flossie had insisted. I shivered, but pushed these wild insecurities aside. I loved Harry. I did . . . didn't I? I felt a sudden urge to be at his side.

"May I see him now?" I asked.

To my surprise, Dr. Thomas shook his head.

"That's why I've requested to speak to you, Mrs. Carlyle. Mr. Carlyle was so ill, we had to sedate him. He is resting. And as his doctor, I have decided that he is too unwell for visitors today. I'm afraid I have to ask you to come back another day."

I realized: he was banning me from Harry's bedside.

"I informed him of my diagnosis—yesterday, before the illness struck again with such vengeance," Dr. Thomas continued. "I recommended he allow the police to open an investigation, but he won't hear of it."

"He won't?"

Dr. Thomas shook his head again.

"Yes. Goodness knows why, but he was quite adamant. He must believe that there's a possibility it's an accident. Or else, I suppose, he means to deal with this matter privately."

The doctor gave me a meaningful look.

Was he threatening me? Warning me?

"That's all I can tell you at the moment, Mrs. Carlyle," Dr. Thomas said. "For now, I'm asking you let your husband rest."

"I—oh, yes. If that's what's best for him," I murmured.

"It is."

He rose, and I understood this to be my cue to leave. I stood and crossed the room in a daze. Just before I reached the door, Dr. Thomas spoke again.

"Of course, if Mr. Carlyle comes to a fatal end—God forbid—that's another story altogether," he added.

Shocked by his casual tone, I turned back slowly.

He shrugged, but the steely look in his eyes was deadly serious.

"I only mean that, if something more severe happens to Mr. Carlyle and arsenic is still suspected, well . . . then, an investigation would most certainly be opened. He'd have nothing to say about it."

Again, I could not tell whether I was being threatened or warned. I had an impulse to stay and stand up to Dr. Thomas, but in the next moment, the room began to spin. I staggered to the door, trying to hide my sweaty brow and the terrifying feeling of a spell coming on. Once outside, I gulped at the fresh air until my heart settled. I looked at the entrance and contemplated going back inside. But what was there to do? I knew I had to respect Dr. Thomas's orders.

Finally, I turned and skulked away, feeling like a criminal.

43

The note—the first note I'd received, the one I'd found in my bedroll in Golden Gate Park—had read: *I KNOW ABOUT THE ARSENIC.* Arsenic. Specifically arsenic.

Once I left the hospital, I found I had little wish to hurry home to the Carlyle mansion, and so I did as had become my habit: I ran to find Flossie. I would tell her everything, I decided—about all the things I'd been hearing and seeing at the mansion. About Miss Weber's eerie insistence that Madeleine was not secretly in Italy, and about her belief that Madeleine's spirit still somehow ruled the Carlyle estate. And—as long as she was alone—I would tell Flossie about the arsenic the doctors had discovered, and how I'd even begun to worry about my own sanity.

Luckily, I found Flossie as I'd hoped—home, and alone. Once I'd unburdened myself, she frowned, trying to make sense of it all.

"I don't know what to make of the things Miss Weber said," I admitted. "She was acting so strange that night; and my memory of our conversation is odd, too. I wonder if I didn't dream it, Flossie."

"But she denied knowing that Madeleine is secretly in Italy?" Flossie prodded.

"Yes—that is, if it wasn't all just a dream after all. Either way, I don't believe it. I think she means to protect Harry."

"What about the things she said about the house, Violet?" Flossie asked. "You've been hearing things and seeing things, haven't you? Eerie things?"

"Yes, but I've been wondering about that, Flossie."

"What do you mean?"

"What if . . . well, what if *I'm* the disturbance in the house?"

"Oh, Violet—you poor thing," Flossie said. "You have so much weighing on you!" She gave me a quick hug. Her sympathy triggered a flood of emotions in me.

"Flossie, what if I'm having my spells again? What if I'm losing my mind? How do I even know if I've really seen or heard the things I believe I have? When I tried to show Harry the candle, it wasn't there. When I tried to show him the sheet music, it had vanished. Miss Weber claimed to have heard the piano keys . . . but what if . . . what if that was just *me*, and I simply can't remember?"

Flossie was quiet. She held me in her gaze a long time. Finally, she took a nervous breath and spoke softly.

"I think I know what you are really worried about, Violet."

I waited.

"You're worried there's a connection between you and the arsenic the doctors found in Harry's system," she continued. "Something you would never do if you were in your right mind."

At this, the wave crested and broke, and I began sobbing.

"I love him, Flossie. I feel as if I'm losing my mind. What if I can't be trusted?"

"*Shhh*," Flossie urged. She put an arm around my shoulders and did her best to soothe me.

A few moments passed as Flossie allowed me to weep.

"I have an idea," she said, when the worst of my sobs had subsided. I wiped my eyes and blinked up at her.

"You shouldn't be alone in that house," Flossie diagnosed. "I'll come stay with you tonight. And what's more, we'll set some traps to see if anything eerie happens. If it does, I shall be your witness."

I gazed at Flossie with wide-eyed appreciation. She was right! If she heard and saw the things I did, too, then I could be sure of my sanity—*some* part of it, at least.

We continued to talk, shaping a plan. As we strategized, I began to feel my confidence returning to me. Flossie's faith in me made me realize it was much too soon for *me* to give up believing in myself.

I grew more animated as we plotted the details. I proposed to move several objects and rig up my strings and bells for good measure, just as I had done before. But this time, I came up with a masterstroke.

"Madeleine's portrait," I told Flossie.

"Madeleine's portrait?"

"We'll take it down and move it," I said. "It's much too large and heavy for a lone person to carry. If we find it has mysteriously returned to its 'proper' place, well, then at the very least, I will have eliminated Miss Weber once and for all."

Flossie considered this, nodding. I looked at her and managed to muster a smile.

"Thank you, Flossie. I feel better already. It's possible nothing will happen. But if something does, and you witness it—then at least I'll know I haven't gone completely mad. And either way, I won't feel so alone tonight, with nothing to do but worry about Harry. You have made all the difference."

"Of course," she reassured me. "That's what sisters are for."

We arranged to meet on the pavement outside the mansion at nine o'clock; I had no wish to disturb Miss Weber, or let her in on our plan.

Flossie and I hugged one last time, and I stood to take my leave. I had not been to Flossie's apartment in some weeks, and in that time, it had grown barer. As I looked around, I noticed that her beautiful button-backed settee was missing, along with several lamps.

"Flossie, we always discuss my predicaments, but are you certain everything is all right with you?"

"I'm moving soon to a different apartment," she said, waving a hand around the depleted room. "It's much nicer than this, and I should like to get new things to match."

"Oh," I replied. "How wonderful! I look forward to seeing it."

Flossie smiled. "For now, I'll meet you in front of the Carlyle mansion at nine o'clock sharp."

When Flossie arrived later that evening, she was accompanied by Cora.

I bristled when I stepped outside and caught sight of not one but *two* figures waiting near the hedges. They were both wearing long capes, but I recognized the coil of red hair cascading over one of Cora's shoulders instantly.

"She insisted," Flossie said in greeting. "She wanted to come along because she's worried about you."

The last time I'd seen Cora, I'd been coming from the hospital, distraught. She'd tried to comfort me and even tried to apologize, but I found I was still feeling rather prickly towards her.

"She can help us keep watch," Flossie added, eager to persuade.

"I hope you're not still cross with me, Violet," Cora said. She pulled the hood of her cape down, tossed her red hair, and smiled winningly.

I frowned. "Did Flossie explain our plan?" I asked.

Cora nodded. "If anything peculiar happens tonight, we'll be your witnesses."

She moved in the direction of the front door.

"Wait! I want to know, once and for all, Cora, what you believe," I demanded, wary.

She halted and cocked her head at me.

"About?"

"About all of it."

Cora sighed. "You already know I believe there's a possibility that Madeleine Carlyle *isn't* in Italy," she replied. "But I can't say I've ever put much credence in the spirit world, either."

"So, you've come to . . . what? Ridicule me? Look for proof that I've gone mad?"

"No, Violet!" Cora insisted, recoiling. "I *worry* about you. It's merely that I'd like to help look for an explanation—all three of us, *together*."

I relented. I knew there would be no sending Cora away; she would refuse, and her will had always been far more powerful than my own.

"All right," I relented, and led them both into the mansion. "Quietly, now . . ."

It was a strange feeling, creeping around my own home like a thief. But together the three of us set about moving objects and setting traps—just as I had described the plan to Flossie. We finished by taking Madeleine's portrait down from where it hung in the foyer at the top of the stairs.

"Where shall we put it?" Cora asked.

"The library," I decided. I led the way.

Once all was completed, Cora "offered" to show herself upstairs— mainly because she had no wish to help make tea. Flossie and I crept quietly around the kitchen, trying not to wake Miss Weber. We carried the tray upstairs, to the bedroom I ordinarily shared with Harry, where Cora was waiting.

I was hardly surprised to see that Cora had immediately helped herself to my bed; she'd flopped onto it with a carefree air and was presently occupied in brushing her long red hair with the silver brush Harry had given me as a wedding present. I bit my tongue and ignored this violation. Flossie rolled her eyes at Cora and perched in an armchair near the fire.

Fifteen minutes into our vigil, Cora was bored. I had laid out the rules: we were to remain dressed and awake, ready to investigate the slightest sound. But Cora was unaccustomed to such a stark lack of amusement.

"Haven't you any magazines or sweets?" she complained, sipping her tea.

"I'll never understand how you keep your figure," I said, half-ignoring her question.

"Sweets are how I got it in the first place!" Cora said with glee. She gestured to her bosom and hips.

This was ridiculous, of course, for I knew that, more often than not, bon-bons took up residence in *other* regions of a woman's body. Cora was merely lucky. She gave an irritated sigh and plopped two extra sugar cubes into her tea.

The three of us began to pass the time by chatting softly. Anytime our voices rose in decibel, I took pains to hush the group. I wanted to be able to hear the house . . . and, more importantly, whomever or what-ever it held.

It seemed, for a while at least, that all was abnormally still. I had been so certain that moving Madeleine's portrait would ensure an in-cident, but now the cold dread of doubt crept back in. *What if nothing happens?* I worried. *Cora and Flossie will think that I am really and truly mad.* If I was being absolutely truthful . . . I might worry the same.

The night wore on.

Despite having drunk two large cups of tea laced with five lumps of sugar each, Cora began to nod off. As Flossie and I continued to keep our vigil, Cora sunk further and further into the eiderdown bed, until she was lightly snoring, her empty teacup still clutched in her hand.

"Let her sleep," Flossie urged. "We'll rouse her if something happens."

I acquiesced, still worried that nothing would.

We waited.

And waited longer.

But then . . . when the hour had grown so late it was early and I had all but given up, a terrible loud noise rang out.

CRACK!

The sound was so loud, it ripped through the mansion like a thunderclap. It was followed by the smallest tinkling of glass, like a splash of water. Flossie and I jerked to attention, while Cora gave a drowsy groan from the bed.

"*Flossie!*" I whispered urgently.

"I heard it, too!" Flossie hissed back in a frightened whisper.

"I think it's happening!" I said. "Let's go see . . ."

Cora had roused herself slightly, but still seemed sleepy to the point of inebriation.

"Cora!" I gave her a tap on the shoulder, but she only gave me a sleepy smile and rolled to her side with a snore.

"Leave her—she's safer here." Flossie shook her head and waved urgently towards the door. I obeyed. We crept quickly and quietly along the hallway. When it eventually opened up to the cavernous foyer, I heard Flossie gasp, but I was not surprised by what I saw there. Frozen forever in oil, beautiful Madeleine stared back at us, as haughty and imperious as ever, her painted eyes glistening defiantly.

"Someone put her back," Flossie murmured. "Just as you said they would! But . . . who?"

I shook my head, still stunned.

"Not Miss Weber, after all. You're right, Violet: it would have required more than one person to lift it back into place," Flossie whispered. "But . . . the sound . . . I don't think it came from here," she observed.

"No," I agreed. We continued quietly on.

As we padded along, I noticed a strange draft from one of the downstairs corridors. It felt as though the clammy night wind was blowing directly into the house. It was coming from the drawing room. When I remembered what was in the drawing room, my heart clenched and I shivered.

"This way," I whispered.

We turned into the open door and I immediately felt the wall for the light switch. I pushed the button and light flooded the room.

One of the large glass windows was broken. It was a Tudor window, and an enormous hole had been punched out of the diamond-paned glass.

"What broke it?" Flossie gasped. "Was someone . . . trying to escape?"

"No," I said, suddenly certain. "An object was hurled at this window, and with great force."

I crossed the room and approached carefully. When I peered out, I spied an object smashed upon the pebbled path. *Harry's portrait of me.*

"It wasn't finished. In fact, I'd only just started sitting for it," I explained to Flossie as she followed me and peered through the broken pane, too.

"Oh, how awful," Flossie said. "Violet . . ."

Inexplicably, I began to laugh. Flossie stared at me, taken aback by my reaction.

"Are you all right, Violet?" she asked.

"I have to admit, I was terribly uncomfortable sitting for that portrait," I said. "And even more uncomfortable to think it might someday hang beside Madeleine's. I never imagined it would come to quite so violent a demise, but . . ."

My laughing had turned maniacal, and I was trembling all over. I saw Flossie peering at me with concern, but reading the worry in her face only further unleashed my frazzled terror: the laughter wouldn't stop, nor would the trembling. I felt tears streaming down my face.

"Violet, get ahold of yourself!" Flossie said, sounding panicked.

"What's going on here?" a voice interrupted us.

I spun around and saw Miss Weber in her night-robe, clutching an oil lamp. She took in Flossie with a look of unwelcome surprise.

"Who is this person?" she demanded. Her eyes flitted to the broken windowpane, then to Flossie, and back to me.

I wanted to answer her, but my laughter had turned to sobs. Each time I attempted to speak, I choked on my own heaving breath. It didn't matter, anyway: Miss Weber's eyes left Flossie's face and darted to the broken window, the shards of glass glittering on the lawn beyond. She gasped, and threw her hands before her face, as though guarding herself.

"*I told you not to disturb the house!*" Miss Weber scolded in a hiss. "*Now look what has happened!*" She jabbed a finger in Flossie's direction. "*And you brought a stranger here! You have brought this upon yourself!*"

"Please, calm down," Flossie coaxed, but she refused.

"*No! I'll have none of this!*" Miss Weber insisted, shaking her head. She turned to go. "*I told you not to disturb the house, but you wouldn't listen. I'm washing my hands of you!*"

Clearly terrified, she vanished back into the gray darkness beyond the doorway, ostensibly to hurry back to the safety of her own familiar quarters.

Flossie remained with me. She sat me down on the settee and held me close, stroking my back until I slowly ceased my sobbing.

"At least you saw it, too," I said, once I had caught my breath.

"Yes," she said, looking again at the broken glass. "I see it, Violet."

I sighed, and after a moment, I chuckled again. Flossie looked at me with alarm, worried I was about to cascade into another bout of hysterics. I shook my head.

"Miss Weber," I confided to Flossie, sighing. "If she didn't have it in for me before, she certainly does now."

The room would need repairs. I went around to the kitchen and let myself out into the garden to retrieve the tattered remnants of my unfinished portrait. Back inside, Flossie helped me put the room in order as best we could. I would have to send for a glazier the next morning, in the hopes of having the window replaced.

We went back upstairs to find Cora still snoring. It was incredible: she had slept through all of it.

"I can't believe her," Flossie remarked.

I nodded. "Still, though, Flossie—I am grateful *you* were here," I said.

Flossie and I crawled into the enormous bed, one on either side of a snoring Cora.

"I'm here, Violet," Flossie whispered. "Now I've seen it, so you *aren't* alone. We'll keep each other safe. Now get some sleep."

I closed my eyes and willed sleep to come. My mind was whirring with questions. Did I honestly believe a malevolent spirit was behind these otherwise inexplicable disturbances in the mansion? And . . . if so . . . did I truly still believe Madeleine was in Italy, as Harry had always insisted?

Simply opening my mind to these questions caused a deep sense of exhaustion. A poignant weariness came over me.

Sometime during the break of dawn, Flossie stirred. She woke up Cora.

"I'm sorry, Violet," Cora whispered, still looking groggy. "I don't know what came over me. I can't ever recall being this tired."

Before I could reply, Flossie stepped in. "You missed quite a lot, I'm afraid."

Cora's eyes widened. "Something happened?" She looked to me for affirmation.

But Flossie had seen the exhaustion in my face and understood now was not the time. "Shh, Cora. We all have much to discuss, but for now we need to leave, and Violet must rest."

Together they bade me a temporary farewell. Flossie kissed me on the forehead as I thanked them. Then I rolled over, still saturated with fatigue, and slept with all the dark velvet oblivion of the dead.

When I opened my eyes again, the sun was streaming through the windows, stretching long golden bars on the rugs, and informing me that the hour was already surprisingly late. It was afternoon, in fact. I guessed that Miss Weber was at the hospital; she must have hurried there at first light to tell Harry about the portrait, the broken window—and how I was likely to blame for all of it.

Still, when I rang the service bell, I was surprised when no one came at all. During the daytime, the mansion often had as many as eight servants at hand . . . surely there was *someone* downstairs. I rang again, but to no avail.

Finally, I gave up and hooked myself into my corset alone, then dressed myself to go downstairs. I got as far as the staircase when I heard another bell—a different bell—ring. It was the doorbell, I realized; someone was standing outside on the front stoop. I could see a shadow through the tessellated window in the enormous, Gothic door.

"Mabel? Bess? . . . Davies?" I called, assuming one of the servants would be along to answer the front door.

The bell rang a second time, and I realized I would have to answer it myself.

The bell rang a *third* time.

I became slightly chilled by the sound: a third ring implied urgency, impatience. Had something happened? I took a breath, smoothed my rumpled dress, descended the remaining stairs, and crossed the foyer to the front door.

My hand had begun to jitter with nerves by the time I reached for the bolt and latch.

Never in a hundred years could I have guessed what—or who—awaited me on the other side. But when I swung the door open and gazed upon her features, I knew immediately. She was no ghost after all. I was staring at a living, breathing woman.

Madeleine Carlyle.

44

A bolt of shock ripped through my body.

"From the expression on your face, it seems I need no introduction," the woman said. Her figure cut a svelte black silhouette against the blaring sunshine behind her.

It took a moment for my eyes to adjust so I might get a better look. It was as if she had stepped right out of her own portrait. Her clothing was different, of course: in the painting she wore an extravagant ruby-colored ball gown; standing before me, she wore a tailored women's suit of white and navy. But her silky dark hair—hair so dark it might be called black, really—was pinned up in that same elegant, swirling Gibson Girl bun. The only difference was a small hat pinned atop, instead of the jeweled tiara featured in the painting. It was uncanny.

I didn't answer right away, and the woman's long black lashes flicked up and down as she looked me over. Her mouth twisted into an amused half-smile. The gesture reminded me of Cora somehow—the only other woman I'd met who was so beautiful, she could make a smirk appear pretty.

"Madeleine . . . !" I finally managed to stammer.

Her eyebrows shot up.

"I didn't realize we had entered into a first-name understanding already," she said, with a hint of devilish glee.

"Oh!" I gasped, surprised and uncomfortable. "I mean to say, Mrs. Car—" I began to correct myself, but stopped short.

To my horror, Madeleine laughed aloud.

"Ah, yes," she replied. "I quite see your point. Two Mrs. Carlyles— both living. That will never do, will it?"

I was flabbergasted. I stood staring until Madeleine began to fidget and sigh, obviously impatient.

"As it is my home, I suppose I *could* invite myself in, but I would much rather if you would do the honors."

"Oh . . ." I said, trying to hide the trembling that had gripped my body. I couldn't make sense of what was happening. I had no idea what I should do. "Come in, I suppose . . ."

I choked on each and every word, still suffering from the acute shock of it all. But Madeleine only tipped her chin politely and sailed through the open door.

"My, my . . ." she said, once she had stepped inside. "One would never guess they rebuilt all of this," she commented. "Razed to the ground—or so I heard."

Shocked as I was, I nonetheless wondered, momentarily, if I was witnessing her permanent return to the mansion. There had been no steamer trunks on the doorstep; in her hand she carried a lone attaché case. She turned to face me again.

"Well, no matter! As we both seem to answer to the name 'Mrs. Carlyle,' we've more pressing matters than the architecture to discuss, haven't we?"

"Is it . . . is it really you?" I finally managed.

She laughed. "Were you expecting someone else? Has Harry a third or fourth wife I don't know about?"

She leaned closer as though confiding a secret.

"My dear, no matter how many 'Mrs. Carlyles' exist, I think you know as well as I do there has only ever been *one*. And a memorable one, at that. Somehow, I have the feeling that you already know quite a lot about me—more than I shall ever bother to learn about you."

I was having trouble finding my tongue.

"Either way, we are in need of a chat—you and I," Madeleine said more bluntly.

My head was spinning. It was all I could do to keep breathing and avoid fainting. She sighed impatiently, as if I were a child and explaining things to me was quickly growing tedious.

"Well? Shall we?"

My tongue still felt too sluggish.

"I was always fond of the conservatory," Madeleine continued in a breezy tone, taking charge. "Shall we have our talk there? You *might* offer me a spot of tea. I'm still recovering from a long journey."

"I haven't been able to find any of the help . . ." I murmured, in a daze.

Madeleine gave me a look that suggested such things had never happened to her during her own tenure as mistress of the house.

"Very well, then," she said. "I'll wait in the conservatory while *you* make the tea."

She strode away—she knew her way around the mansion, naturally enough—and left me staring, open-mouthed, after her.

I went to the kitchen, boiled some water, and made up a tea tray. My body went through the motions as if in a trance, while my mind raced. Too much had happened in too short a time, and somehow I'd gone from hiding Madeleine Carlyle's portrait from her supposed ghost, only to have Madeleine herself turn up on my doorstep in the flesh! My thoughts were pulled in so many directions, nothing felt real.

When all was ready, I carried the tea in with trembling hands. The cups and saucers chattered as I walked, and chattered some more as I attempted to place the tray on the table. All the while I toiled, Madeleine eyed me with obvious amusement. When she took a sip of the tea, she wrinkled her nose. She pushed her teacup and saucer away, then took a deep breath and sighed. She lifted the attaché case from her lap and placed it on the table where the teacup had been.

"Let's address our little predicament," she commanded. "I'll be frank with you, Violet: it seems I have returned at a critical juncture— though I hardly planned it that way."

"You mean with Harry . . . newly remarried?"

She didn't answer right away. Instead she studied my face, giving me another bizarre half-smile before continuing.

"As someone who grew bored of Harry myself, I can't say I blame you, although it is rather bold. Whatever makes you think you won't get caught?"

"I—Harry insisted you had no intention of ever returning, and that we'd never find ourselves accused of bigamy."

"Oh, I don't mean *that*."

I blinked.

"What *do* you mean?"

"Come, now, Violet. I know Harry's presently in the hospital. What-ever made you think you wouldn't get caught attempting to *poison him to death?*"

I gasped.

"I didn't . . . I haven't . . ."

Madeleine shook her head and extracted an official-looking sheaf of paper from her attaché case.

"When I left Harry, I had a copy made. You see . . . I imagined it might come in handy someday. I was thinking I'd need it much farther into the future of course, and I never pictured a dramatic scandal quite like this one."

"What is it?" I asked.

In answer, she merely began to read aloud from the document.

"*In the event of my death, I bequeath my servant and friend, Miss Ina Weber, ten thousand dollars. To my loving wife, I bequeath the remainder and large majority of my fortune—including all bank holdings, business interests, mansions, and other properties.*"

Madeleine stopped and looked up at me.

"All told, it amounts to quite a lot—Harry's fortune. But I'm sure you know that already; perhaps you've even managed to riddle out the precise figure."

My mouth fell open.

"You've the wrong idea about me," I insisted.

"Have I?" Madeleine replied, chuckling lightly again.

She reached across the table and patted my hand. I recoiled.

"Woman to woman, I admire your boldness, Violet—that's one way to make a marriage worth the bother! Very conniving. And you hardly look the type!"

She grinned, then sighed.

"But, alas . . . the will says *'to my loving wife.'* Harry can only have one wife, you see—and I am very much alive."

"What . . . what will you do?" I stammered. "You mean to tell everyone?"

Madeleine blinked at me dumbly, as though I had just uttered an absurdity.

"Well, I don't see any way around it—do you? I have no intention of skulking around San Francisco, keeping hidden. Not for very long, at least. *I am Mrs. Harry Leland Carlyle.*"

Madeleine gave me a cheeky smile, as though a naughty thought had occurred to her.

"Can you just imagine the shocked faces of the ladies down at the Francisca Club when they discover I've risen from the grave?" She laughed.

I stared at her, perplexed by her amusement. She caught my expression and shrugged.

"At first I was rather perturbed to hear that Harry had me declared dead. What an insult! But I suppose I ought to have anticipated it: Harry's always been sensitive, and divorce would have been an embarrassment, too brutal a blow for his pride. The earthquake must have looked like a clean slate from his vantage. When I heard he'd told everyone that I'd died in the 'quake, then turned around and married the first little ninny of a shop-girl who'd batted her eyes at him, I admit, I was so insulted as to vow revenge."

She paused, and flippantly picked a stray piece of lint off her tailored suit.

"But I'm feeling more sensible, not to mention more generous, at the moment. I *have* decided—just now, as I was sitting here—to do you a kindness," she finished.

"A kindness?"

"Well, yes," Madeleine replied. "I will let you be the one to tell Harry."

"Tell him?"

"That I've returned, of course. I'll let *you* break the news to him," she said. "Although it's a shame—I would love to see the look on his face. It's bound to be quite something."

I was silent, digesting all. I couldn't imagine delivering this news to Harry.

"Well?" she prodded. "Wouldn't you prefer that?—to tell him, in private?"

Before I could decide how to reply, we were interrupted by a great clatter.

I twisted in my chair and saw Miss Weber. From the looks of it, she had brought a tray of tea. She'd heard voices in the conservatory upon her return home, no doubt, and supposed that I was receiving a visitor. It was almost kind.

But one glance at Madeleine, and the tray had gone crashing to the ground. Miss Weber was pale and visibly quivering.

"*Madam!*" Miss Weber exclaimed. "You've come back to us!"

She stood surrounded by a heap of teaspoons, butter knives, and the debris of broken teacups, saucers, even a teapot that I recognized as Limoges. I tried to read Miss Weber's expression. Was she shocked?

Frightened? Looking at her face, I thought Miss Weber was trembling with . . . *joy*. Yes. That's what it was: the corners of her eyes crinkled in a way I'd never seen before. I realized that her eyes were *smiling* and brimming with happy tears.

As she glanced at the wreckage at her feet, however, she frowned.

"Oh! Mrs. Carlyle!" Miss Weber exclaimed in apology, taking note of the haphazard heap of broken Limoges. "I know it was your favorite!"

I was not foolish enough to think she was talking to me.

"It's quite all right, Ina," Madeleine said in a cool, pleasant voice.

It took me a moment to understand that she was replying directly to Miss Weber; until only a few moments earlier, when Madeleine had read Harry's will to me, I had never heard anyone speak Miss Weber's given name aloud.

Before I knew what was happening, Miss Weber had rushed to Madeleine's side. Whether she stumbled or it was intentional, I'll never know, but Miss Weber lurched to a kneeling position before her former mistress, as though Madeleine were a queen sitting upon a throne.

"We've missed you terribly, Mrs. Carlyle!" Miss Weber declared.

Madeleine leaned over the arm of her chair, gripped Miss Weber's shoulder, and planted an airy kiss on the older woman's cheek.

"It is a pleasure to see you again, too, Ina," Madeleine said.

"Miss Weber?" I said, finally finding my voice. "Where have you been?"

Miss Weber's head swiveled from Madeleine to where I sat. The shining gleam in her eyes slowly died. Her jaw hardened. It was clear where I fell on her list of loyalties. She stood and cleared her throat, her spine becoming more erect. Her whole body seemed to reject me in military fashion.

"You gave the servants the morning off, ma'am," Miss Weber reported in a bored tone. The switch between how she spoke to Madeleine and how she spoke to me was jarring. "Don't you recall?"

I didn't. But in front of Madeleine, I was too embarrassed to say so.

Suddenly, the events of the past few days began to overwhelm me. My head hurt. I stood up from the tea-table abruptly, rubbing my temples.

"Are you all right, Violet?" Madeleine asked, the mocking tone never leaving her voice.

"I need to talk to Harry," I blurted, pain throbbing at my temples and behind my eyes.

"Oh, good," Madeleine replied. "You've decided to take me up on my offer."

"I . . . I . . . I must go to him," I repeated. "Now."

"By all means, please do."

I began to back out of the room. I was aware of Madeleine and Miss Weber watching me as I moved, as if I were some kind of wild animal, but I didn't care. I turned and staggered in the direction of the conservatory door, still dizzy with disbelief. Just before I reached the hall, I heard Madeleine's voice calling my name.

I turned back.

Her eyes roved over my figure and face one more time.

"I hope I'm not being rude, but you really *must* consider applying a bit of rouge, dear. You look as though you've seen a ghost."

She gave a satisfied smile. I closed my eyes, turned, and strode away as fast as I was able.

45

You look as though you've seen a ghost, she said. The night before—with the switching of the portraits, the broken window—in many ways, I thought I had. But *she* was not a ghost; Madeleine had rung the bell at the front door with a very real hand. She had sat before me, in the flesh, dark-haired and beautiful, and announced that she was back in San Francisco to stay. I'd been completely spun around.

It wasn't until I arrived at the hospital that I remembered the events and exchanges of my last visit. As I entered the outer doors, my last conversation with Dr. Thomas came back to me.

I hastened my step, avoiding the nurses. When I reached Harry's room, I heard his soft, snuffling snores. I entered quietly and closed the door behind me.

"*Harry!*" I whispered urgently. "Harry, wake up!"

To my relief, he stirred.

"Violet?"

Once again, Harry struggled to sit up, confused by my unexpected appearance and panicked whispers. As I took in the sight of him, I suddenly felt the need to be near him—to touch him and hold his hand and kiss him, perhaps for the last time. What would he say once I told him about Madeleine's return?

Though he was still weak, Harry squeezed my hand and kissed me back, but to my chagrin, I began to cry as our lips touched. I felt the hot tears on my cheeks and our kiss began to taste of a sad, sad sea. Harry pulled away.

"Violet—what's the matter?"

"I don't want to lose you," I blurted out.

Harry's eyebrows knitted together. I could see that he was both dismayed and perplexed. I continued as best as I was able.

"Whatever happens next, Harry, I'll always treasure our memories. That silly monstrosity of a hat we laughed about. That thoughtful nosegay of violets you wore in your lapel on the morning we went to City Hall . . . Our first nights together in Hawai'i. I love you, Harry . . . I truly do."

Harry shook his head and waved his hands before his face.

"Stop this, Violet! I don't understand what you're about, but I don't care for the way you're speaking—as though you're giving a eulogy." He paused and gazed at me earnestly. "Are you . . . are you leaving me, Violet?"

"Harry, I don't *want* to leave you! Believe me!" I said.

He frowned. "Then, don't."

"It's not so simple."

"But it is, Violet. It is."

"No," I insisted. "For what I tell you next will undoubtedly change everything . . ."

Harry's face fell. He looked at me with clear, sad eyes.

"Harry, *Madeleine has returned.*"

Harry sat bolt upright in the bed. I was surprised he was capable of such a surge of strength.

"What? No! I'm sure you are mistaken, Violet."

"I've seen her," I said with solemn resignation.

"Violet . . . I fear I've failed you again; I ignored the things Miss Weber has been saying . . . She is worried about you hearing and seeing things while all alone at the mansion. I brushed off her concerns and told her you were just an imaginative girl, as I have always known you to be, but, Violet—oh, Violet—perhaps I ought to have heeded Miss Weber! I didn't know you were having such visions!"

"I'm *not* having visions," I insisted. "I saw Madeleine not thirty minutes ago, at the mansion. Miss Weber did, too."

A shadow fell over Harry's face and he stiffened.

"That's *not possible!*"

Before I could insist, the door flew open and suddenly we were not alone. I turned to see Dr. Thomas standing in the doorway, accompanied by two male orderlies and a harried-looking nurse.

"I told you I saw her slip in and shut the door!" the nurse said with a terse, righteous nod.

"Yes, thank you, Nurse," Dr. Thomas replied in a quiet tone. He cleared his throat and addressed Harry and me. "I'm afraid Mrs. Carlyle is no longer welcome in our ward," he said, and turned to the men. "Orderlies?"

Harry, already under duress from my news, now strained to sit up even further.

"What? This is absurd!" he protested. "Violet is my *wife*, and you have no right barring her from my bedside!"

Harry reached for me, but as I embraced him back, I felt his body begin to go limp. He was still weak, and had suffered too many shocks; his skin was clammy and I could see he was on the verge of losing consciousness.

I felt someone else grip my arm firmly. It was one of the orderlies.

"Violet . . ." Harry moaned, his eyes beginning to roll back in his head.

"Harry, I'll come back to you—I promise," I cried as the orderlies pried me from his arms.

"A word, Mrs. Carlyle," Dr. Thomas called after me as the orderlies walked me along the hallway.

We halted. Dr. Thomas gave a nod and the orderlies strode a few paces away, watching us from a distance.

"I see no reason for this treatment. You asked me to let him rest yesterday," I said. "And I did. I returned today because my husband and I have urgent matters to discuss."

"I'm certain you do," Dr. Thomas replied.

His tone struck me as patronizing. I took a step back, my brow raised. Dr. Thomas continued.

"I don't believe this will come as any surprise to you, Mrs. Carlyle," he said, "but I should inform you that arsenic is the ongoing cause of Harry's illness."

I was slow to comprehend his meaning. "Why *would* it come as a surprise? You've already informed me as much," I said. But Dr. Thomas shook his head.

"No. I told you that Harry's illness was caused by arsenic poisoning. But what I'm telling you now is that we've been able to determine that *the poisoning is ongoing.*"

My skin went cold.

"You mean . . . ?"

"I don't know why you would be so bold. Nothing can be done without proof, but I'll be damned if I let you poison one of my patients to death while in my care. For now, you are to keep away from this hospital at all times, do you understand? And you should also know, we've informed the authorities of our concerns."

By now, my mouth had gone dry. For a brief second, it felt as though all the blood had drained from my cheeks. Then, suddenly, every fiber in my body came roaring back to life. There was only one thought in my brain: *Harry! He was in danger.* I needed to get back to him immediately.

As my whole body surged in the direction of Harry's room, Dr. Thomas stood frozen with shock—but the two thick-necked orderlies did not. I took only a handful of steps before I felt their rough touch upon my shoulders again, this time unrelenting.

"Remove her at once," Dr. Thomas barked, when he finally recovered himself. It was merely a show of vanity. The orderlies hardly needed directions at that point; they appeared to know exactly what they were expected to do with me.

"This young woman is banned!" I heard Dr. Thomas call after us. "*Permanently.*"

———————

When they finally deposited me on the street outside the hospital, I was still frenzied, panting, and undignified. I caught several passersby staring at me, but I didn't care. I gave the now-forbidden hospital entrance a leery glance and my heart cried out for Harry. I needed help.

46

t was plain from the expression on Flossie's face that she wasn't expecting to see me again so soon.

"Violet!"

"Harry's in danger!" I blurted, not even mustering a polite greeting first. "It's certain now: he's being poisoned!"

Flossie blinked at me dumbly.

"The doctor just informed me that the situation is, well . . . *ongoing*!"

Flossie still appeared bewildered, but poked her head out and peered up and down the length of her apartment hallway. I knew I was speaking loudly—too loudly—but I couldn't help it.

She reached for my arm as if to gently usher me within. At her touch, I suddenly felt like the old, meek, childlike version of myself. I burst into tears.

"They've banned me from the hospital, Flossie!" I half-wailed. "I can't even get to Harry's side!"

"*Shhhh, shhh, shhh,*" Flossie urged, quickly closing her door behind us. "Violet, come, now. You're in absolute hysterics. Come sit and catch your breath."

I followed her further into the sitting room of the apartment. She'd gotten rid of her sofa, so there was only a pair of chairs left to sit on, and we collapsed onto them.

"That doctor, he hates me!" I said after a few seconds had passed. "He made no bones about it: they believe *I'm* the poisoner, Flossie."

Flossie was quiet a moment. "But . . . you're not," she said in a hushed voice, when she finally spoke.

To my tired, defensive ears, the statement sounded unnervingly like a question. A violent trembling overcame me.

"Oh, Flossie!" I managed to choke out. "What if . . . what if I am?"

She shook her head. "No."

"What if I am, and I simply don't know it?" My breath came in heaves until I was utterly sobbing. Somewhere deep within me a dam was breaking. "What if I don't deserve the faith you've placed in me? My history of spells . . . and then all these strange happenings . . . What if I'm losing my mind?"

"But I've seen those things, too, now!" Flossie protested, her voice full of compassion. She paused, then pressed on. "The notion of spirits still frightens me, but I believe something truly eerie happened last night. And, more importantly, I believe in *you*, Violet."

Sniffling, I tried to collect myself, realizing I hadn't told Flossie everything yet.

"There's more . . ." I said. I hardly knew how to deliver my next news. "I saw Madeleine," I finally choked out.

Flossie paled. She reached for my hand and gave it a trembling squeeze.

"Do you mean to say, Violet . . . that you saw Madeleine's *ghost*?"

"No," I said. "No. I mean Madeleine, the *real* Madeleine—a living, breathing woman—came knocking at the mansion's front door!"

At this, Flossie froze. She studied my face carefully.

"Are you *certain*, Violet?"

I nodded. "Unless I *have* gone mad, Flossie."

"You haven't," Flossie affirmed again. Then, after a moment of silent reflection, she asked, "What did she want?"

"Madeleine? She . . . well, she's come back," I said. "And she wanted me to know there could only be *one* 'Mrs. Carlyle.' I was so frazzled, I ran straight to the hospital to tell Harry!"

"What did *he* say?" Flossie asked with a slight gasp.

I paused, feeling my headache return like two knives to my temples.

"He insisted it wasn't possible," I replied. "You should have seen him, Flossie! I gave him such a start; his face turned purple. As if that weren't bad enough, we were interrupted when the orderlies burst in and they banned me from the hospital. Poor Harry . . . I doubt he knows *what* to make of me anymore! But, weak as he was, he tried to fight for me to stay. Despite that awful doctor's accusations, Harry has remained on my side. I don't know what I'd do if Harry ever suspected that the doctor's terrible suspicions about me were true."

"He loves you, Violet."

"And I love *him*! All I truly have is him, and you and Cora."

A strange, pained expression flickered over Flossie's face.

"What is it?"

"Well, *I* believe in you—truly, I do, Violet. But Cora . . ."

"Cora?" I was equal parts surprised and leery.

Flossie sighed.

"I may as well tell you the whole truth, Violet. She's been at it for some time now. Cora doesn't believe there *have* been any strange occurrences at the Carlyle mansion."

"But, Flossie, you saw it all with your own eyes."

"Of course, Violet! Of course I did. But Cora didn't. She insists you somehow *planned* it."

"That's outrageous!"

"I know, I know. But, Violet, even *you've* doubted yourself. Why, just listen to how you went on only a moment ago!"

Flossie paused, and a tense silence filled the room as I tried to fathom Cora's betrayal.

"So . . . Cora truly believes I would poison my own husband," I said finally.

"I'm afraid so," Flossie said, casting her eyes guiltily down to the floor. "She's constantly pointing out how much you would benefit if Harry were to pass away; she knows an awful lot about the Carlyle fortune, it seems."

I frowned.

"But it just doesn't make sense—especially now! If I were responsible for the strange occurrences around the mansion, and if I were feeding Harry arsenic to get at his money, then why on earth would I claim to have seen Madeleine now? I really *did* see her, Flossie—in the flesh! She walked right into the mansion and made herself at home. In fact, speaking of this so-called 'fortune' Cora thinks I wish to inherit, Madeleine herself produced a copy of Harry's will and read it aloud to me, pointing out that in naming his wife as beneficiary, it refers to *her*—not me."

As the words left my mouth, I froze.

"What is it?" Flossie asked.

"The will!" I said. "She read it to me! *Madeleine read it aloud to me!*"

Flossie only blinked, not comprehending, but I felt my doubts replaced by a forceful new conviction.

"I have to go back to the mansion, Flossie!" I said, scrambling for the door.

Flossie's brow furrowed with concern. She rushed to throw on her shawl and followed me out the door.

"I'm going with you, Violet," she vowed.

I ran for the street, suddenly full of grit and determination, and galvanized by the feeling of Flossie at my heels.

47

The rest of the mansion was empty, but I could hear the sound of voices coming from the library. I hesitated in the foyer, deciding how to proceed.

"*Shhh*," I said, motioning for Flossie to follow me. I tiptoed carefully to Harry's study. It was a perpetually dark, musty room, but I dared not draw the heavy curtains or switch on the electric lights. I crossed over to Harry's desk, breathing in the faint scent of old pipe tobacco.

I paused for a moment, steadying myself. Then I pulled open the drawer and lifted out the case I knew contained his revolver. When Flossie made out the shape of the gun in the gloom, she gripped my elbow with fresh alarm.

"Violet—what do you plan to do?"

"Nothing grave, Flossie—don't worry! There aren't any bullets in it. See? I'm leaving them right here." I pointed to a small box still nestled inside Harry's desk drawer, then pushed the drawer shut. I tucked the revolver in the pocket of my skirt and arranged the folds to hide the heavy tug of its weight.

I could still feel Flossie fretting, her worry emanating from her body in near-palpable waves.

"If you'd rather remain in here, that's all right, Flossie," I instructed her. "I have to confront her, but I wouldn't blame you if you'd rather stay out of it."

Flossie was dithering and biting her lip, but I couldn't wait. I headed for the hall.

The library had always been the one place in the Carlyle mansion I'd felt most at home. But as soon as I neared the open door, I recognized Miss Weber's voice engaged in conversation, and I knew that Madeleine had decided to stake her claim.

There, upon one of the cozy button-back leather sofas, sat Madeleine. When she spied me hovering, she smiled.

"Why, *do* come in, Violet!" she called.

She patted the seat beside her. I entered but opted instead for the matching sofa opposite her.

"I never much cared for this room," she said, casually glancing around. "But Miss Weber tells me you spend all your time here. I thought there might be some quality I'd overlooked."

It was jarring to think that Madeleine had been asking questions about me—and even more jarring to know Miss Weber had been happily answering.

"I'm still not sure I see the appeal," Madeleine continued. She wrinkled her nose. "I can never get the smell of dusty, moldy books out of my hair."

"I love that scent," I countered.

She turned back to regard me and gave a shrug.

"Well, after all, we *are* very different—aren't we?"

Miss Weber let a bitter grunt of amusement slip. I glared at Madeleine in response and debated how best to confront her. I sensed Flossie standing in the doorway, cautiously poking her head in. Madeleine followed my gaze. For the first time, her unflappable demeanor betrayed a jolt of surprise.

"You . . . you've brought a guest?"

"My friend," I answered. "Flossie. Come, Flossie—join us." The sight of her strengthened my resolve.

Madeleine and Flossie exchanged a stiff nod, each looking equally uneasy. Flossie looked uncharacteristically rattled as she edged further into the room, but she came faithfully over to my side.

"In any case, there is a matter I wish to discuss with you, *Madeleine*," I said.

"Oh?" Madeleine replied, arching her elegant black brows. "This sounds rather serious." She glanced again at Flossie, then turned to address Miss Weber. "Would you mind terribly, Ina, pouring the three of us a nip of brandy?"

I bristled at how Madeleine continued to play the hostess. Miss Weber held Madeleine's gaze for a moment, then gave a quick curtsy. "Ma'am," she said.

She extracted three snifters and a cut-crystal decanter of brandy from the liquor cabinet and filled them with a finger each. Then she set one before each of us and excused herself, giving me a cold glance as she bustled out of the room.

A thick silence settled among the three of us who remained.

Madeleine took a long sip of her brandy, nearly draining the glass. Then she turned to me.

"I imagine you've come from the hospital."

I nodded hesitantly.

"Did you deliver the news to our dear husband?"

"I did," I replied.

"How did he take it?"

"He insisted it couldn't be true. In fact, he was so adamant it couldn't be true that I fear he is worried for the health of my mind and believes I am suffering from a hallucination."

Madeleine laughed. "Well, that sounds like Harry," she said. "He adores you—until he has a reason to doubt you."

"Perhaps," I replied. "But the more I mull things over, *Madeleine*, the more I believe Harry may be on the right path."

She straightened up.

"What do you mean? Obviously, I am no figment of your imagination, Violet. I am sitting right in front of you. You need only ask your friend there"—she nodded at Flossie—"who can also see me, plain as day."

"Yes," I agreed, "that much is true. *But I don't believe you are Madeleine Carlyle.*"

She tried to keep her composure, but I could see I had rattled her; the tendons at the base of her neck visibly tightened. Her eyes darted nervously to Flossie, then back to me.

"I don't believe you *are* Madeleine Carlyle," I repeated.

"You're talking nonsense," Madeleine said with a snort. "I realize it would be much simpler for you if I hadn't decided to return to San Francisco."

"You read Harry's will aloud to me," I countered.

"What of it?" Madeleine shrugged. "You know perfectly well why I read that off to you."

"Oh, I know *why*..." I said. "It is *how* that presents a problem. You see, I also happen to know that Madeleine—the *real* Madeleine—was so nearsighted, she was almost blind. She needed inch-thick spectacles to read—spectacles she despised wearing in front of others."

At this, the dark-haired beauty hesitated.

"It was a familiar read, my dear," she said haughtily, recovering. "I could've recited that will in my sleep!" She forced a laugh, but already she was beginning to crumble. She looked around the room for an impartial party, giving Flossie a pleading glance, after which she eyed the door. "Of course I'm Madeleine," the woman insisted, now with a hint of desperation. "Ina knows me."

Her words—*Ina knows me*—struck my ears like a thunderclap. *Miss Weber!* How had I ignored what was staring me in the face the whole time? Miss Weber knew the real Madeleine, and yet she had accepted this impostor! She had embraced her, even flouted their cozy rapport.

"Flossie!" I shouted, my eyes wide.

But Flossie had already read my thoughts. She sprang to her feet.

"I'll find her," Flossie said, hurrying towards the library door.

She disappeared into the hall, the patter of her urgent footsteps echoing back to where I remained with "Madeleine," whom I now knew to be a perfect stranger. I took a breath, hoping to steady myself.

"Well," I said, with apprehension. "We still haven't been properly introduced. Would you care to tell me what your real name is?"

The woman's lips twitched nervously.

"Madeleine Carlyle," she insisted. But I could tell that her conviction was waning.

"I think we both know that simply isn't true."

"Prove it," she said, her voice quivering. She forced a smug smile. "I've been hearing plenty of gossip that you may not be in your right mind anyway, Violet."

I smiled in return, then reached into my skirt pocket for the revolver. Her eyes went saucer-shaped to see it.

"You're right—I don't feel I *am* in my right mind," I admitted. "But either way, I expect you to tell me your name. Your *real* name, that is."

The smug smile remained frozen on her face for a full ten seconds longer; then, all at once, it gave way and crumpled. She glanced nervously at the revolver, then again at the empty doorway where Flossie had recently disappeared. She let out a small, exhausted sigh.

"Helen," she said finally. "Well, my stage name is Helen Beauchamp. I'm part of the musical revue down at the Imperial."

"The Imperial Theater?" I echoed, slowly putting the pieces together. "You're an actress."

"Yes—that's where she saw me."

I didn't answer right away, mulling this over. Helen gave a nervous chuckle.

"Don't you think you should put that revolver away now?"

I ignored this, keeping the gun pointed at her. "Where *who* saw you?"

Helen rolled her lips into a tight line and cocked her head at me. Then, after a moment, she asked, "Who do you think?"

"I see," I said, nodding. "Miss Weber."

Her entire demeanor had changed, and so had her accent. Gone was the elegant, eloquent, glamorous Madeleine, and in her place sat a chorus girl—still a beauty, but a common one. She had been acting a part.

"You say Miss Weber found you at the theater?"

"Yes."

"Explain," I demanded.

"Well, she insisted I looked so much like her dead mistress, it was like seeing a ghost. We talked and made some arrangements, and she dressed me and tutored me as to how I ought behave."

"And then you came to me. You rang the bell knowing I would answer."

"Yes."

"You intended to give me a fright?"

"Ina—Miss Weber—she said you were going mad and needed to be removed for the good of the estate. She told me you were half-convinced Madeleine was still alive, and half-convinced her tormented spirit was haunting this mansion. She thought if I were to turn up, the sight of me might give you a little shove—so to speak—and send you over the edge."

I shook my head, incredulous. "Send me over the edge," I said. "You mean *put me in a madhouse*."

Helen nodded cautiously.

"Why did you agree to do it?"

At this, she gave a snort.

"Well, an awful lot of money, to start."

"But . . . how? *Miss Weber* offered to pay you a large sum?" I asked.

Helen shrugged. "She said if I did my job properly, she would be coming into a great fortune."

Where was Flossie? Why hadn't she returned with Miss Weber yet? I began to think through everything Miss Weber must have orchestrated. I was sure, now, that she had something to do with the eerie things I'd been seeing and hearing at night. I thought back, too, to our visits to Harry in the hospital . . . Miss Weber had desperately wanted him moved to a more private, less central room. All that fussing over him, the water pitcher she insisted on constantly refilling. An ominous feeling settled over me, and I had a sudden urge to find Flossie and make certain she was all right. But what to do with Helen? I didn't want to leave her alone and risk having her escape.

"You *do* look an awful lot like her," I remarked, making a more studied inspection of her features.

It wasn't intended as a compliment, per se, but Helen surprised me with a proud grin.

"I've heard it before; everyone's seen Mrs. Carlyle's face all over the papers." She paused, and blinked her long lashes sheepishly at me. "The *first* Mrs. Carlyle, that is. I've been told it's uncanny. I think that's how she knew to come to the theater looking for me."

She meant Miss Weber. My quiet panic began to intensify. I got up and peered into the hallway.

"Flossie?" I called. "Flossie? Where are you?"

I heard a rustling but couldn't tell where it was coming from.

"Flossie?" I called again.

Finally, I heard her footfall. She was running.

"She's gone!" Flossie exclaimed as she hurried towards me.

"Gone?"

"She must've realized you'd figured out the truth."

"Where did she go?"

"Impossible to know. But it's a fair guess that she's gone for good, Violet."

"No—that can't be!" I darted my eyes about desperately. "Here—take this." I handed the revolver to Flossie. "Watch her!"

I made my own frantic search of the mansion, heading directly for the one portion of the house I had never permitted myself to explore: the servants' wing.

It was strange—a whole wing I'd never dared to enter. I'd often wondered what it looked like, and what Miss Weber got up to when there was no one else around. Now I hurried down a staircase and along a narrow hallway. I noted a bathroom and three very tidy, empty bedrooms. They possessed beds and mattresses, but none of them were made up with bed-clothes, and not a single painting or even postcard hung on the walls. There was another room meant to facilitate the washing of laundry, with great tubs and washboards and a hand-cranked ringer. There was also a small cupboard-sized room with an ironing board, and another tiny room that housed an additional oven and several sacks of flour.

I moved along frantically until I reached a fourth and final bedroom. Surely, this was Miss Weber's room. I slowed my step and peered inside. The bed boasted a pale blue chintz spread, and the walls were sparsely decorated with seaside paintings of some distant, cloudy, European shore. I entered cautiously on light feet.

"Miss Weber?" I called.

I saw that the wardrobe had been left ajar. A glimpse inside revealed that it had recently been emptied; only a few stray items hung abandoned on idle hangers. I crossed to a dresser and tried one of the drawers.

It, too, appeared to have been ransacked. Flossie's guess was right: Miss Weber had indeed packed her belongings and left.

If I had been harboring any doubts about the full extent of Miss Weber's guilt, they evaporated there in her room, as I stared down into an empty dresser drawer.

I shut the drawer and looked around once more, feeling utterly empty-handed. I was no longer looking for a person; I was looking for an explanation. To my deep surprise, I spied a folded slip of paper propped up on the nightstand. I seized it and read it with shaking hands.

> *You little fool, he could never belong to a wretch such as you.*
> *I offer no apologies. I care little if you come looking for me. The*
> *others did it for want of fortune. I did it for love.*

I blinked, reading the lines over a second time, troubled by one line in particular. *"The others did it for want of fortune."* I read and reread that sentence several times. I couldn't help but wonder: *The . . . others?* It was clear that Miss Weber had been working in concert with the woman who presented herself as Madeleine, but . . . was there someone else in addition to those two? "Others" implied a greater plurality. It was troubling, and there was only one person left who might provide answers.

I scrambled back upstairs to the library. Helen was still there—much to my relief—and she and Flossie were locked in a long, hard stare as Flossie continued to point the revolver at her. I broke the spell, rushing into the room like a gale of mad wind, and accosted Helen.

"What did she tell you about her reasons for hiring you?" I demanded.

Helen blinked stupidly at me. I yanked the revolver out of Flossie's hand and made certain that Helen got a closer look at the barrel. She paled and sputtered, then began to talk.

"She always used the same words, '*for the good of the Carlyle estate*.' I got the impression she loved Mr. Carlyle and wanted to protect him. They'd been children together, she said. She insisted the night of the earthquake had deepened their bond. Afterwards, she helped Mr. Carlyle rebuild his home, and in return he finally treated her as though she were the mistress of the mansion."

Helen hesitated and shot me a nervous look.

"I guess . . . until he married *you*. She seemed . . . well, *furious*. She didn't feel you deserved to call yourself his wife. Later, she didn't trust you, and she said she'd found out you had your own checkered past. She told Mr. Carlyle about it, but he didn't care. That enraged her further, I think. By the time we met—she and I, that is—she said she'd found a way to turn your checkered past to her own advantage. If she could get enough people to believe you were insane—so insane that you were having conversations with ghosts—then locking you away in the madhouse would be a cinch."

Helen paused. She looked down at her hands, then nervously at the revolver.

"I believe she was hoping to keep him safe. After he went to the hospital, she insisted he wouldn't get well until you were safely locked away. She mentioned . . ."

Helen hesitated. She shot me a fearful look.

"She mentioned it might be arsenic. Please . . . if you let me go, I won't tell anyone, I promise."

I shook my head at Helen. "You *can't* be that big a fool," I insisted. "You weren't helping Miss Weber prevent a poisoning. Don't you see? You were helping *commit one*. How do you think Miss Weber was going to procure the money to pay you?"

At this, Helen paled. She shifted where she sat, looking genuinely uncomfortable.

"That can't be . . . I always had the impression she loved him," Helen murmured aloud. "She even insinuated that the two of them were . . . rather intimate, on occasion."

"That's a *lie*," I snapped, enraged.

She looked at me, frightened by my sudden vehemence.

"That's simply not true."

I realized that I *had* always wondered; moreover, Miss Weber knew she'd put the question in my mind, and the mere thought of it felt like a violation.

I felt myself growing more and more upset.

"Violet, calm your breathing," Flossie warned gently. "You're beginning to look faint . . ."

She was right. I tried to calm down, but the flustered feeling wouldn't go away. Flossie reached for my untouched snifter.

"Here, drink this," she urged, handing it to me.

I took a sip and felt the warm fire of the brandy slip down my throat. Then, after a brief hesitation, I swallowed what remained, hoping for more fortification.

"That was a lie," I repeated, glaring at Helen. "If Miss Weber ever said that about . . . about . . . her *relations* with Harry, she was lying to you."

Helen was silent, nervous to see me unraveling, gun in hand.

Abruptly, the brandy turned on me. My stomach lurched and I felt light-headed. I tried to calm myself, as Flossie advised.

I recalled the lines in Miss Weber's note. *The others did it for want of fortune. I did it for love.* I attempted to focus.

"Miss Weber left a message," I said now. I produced the slip of paper from my skirt pocket.

"She left a note?" Flossie asked, surprised.

I nodded and tucked the note safely away again; it was precious. Though the language was vague, it was one small piece of written proof that I had nothing to do with Harry's poisoning. I turned back to Helen.

"The note mentions 'others'—*plural.* Clearly, you were involved, but who else did she enlist?"

At this, Helen's eyes widened, and a brief flicker of panic rippled over her face. She glanced at Flossie and then back at me.

"Helen . . ." I said, a warning note in my voice. "Or should I say 'Madeleine'? You agreed to be part of a dangerous confidence trick. You are a pretender, that much is certain, but you cannot pretend you're above it all now—not to me, unless you'd like police charges brought against you."

She looked near to fainting, but I stared her down regardless, and she squirmed in her seat. She looked one last time from Flossie to me, but evidently found no mercy in either of us.

"There *was* another," Helen admitted finally. "A third woman. She said she was a friend of yours, in fact, and told us all about you. She was privy to every detail of your life, it seemed—your life before meeting and marrying Mr. Carlyle. She knew how your past might be used against you, and *she* was the one who gave Miss Weber the idea to do what she did. She didn't believe you deserved the enormous fortune you'd married into."

A prickly chill ran over my skin. Flossie and I exchanged a meaningful look.

"And her name?" I demanded.

Helen hesitated.

"She called herself Blanche, but from the very first, I had the impression this was a false name, anyway."

Flossie cleared her throat and stepped forward.

"Tell me now, Helen . . . was this woman quite pretty, with scarlet hair?"

Helen stared at Flossie, and Flossie held her gaze in return.

"You *must* tell us, Helen," I implored. "Did she have red hair?"

Helen took one last look at Flossie and lowered her eyes to the ground.

"Yes," Helen said. "Yes, she did."

There was no longer any doubt who Helen meant.

48

Cora.

The answer hit me like a wave. But I felt a wave of something else hit me, too—a wave of severe nausea. I wobbled a little on my feet and realized I was feeling quite ill, indeed. I fell to the rug and fought the urge to vomit, but eventually failed.

"Violet!" I heard Flossie's voice calling, but already the room was floating away from me, spinning in such a way to make my queasiness worse. The black spots in my vision were crowding together, threatening to blot everything out. Two pairs of hands attempted to catch me as the fainting spell hit me in full. Was Helen attempting to help? What was happening?

But as I strained to comprehend the circumstances, all the sound in the room was moving further and further away. I struggled against the sensation of spinning . . . until I could struggle no more.

Endless black enveloped me.

When I woke, dusk had fallen and night was rapidly settling into the mansion. I was lying on one of the two library sofas, while poor Flossie was thoughtfully scrubbing the rug beside me.

I blinked, searching for signs of Helen.

"Where is she?" I demanded.

Flossie looked up, surprised to see me awake.

"She helped me lift you to the sofa," Flossie said. "For a moment, I considered perhaps she was not the unscrupulous character we took her to be. But as soon as my back was turned, she ran away. I'm sorry, Violet. I was too preoccupied to stop her."

I was too upset to speak. I struggled to sit up.

"Shhh—no, Violet," Flossie urged. "Just rest."

"I have to get back to Harry!"

"You need to rest, Violet! You've been awfully ill!"

"There was something in my brandy," I said, realizing. "Miss Weber put it there—I'm certain of it!"

I tried again to sit up, but Flossie came to my side and gently pushed my shoulders back down.

"No, Violet. *Rest!*"

"But we have to do something, Flossie! I have to go to Harry!"

"Don't worry about Harry. I telephoned the hospital, Violet, and explained everything. I warned them not to let Miss Weber get anywhere near him. We'll go to the hospital together, but first you need to recover some of your strength."

I ached to argue, but my body took Flossie's side; a jarring pain filled my head and my muscles quivered.

"I promise I'll help you, Violet," Flossie repeated. "As long as you take a few moments and let me get some food into you."

I looked at her with a mixture of gratitude and anguish. Finally, I nodded my assent.

"It's awfully chilly in here," she remarked. "I'm going to light a fire and make some tea, but you stay where you are. Just rest."

I watched as she piled wood and lit a fire in the library fireplace. I was glad for it: the gloomy, foggy day had left a clammy chill in the very bones of the house. When the flames were leaping, Flossie scuttled off to make some tea; I listened to the echoing sounds as she found her way around the kitchen. The house was still empty. I knew now that it was Miss Weber who had ordered the servants to take the day for themselves. It was unlikely I would see any of them until the next morning, at the earliest.

When Flossie returned, she placed a tray of hot tea and beans on toast before me.

"Simple comforts to help you regain your strength," she explained.

She stuffed some pillows behind me on the sofa to prop me up and tucked a wool blanket around me. I wasn't in the mood to nibble at anything, but I took a couple of polite bites before sitting in silence with my eyes closed and my face turned towards the glowing hearth.

All was silent, save for the satisfying crackle of the fire. My eyes fell upon some papers lying idle on the library desk. In her hasty departure, "Madeleine" had left behind her copy of Harry's will. With some effort, I stood and crossed the room, scooping the pages up and reading them.

I found the passage Helen had read to me aloud, but as I read on, I saw what followed.

"Flossie . . . if 'Mrs. Carlyle' was deceased or otherwise 'declared unfit' for some reason, Harry's entire fortune was to pass to Ina Weber, 'to keep in trust and utilize how she deems necessary.'"

There it was: the truth made crystalline. Had I been committed to the madhouse, Miss Weber would have inherited everything. It was all unequivocally confirmed: the way Miss Weber must have been slipping Harry arsenic all along—and, moreover, the way she must have planned to slip him one large and final dose in the hospital after ensuring the doctors already had their suspicions about me.

"Without a doubt, she intended to kill him," I said.

"You guessed as much already, Violet," Flossie reminded me. "The money she'd promised to pay that actress—where else was she going to get it?"

"Yes," I agreed. "Still, it is a shock. Miss Weber . . . well, she really *did* seem to love Harry. Moreover, she often seemed, well, *in love* with Harry."

Flossie only nodded and nudged me to take a sip of my tea.

"The note she left even said something about love," I confided. "Miss Weber wrote about how the others did it for money, but she did it for love . . ."

I reached into my skirt pocket to pull out the note again. I didn't feel it, and rummaged more rigorously.

"Flossie! The note! It's gone!" I said, alarmed.

She looked at me, wide-eyed. "Oh, no—Helen must have taken it when she helped me lift you to the sofa!"

"Flossie, that letter was all I had!" I said, feeling my throat constrict, overwhelmed. "My only real proof!"

"That's not true," Flossie insisted. She reached for my hand and patted it. "I'm a witness. You have me."

I felt hot tears welling behind my eyes.

"Thank you, Flossie," I said. I wanted to say more, but I felt my throat thicken and began to choke on the words. "Truly . . . *thank you*. It means more to me than ever just now, considering . . . well, considering *Cora*."

Flossie nodded.

"Yes. That *is* unexpected," she conceded.

"I'm hurt, of course—and angry. But angry, too, at myself. I'm ashamed to think I've been so blind."

"Don't blame yourself," Flossie urged. "The three of us have been like sisters. When it comes to those we love like family, the heart often wears blinders . . ."

Her words trailed off momentarily, and she took a sip of tea before going on.

"I ought to have done a better job of warning you," she lamented.

"What do you mean?" I demanded.

"I spent some time with Cora two days ago. We talked for hours over afternoon tea. She seemed awful eager to insist you were the one poisoning Harry . . . She kept pointing out how much money you stood to gain."

Flossie paused, hesitant. She bit her lip as she warmed her hands on her cup of tea.

"Violet . . . she also brought up the past. She blamed you for Blanche and Tackett. Even Sister Edwina, and how strange it was you were the last one seen emerging from her room."

I thought back to the day I had run into Cora on the street outside the Emporium. She had pretended to be so worried for me! Now I knew it was all a deceitful performance.

Musing upon this, I frowned. "When did you say you had tea with Cora?" I asked. "Two days ago? On Sunday, then?"

"Yes," Flossie replied. "Sunday."

"Are you . . . certain it was Sunday? I bumped into Cora outside the Emporium on Sunday. She said she had spent several hours ordering hats from my old millinery counter."

"Oh," Flossie said. I couldn't make out her expression. The light of the fire was playing tricks upon her face. "Perhaps it was Saturday."

My thoughts returned to Cora, and her betrayal.

"Cora has always been . . . well, *Cora*," I said. "But I always thought that, deep down, she loved me—that she loved us both."

"I did as well," Flossie consoled me.

We fell back into silence.

"When the time comes, I'm certain we will find a way to confront Cora," Flossie said. "But first things first. When you're finished with your tea, we'll go to the hospital. Beyond that, I don't know. We might go looking for Helen, but I doubt she'll return to the Imperial. Surely she'll leave town."

As Flossie continued, I nodded, lost in my own thoughts. Then, all at once, it struck me: *Flossie had not been in the room when Helen had given her name and told me she worked at the Imperial Theater!* How could Flossie possibly know all this, unless . . . ?

My blood ran cold.

I sat incredibly still, holding my breath, trying to catch up with my own thoughts. My heart was suddenly racing and I was afraid to look at Flossie, lest she glimpse my shivering state of realization. I moved to take a sip of my tea, but as it touched my lips I noticed a familiar bitter note. I froze again, staring with new comprehension at the cups that Flossie had prepared for us. The brandy I'd drunk earlier . . . I'd left Flossie *alone* with Helen when I searched for Miss Weber.

"Did I make it too strong?" Flossie asked, taking note of my reaction to the tea. She looked at me with wide, innocent eyes.

"No," I said. "It's only that I just now realized how deeply tired I am."

I paused, thinking carefully how to proceed.

"Flossie . . ." I said, pretending to stifle a yawn and feigning potent exhaustion, "I don't think I can make it to the hospital tonight. I think I need to sleep first—at least, a little."

Flossie froze. She studied me carefully. Then the frown vanished from her face, replaced by a strange smile.

"Of course," she said. "By all means—rest. I told you I telephoned; Harry's safe, and the hospital can wait." She smiled again and eyed my barely touched teacup and uneaten plate of beans on toast. "You didn't care for the tea or toast."

"Please believe me, I am grateful for all of it," I said.

My jaw felt stiff as I pronounced the words. I wanted to hurry upstairs and be alone, away from her, as quickly as I was able.

"Leave the dishes here," I said. "I'll have the servants attend to this room tomorrow. Will you be all right in one of the guest rooms?" I asked. "You can show yourself?"

Flossie nodded. "I'm sure I'll be just fine. Please get some sleep, Violet. Remember, if I hear anything at all, I shall come running to your aid."

"Thank you," I said.

I stood up and smoothed my skirts. Flossie and I locked eyes, and in that moment, I believe I understood her at long last. I turned and walked in the direction of the door, feeling her sharp gaze still on me as I made my way out.

49

Once upstairs, I closed the bedroom door and stood in the middle of the room, quietly panicking.

Was I paranoid? I thought back over the events, and still had a clear memory: Helen had only told me her name and profession when Flossie was out of the room; Flossie had gone to search for Miss Weber. *Alone.* And it had taken her quite some time to return. Why? I wondered. Now it only made sense that she was tipping Miss Weber off, knowing I wouldn't want to turn my back on Helen and ensuring Miss Weber had ample time to flee.

My heart was pounding with terror, and at the same time, my eyelids felt heavy. My exhaustion terrified me further—I had taken a couple of sips of tea before realizing I ought not to. In retrospect, the familiar bitter flavor might have even been laudanum. But even if this were true . . . laudanum, not arsenic? What did Flossie want with me?

And how long would she keep up the ruse? I feared the ruse was now the only thing keeping me alive.

And Harry! Now I could be certain Flossie hadn't made any such telephone call to the hospital. Worse . . . what if Flossie had sent Miss Weber there? My heart beat in wild agony: I knew that, above all else, I needed to get to Harry.

I made up my mind to sneak out of the mansion. I cast about desperately for some way to thwart Flossie's discovery of my absence. My mind drifted back to Helen and how she had been made to look so much like Madeleine, and then an idea came to me. The bed! I pulled back the bed-clothes and lumped a number of pillows together, then covered them back up again. I stepped back to inspect my work. With the covers pulled up high enough, it could indeed pass for my body in the bed. I padded quietly to the door and laid my head against it, listening. The house was still. If Flossie was keeping an eye on me, she was doing so from a distance.

I carefully turned the knob and crept into the hall, gently closing the door again behind me. I said a silent prayer that by the time Flossie realized I was not in my bed, I would be halfway to the hospital.

Using the grand staircase was out of the question: it was too open, too central. I elected to try one of the back staircases instead and made it successfully down to the first floor. I paused briefly, deciding which way to go. Like the grand staircase, the front door was too exposed, and the enormous door often shut with an echoing clatter. Exiting via the servants' entrance would take me back through Miss Weber's lair, and the memory of the candle flickering in the rose garden still chilled me, prompting me to rule out the kitchen door on instinct. I decided: the conservatory was on the opposite side of the mansion, and its glass door opened onto a narrow garden that eventually let out to the street. I would slip out there, run for the street, and never look back.

I only knew that I *had* to get to Harry. But as I held my breath and continued to soft-shoe my way through the halls, I heard a stirring, followed by the sound of footsteps. I froze, my skin suddenly prickling with cold perspiration.

"Violet . . . ?" Flossie called.

Panicked, I sprang into action. The conservatory was still some distance away; presently, I was in a hall lined with several of the downstairs guest rooms. I turned and dove into the nearest one, hoping to hide. It was a dark room, intended for male guests, with lots of heavy furniture and several heads of various big-game animals mounted on the walls. I'd entered this room only once before, when Harry gave me my official tour, and I'd taken an immediate dislike to it. The bulky furniture felt designed to push you out. The mounted lion's head was frozen in a snarl, its teeth garishly bared. Even the stuffed hawk gave a phantom scream.

But now this room was my only refuge. I cast about for anything that might help me, and picked up an ivory-handled letter opener. I debated hiding under the bed. I heard Flossie's steps drawing near, and opted to hide behind the heavy silk curtains that framed the far window. Pressed so near to the frigid windowpanes, I could feel the cold, fog-laden night air seeping in, and I shivered. I waited, watching the door through a tiny crack in the curtains. I tried to hold my breath, but my teeth began to chatter.

I heard a shuffling in the hall, and Flossie appeared in the doorway.

She was holding an oil lamp at waist level, casting an unsettling, devilish glow upon her face.

"Violet?" she repeated, this time more softly.

Her mouth twisted with a sly smile, and she stepped into the room. I barely recognized her. There was something different—even in her posture, the way she moved. I'd always known Flossie to have a very demure way about her, but now she prowled with all the carnivorous confidence of the lion snarling on the wall. Her eyes, too, looked darker and stranger than I'd ever seen.

It finally dawned on me: *I had never truly known Flossie at all.*

I watched this stranger with grim wonderment as she peered under the bed and shined the lamp into an empty wardrobe. Once she had made her search of the room, she turned as if to go. My heart leapt with elation. My tactic had worked!

But then . . . when Flossie reached the open door, she paused. Her shoulders shook—faintly at first, then with increasing vigor. To my surprise, she began making a sound. At first, it sounded like a low rumbling, but then I realized she was laughing. *She was laughing.* In the next instant, she had spun around to face the curtains.

"All right, Violet, you can come out now," she called gleefully.

I didn't move. I was still holding my breath, though it was obvious she knew exactly where I was hiding. Flossie laughed again and extracted an object from her skirt pocket. I stifled a gasp. The cold perspiration of dread prickled my skin again.

I had forgotten about Harry's revolver.

"Don't make me *persuade* you, Violet," Flossie urged in a delighted tone. "You may prefer to make empty threats with no bullets, but I think we can both agree, I'm far more shrewd." Another second ticked by, and she added irritably, "Hurry up, now!"

I staggered slowly out from behind the curtain. Flossie looked me over. When she caught sight of the letter opener, she laughed again.

"Were you hoping to stab me to death?" she said. "With that!" Her tone was light and teasing—and turned my stomach. "Please put that silly thing down."

I didn't move and Flossie gestured again, this time with the revolver. I did as I was told: I dropped the letter opener, and it landed on the Oriental rug with a dull thud.

Flossie sighed.

"I *was* trying to go about this in a compassionate manner, Violet." She shook her head. "The fire, the tea . . . a dear friend by your side."

"You poisoned the brandy," I said, putting the pieces together. "And there was something in the tea, too."

"The brandy merely had a splash of ipecac and laudanum," Flossie said.

"Why?"

She shrugged. "I needed to have a look at the note Ina left behind and decide what to do about it."

"And decide what to do about *me*," I said with a slight tremor in my voice.

Flossie nodded calmly, as though we were discussing the weather. "You changed everything when you figured out that Helen was an impostor," she said. "No more locking you away in a madhouse if you could prove Helen was an actress. But we might still have been able to salvage things if Ina had just kept mum. Instead, when she fled, she left that infuriating note."

She paused and changed demeanor with a forlorn sigh. "Now there is only one thing that can be done."

"Do you mean to shoot me?"

"I'd rather not. The madhouse isn't an option for you anymore, of course, but I also can't have you dying in just any old way. I'm aiming for a specific result, and death by gun doesn't suit you. That would make for a rather implausible suicide, really."

"You expect me to . . . kill myself?"

Flossie nodded. "It's the only way for you to show how deeply you repent poisoning your husband."

"I didn't."

"Oh, but you have! And you've explained it all, in your letter!"

"My letter?"

"I visited your bedroom and saw it with my own eyes," Flossie said. "It's there on your nightstand. Don't you believe me?"

I glared, wary. It came back to me—how Flossie had been able to perfectly imitate Sister Edwina's penmanship. I thought, too, of the note I'd found in the camp.

"We'll go there now," Flossie insisted. She gestured with the gun. "Go on! Back upstairs! You lead the way."

I hesitated. I knew it was not in my best interest to go anywhere Flossie commanded. But she cocked the hammer of the revolver, reminding me that my choices were extremely limited at the moment. I obeyed and, with Flossie pointing the gun at my back, proceeded up the grand staircase and down the hall to my bedroom. Once inside, Flossie nodded her head at an unfamiliar envelope propped against a water pitcher on my bedside table.

"It really *is* a moving letter, Violet. You see . . . you've been feeling the weight of your own guilt for so long. The family that could not keep you because of your wicked ways . . . the orphanage you burned down for spite . . . the boardinghouse owner and his mistress whom you couldn't stand . . . and now, poisoning your wealthy husband to have at his fortune. You've done terrible things, Violet. And the only way you know to make amends for all the lives you have hurt is to pay with your own."

My jaw dropped.

"*You . . . you* were the one who poisoned Tackett and Blanche."

She didn't say anything. A smile played at the corners of her small mouth.

"*You* burned down the orphanage," I continued.

Still, she said nothing, that eerie curl of her lips unmoving.

"And Cora . . . Cora had nothing to do with any of it, did she?" I demanded. "You kept us busy with suspicions about each other . . . *you* convinced *her* not to meet me in Golden Gate Park—not the other way around. Isn't that so?"

Still, Flossie said nothing. She only looked at me, unflappable and unmoved. It was as though she was patiently waiting for me to catch up to her.

"And when I bumped into you on the street that day . . . our reunion was no accident, was it?"

"Of course not," Flossie finally answered. "You must know, Violet, I'm very impressed that you were able to get a man as filthy rich as Harry Carlyle to marry you! I'd have put my money on Cora. But I'm afraid it's what's landed you in your current predicament."

"My predicament?" I repeated, shaking my head. "I don't feel entirely persuaded to take my own life, I'm afraid."

She smiled at me, cool as ever.

"You might have spared yourself the trouble if you'd simply eaten your toast and drunk your tea. But I couldn't help but notice how you suddenly lost your appetite."

"To do all this, Flossie . . . do you hate me?"

"No, no, Violet! I don't hate you!" Flossie protested, indignant. "I find you weak, yes; that much is true. But I have cared for you deeply over the years—I *love* you, Violet!"

I shook my head, feeling dazed.

"You tried to feed me poison, not more than two hours ago . . ."

"Yes." Flossie nodded. "But I added laudanum to your tea as well, Violet. You see? I didn't wish for you to suffer!"

Now it was my turn to laugh.

"And this is your idea of *love*, Flossie?"

Her mouth tightened with displeasure.

"It is all the world has afforded me, Violet," she said. "You know as well as I do, we women are forced to live on the fortunes of men. I'd rather steal it for myself than beg."

"But why hurt *me*, Flossie? Without Miss Weber, you won't be able to get at Harry's fortune."

"I know it. I'll have to settle for your safety-deposit box, Violet," Flossie said. "A pittance, but still. Either way, the doctors will want to know *who* has been poisoning Harry. At the very least, I'll give them a resolution to that little mystery."

"But we can go to the police together, Flossie, and tell them that Miss Weber did it!" I urged, trying to keep my voice even. I was aware that I was pleading for my life. "I won't tell anyone about the rest of it, Flossie—I promise."

She sighed, and my spirits sank.

"I wish I could believe that, Violet," she said. "But I'm simply not that big a fool." She lifted the revolver and pointed it directly into my face. "Sit on the bed."

My body began to tremble violently. I sat. Flossie sighed again and reached into her skirt pocket to produce a small brown glass bottle. I hardly needed to ask what it contained. She set it down on the night table beside me.

"I've some laudanum as well," Flossie offered, producing a second bottle. "It doesn't have to hurt . . . This won't be any different than falling asleep, perhaps."

I somehow very much doubted that would be the case; laudanum had one effect on a person, but arsenic quite another. It was bound to be like slipping into a nightmare. But I was also beginning to come to grips with Flossie's determination. As if reading my mind, she cocked the hammer on the pistol.

"As I said, Violet, a gunshot to the head is much less ideal, but I'll do what I have to. Please believe me."

I was silent. My mind was racing for some way to break free of the room, but I could think of nothing. Flossie appeared utterly prepared to fire the pistol the second I twitched. She was never going to let me out alive.

"Here, now, Violet," she coaxed, handing the laudanum to me. There was a glass of water sitting on the night table where she had left the forged letter. She pointed to it. "A few drops of laudanum in there, and drink half. When you grow sleepy, we'll have to add some from the other bottle."

It was a macabre recipe. I stared at her.

"Hurry, now," she said, impatient. "Don't dawdle; best to have it over with, and we've got to beat the sunrise."

The realization settled in even further. She wanted to beat the sunrise—*a sunrise I would never see.* I thought of Harry, and of never seeing *Harry* again. Would he believe the terrible things in Flossie's counterfeit letter? Tears sprang to my eyes and my hands began to tremble. What could I do?

"Violet!" Flossie barked in a stern tone, sensing my desperation.

I reached with shaking hands to unscrew the top of the bottle and extracted its dropper.

"That's enough!" Flossie snapped when I had added as many as eight or nine drops to the water. "I need you awake enough for 'dessert,' my dear. The arsenic isn't going to swallow itself!"

I stopped and put the dropper back in the bottle.

"Now, *drink*," she commanded.

I sat unmoving, staring at the glass.

"I can't . . ." I finally managed in a hoarse whisper.

"It's only laudanum; you're accustomed to that much," Flossie reminded me. "Now drink. *Or else.*"

There was nothing to be done. Slowly, I lifted the glass to my lips. I took one sip, then a second. Flossie sighed with what sounded like . . . *satisfaction? Happiness?*

"You have no conscience," I said in a low, accusing voice.

Flossie laughed.

"Thank God, I haven't," she said. "But you may as well get that— and anything else you'd like to say—off your chest."

"You're vile."

"Better to be vile than to be meek."

I inhaled bitterly, but bit my tongue. She raised her eyebrows.

"What?" she jeered. "Were you about to quote some scripture at me: *'The meek shall inherit'* and all that claptrap?" She chuckled. "I don't think you'll be inheriting anything at all now. You don't see the irony?"

Already the laudanum was working. I felt a heavy wave of drowsiness, almost like a blanket smothering my senses. Flossie smiled as my eyelids began to droop.

But then I thought I heard something rustling elsewhere in the house. It sounded a little like the noises I'd heard on so many previous nights.

I was so tired: Was I imagining it? But no, Flossie frowned and glanced at the open bedroom door. She had heard it, too. The rustling resolved into the sound of footsteps. Someone was in the house. They were coming closer. My head spun with lethargy but I struggled against it.

A figure appeared in the open doorway. I squinted at it, and saw . . . red hair, a crisp silk dress, a shapely bosom, and a very worried expression.

"Cora?" I managed to croak.

"Violet!" Cora exclaimed. "Are you hurt?"

My heart leapt. She began to rush to my side, but as soon as she stepped into the room, Flossie turned the revolver on her. Cora froze.

"Flossie," she said. It was not a question; it appeared Cora was not surprised to see Flossie, or the gun, though the latter plainly intimidated her as she stood frozen, staring at it with bulging eyes.

"I'm impressed, Cora. I can't imagine how *you—of all people—* found me out."

Despite her obvious fear, Cora kept her composure.

"Yes. Either I'm not as dull as you think," she said in a cool voice, "or else you're not as clever."

Flossie's mouth twitched; I knew Cora had caught her by surprise.

"Always pitting Violet and me against each other . . . Could you have done any of this without us? I doubt it."

Flossie's irritation was growing. Her face was as placid as a lake on a windless day, but I knew her better than that, and could make out the telltale grinding of her teeth.

"What will you do now, Flossie? Whatever you have planned for Violet, she's not the only one who has seen through you and can tell the police what you have done."

Cora was holding her hands up and inching backwards towards the open door, and Flossie—in her rage—was advancing in lockstep, the gun trembling in her hand with fresh fury. Cora's eyes darted once in my direction, and I grasped what I needed to do; I only hoped I was not so woozy now that I would fall flat on my face.

In the next second, I mustered all my strength and surged up from where I sat on the bed, launching my entire body at Flossie. Too late, Flossie tried to whirl about and fend me off. Cora lunged in and wrested the pistol from Flossie's grip. A chaotic scuffle ensued. It was difficult for me to track what was taking place; the laudanum made me feel as though I were watching it all from somewhere deep underwater. I felt an elbow strike my shoulder and stumbled backwards, struggling to get back into the fray.

Eventually, I heard an earsplitting *CRACK!* as the gun went off. Two screams rang out, and the two shapes I'd been watching disentangled themselves from each other. One slumped to the ground, and the other . . . the other hurried away and was gone.

50

"Violet? Violet?"

I was lying in my bed with the sheets tucked around me. Someone was lovingly sponging my forehead with a damp cloth and gently shaking me awake.

"Violet," Cora's voice urged. "You'd do well to get as much of whatever Flossie gave you back up. Can you try?"

She rolled me on my side, and I opened my eyes to find myself staring into a sick-pail. As it turned out, not only could I try, I was able to succeed with great vigor. Cora kindly held the pail and stroked my back to soothe the strain of the convulsions.

Once I had exhausted myself, I was still exceedingly dizzy and tired. I rolled onto my back in the bed.

"You'll likely have to sleep the rest off," Cora advised.

"Where is Harry?" I demanded with fresh panic.

"Safe," Cora said. "Still in the hospital, but very, very safe, now that they know the truth."

"When can I see him?"

"Soon," she promised. "I'll take you there myself, just as soon as you're stronger."

She wiped my mouth and face clean with a damp rag, and as she did so, I caught sight of a bright red stain that bloomed along the entire length of her sleeve.

"You're injured!" I exclaimed. "The revolver?"

She shook her head.

"It went off," she said, "but that's not my blood."

"Flossie . . ."

"Yes," Cora replied. "We struggled, and she was struck in the arm. Once she realized she was shot, she tried to run."

Alas, the shape I'd spied fleeing had been Flossie, after all.

"*Tried* to run?" I repeated.

"She was caught just outside the mansion. The police nabbed her."

"*The police?*"

"Yes. They're here. And I'm afraid you'll have to speak with them. Flossie's trying to play the victim, of course. I don't think they're inclined to believe her, but you know how clever she can be. They'll need you to set the record straight about what went on here."

"But . . . how?" I stammered. "How did they get here, and why would they believe *me*?"

Cora smiled.

"As it turns out, Violet, I'm not the only one who was worried about you. When you visited Harry and told him a woman claiming to be

Madeleine had come to the mansion, he grew frantic and demanded that the police pay a visit to the house and interview the impostor. They fobbed him off at first—the story *does* sound outrageous, certainly—but eventually Harry was put through to someone who recognized the Carlyle name and agreed to do as he asked."

Cora paused. I heard muffled voices coming from the hall outside my bedroom. She tipped her chin in the direction of the closed door.

"A few of them are here and waiting right now. I told Detective Stanhope they could talk to you just as soon as you were awake and feeling up to it."

I nodded, willing to help.

"But, Cora . . . I still don't understand. How did *you* know to come here tonight?"

"I've been wondering about Flossie for a very long time," Cora said. "It was little things at first: little white lies she told back when we were all at St. Hilda's. She told you she stole that bottle of laudanum in order to help you . . . but really she stole it in order to put drops in Sister Edwina's tea. Once Sister Edwina nodded off, Flossie went through all the drawers in Sister Edwina's desk, looking for anything she might scavenge or use as bribery."

"When I confronted her tonight, I accused Flossie of burning down the orphanage," I said. "She didn't deny it."

"For a long time, she suggested *you'd* done it during one of your spells," Cora said. "But I could never quite picture it."

"I didn't!" I recalled the charred matches I'd found in my pocket, and realized just how easy it would have been for Flossie to put them there.

"I know that now," Cora said, nodding. "But I admit, at the time . . .

I wondered. Afterwards, it was Flossie's idea that we become dancing girls—although, quite frankly, she hated it every bit as much as I did in the end. We girls didn't get to keep much of the coin we earned. She set her sights on discovering the combination to Tackett's safe."

"She told me *you* were the one to get it out of him," I said.

Cora sighed. "Of course she did! I can see why she would've wanted you to think that, but it wasn't me."

"But . . . once she learned the combination, why didn't she just steal his money and leave?"

"I've mulled that one over, too," Cora admitted. "But I believe the answer lies in the way Flossie thinks. She doesn't like to leave things open-ended. She wanted to kill Tackett. There was no official record of Tackett's riches; once he was dead, no one would know to come looking for the missing fortune. And . . . well, I believe Flossie kept us close in case she needed someone to blame." Cora looked at me apologetically. "I believe Flossie meant to lead any official police inquiry straight to *you.*"

As Cora spoke these words, I knew that they were true. I shuddered to think of how guilty I would have looked.

"But then the earthquake struck," I said, comprehending.

Cora nodded. "Yes, and that changed everything. Flossie no longer needed you to take the blame."

I thought of the blackmail note I'd found in the camp. "But why did she go to such trouble to drive me away?"

"I think she knew she needed to keep the two of us—you and I— separated so we would never piece together the truth about her," Cora explained. "And I think she chose to send you away and keep me close for a number of reasons . . . because she felt I was dimmer than you and less likely to figure her out. And because she believed I would prove useful to her again, perhaps if I married well."

"But then *I* met Harry . . ." I said.

Cora nodded again. "I think Harry Carlyle was too big a mark for Flossie to ignore. And she 'happened' upon you on the street right around the same time she'd begun to lose quite a lot of her money in the mah jong parlors. I think she ran through her share of Tackett's fortune faster than one might think possible."

"Cora . . . between what happened to Tackett and Blanche, and Harry's illness . . . did you believe I was capable of poisoning people? Flossie certainly made it seem like you did."

Cora took a breath, and sighed. "I admit, Violet . . . there were times I wondered if it wasn't true. But the night we came to stay here together—the night we took down Madeleine's portrait and hid it in the library—I drank some tea to keep myself awake . . . and afterwards I felt awful. I was so drowsy, and I slept like the dead! Flossie poured my tea; I told myself I must have simply been exhausted. But then Flossie rushed me out of the mansion the second you woke up. She had a lot to say about you once we'd left. She insisted that you'd gone mad—that your so-called 'hauntings' were staged, a result of your spells. She wanted me to agree that you were going mad in earnest and that it might be prudent to get you to a doctor."

"That would have helped her and Miss Weber in their plan to have me committed."

"Indeed," Cora concurred.

"There were so many wedges driven between us by then," I lamented. "You seemed to despise me for marrying Harry."

Cora shook her head. "I was only ever worried about you, Violet. I didn't like the idea of you marrying Harry, but only because I'd heard the gossip about Madeleine. It was Flossie who pushed me to confront you with the fact of Harry's previous marriage, you know."

"I wouldn't have guessed," I admitted. "I'm sorry, Cora. I mistook your concern for hostility."

"And that is exactly what Flossie wanted, Violet! But Flossie went too far, I think; she told me you'd begun seeing Madeleine Carlyle in the flesh. Something gnawed at me. I remembered something . . . I recalled how it had been *Flossie's idea* for Jasper and me to dress up like Tackett and Blanche to collect on his old debts. The more I thought about it, the more I realized that there was an awful lot to gain from deceiving you."

I was quiet for a moment.

"There's more," Cora said. "I've been wondering about Flossie for so long. Two weeks ago, I decided I needed to know who she was, once and for all."

"What do you mean?"

"Like you, Flossie was not always an orphan. She arrived at St. Hilda's only a few months earlier than you did."

My eyes widened. I had never known this. As long as I had known her, Flossie had kept a tight lip about her past.

"She told me the story of her family one day—only that one time, when Flossie first arrived. It was a sad tale: Flossie's people were farmers. She'd had a father and a mother, and one sister close to her own age. They were a happy family until tragedy struck. It seemed their well went rancid, and everyone but Flossie died." Cora paused and shook her head. "It never quite sat right with me," she admitted. "As so many things with Flossie never did. I hired an investigator to trace the details . . .

and, lo and behold, I learned that Flossie's sister did not die that day when Flossie's parents were poisoned by the well."

"She lived?"

Cora nodded. "She lived . . . and *she was committed to an asylum, there being proof that she had dumped arsenic into the well.*"

My jaw dropped. "You believe Flossie arranged for her sister to take the blame even back then?"

"I think Flossie is far more dangerous than we know," Cora said.

A heavy silence settled over the room. Finally, Cora took a deep breath and sighed. "I've told the police everything I know—including what I had the investigator turn up about Flossie's past. But do you feel able to talk to the detective now, Violet?"

I nodded, but then remembered. "Miss Weber!" I said. "Have they found her at all?"

"No," Cora said. "But they understand she played a large role in this. After you told Harry that Miss Weber also saw 'Madeleine,' he put the pieces together and informed the police that she was not to be trusted, either."

"When I told him that Madeleine had returned to San Francisco, he insisted it was impossible," I murmured. "He knew she was an impostor right away."

"Did you uncover anything about the impostor's identity?" Cora asked.

"An actress. I had to threaten her to get it out of her, but she said her stage name is Helen Beauchamp, and she sings in the musical revue down at the Imperial."

Cora gave me a smile tinged with pride and affection.

"Well, that's precisely the sort of information that Detective Stanhope will want to know—and sooner rather than later. Shall I send him in?"

"All right," I agreed.

Cora laid the damp cloth gently on my forehead and stood from where she had been perched on the edge of my bed. She moved for the door.

"Cora?" I called, just before her hand turned the doorknob.

"Yes?"

"I'm sorry, that . . ." I tried to think of the words to describe how terrible I felt for eating up all the bad things Flossie had fed me about Cora. "Well, I'm sorry we didn't confide in each other sooner."

We exchanged a long gaze.

"We have an awful lot to catch up on, it seems," she said. "But, for now, it will have to wait—until the police have done."

I nodded. She moved to turn the knob, but paused again. She turned back to me.

"She did a very good job keeping us apart." Cora smiled. "Let's not let that happen, ever again."

"No," I agreed. "We won't."

She smiled one last time and opened the door. I watched the ruby glow of her scarlet hair disappear into the hall, and a few seconds later a tall, gangly, white-haired man entered the room with an apologetic air and introduced himself as Detective Stanhope.

51

The day finally arrived for Harry to come home from the hospital. Without regular visits from Miss Weber, his health finally and "miraculously" improved. His strength had returned with each passing day, until Harry grew restless, and his hospital bed was more of a shackle than a true respite.

"He may still have suffered damage to his nerves," Dr. Thomas warned. He still frowned at me every time I visited, as though not convinced that I'd had nothing to do with the arsenic, even after Miss Weber's guilt had thoroughly come to light.

"You will want to watch carefully for signs of lasting damage," Dr. Thomas warned. "Heart palpitations, tingling in his limbs, or loss of muscle control."

Harry and I promised to be on the lookout for the long list of symptoms Dr. Thomas exhorted us to remain vigilant against, and a great many more, besides.

Then, together, we left the hospital. Mr. Davies met us out front, dressed in his chauffeur's uniform, and we climbed into the same motorcar that had carried us from our honeymoon ship to the Carlyle mansion for the first time as a married couple.

"Davies lives-in now," I told Harry as we traveled home. "So do four others—new people whom I interviewed and hired. It only made sense, now that . . ."

"Now that Miss Weber is no longer with us," Harry finished my sentence for me.

"Yes."

Harry nodded. I was silent. I knew Harry was still struggling with Miss Weber's betrayal. Flossie had been arrested, Helen had been arrested, but the police had yet to find Miss Weber.

Later that same day, once we were alone together in the sanctuary of our bedroom, I dared to ask Harry what he thought of Miss Weber. It was still early, and the sun peeped in through cracks in the curtains, but we were lying together in the bed, naked and vulnerable.

"Why do you think she did it?" I asked, after much speculation of my own.

At the mention of her name, I saw Harry's jaw clench. His cheeks flushed, and I realized his anger was mingled with a measure of embarrassment. I stiffened without meaning to.

"When we were children," Harry began, "I never imagined Ina might have any affection for me beyond a brotherly-sisterly bond. She was several years older. I was a child—I assumed I was only a nuisance in her eyes." He paused, and swallowed. "But then, when we had just crossed the threshold of adulthood—or at least, when I had finally joined her there—she let it be known that she harbored deeper feelings for me."

I blinked at Harry, surprised by his confession. He shook his head.

"Her love went unrequited," he rushed to assure me. "And when I met and married Madeleine, Ina came to me and told me she not only accepted the match, but wished to offer her services to us as head housekeeper. She appeared sincere. I think she believed Madeleine was above her in station and class, and for whatever reason, the social gatekeeper within Ina was able to accept another woman by my side—so long as Ina perceived the woman superior."

Harry paused. I said nothing. He swallowed.

"But then, as the years passed, Madeleine began . . . well, *acting* as she did. It was unladylike, to say the least. Ina did not approve. Her love for Madeleine quickly turned to hate. The night Madeleine left—the night of the earthquake . . . I'm afraid to say, Miss Weber did not mourn her mistress's absence. Not in the least."

I frowned. "But . . . Miss Weber was always carrying on as though she *adored* Madeleine!" I said.

"I know it looked that way," Harry conceded. "At first, I assumed Ina was helping keep up appearances; it was *her* idea to spare me the humiliation of divorce and have Madeleine declared dead. But in retrospect I believe she also meant to control me after a fashion, reminding me of the mistake I had made . . ."

"What do you mean?"

"She may have hated Madeleine, but Madeleine's *ghost* proved useful to her. After all . . . who desires a widower?—much less a widower whose temper has become the subject of all the idle gossips? Who would want to enter into a house reconstructed in the exact fashion the dead wife left it? And yet, this was what Ina insisted upon. I was so beside myself with grief that my marriage had ended, I was simply grateful that Ina helped me put the pieces back together, whatever their order. In return, Ina was given dominion over the house, until . . ." He trailed off.

"Until we met," I said.

"Yes." He nodded. "Until we met. I think that may have been the tipping point for her. She was outraged I should marry again, and somehow she found out . . . well, where you came from, I suppose." Harry glanced at me, sheepish, apologetic. "She wasn't content to stand aside as mistress of the house for an individual she did not consider her superior. We argued about it, but ultimately, I told her to keep her feelings to herself."

I nodded, picturing all this.

"And then Flossie approached her," I said.

"I suppose that's the way of it," Harry agreed. "Right around the time your friend got to her, Miss Weber must have been quietly seething and was ready to turn on me—or anyone, really."

"Her love had turned to hate."

"Yes—I think so. And now I understand she *would* have seen me dead, if it meant she did not have to suffer further insult to her rather backwards sense of love and morality."

We fell into silence and snuggled closer to each other on the bed. The conversation was over, but I went on thinking about Flossie. Almost a month had passed since the night I discovered Flossie for who she really was, but I still couldn't fully bend my mind around the shape of it. *Her rather backwards sense of love and morality,* Harry had said, in describing Miss Weber's powerful fury. But Flossie . . . Flossie was different. Flossie was *cold.* I recalled the black look in her eyes when she ordered me to swallow a lethal dose of arsenic. There had been nothing there—an eerie, absolute void. It chilled me to realize this had probably always been the truth of Flossie: every bond of affection forged solely for its utility, every show of coming to my aid a manipulation to be exploited later. She moved through life taking risks and breaking things with brutal indifference. And when things didn't go her way, she sacrificed those closest to her with that same brutal indifference.

I'd loved her so blindly.

I'd come very near to believing myself capable of *poisoning* someone.

As this thought passed through my mind, I shivered. I pushed it away and wiggled so that even more of my body was in contact with Harry's warm skin.

At first, I found that I was still shy to move things.

"It's time for you to make a real home there, Violet," Cora insisted. She had come around to approving of Harry, ever since the night he'd grown so worried about me that he sent the police to our rescue. "*You* are the mistress of the house now," she added, with a toss of her hair. "*Act* like it."

Harry agreed, and after a while, he encouraged me to dispose of entire pieces and even sets of furniture and buy new ones instead. I filled the house with new vases overflowing with flowers—none of them lilies. Harry laughed, delighted. Without Miss Weber to haunt the house at night, it was all quite peaceful.

Then, one late summer day, when the weather had turned surprisingly balmy, and I had opened all the windows to let in the sea breeze, I stood at the bottom of the stairs, staring upwards at the great portrait on the wall above.

After a while, Harry came along and stood beside me, also gazing up.

"Shall we take it down?" he said.

"That's for you to decide," I answered.

He gazed at the painting for one long minute more, then said, "We shall."

The portrait was helped down by the gardeners, who carried it out to the toolshed. We never discussed it again, but I knew we had silently decided it would remain there indefinitely.

A wonderful, peaceful, uneventful month passed. I finally felt like the mansion was my home. The only thing missing was a child.

"We'll keep trying," Harry promised—a favorite line of his, usually delivered with a kiss and a wink.

"When we weren't having any luck, and Miss Weber was tricking me into believing the house was haunted, I began to worry that I was cursed," I confessed.

"You are anything but, Violet," Harry said.

His hair was damp from his recent bath, and he'd parted it down the middle and slicked it temporarily down with a comb. For the slenderest of seconds, I saw a flash of Tackett, and shivered. I looked again, and all I could see was my handsome Harry.

Harry and I enjoyed our evenings together, and when it came time to sleep, the house was blissfully silent—even with all the servants living in now.

All had come into harmony, until one night, when I fell asleep, I began to suffer a terrible nightmare. I can't say what the dream was about, only that when I woke, all memory of it was gone, leaving me in a sweaty panic, an awful, torturous residue.

The more I tried to recall the dream, the more I could only remember that day when I had visited Harry in the hospital, and informed him of Madeleine's return.

I kept remembering the way Harry had reacted upon being told that Madeleine had turned up on the doorstep in the flesh . . . the way he jolted upright and shouted out, *That's not possible!* Why had he been so very sure?

As I thought this over, I heard a strange rustling downstairs. It sounded rather like pots and pans rattling. Though they were usually very discreet, I guessed that it might be one of the servants unable to sleep or perhaps hankering for a midnight snack. But something compelled me to go down and see anyway—the bad dream, perhaps.

When I got downstairs, I moved in the direction of the kitchen—the place from which I'd thought I'd heard the stirrings emanating.

The lights were extinguished. I peeked in anyway, and to my shock,

I saw the door to the garden ajar. My heart gave a terrified squeeze, and my blood ran cold.

By the time I worked up the courage to step out into the garden and make my way to the rosebushes, I already knew what I was likely to see.

The light of a single candle, burning upon the brass compass. A candle that flickered and guttered, and managed to stay lit despite the wet ocean breeze.

ACKNOWLEDGMENTS

My thanks to Tara Singh Carlson and everyone at Putnam for acquiring this novel, and deepest gratitude to Helen Richard O'Hare for slogging through several drafts of edits with me. FACT: Writers can never thank their editors enough.

I am thankful to Emily Forland and everyone at Brandt & Hochman. Thanks, too, to Michelle Weiner of CAA, who has always provided encouragement for my endeavors.

I am lucky for friends who have cheered, championed, counseled, and consoled along the way: Jayme Yeo, Atom Crimi, Elizabeth Romanski, Brendan Jones, Olga Zilberbourg, Julie Fogh, Melissa Rindell, Julia Masnik, Eva Talmadge, Amy Poeppel, Joe Campana, Susan Wood, and Sophie Weeks. I am grateful to my parents, Sharon and Arthur Rindell, for their love.

Finally, I am incredibly indebted to the readers who have picked up my books over the years. You keep me alive. ALSO, FACT: Writers can never thank their readers enough.